Residuum of Ravenstone

Part One of the series:

THE RUINS OF RYTUS

By Emily Reading

First Edition

Copyright

eBook ISBN 978-1-326-64369-0

Paperback ISBN 978-1-326-64486-4 – First printed 2016

Discover more about the series: www.RuinsOfRytus.com

Dedication

To my loving husband, Jamie.

Thank you. Without your support and patience,
I would have never achieved my dream.

Acknowledgements

I would dearly like to thank my friends and family for their hard work and dedication. They have helped me to not only overcome the emotional struggles of depression and anxiety, but they have also stuck by me through it all.

There were times when I wanted to give up, give in and abandon hope. They stood by me, guided me through the darkness and never treated me any differently to their other friends or family members.

I would also like to dearly thank my friends who took the time to sit down and read my book. They helped me understand how to improve my writing, but also put my mind at ease. Without their guidance this would have not been possible. Their belief in me, their guiding words and their understanding will never be forgotten.

In particular I would like to thank:

Carole Bell	Jim O'Brien
Anthony Bell	Glenn Reading
Beverley Brant	Helen Reading
Maria Brant	Gary Skipp
Vicky Brant	Sarah Turner
Andy Milne	

Preface

Set in a time ruled by gods, rituals and sacrifices; before the influences of foreign nations and their allies, Rytus stands poised. Now a catalyst, triggered by the fall of Ravenstone, ignites the foundations of this ancient nation.

The Ruins of Rytus: Part I - Residuum of Ravenstone, features a glossary as the last section, to help explain the terminology of this ancient and forgotten land. Though the pronunciation of the names, armour and clothing have been forgotten over time, it is hoped that you can make these your own, and breathe life into them once more.

May the gods bless you, as you begin your journey through this once great nation.

Maps

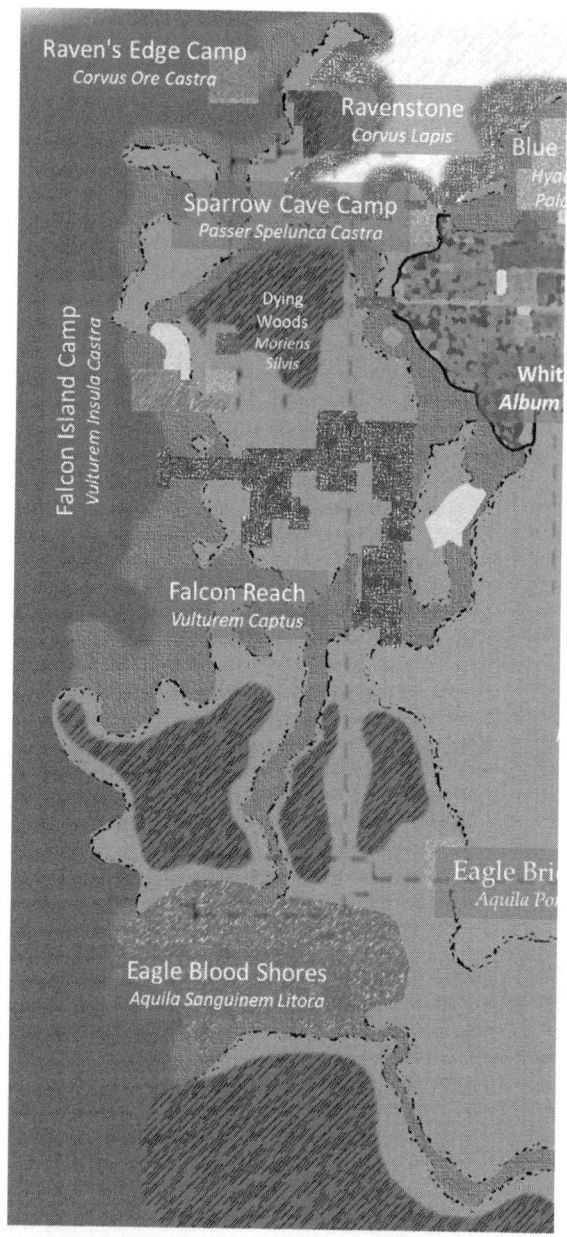

Raven's Edge Camp
Corvus Ore Castra

Ravenstone
Corvus Lapis

Blue
Hya
Pal

Sparrow Cave Camp
Passer Spelunca Castra

Dying
Woods
Moriens
Silvis

Falcon Island Camp
Vulturem Insula Castra

Whit
Album

Falcon Reach
Vulturem Captus

Eagle Bri
Aquila Po

Eagle Blood Shores
Aquila Sanguinem Litora

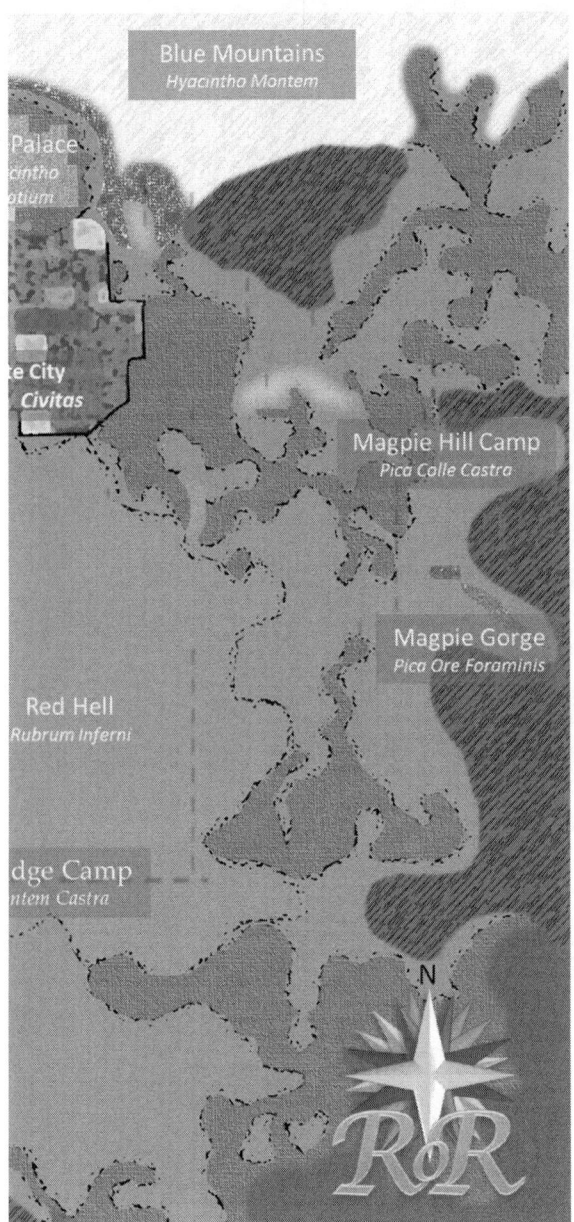

Blue Mountains
Hyacintho Montem

Palace
cintho
otium

e City
Civitas

Magpie Hill Camp
Pica Colle Castra

Magpie Gorge
Pica Ore Foraminis

Red Hell
Rubrum Inferni

dge Camp
ntem Castra

N

Map of White City

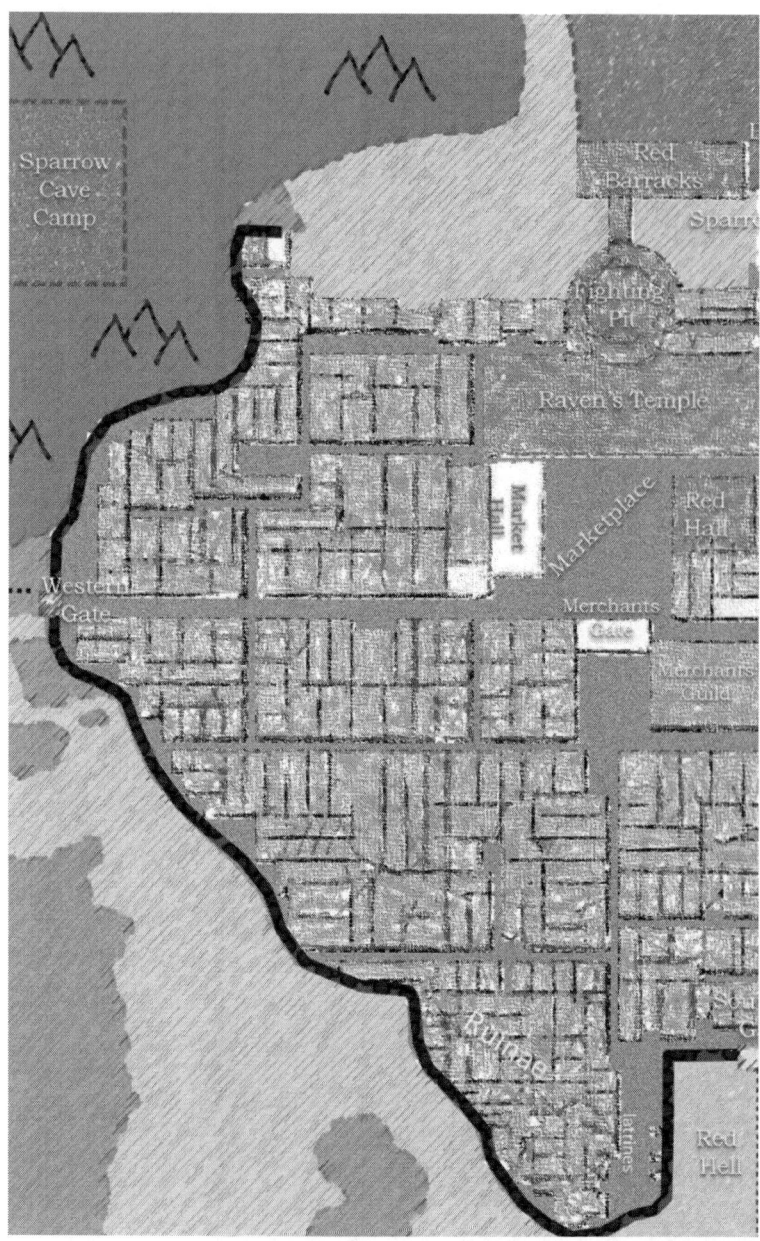

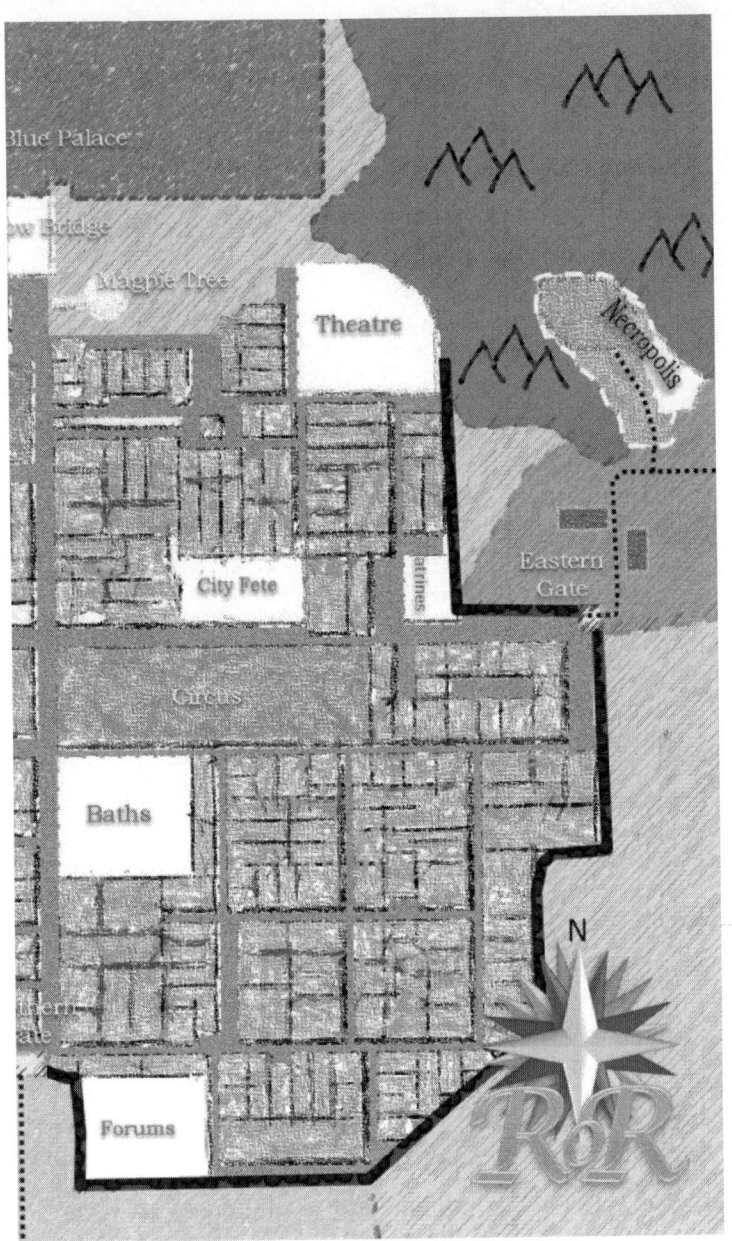

Blue Palace

w Bridge

Magpie Tree

Theatre

Necropolis

City Pete

atrines

Eastern
Gate

Circus

Baths

N

ern
ate

Forums

RoR

The Ruins of Rytus
Part I - Residuum of Ravenstone

#RoR

Chapter One

14 days after the eclipse.

Darius braced. He stood, just as he had been trained to by his White Blood doctore, from the day he could walk. His red eyes narrowed, as the galloping of hooves and the screams of his fellow Red Guards, became drowned out by the beating of his own heart. His breathing slowed but his vision remained focused on the Black Blood rider, charging in his direction. Darius did not know the name of this mounted warrior, his black eyes and long black hair were foreign to him. His strange light armour flexed with the rhythm of the horse, and his opponent's cry was in a language that Darius did not understand.

Darius's armour in comparison was heavy and the conditions were arid. His red crested helmet shimmered in the unforgiving blazing sun, as the red desert sand grasped at his disfigured brow. The blood that had splattered on to his face, dried instantaneously in the heat. His throat was parched, his eyes were sore, and the wound in his side was excruciating. However, he knew that as the mounted warrior's black horse cut a line through the swirling desert sand, he would only get one opportunity to bring his enemy's charge to a crashing halt. He had to stay focused.

The mounted Black Blood gripped the reins with his left hand. He steered the horse to the right of Darius and aimed his sword, poised to strike with the tip. This played perfectly into Darius's hands; with the narrowing of the blade, the chances of the mounted Black Blood making a successful strike were dramatically reduced. He smirked, as the seemingly clueless Black Blood continued to close the gap.

Darius dropped to his knees. He spun around the axis of his right leg, rendering him side on, further reducing his enemy's target. Darius glared into the black eyes of the rider, his horse now so close, Darius was sure he could feel the charging snorts of the animal against his skin. He repositioned his sword to strike the horse's front legs, hoping to bring the beast to a sudden and unfortunate halt. A successful strike could stop the horse and rider, but a poorly executed one could bring the beast crashing down on top of him.

Just as he prepared to counteract the sword's bite of the horse's flesh, the mounted rider jumped upward. His toes perched on the back of the saddle before leaping into the air with the grace of a grasshopper.

Equally unexpected, Darius's sword remained untouched, as the once very real horse turned to a black smoky silhouette. The black smoke washed over the blade of the sword, as the beast continued on its way, undisturbed by the Red Guard in its path. Darius did not know what to do or what to think. He froze to the spot.

He looked upward, as the Black Blood loomed in the air above him, his sword now firmly aimed at Darius. With almighty strength, the Black Blood forced the sword through the tight gap between Darius's helmet and cuirass; deep into the base of his neck, shattering the collar bone. With the full weight of the Black Blood now behind the strike, the sword tore its way through flesh and bone, with seemingly little resistance.

The rider used the momentum this manoeuvre had given him to leap again. This time he leapt from the handle of the sword. This not only compounded the impact, forcing the sword into Darius's heart; but also allowed the rider to gracefully land on his now solidly formed horse, before continuing on his way.

The red eagle embedded into the handle of Darius's sword, let out a cry, as it slipped from his hand, landing in the sand at his side. Blood filled his lungs before spilling from his mouth. Like a slain bear, Darius dropped to the floor before rolling on to his back. His eyes were now fixated on the sky above him, and the gods who had been left with no choice but to punish Rytus for her disobedience.

As Darius lay in the bloodied sand, the Black Blood's sword still embedded deep into his core, and the bodies of his fellow Red Guards scattered around, only one thought prevailed. The ruins of Rytus belonged to no man; the ruins of Rytus were truly for the gods alone. They had made that perfectly clear.

1,000,475 days after the eclipse.

Just a few short steps from where Darius fell, a small group of tourists filed off the shuttle, following the travel agent's appointed guide. The group made their way along a dusty path, through the ruined stonework and fallen masonry. The guide herded the group into the remains of an open air theatre, cut into the hill side. He then gestured for each of his patrons to find a seat among the ancient rubble.

"Welcome one and all, to the glorious ruins of Rytus," announced the guide, as the stragglers of the group hurried to find a spot. "You are now in all that remains of the once sprawling White City, capital of Rytus. Home to the six blood gens that once lived and worked here," the guide knew the script well, spoke with confidence, and still clearly possessed some enthusiasm for the job. The small group of intrepid adventurers remained seated, as some stared wide eyed at the ruins around them, some transfixed on the guide, and others who began tucking into their pre-prepared lunches.

"Behind us once stood the beautiful Blue Palace, and to our right, the awe inspiring Raven's Temple. Ahead of us lay the arena, circus, great halls, and the homes of thousands of the ancient White Blood citizens," the guide raised his hands slightly, while gesturing with minimal effort to the directions in which he referred.

A few rows back from the front, sat a family, consisting of three members; Mother, Father, and their fat grubby son, Max. Mother and Father listened intently, while Max sat with his chin resting on the palms of his hands. His elbows were perched on his knees and his cheeks bulged with each breath like a toad. From time to time, he would let out a loud huff, to ensure those seated immediately near him were well aware of his complete and utter boredom.

The guide was well worn to this kind of behaviour, and the effect it could have on his tips at the end of the tour. Therefore, he set in motion a plan to alleviate his young guest's boredom.

"The ancient Blue Bloods ruled over the White Blood citizens of Rytus, with the help of a well-trained and ruthless army. The ancient Orange Bloods, under the sigil of the falcon, were once fast, covert hunters. They utilised small blades for close combat, and the bow and arrow for distance," the guide explained, before he pretended to fire an imaginary arrow into the air. "The ancient Red Bloods were strong and powerful, fighting with swords and brute strength, under the sigil of the eagle," the guide declared, as he pretended to swing a sword around. "The ancient Green Bloods fought using magic, under the sigil of the magpie."

The guide brought his hands together, before he simulated a puff of smoke rising into the air, causing a few people in the crowd to applaud. Sure that the boy would be impressed, the guide looked toward him expecting awe, but instead was greeted with the loudest huff the boy could manage.

The guide remained undeterred, he wasn't finished yet. "However, no-one could ever expect to become more powerful and more commanding than one blood gens in particular. A gens so powerful, they held the power to decide who would live and who would die. They commanded mountains to spew lava and the ground to open up below our very feet. They bought Rytus to her knees and destroyed her, free of regret or guilt. A blood gens so powerful, the gods only permitted one of their kind to walk these lands at any given time; before banishing them forever."

The guide, now in full flow, paused momentarily to glance up past the boy, before nodding discreetly. He continued with ever increasing dramatic body language, playing out his words as he spoke.

"Serving as the voice of the gods, this powerful creature, secretive and mysterious in nature, would often take the form of a single black raven. He would observe, spy, and whisper in the ears of the people of Rytus. Other times he would be seen walking the streets, a hooded figure, his purple eyes piercing the souls of any citizen unfortunate enough to be in his path. He rarely spoke, but his words could be deadly." The guide began to smile, as he glanced up at the boy, head still resting in his palms, but no longer huffing loudly.

"Even the respected Blue Bloods feared the Raven, and rightly so. After all..." a dramatic pause, "legends tell us, that he murdered them all!" Just then, a man in a hooded cloak, wearing a large plastic raven mask, screeched loudly into Max's ear. He immediately turned around causing the beak to brush his fat cheeks. Max screamed, shot up, ran down the ruined steps, and disappeared behind a wall.

The guide and a few people in the small audience began to laugh and applaud. Mother stood up and called after him, "Max! Wait!"

"It's OK. He'll be OK," said Father, grasping her arm to encourage her not to follow the boy.

The guide smiled at the couple, "I'm sure he will be fine. He can't go far."

Mother sat back down and the guide continued his speech, now without the interruptions of Max. "The White Bloods were effectively slaves, owned by the Blue Bloods..."

5,262 days before the eclipse.

Cardea called out for her friend and blood gens sister, "Ana! Ana! Where are you?" Anatola giggled, as she ran further into the city's market. She ran through the unusual and unprecedented snow fall. She passed fellow White Bloods, as they struggled to complete their work, among the tall insulas and shops at the heart of White City. She crouched down behind a box, before an angry White Blood moved her on with a kick and a hiss.

"Ah ha! Found you!" shouted Cardea, mistakenly believing Anatola to be a few stalls over. Another angry White Blood barked at Cardea to move along.

Anatola, still a few steps ahead, ran out of the market into the theatre. She pushed past the White Bloods, as they excitedly debated in the corridors about the new Blue Blood Imperator, due to be presented later that day. Convinced this time she had the perfect spot to hide from Cardea, she ducked behind a door, into the long L-shaped room, hollowed out beneath the theatre. She attempted to silence her own giggles, before sitting down on the cold stone floor.

The excited chatter outside began to fade, as the White Bloods made their way out of the theatre, towards the palace. Anatola still pleased with her evasion skills, giggled excitedly, before she was unexpectedly interrupted by the sound of a child crying. She listened for a short while to determine the direction of the sound. It was behind her, deeper into the hollowed out room.

24

She stood up and began to follow the sound, being sure to carefully place her feet in the poorly lit room. She turned the corner and there at the end was a boy, sat on the floor, crying. Like the other White Bloods, the boy had white hair and white features, but unusually, he was quite well dressed in clothes unfamiliar to her.

1,000,475 days after the eclipse.

Max, sat in the dirt just out of ear shot of the tour guide, wiped his runny nose on his sleeve, before drying his eyes with the other. To his left he felt Mother's doting presence, or perhaps this time it was strict and unforgiving Father? No, wait. It can't be, he thought. To his left was an aging rusted gate, blocking the path of anyone wishing to venture into what remained of a collapsed room. The room had no way in and no way out, not with the old gate in the way. So what was it that he could feel, staring at him, watching him?

He peered through the gate. At first there was nothing, so he dismissed it. The more he thought about it though, the more he felt sure he was being watched. He stared again, and this time could just about make out a shape, a figure, a girl dressed in rags, staring back at him. He wasn't gripped with fear, unlike when that idiotic man appeared in the fake mask. This time Max was gripped with curiosity. What is it that I can see? Who is this girl? Why is she there? Why is she staring at me?

5,262 days before the eclipse.

Anatola looked at the boy, now staring back at her. "Why are you crying boy? Are you an immortal spirit?" she asked. The boy did not answer, but instead continued to stare back. At least he has stopped crying now, she thought. Curiosity had also captured Anatola, who is he? Why is he here in this room? Anatola stepped forward to get a better look at the boy.

1,000,475 days after the eclipse.

The figure of the girl stepped closer. Max stood up gingerly. The girl stretched out her hand. Max began to grow nervous, unsure of what would happen if the two were to touch. He stepped forward to the gate. The girl stepped closer, with only a pace or two between them. Max put his hand through the bars and reached out to the girl. She was so close, almost now within touching distance.

5,262 days before the eclipse.

The boy was now so very near, seemingly unwilling to move forward. Is he afraid? she wondered. As he stretched out his hand, she leant in closer. Their fingertips once separated by nearly three millennia, were now just millimetres apart. The air fell silent as her concentration became fixated on the boy's hand. She held her breath, anticipating the touch, the moment.

"ANA! There you are!" Cardea exclaimed, grabbing her by the shoulder. Anatola instinctively turned to look at this rude interruption, before looking back at the boy. It was too late, he was gone. "Come on Ana, what is wrong with you?" demanded Cardea. Anatola continued to stare into the void once filled with the light of the crying boy. "Ana! – Snap out of it! We have to go; we are being called to the palace. We will play later." Cardea tugged at Anatola's arm, pulling her towards the door. It made little difference, as Anatola continued to stare into the now barren spot at the end of the room.

1,000,475 days after the eclipse.

The girl drifted away. Max tried desperately to reach further through the bars. He strained trying to reach her, the rusty bars scratching his skin. It was no good, she was gone. In the distance behind him, he heard Mother calling out. "Max! Where are you? We have to go now!"

Confident this phenomenal event was now over, he decided it would probably be wise to return to Mother, before Father became involved. He attempted to pull his arm back through the bars before realising he was now well and truly stuck. He began to panic.

"MOMMY! HELP ME!" he cried out.

"What have you done? Why are you stuck in that gate?" she asked. She grabbed him by his other arm and attempted to pull him free. The rust dug deeper, causing him to yell out in pain. "Oh for goodness sake Max; we can't go anywhere without you showing me up. I'll have to go get your father!" his mother said in frustration. "Stay here!"

"Well yes mother," he replied, rolling his eyes. She gave him a disapproving look before disappearing to get help.

Chapter Two

5,262 days before the eclipse.

Her grey palla dragged along the snow, getting increasingly heavier with each footstep. She hurried along the stone path, making her way to the Blue Palace. Stepping quickly, she hopped along the embankments of the public fountains, ducking through the busy marketplace. She picked up pace as the palace drew into sight, now running on her tip toes. She pulled her hood tighter as her fingers turned almost entirely white. The guards waiting at the end of the bridge, waved her across. Like a flash of grey, she cleared the frozen Blue Lake surrounding the palace. She raced up the steps, being careful not to drop her precious parcel. She turned the corner, narrowly avoiding a crash with an oncoming White Blood. "I beg your forgiveness!" she yelled back before turning the corner, up the final flight of stairs.

Inside the lavishly decorated room, Quinta waited impatiently. She tutted loudly, as she picked through her large collection of jewellery. "Finally!" she exclaimed. "Give it here!" she said, snatching the neatly wrapped parcel from the nearly exhausted White Blood girl. Quinta unwrapped the parcel and held aloft the swan fibula, handed down through the generations of her family. "You better not have dropped it!" she snapped, before passing it on.

The rest of the White Bloods began to swarm around Quinta, busily working away. A carefully selected group of ten began to style her hair, while another carefully positioned her jewellery. Others fastened up the many elaborately decorated buttons on her black tunic, while another laced Quinta's shoes. Eventually, she stood to her feet. The finishing touches were applied and her blue palla was drawn over her shoulders. The fibula was presented. Quinta nodded in agreement before taking it; only to then roll her eyes and thrust it back into the White Blood's hand. At first the girl was confused, then realising her mistake, she quickly opened the pin, and presented it back to Quinta.

Without thinking through what she was about to do, Quinta snatched the fibula back, pricking her finger on the sharp point. Quinta looked down in horror as a pool of blue blood began to form on her index finger. She let out an almighty scream before dramatically fainting.

Tita came running in, pushing White Bloods in all directions. "What have the ineptus done now?" she demanded. The White Bloods dispersed quickly to the edges of the room. Tita sat Quinta up. "There, there my child. What happened?" she asked.

Quinta still somewhat drowsy, could only mutter one word, "Blood."

Tita looked around frantically, expecting to find a gushing wound. Eventually she found her pricked index finger. "Oh really Quinta? You are being quite ridiculous. Get a move on, you silly girl. The procession leaves shortly. With or without you." Tita stormed out of the room, but not before giving the already terrified White Bloods another ear full.

The White Bloods helped Quinta to her feet, before a petrified girl carefully pinned Quinta's palla. All of the White Bloods parted to the edges of the room, allowing Quinta to leave in all her resplendence.

Outside, the steps to the private Blue Temple were lined with Red Blood signifers, proudly holding aloft the banners of each of the blood gens. Their red tunics, bronze cuirass and silver helmets, were a welcome contrast to Quinta, against the almost blinding amount of white snow, white stone work and white marble, now towering above her. A cold wind twisted and swirled around the Red Bloods, fluttering the banners loudly. The Eagle of the Red Bloods, the Falcon of the Orange Bloods, and the Magpie of the Green Bloods, set against white backgrounds to symbolise their dominance over the White Bloods, flew proudly. The White Bloods in turn were represented by a small white sparrow, set against a black background. At the top of the stairs, fluttered the banners of the Blue Swan and the Purple Raven, with edges decorated with golden thread.

Quinta quickly rushed into position alongside Lucius, who sniggered at his sister's late arrival. Tita turned and glared at both of them, instantly silencing the pair.

Inside the temple, lay the body of Decima, dressed in a white tunic, a golden stola and a blue palla. The ceremony had already begun, led by the Will of the Gods, the Purple Blood, known simply as the Raven. On command the Blue Bloods gathered silently around Decima. Servius wiped a tear from his cheek before stepping forward. He presented a single blue rose, which he lovingly placed on his wife's body. The Raven then signalled the six waiting Red Bloods to move into position. The Blue Bloods took a step back, allowing the Red Bloods to pick up the bier carrying Decima.

The Raven, in his purple paenula, pulled up his hood, and took his position at the front of the procession. The six Red Bloods, in their gloriously polished ceremonial armour, followed with Decima. Behind them came the Blue Bloods, in their blue togas and pallas. Next the signifiers, carrying the gens banners. Then followed the senior representatives of the Red Bloods, in their red lacernas, Orange Bloods in their orange birrus cloaks, and Green Bloods in their green paenulas. The procession concluded with the White Blood musicians, actors and trusted advisors, with little more than their tunics to protect them against the harshness of winter.

The bitter wind swirled around the colourful procession, bringing with it a heavy snowfall. Carefully, they made their way down the polished stone steps of the temple, and across the courtyard. The White Bloods of the palace, who had gathered in the snow to pay their final respects to a much loved imperatrix, joined the back of the group. Two lines of guards waited in position on Sparrow Bridge, before taking their places in the procession, in front of the growing number of White Bloods.

The route through the city to the Necropolis was now lined with citizens of every blood gens. Young children looked on in awe as the procession passed by. Quinta smiled as members of the crowd began to shout out praise for the Blue Bloods. The Raven led the procession past his temple, where his attendants had been waiting patiently in the storm. Dutifully, they took their places in the group.

Through the driving snow, the procession marched on, as more citizens joined the back of the group. At the Eastern Gate, the Red Bloods proudly held open the doors, as the Raven led the group through, out of the city.

Now outside the city walls, everything seemed so unfamiliar to Quinta. She had only ever been outside the city for Blue Blood funerals. She marvelled at the change in scenery, everything seemed so beautiful, now painted with virgin snow. A sharp jab in the back from her younger sister, Numeria, served to remind her to keep up.

The first of the group passed through the gates to the private Necropolis, reserved only for the Blue Bloods. Quinta caught the gaze of a very handsome Red Blood on the gate. She smiled back suggestively, knowing full well, that if Tita caught him, he would be flogged in the streets. When all but a select few White Bloods had passed through, the guards pushed back the crowd, and sealed the gates shut.

The Red Bloods carrying Decima, carefully laid her down upon the funeral pyre, next to a single white slab of marble. Everyone took their predetermined positions. White Blood actors stood around the perimeter, wearing masks of the ancient Blue Blood ancestors, the original ten. They were dressed in white tunics and blue togas for the men, and pallas for the women. Between them stood the musicians and the signifiers. At the front stood the living Blue Bloods.

The Raven stepped forward, reading aloud from a scroll, "Imperators, Caesars and citizens, we gather here to give thanks to the gods. We share with them a sacred bond, one that can never be broken by man. For it was written in stone by the gods themselves, the bond, a blood bond, one that binds us all..." Quinta rolled her eyes. The Raven's speech was just as boring as she had remembered from her childhood. "...for every life given, one must be taken. This is the bond. This is the word of the gods, and I am their will," the raven continued.

Quinta's gaze drifted away from the Raven, and happened to meet the red eyes of the guard from earlier, who was now stood within the walls of the Necropolis. This time he reciprocated her smile, causing Quinta to giggle. It then quickly dawned on Quinta, that everyone was now looking at her, including her furious mother, Tita. Quinta gasped and immediately pressed her hands tightly to her lips. She focused solely on the ground at her feet.

"Please continue!" Tita said apologetically to the Raven.

"Very well," he said, before clearing his throat. "As with every blood gens of Rytus, we are granted but just one lifetime in this mortal world. It is therefore, with a heavy heart, that at the start of the new day, we must see Decima to the afterlife. As she bore no child in her time, we can take comfort knowing that her mortal spirit will go on, through a gift from the gods, in the form of the child Decimus," The Raven pointed to one of his attendants, who dutifully placed a bundle of swaddling cloth on the marble slab. On cue, Decimus filled his lungs with air, but let out only a meek cry.

"Who claims the mortal spirit of Decima?" asked the Raven.

"I do!" replied Servius, stepping forward.

"Gods, grant this man the power to raise this child as his own. Allow him to teach Decimus the ways of the Blue Bloods, to care and to love. To cherish and to rule fairly," he loudly proclaimed. "And you, Blue Bloods of age, do you pledge to give your service in the teaching of this child?"

"We do!" Tiberius, Tita and Lucius replied.

"Very well, Servius, you may take the child," declared the Raven.

As instructed, Servius lent forward, and carefully picked up Decimus. He stopped for a moment to look at the child. He was so pale and weak, he looked desperately ill. However, before Servius could question the health of the child, the Raven continued.

"Let the blood debt be sealed," the Raven commanded, signalling his attendants waiting with flaming torches, to step forward, and light the funeral pyre. Each did as instructed, but the pyre struggled to light. The wood, now damp with the continued snowfall, smoked before extinguishing.

Those gathered began to look to the Raven for answers. He snatched a torch from one of his attendants, before lighting his scroll on fire. He tossed the scroll into the pyre followed by the torch. Tita raised an eyebrow at the Raven's rash behaviour. But before she could vocalise her thoughts, the pyre burst into life.

"There we go," the Raven muttered to himself, as the fire took hold.

The snow storm melted away as the smoke began to rise into the skies above. The wood crackled and popped as Decima's body became consumed by the flames. Servius's gaze remained fixed, seemingly frozen. A White Blood Nutrix offered to take the child from Servius but instead he dismissed her. He continued to cling tightly to Decimus, the child was now all that Servius had left of Decima's mortal spirit.

At the far end of the Necropolis, inside the tomb, where the funerary urns of all the Blue Bloods who had already paid their blood debt were housed; the procession gathered around the large table in the feasting hall, waiting for Servius to arrive with Decimus. Tita used the opportunity to scold Quinta for her behaviour. "What do you think you are playing at?" she demanded. Quinta remained silent, embarrassed by her own actions. "Here we are, in the presence of all your ancestors, and the gods themselves, and you think it is what, funny?" Quinta again remained silent. "This is wholly unacceptable behaviour!" But before Tita could continue her barrage of words, Servius entered. The room fell respectfully silent. Tita returned to her position by the table. Servius, as per the custom, sat down first.

"Let us celebrate her passing to the Blue Palace of Asphodel," he said, signalling the start of the feasting, music and plays. Quinta remained rigidly still, terrified of invoking the wrath of Tita again. To their mistake, the White Bloods behind her took this as a sign that Quinta wasn't listening; in fact, Quinta froze with a new deadlier fear, hearing every treasonous word they uttered.

"They feast, while we starve," they commented. "There are far more debts to be paid, more blue blood will yet be shed before the next passing."

Chapter Three

"I have always loved you," Alpheaus whispered. He gripped Diana's hand tightly, as the last essence of life left her body. His world grew mute, as the tears fell from his cheek, onto the fading mortal embodiment of his wife.

"Do not despair father, I am still here," Petrina said gently.

"I know," he replied, "and I am lucky to have you. I will miss her dearly though. I loved her so very, very much." He lifted Diana's hand and kissed it softly before placing it at her side. I must be strong for Petrina, he thought, as he wiped the tears from his eyes. He took a moment to compose himself, and rose from the stool at Diana's bedside. Petrina threw her arms around her father's waist; he lifted her chin, and saw her trying to fight back the tears.

"Do not be discouraged child. Do not be afraid to cry," he said, stroking her cheek.

"Where will she go now?" Petrina asked.

"To the after-life," he replied, "but first we must prepare her for the journey. I shall then carry her to the Necropolis, so that her blood bond may be severed and her immortal spirit allowed to enter the plain of Asphodel."

In the distance, the funeral procession of Decima, could be heard approaching. "Father, will she have a procession like the Blue Bloods?" Petrina asked.

He sat Petrina down. "No child, every day a White Blood severs their bond to the gods. The lives of the citizens of Rytus will not change because of another White Blood passing. Instead we will rejoice her name, we will remember her, and she will live on in us."

"I do not understand," she replied.

"You will in time," he explained, uncertain that he himself truly understood.

"Will you die too father?" she asked.

He pondered the question for a moment, deciding that perhaps this was not the best time to explain, that he too, was sick.

"Will you help me dress her?" he replied instead.

Petrina made her way into the second room of their tiny home, to retrieve Diana's belongings. Alpheaus took the time this gave him, to ponder what would happen when his final day as a mortal came. Were the stories they were told as children truly real? he wondered. Or were they a result of situations like this, lies repeated through the years, to comfort children and adults alike, at times of great difficulty? Before he could answer his own questions, Petrina returned with a grey tunic, grey stola and well-worn palla.

Together they lovingly prepared Diana, cleaning her skin with oils and a strigil. With great respect for their dearly departed, they carefully dressed her in the tunic, stola and palla, so that she would enter the afterlife with full dignity. Alpheaus lifted Diana into his arms. Petrina opened the door, and guided her father down the five flights of stairs, out on to the street. A few dawdling stragglers of Decima's funeral procession passed by, as Alpheaus stepped out carefully into the deep snow. His worn out sandals did little to protect his feet from the cold.

Dutifully, the pair followed as the procession quickly disappeared into the distance. Alpheaus struggled in the snow, to not only find his grip, but to deal with the almost crippling pain in his feet, as the cold bit down into his flesh. He slipped. Petrina quickly did what she could to catch her father. It was close but it was enough. He regained his balance, and breathed a sigh of relief as the Eastern Gate came into view.

A kind Red Blood held the gate open, as they made their way out of the city. In the distance, the Raven could be heard giving his speech. They made their way through the crowd gathered, all waiting for a glimpse of the Blue Bloods and their vast entourage. Swept up in curiosity, Petrina approached the gate to the private Blue Blood Necropolis, much to the annoyance of the Red Blood posted there.

Alpheaus whistled to her, "This way." Petrina did as instructed and returned to her father. He uttered a small prayer, before crossing the threshold into the walled yard with Diana. Petrina waited patiently by the gate as the snow continued to fall.

Seated in the corner, near a small fire pit, sat a White Blood administrator. His grey eyes were firmly fixed on the documents before him, as he desperately tried to write down the last few sentences, before his pen froze to the animal skin.

Alpheaus approached the man and waited patiently before announcing his arrival with a loud cough. The administrator briefly looked up before again attempting to complete the sentence he was so desperately trying to finish. Alpheaus coughed again, causing the administrator to throw down his pen.

"YES?" he barked, before remembering where he was. "I mean; how can I help you?" he said more softly, before noticing Diana in Alpheaus's arms. "Ah, today's White Blood death is?"

"Her name was Diana," Alpheaus dutifully replied.

"Occupation?" the administrator demanded.

"Cook, at the palace. And loving..."

"Very well," the administrator interrupted. "Place her there, please. An attendant will be along shortly to deal with her." The administrator waved to a Red Blood in the distance to fetch an attendant.

"Where?" Alpheaus asked, confused.

"There!" the administrator replied, pointing to the floor by the unprepared snow covered funeral pyre.

"On the floor?" Alpheaus questioned.

"Yes," the administrator replied.

"There on the floor?" he asked again.

"Do I not make myself clear? Yes. On the floor over there where I am pointing," the administrator explained, annoyed by his apparent lack of understanding of a simple instruction.

Alpheaus stood for a moment, confused and angry.

"Look," said the administrator with a change of heart and tone. "I appreciate this is not normal but Decima's cremation is taking place. All of my staff have been taken away from me. I am here on my own as you can see. I promise she will be seen to as soon as they are finished. You have my word." Unsure what other options he had, Alpheaus obeyed, and carefully laid Diana down as instructed.

He kissed her gently on her forehead, and placed her arms at her side. Her skin felt so cold. He looked at his own hands, his fingers were now almost frozen white. Alpheaus tried to clench his fists, but his fingers disobeyed. He drew them into his chest, longing to feel her warmth one more time. He felt frustrated and betrayed.

The smoke from the administrator's fire pit drifted towards Alpheaus, the soot stinging his eyes. He wiped away the tears and rose to his feet. The sparrows singing in the trees were silenced, as the musicians on the other side of the Necropolis's wall burst into song, signalling the end of Decima's funeral.

Alpheaus approached Petrina at the gate. Before he could comfort the tearful girl, the administrator in turn coughed loudly, to gain Alpheaus's attention. He turned to face the administrator who pointed at the Raven's attendant, standing alongside Diana, holding a bundle of swaddling cloth.

"Her replacement," explained the administrator. "Raise him to fulfil Diana's duties as er?" he consulted his notes again, "cook, yes as a cook."

Alpheaus approached the Raven's attendant. He was immediately captivated by her long white hair, as it fell from her raised hood; her grey eyes piercing into his soul. She stretched out her hands, offering the bundle to him. He stood speechless for a moment, before accepting the gift. He carefully unwrapped it, to find two grey eyes staring back at him. Alpheaus looked back up to thank the attendant but she was already gone, and so was Diana. Lost for words, he carefully wrapped the child up to protect him from the cold.

"What is it?" asked Petrina.

"A boy, a baby boy," Alpheaus explained with a smile. He turned back once more to the necropolis and whispered, "Goodbye".

"Forgive me, I have become a burden," he said apologetically, upon their return home.

"Father, you will never be a burden," she said reassuringly, as she guided him to his chair.

"Thank you my child," he replied gladdened.

They both admired the baby boy in his arms.

"Dianus. His name shall be Dianus," Alpheaus declared. "He will carry on the mortal spirit of your mother in his name. Who knows, he may even rise to the position of cook, in the Blue Palace, just as she did."

"What is my future?" Petrina asked.

"That I do not know, child. Your future has always been uncertain, ever since the day I found you. However, I believe the gods intend great things for you," he explained with a smile.

"Like what?" she asked.

He laughed, "Only the gods know the answer to that, my child. There is something burning inside of you. Something I have never seen in any other. I feel it within my heart..." Alpheaus, unable to continue, became gripped in a painful coughing fit.

"Father!" Petrina cried out, as Alpheaus gasped for air.

Chapter Four

5,261 days before the eclipse.

Aulus looked to the Blue Palace, its gleaming white marble columns towered into the skies above the group, casting a long shadow as the sun began to rise. The echoes of heavy footsteps approaching drew his attention back to the smaller, red tile topped barracks before him. In the distance a vast and powerful figure approached. Aulus had heard stories of the boys that go to the city, never to return. He had also heard the stories of the Red Blood leader stationed here. He had no time for nonsense and ruled with a heavy fist.

This was nothing like Eagle Blood Shores, his home until today. There, he was above the White Bloods who trained him. He rose through the trainees quickly, and he had made his doctore proud. Not here though. Here he was bottom of the pile. A New Blood with no battle experience and no respect, he could feel it already.

Publius strutted up to the group, sure footed and large in stature. "Listen up New Bloods, I am not your nanny," he bellowed. "I am not your father and I am never going to give a concacavi how you feel. Do I make myself clear?" he boomed. The boys looked around to see if anyone would respond to this monster of a figure before them.

Aulus looked to his childhood friend Darius, who simply shrugged his shoulders in reply.

"Good. Follow me!" Publius commanded.

The boys followed Publius into the barracks. Inside, smaller rooms for the seniors lay off a corridor to the right, and at the back of the barracks lay the baths, the Eagle shrine, and the hall of honours. The middle of the modest building was laid out as a dormitory, lit by red candles. The bunks were arranged in formations and at their feet were small wooden chests. The walls were filled with racks for weapons and armour, while banners of the Eagle hung from the columns. The barracks served as a base and home, for all the Red Bloods of White City.

As they passed, Aulus noted the battle scarred Red Bloods sat on their beds. They were mostly occupied preparing for the day ahead, cleaning down their pilums and wiping blood off their shields. The air was thick with the smell of bodily odours and stale blood. Another boy, Velius, began to explain how his doctore was regarded as one of the best trainers in all of Eagle Blood Shore. "I am not afraid of any of this," he gloated.

Aulus made the unfortunate mistake of catching the glare of Gaius. He couldn't help himself. Gaius had a large scar running from the top of his head, down through his right eye, continuing down to his chin. Gaius met the curious gaze of Aulus with a growl, while gesturing to slit his throat. Not wanting to give him a chance to carry out this threat, Aulus caught back up with the group, as they made their way through the large dormitory.

The boys gathered around Publius, now positioned in the middle of the hall of honours. "These are the Red Bloods you should be proud of, well what is left of them," he declared, as he gestured towards the armour hanging from the wall, with large holes gouged out of it, a shield with an axe still buried deep in the wood, and a splintered pilum. Pride of place was granted to a well-polished sword, crafted from Invictus steel, embellished with an eagle in the handle. "Ah yes! The sword of Ravenstone, hell of a story to go with that, boys. Perhaps I will tell you someday," Publius resounded as he lovingly ran his index finger along the sword's edge. He lent back, opened his arms out wide and took a deep breath, "Breathe it in boys. Death. It comes to us all. Just be sure you are on the right end of it when your time comes." The boys exchanged puzzled looks.

"Listen closely, I am not one for repeating myself," Publius explained, leaning down to the boy's level. "Each of you were born as Red Bloods, raised by the pathetic White Bloods. I am hoping they, at least, taught you the basics of combat, so that today you can earn the right to truly call yourself Red Bloods," he bellowed, as he gestured out of the door and across the bridge, to the famous fighting pit of White City. "Forget any allegiances you forged at Eagle

Blood Shores; after today you will no longer be known as boys, you will become men."

"Yesterday we lost six good men and women, any of you that can count will realise there are in fact ten of you. Therefore, to test your resolve, you will fight to the death until only six of you remain. Do I make myself clear?" Publius asked. Velius, still unwilling to conceal his smile, laughed in the face of a smaller weaker boy.

The Old Bloods passed through the room, carrying their swords and shields, making their way to the pit. Varia stopped to look at the new stock. "This is what they send us?" she sneered. "A bunch of snivelling children? Every time the gods mock us, sending us weaker ones. Bah!" she said dismissively. "I bet none of you will last a day out there in the real world!" she said, pointing her index finger at the smallest boy in the group before leaving.

Publius sighed, "Prepare yourselves boys."

In the pit, the experienced Red Bloods began beating the butts of their swords against their shields. The sound echoed through the corridors to the boys, who stared back in anticipation. Aulus closed his eyes to visualise victory, before Velius intentionally knocked him off balance. Aulus shoved him back. "Save it for the pit, boys," Publius barked. An attendant from the Raven's temple stepped forward from the Eagle's shrine, where she had been preparing, and blessed the boys with water and bone dust.

Publius picked up a box and presented it to the group. "This is it boys, no time like the present. Each of you place your bulla in here. Say goodbye to your childhood." The boys, as instructed, one by one, lined up to place their bulla in the box, before heading out across the bridge towards the pit. The sound of the shields being drummed filled the air; as a flock of sparrows flew from the Raven's Temple casting its imposing shadow on the pit below.

The small crowd that had gathered, applauded the boys as they entered. Aulus looked around; this truly was nothing he had ever seen before. His heart began to race. His breathing increased. His chest felt tight with anticipation. The boys began to spread out around the pit.

A group of White Bloods carrying wooden boxes entered, and began to distribute poor quality swords among the waiting boys. Velius scoffed, "What am I to do with this? Batter someone to death? It certainly would not be much use to cut with."

Publius entered the pit, raising his hand to signal the boys to wait. He peered up to the Swans Nest above, and waited for the arrival of Tiberius and Tita. "Boys, we are blessed this day. For I present to you the legates of the Red Bloods," Publius declared, before bowing respectfully. Aulus

51

dutifully dropped to one knee and bowed his head. The other boys followed suit.

Tiberius walked to the front of the platform and bellowed out to the crowd. "Red Bloods and citizens of Rytus, I present forth these boys..." He sneered at the boys scattered in the pit, before addressing them directly. "You were born as Red Bloods. You were trained to fight in the pits of Eagle Blood Shores. You have learnt how to wield a sword. You have learnt how to use a shield to your advantage. You have learnt the art of fighting with sticks against wooden posts," he paused and smiled, as the crowd laughed and cheered. "In the past your kind were forced to fight before the gods, in the Eagle Blood Arena. For days, the battles would rage on, as those who failed the test were ground into the clutches of Orcus. Now that I, Tiberius Hyacintho Olor, stand as Imperator and Legate to the Red Bloods, I have been forced to move the trials here to my home. The traditions of old remain valid. Only the greatest Red Bloods can protect the Blue Bloods. Only the best can fight for our liberties. Only the strongest can keep the peace. Only the brave can stamp out rebellion. You have come of age, but are you truly ready to be Red Bloods? Are you ready to earn that honour? Who will rise from the ashes of their enemies and soar into the ranks of men? Today we will discover who among you is worthy to fight for Rytus, and all that she represents!"

Publius promptly left the pit and the gates were closed behind him.

Tiberius dropped his hand. "Begin!" he shouted.

At first no-one was really sure what to do. It had all come as a bit of a shock for them. "I swear the gods laugh at us, every day they send us weaker and more idiotic boys," Tita muttered, before rising from her chair. "Do something! We have not all day," she shouted, unimpressed by the lack of action.

Velius didn't need telling again. He ran at a smaller boy, striking him in the stomach, causing a slight flesh wound. Tita clapped. Velius smiled up at her. Darius saw his opportunity and struck Velius with the butt of his sword, causing Velius to drop to the floor, face first into the slushy snow and wet sand. Darius helped the smaller boy up, before defending himself from another.

Aulus spotted a boy approach his friend from behind. He threw his useless heavy sword down, and raced over to Darius, grabbing a handful of sand. He launched the sand into the face of the boy, temporarily blinding him.

"Thank you brother," Darius said gratefully.

"Anytime friend," Aulus replied.

Darius immediately kicked his crippled attacker in the gut, sending him flying into the towering walls of the pit.

"One down, three to go," Tiberius announced.

Aulus turned, just as one of the boys fell to the floor at his feet, clutching his own throat. Darius and Aulus watched as the red blood began to pool in the wet sand. Aulus bent down to pick up the boy's sword. He immediately beat back another attacker, taking a slight cut to the abdomen. The other boy, thrilled at drawing blood, caught Aulus off guard, pushing him to the floor. The boy held the sword above his head, exposing his abdomen, giving Darius the opportunity to strike. Darius used his full might to launch his useless but heavy sword into the boy, winding him. The boy dropped to the floor, gasping for breath.

Before Aulus could strike, Tita cheered, as her new champion, Velius, struck the boy down with the butt of his sword, breaking his jaw. Teeth and blood scattered on to the sand as Velius delivered a fatal blow with his foot, breaking the boy's neck.

"Unconventional, but it gets results," commented Tiberius, "two down, two to go!"

Velius wiped the blood from his face, and turned his attention to Aulus and Darius. "You are not beating me," he scowled.

"Watch out!" Darius cried.

Aulus turned to see another boy, running at them with a rock he had found. He charged towards Aulus, his eyes narrowed. Instinctively but reluctantly, Aulus cut the boy down.

Tita sat up straight, "Perhaps a *new* candidate for my guard emerges?"

This infuriated Velius, who screamed at the pair, before charging for them, sword held aloft. Another boy, tripped Velius as he ran, causing him to come crashing down in a heap on the floor. Darius laughed at Velius.

Velius climbed to his feet, his face red with anger. Once again, he charged for the boys. Aulus almost felt sorry for him, though it didn't stop him lowering his sword into prime position for Velius to impale himself.

Velius drew so close, that Aulus could see clearly into his furious red eyes. Aulus braced. Time to end this nonsense once and for all, he thought, preparing for the bite of the sword.

"STOP!" Tiberius declared.

Aulus immediately dropped his sword, grabbed Velius by the shoulder and forced him with all his might, over to the side. Darius turned to face Tiberius, just as Velius came crashing down next to Aulus.

"We have our six new Red Bloods!" Tiberius proudly declared, gesturing to the back of the group, as a final boy dropped to the floor in a heap.

The gates swung open and Publius returned to the pit, "Well done men, you have earned the right to call yourselves New Bloods. Now only the gods themselves can strike us down!"

The Raven, watching proceedings from the temple, laughed. "We will see about that, soon enough dear Publius," he sneered.

Chapter Five

Marcus hurriedly examined a scroll in the flickering candle light. He consulted the etchings in the stone wall of his dimly lit private quarters, deep below the intricate marble floor of the Raven's temple. "No," he muttered to himself, "this will not do." He put the scroll back down on the smooth surface of the once jagged stone, jutting from the foundations of the temple above. He walked over to the oldest scrolls in his collection, hidden in the far corner. He ran his fingers along the old forgotten leather and wax bindings, leaving a trail in the dust. This one, he thought, grasping at the most worn of them all. He blew the dust from the casing before rolling out its stained animal skins. He stamped his position on the scroll with his index finger, and marched back over to the etched wall.

He stared intently at the scroll for a moment before muttering a phrase to himself. He looked up from the scroll to see if any affect had been made. He cleared his throat, put the scroll down, and stood facing the wall with both arms outstretched. "Indica mihi," he proclaimed. Nothing. Marcus took a moment to rethink his steps, and began pacing the room, muttering to himself. "But of course!" he cried. He picked up the old scroll again, put on his purple paenula, and stood over the bronze plate in the centre of his quarters. "Corvus calls," he chanted, right hand over the plate, as if he were trying to benefit from the warmth, with his left hand still grasping tightly at the scroll. "Diis exaudi me," he chanted.

His face began to cut through the darkness as the plate came to life with light. Soon it filled with a bright ball of purple aura. "YES!" he excitedly declared, "Yes this will work!" The purple aura stabilised. Marcus picked it up with his right hand. Carefully he carried it over towards the etched wall, and once again he spoke, "indica mihi." Unlike the first attempt, the aura left his hands and dissipated into the wall. Gradually, one by one, the etchings began to glow.

Marcus, overcome with joy, laughed as the wall lit up with over a thousand names, etched into the stone. He ran his fingers along the gritty wall, feeling the indentations of the letters.

The aura began to fade away, plunging the room back into darkness. Marcus took a moment to take in all that he had achieved before leaping for joy, punching the air. He laughed with an almost menacing tone.

He suddenly became aware he was not alone. Aegle, one of his attendants, waited patiently at the bottom of the stairs, respectfully transfixed on the floor. "Yes?" Marcus asked, not appreciating this interruption at such a pivotal time. She looked up sheepishly.

"I beg your forgiveness Dominus, Servius the Blue Blood, demands your counsel," she explained.

"Tell him I will be available in the temple shortly," he replied, "and stop calling me Dominus. Call me Marcus."

"Forgiveness," she stopped, unable to think of another more appropriate way to address the man she served.

Servius pushed her aside, knocking her off her feet. Marcus gave Servius a displeased glare. "And how may I counsel you, Imperator?" Marcus asked, through gritted teeth.

"What right, Raven, do you or your gods, have to take the life of a Blue Blood?" Servius demanded stomping around the room, examining Marcus's belongings, squinting in the dim light.

"Imperator, it is the will of the gods. The blood debt must be paid," Marcus replied calmly, trying to discreetly draw the hangings back over the etched wall.

"She was a Blue Blood. Why not take the life of one of these worthless White Bloods?" Servius barked back, pointing in the direction of Aegle.

"To the gods, all blood gens are equal. To give Decimus life, I had to take from Decima. It is the will of the gods and I am their voice," Marcus replied continuing to keep calm.

"You and your gods are nothing to me. Decima was my everything. She was my world. I loved her in a way, you, a destitute Purple Blood, could NEVER understand!" Servius continued, squaring up to Marcus.

"Imperator, we agreed..." Marcus tried to respond.

Servius placed his right hand around Marcus's neck, and lifted him up, clear of the floor. Marcus began to kick out, while desperately grabbing at Servius's hand. Aegle gasped in horror as she ran to the aid of her master. Servius, without breaking his stare, struck out; knocking Aegle to the floor.

"Listen to me Raven," Servius sneered. "If you ever trick me, or my family again, this dark stone pit will become your tomb!"

Marcus struggled, spluttering a sound which Servius took as confirmation that Marcus understood the deal. Servius dropped him in a heap on the floor and left.

Aegle ran over, "Please, Dominus, are you hurt?"

"I am fine," he replied hoarsely, as he sat up rubbing his neck.

She turned to run, "I will fetch a Green Blood."

"No," he replied, grabbing her hand. "Please. I will be fine. I just need a few moments to think, alone."

"Very well," she replied, "I will close the temple."

"No," he pleaded, "I will see those waiting. Just give me some time, please."

"As you wish," she paused, momentarily, "Marcus."

He smiled. She giggled shyly before leaving as instructed.

Marcus picked himself up, gathered up his belongings, and returned the scrolls to their rightful place. Just as he was about to leave for the temple above, a faint purple aura behind the hangings caught his attention. He drew them back revealing a new name on the wall. The aura faded before Marcus could read it. He collected a candle from the opposite side of the room, and lit it using the smouldering torch, positioned nearby. He walked it over to the etched wall, carefully protecting the precious flame from being extinguished prematurely. He offered the light up to the wall. There, etched in the stone, a new name, 'SERVIUS'. Marcus took a few moments to absorb this seemingly simple instruction, before blowing out the candle and drawing the hangings once again. He dusted off his clothes, drew up his hood, composed himself, and began ascending the stairs to the temple.

The temple was bathed in unusually warm winter sunlight. He squinted as his eyes took a moment to adjust to the change. Before he could continue, he caught sight of a familiar figure, lent against the wall; a woman, with two Red Bloods at her side.

"Hail Raven," she greeted.

Marcus, without thinking replied, "Hail Tita," causing one of the Red Bloods to growl with discontent. "Imperatrix," Marcus said, correcting himself.

"Raven, the crop yields were down again at the harvest. There will not be sufficient food to see this winter out," She explained, as the group walked through to the public section.

"Imperatrix, what is it that you wish me to do?" he asked, slightly puzzled.

"Tell the White Bloods they must go without. If we are to survive this winter, they must not gorge on the food they have," she said.

"Apologies Imperatrix, but that will not solve this crisis. If the harvest was not bountiful, then it is already too late, they have very little as it is," he replied, attempting to commence his duties.

"You will do as you are commanded!" she barked, blocking the way.

"I beg your forgiveness," Marcus replied, trying to conceal the anger welling inside of him. "I did not mean to be obstructive. Just that I do not understand what it is that you wish the White Bloods to do? You already had their homes in Falcon Reach burnt to the ground to clear room for more crops. Now they live in hovels on stilts in the swamp. They eat only a small amount of oats mixed with water once a day; most have never tasted meat. They are sick and now they starve." Marcus tried again to return to his duties.

"Listen here Raven," Tita snapped, "With Saturnalia fast approaching, we cannot be wasting good food on White Bloods. Do as your Imperatrix commands, or else I will have your temple burnt to the ground, and you too will find yourself living with the rats in the swamps."

Marcus somehow managed to contain his anger, as Tita and her guards left, one of them barging him aside in the process. He took a deep breath before muttering to himself.

He turned back towards the altar, as the rays of sunlight pierced the cloud, illuminating the highest point, the Raven's perch. A sign from the gods perhaps? he thought. He used the short walk up the steps to contemplate what he would say. Would he do as commanded by Tita, biding his time until cold justice could be paid out, or would he take this sign as the time to strike, and set in motion a lifetime of planning? he pondered.

The rays of sunlight felt warm on his face, like a loving hand guiding him into position above the crowd. Below him citizens of almost all the blood gens gathered.

White Blood mothers with children, some their own, some of other gens being raised and trained by the White Bloods, looked upward. Orange Blood archers stood gathered toward the edges; Red Bloods wishing the blessings of the gods before going on patrol, and Green Bloods praying for greater understanding of their healing powers, waited patiently. Everyone but the Blue Bloods, anticipating his words, staring up at the hooded man basking in the light of the gods, hoping for guidance to get them through another cold winter's day.

"Friends," he proclaimed. "The gods bless you all with good fortune this day. Winter can be harsh for us all. The gods must now test Rytus and her strength of devotion so that you, the citizens, can enjoy the pleasures that spring and summer will bring. Go forth this day, spend time with your loved ones and enjoy the day we have granted you. Spread this message, conserve and share. This is the will of the gods and I am their voice," he declared with convincing tone.

The small crowd began to disperse as Marcus descended the stairs, he felt like he had betrayed them all. The guilt burnt inside him, turning to rage. He struck out at the foundations of the steps. He pounded his fists against the hard unforgiving stone, until blood began to seep from his wounds. Acquilina, an attendant, rushed to his side, placing herself between him and the stone. She instinctively placed her arms around him, her head against his chest. Marcus stopped, and recoiled his hands. He felt the warmth and affection of Acquilina calming his soul. He bowed his head, embracing her spirit. His breathing slowed down to a normal pace, and the pain in his chest subsided. For a moment he felt completely at ease. This was warmth he had not felt for a very long time. He closed his eyes, and he became immersed in the sensations pulsing through his veins.

Aegle turned the corner to be greeted with a sight that made her heart sink. She felt the flame burning inside her had now been almost entirely extinguished. She turned and ran to the attendants' quarters in a flood of tears.

Completely unaware of the pain inflicted on Aegle, Marcus continued to embrace the moment, now with his arms around Acquilina. He took a deep breath. The smell of incense burning in the temple, the smell of her hair, it all filled his being. He had never noticed before how sweet it all smelt. He ran his fingers through her long white hair, evoking inside feelings he had forgotten long ago. Here lay in her some form of peace, a hole in his soul that had laid barren for so long.

That was until the memories that haunted his nightmares began flooding back. The pain of love lost, snatched from his hands by the Red Bloods. Her screams as she was dragged kicking and screaming from his arms. The painful memories that he had tried so hard for years to forget, now filled his mind in all their agonising glory. With a deep and terrifying passion Marcus yelled out, "NO!" pushing Acquilina back into the blooded stone. The pain crippled Marcus bringing him down to his knees. Acquilina, realising now what she had done must have been terribly wrong, ran away in fear. Marcus doubled over in pain on the floor, his bloody knuckles now clenched in tight fists against his chest, seemingly trying to extract the pain. He let out an almighty cry, howling like a wounded bear.

Marcus climbed to his feet still clutching at his chest, tears streaming down his face. He staggered down the stairs into his quarters. He threw himself against the etched wall, accidentally tearing down one of the hangings.

"I cannot live this lie any longer," he cried as he clutched at the torn hanging, feeling it crumple in his hands. He looked at his blooded fists. "Why?" he demanded, "How could you?" He paused, his face contorted with pain. "You were all I had, you were the only person who knew me, who I really am." He sat in almost total darkness, his knees now brought up to his chest. He sobbed uncontrollably into the hanging he still clutched in his hand.

A wave of clarity washed over him. He hurried to his feet discarding the hanging. He wiped away the tears, brought the torch closer and pulled up a chair. He began hurriedly writing down a long list of names.

Once the list was complete, he emerged from his quarters. He was greeted by a crowd of his attendants all looking concerned, with the exception of two. Aegle stood emotionless, with a blank expression on her face. Acquilina hid towards the back, hoping no-one would find out it was her who drove her master to madness, this time.

Marcus pushed the list into the hands of Aellae. "Take this to her," he explained. "It is time for old debts to be paid. The gods will have their blood!" Marcus returned immediately to his quarters, without saying another word. His attendants looked at each other with confusion. Aellae did as instructed and left immediately.

Chapter Six

5,261 days before the eclipse.

Acernis sat at one of the many desks neatly arranged around Magpie Hall, surrounded by his peers. He scribbled down, as fast as he could, the information being presented to him by the more senior Green Blood, Ulmus. In the middle of the hall, on the floor lay a White Blood woman, desperately sick. Her skin was soaked with sweat. Her face was entirely white, even more so than normal for a White Blood. Her lips were dry. Her breathing was shallow. Her words were faint and garbled. Her expression was dazed, and her body lacked in even enough strength to lift her own arms.

"Medicine has failed to cure her," Ulmus declared, pointing to the woman. "Now her fate lies with the gods," he paused, "or does it? Close the doors!" he commanded. Dutifully the White Bloods obeyed their master's demands and sealed shut the large wooden doors of the hall.

"Watch closely," he instructed, before kneeling at the woman's side. He ran his fingers along her arm, disturbing the beads of sweat. He fell silent for a moment while tightly gripping her hand; bowing his head and quietly chanting.

Acernis leant forward, trying to hear the words being uttered. Ulmus replaced the woman's hand at her side and began to rise from his knelt position. "Acernis," he said softly, "do not know the words. Feel them within your heart." Acernis returned only a look of confusion. "Come here," Ulmus commanded, "feel for yourself." As instructed, Acernis approached with intrigue. "Kneel, take her hand," Ulmus demanded.

Acernis knelt at her side and, with hesitation in his heart, he took her hand. Ulmus guided him, "close your eyes. Breathe deep. Lose the sounds of all but my voice." Acernis closed his eyes and took a deep breath. The hall fell silent. He heard no sound apart from that of each breath he took; each intake of air now louder than the one before.

"Forget the mind. Forget the body. Feel the ground where you kneel; feel it press against your flesh. Feel the weight of your own bones," his mentor explained. "Look inside yourself; find the swirling essence of your own soul. Do you see it?" Acernis's expression changed to one of confusion, then frustration, before he felt a calming breeze beginning to flurry inside. Out of the dark, a vision of green swirling aura began to twist and turn before him.

"Yes Mentoris," he replied.

"Let it dance in the dark, feel it move with your desires and your hate."

Acernis watched it twist and turn as he explored a whole range of emotions taking control of his body.

"Reach out with your mind and make it still," Ulmus instructed.

Acernis concentrated and, sure enough, he brought the swirling aura to a resting halt. "Now feel her hand in yours. Feel it pressing against your own," Ulmus instructed. "Search your own mind. Feel through the skin and flesh. Peer deep inside, beyond *her* bones. Find it within her; find the soul. Grasp it. Feel it. Let it entwine with your own. Let it swirl around you. Guide it to your own thoughts."

The hall remained silent.

"Something is wrong," Acernis replied, "her soul. It is dim, motionless."

"That is good," Ulmus replied.

Acernis snapped out of his trance. "How can that be good?" he demanded.

"Do not break the bond," his mentor replied calmly, "her soul is not dead. It is being suffocated. Crushed. Held down by a darkness within her core."

Acernis closed his eyes, settled back down and concentrated. This time, sure enough, just as Ulmus had described, there on her aura, lay a black void. Crushing, draining and suffocating her soul.

"Shake the darkness from within. Grasp it and pull it clear. Let her soul rise, let it shine through once more."

Acernis reached out to grasp at it with his free hand but it remained unmoved. His brow furrowed as he tried once again. Those gathered gasped in awe, as a black smoky cloud began to rise from the woman's chest, commanded by the open hand of Acernis. He drew the black aura in to his outstretched hand.

"Yes. Yes. YES!" exclaimed Ulmus with growing excitement. "Hold your commitment Acernis, hold on to the darkness." His mentor carefully took hold of Acernis's hand, turning it over, but so as to not lose his grip on the choking cloud. "Now, let it go." Ulmus released his hand, just as Acernis did as instructed, releasing the aura. Ulmus carefully guided the toxic smoke upward, before releasing it fully from his control. The black cloud rose up, slowly. All eyes remained fixed on the cloud.

The woman coughed and spluttered before gasping for air, as if she had just surfaced from the ocean. Acernis opened his eyes. "Well done Acernis, well done indeed. You are much stronger than I could ever have hoped," his mentor said, praising him while patting him on the back, "and you did not need to call out to the gods to help you, as I had to. You have great strength, even more so than I. I am very proud of you," he paused, a smile now gleaming across his face, "brother." His peers gathered around him to congratulate him, while White Bloods began to assist the confused and dazed woman.

Without warning, one of the doors to the great hall opened just enough for a White Blood to squeeze inside.

"Please accept my forgiveness Dominus," she announced respectfully, "Servius approaches."

The hall was immediately thrown into panic, as Green and White Blood alike began to frantically remove all trace of the events that had just unfolded. No sooner had the woman gained her footing, when a group of five or so White Bloods swept her away, and into another room, closing shut the door behind them.

The senior Magpies ushered the younger members out of sight, picking up scrolls on the way, some even kicked scrolls under desks in the chaos. Acernis was guided back into a seated position at the side of the hall. Others quickly found a spot, any scroll and a companion, to immediately begin a composed debate on the benefits of medicine, over the banned arts of signum altercations.

A knock at the door. Everyone froze rigidly still. The White Bloods nearest the door quickly dispersed, as Ulmus approached it to greet Servius. He took a moment to compose himself. He straightened up his tunic and kicked a stray scroll out of the path of the door, into the waiting arms of a low ranking Magpie called Seniorem, who instinctively, without thinking, threw it out the window. Ulmus looked at the young man coldly before letting out a heavy sigh. He cleared his throat, then threw open the doors.

"Imperator! What a pleasant surprise," he said with convincing enthusiasm. Servius looked around the hall at the various Green Bloods, glaring at him like they were cornered prey. Ulmus coughed loudly, reminding the others to carry on about their business. Servius, though a little confused, continued into the hall, followed closely by his immediate entourage.

"I bring with me Decimus Hyacintho Olor," Servius explained, gesturing for the Nutrix carrying Decimus to step forward, "sent by the gods themselves; Decima's mortal spirit, a future Imperator and my beloved grandson. He is sick. I fear he will not see the night out. Therefore, I present him to be blessed by the Magpies, to guard and protect him, from disease and ill health, from now until the day his blood bond is severed." He paused, looking solemnly at Ulmus. "Make him well again," he said with sincerity.

"And it is with great honour that we welcome Decimus into the world," Ulmus replied, taking the child from the Nutrix. He paused to unwrap Decimus from his bundle, expecting to see a healthy young baby. Instead he was greeted with a sickly, undersized shadow of a child. "And what a handsome Cesar he is too," he commented, trying not to cause offence. He walked with the child to the centre of the great hall, where the light was brightest. Ulmus looked deep into the child's blue eyes. "If he dies, I will invoke the wrath of the Blue Bloods for failing them. If I

73

refuse I will likely be flogged and they will get someone else to do it," he muttered to himself. "May the gods bless this child, let us begin," he proclaimed.

Ulmus ushered Servius and his entourage to the edge of the room, and called the other Green Bloods present forward. "We put on a show. We wave some offerings around and so on. Follow my lead," Ulmus explained to the newer hall members, before dispersing them to collect their green paenulas. White Bloods entered, carrying with them small wooden boxes, containing a variety of items from berries and branches, to bones and minerals; which they then began to distribute to the waiting Green Bloods.

Servius looked on, as the Green Bloods pulled up their hoods, and formed a circle around Ulmus, who in turn, carefully put on his own paenula, while being mindful not to drop the newest member of the second most powerful blood gens in Rytus. The tension within Servius grew, as the Green Bloods drew in closer around Ulmus, now he had to place all his faith in the Green Bloods not to hurt weak little Decimus, his only remaining mortal link to the only woman he had ever truly loved.

Now so close that their shoulders touched, the Green Bloods bowed their heads respectfully, and closed their eyes. Ulmus carefully clung on to little Decimus, before bowing his own head, and closing his eyes.

"Deos, audi nos," they all called out twice, "gods, hear us." Each Green Blood then offered their gift upwards to the gods with their left hand, and this time shouted their demands of the gods, "GODS, HEAR US!"

Panic struck Servius as Decimus, startled by events, began to wail. Concerned for his wellbeing, Servius stepped forward to put a premature end to proceedings. He stopped as the ground beneath his feet began to tremble.

Ulmus looked up, "STAY BACK!" he commanded, "You will put us all in great danger." Somewhat taken aback by being commanded, Servius for once, did exactly as he was told.

Ulmus closed his eyes once more, and searched deep within Decimus's soul for the swirling blue aura of this future ruler. He was struggling. The other Green Bloods held their position, while their mentor and leader's expression turned to one of confusion. "No," he muttered, "this is not right." The Green Bloods lowered their offerings and took a step back, to allow Ulmus space to think, to breathe.

"Acernis!" Ulmus called out, "where are you?"

"I am here Mentoris," he replied.

"You, you should lead this. You have shown great potential in..." Ulmus paused, remembering Servius was still in the room. "Erm? Yes, in your studies," he continued, "here, stand here, hold Decimus."

Servius remained agitated. His concerns for his grandson and the stories of Ravenstone, pulsated through his heart and mind. He clenched his fists and closed his eyes, in the hope that his anguish would ease.

Ulmus ushered Acernis into place, taking his paenula off, and placing it carefully over Acernis and Decimus. "It is traditional," he explained with a smile. Ulmus took a few steps back and instructed the group to continue. "Remember what you learnt today Acernis, use it wisely," he said, while tilting his head in Servius's direction, to hint to Acernis not to overdo it.

The Green Bloods formed around Acernis. They raised their offerings to the gods, while Acernis closed his eyes, and began to search deep within his own soul, for that of Decimus's. He looked into the dark void and saw only his own aura, just as Ulmus had.

Acernis knew that if he invoked the banned art of manipulation, he would likely find himself in the prison below the palace, probably alongside his mentor, but the death of the child could also yield the same result. He took a deep breath and mulled it over for just a few seconds, before calling on the gods. "Gods, hear me. Grant me the wisdom and knowledge to see within this child. To find at his core the soul and life force that you so kindly granted him."

Everyone waited to see what would happen next, all except Servius, who could no longer contain his anxiety, and promptly left the hall, taking with him most of his entourage. The rest remained, too mesmerised by what was about to take place, even at the risk of a scolding from their master later.

Acernis began to lose hope that the gods would hear his demands, when in the distance of the void, a dim, weak and pale blue spark lay flat. Unsure what this truly meant, Acernis reached out and picked up the spark. He brought it closer. Instantly the spark ignited and twisted around Acernis's own green aura, draining it, suffocating it like a poison. He dropped to his knees, still cradling the child. All those gathered gasped.

"Fight it, stand up!" Ulmus shouted.

The spark bolstered and grew into a swirling tornado, draining all but a dim ebb of life from Acernis. He tried to stand, but only found himself back on his knees, struggling to breathe, to speak, to call for help. He opened his eyes and looked down at the child, whose eyes burned bright blue and green, the aura visibly swirling around his pupils. Acernis panicked. What do I do? he thought. If I die and the child remains in this condition, the Green Bloods will surely be banished from Rytus forever.

"I have to fix this," he gasped, finding it increasingly difficult to breathe.

He struggled to his feet and placed his right hand on the child, while cradling him in his left arm. He closed his eyes and confronted the fiery blue tornado tearing into his soul. Unable to offer up his hands to bring down this life sucking monster, Acernis was left with no choice but to bring this battle into a new realm.

Using all the strength he could muster, he began to draw out the aura. Out of the void. Out of his own body. A bolt of blue lightning struck out from Acernis and Decimus, knocking Ulmus and two other Green Bloods off their feet. The rest scattered to the edges of the hall. The remaining members of Servius's entourage ran for the door, to make their escape.

"STOP THEM!" Shouted Iuniperorum, another of the senior Green Bloods, "No-one must break the seal on that door, until this is over!"

The bolts of lightning, now accompanied by swirling clouds of green and blue gas, began to charge the air. "CONTROL THIS ACERNIS!" Ulmus shouted, as he picked himself up off the floor, "Bring this back under control, NOW!"

A deep seated rumble took hold of the ground. Shelves began to split and tear apart, as scrolls continued to tumble to the floor. The large window frames began to groan, as dust and debris began to rain down on the occupants of the hall. A large wooden beam splintered and crashed to the ground, trapping two White Bloods. The glass in the windows shattered and showered the terrified Green Bloods below.

Acernis used almost all the energy he had left to block out the sounds of the static discharge of the lightning bolts, the screams of everyone trapped inside, and the might of those trying to keep the doors shut. He closed his eyes and began to search inside for what remained of the aura. Nothing. No wait, there! A tiny amount of his own soul remained. Acernis surmised that this was all that was left keeping him alive.

"What is wrong?" Ulmus shouted to Acernis, across the chaos.

"My soul, it is weak. I cannot fight this alone," he replied weakly.

Ulmus thought for a moment, then ran to Acernis's side, "Take mine."

"But you said yourself you are not as strong as I am. This may kill you!"

"If we do not fix this, I am sure I am a dead man anyway."

Ulmus reached out and held onto Acernis's arms. Both men now stood together, heads bowed, with Decimus carefully still cradled, while the hall fell into total disarray.

Both men peered into the void; their souls now combining into a stronger aura, turning and switching like a flock of birds, riding the winds.

"I know you can do this," Ulmus whispered, as Acernis began to draw the aura into the hall. It spilled out on to the floor, filling the cracks in the stone work. It bled into the walls before spreading out across the ceiling.

Outside the hall, alarmed by events inside, Servius began to bang furiously at the doors. "LET ME IN!" he commanded, "I am your Imperator, and I demand you to let me in!" Together with his entourage, he began to pull desperately at the doors.

Inside, the hall became entombed within the green aura of Acernis and Ulmus's combined souls. All they needed to do now was to bring it under control. Both men gave everything they had left, all that they could give. With an almighty boom, that shook the walls of the hall and the ground outside, knocking everyone from their feet including Servius; the seemingly uncontrollable energy imploded.

The hall once more fell silent and still.

Acernis immediately checked on Decimus, who despite almost killing everyone in the room, returned a smile and a giggle. Acernis wiped the dust and debris from the child's head, before looking again into his soul. Now, instead of a flat spark, Acernis saw two swirling auras, a blue and a green, twisting, turning, dancing together in complete harmony.

Servius came bursting into the hall, as the others began to pick themselves up. He stormed over furious, demanding answers. Acernis presented the child to Servius. This was the first time he had ever heard Decimus gurgle joyfully. The broad smile across his face, the glow in his cheeks, this was not the weak sickly child he had given to the Green Bloods just moments earlier. His blue eyes however, were unmistakable. Servius took a moment to admire the child.

"Thank you," he said, placing his hand on Acernis's shoulder, "whatever you did, thank you. You have saved my grandson." Servius gently collected Decimus into his arms, as a broad smile grew across his face. The familiarity he so sorely missed, had finally returned. The child had Decima's eyes, and a warmth that made Servius feel immediately at ease. An inseparable emotional bond took hold, as Servius and his entourage left the hall.

Acernis's thoughts turned to his mentor. "Ulmus!" he shouted, looking around the hall frantically. In the corner, lay a twisted heap of a man, dust and scrolls, tangled up with the remains of a wooden chest. Acernis ran across the hall. He tore into the splintered wood, where he found Ulmus dazed, but alive.

"Are you hurt Mentoris?" he asked.

"Mentoris?" he remarked, "You can hardly call me your Mentoris now. You have surpassed all that I can teach you!" he said cheerfully, as he struggled to his feet. Before Acernis could counter the suggestion, Tita marched into the hall, just as one of the doors fell from its hinges behind her.

"YOU!" she demanded, pointing at Ulmus, "You might have my father fooled, but I am not so blind!" she screamed, as she marched up to Ulmus. "The blood of a thousand innocent citizens at Ravenstone not good enough for you? Nearly two lifetimes of the gods refusing us guidance from the Raven just not long enough in your opinion?" she bellowed into Ulmus's startled face.

"Please Imperatrix, I do not..." he said anxiously, before gulping, "I do not know to what you are referring."

Tita scoffed before turning her back on Ulmus, "THIS!" she shouted, throwing her arms out wide, indicating the mess of the hall. "You continue to practice signum altercations, which is bad enough, but you do it here! HERE in the palace grounds, at the head of the largest city in Rytus!" she sneered. "Are you so stupid that you cannot see, or are you so arrogant you think you can better the gods themselves?" she asked.

"I, I, I, erm? Please Imperatrix..." Ulmus stuttered, pleading with Tita.

Tita raised her index finger, pointing it squarely at Ulmus, "I will NOT allow you and your kind to bring Rytus to her knees again! Do you understand?" she said, glaring at him.

"Yes Imperatrix," he replied respectfully.

"How dare you lie to me!" she barked, signalling her red guards to enter the hall.

"Wait, what are you doing?" he asked.

"Taking the hall!" She snapped.

"What? No! You cannot!" he pleaded.

"I cannot have you endangering the lives of everyone here, and the citizens in the city below. Now get out!" she demanded coldly.

"But the hall has stood here long before the palace itself and the city below," Ulmus declared.

"Are you questioning me?" she replied threateningly.

"I just, er?" he replied desperately.

"Take him away," she commanded.

Acernis stepped forward. "Imperatrix," he said as he bowed his head, "with the greatest of respect, this man just saved the life of Decimus," Tita stopped and turned to Acernis. Before she could start berating him, he continued, "I, not Ulmus, used the banned art of signum altercations to peer into Decimus's soul. He was so weak, he had nothing. His spark lay almost dead. Ulmus worked with me. He saved us all and gave everything but the last remaining glimmer of his own life, to restore Decimus, who as we speak, now giggles and smiles for the first time since the gods granted him life in this unforgiving world."

Tita commanded the guards to hold position. She looked at the hooded man before her. "Then perhaps I should take you in his place?" she said, approaching him. She ran the back of her hand softly down Acernis's cheek, while biting her lip. She felt herself oddly enthralled by this stranger before her. Acernis stood frozen, waiting for the inevitable sentence determining his fate. No words fell from Tita's lips. Instead, Acernis felt them press against his own.

As Tita withdrew, a trace of blue aura passed between them. She savoured the moment; while within her, the aura swirled, joining with her own. Tita felt stronger, more awake and invigorated. Who was this man that had such an effect on her inner being? she wondered. She gazed into Acernis's terrified eyes before turning to leave.

"You have four days before we take the hall," she declared, releasing Ulmus and taking her guards with her as she left.

"What was that?" Ulmus jested, as he sat down on the floor to catch his breath, before being surrounded by fellow Green Bloods.

"What will we do?" a young Green Blood asked.

"Where will we go?" another asked with growing concern.

84

"Calm yourselves. We will go to Magpie Gorge. We will be welcomed there," Ulmus said reassuringly.

"This is an outrage," Cinis declared. "You cannot be seriously considering surrendering our hall and our home to these gluttonous monsters?"

"What choice do we have?" he replied.

"First they ask us to save their child; then they kick us out of the very same hall? And this seems somehow acceptable to you?" she continued.

"No, it is not acceptable to me, but they have an army, we are unarmed, and skilled in a banned art. We are vastly outnumbered here. We will be safer in Magpie Gorge," he reasoned.

Cinis dismissed his explanation, and instead began taking out her frustration on the furniture, smashing a chair to pieces. Ulmus, still weakened from earlier events, decided it would probably be safer for all to leave her to it.

Another knock at the remaining door. "What do they want now? Our clothes?" Cinis snarled across the hall, towards the door, where now stood one of the hooded Raven's attendants, carrying a small bundle of swaddling cloth.

"What is it child of the Raven?" Ulmus asked.

"A gift from the gods," the attendant explained, as she approached. She carefully placed the bundle on the floor, in the middle of the room. Ulmus looked confused. "Katlia's blood debt," the attendant explained, "Your attendant who died yesterday? this is her replacement."

"Ah yes!" Ulmus said, suddenly remembering the woman hidden in the side room.

Satisfied her work was done, the Raven's attendant left. Ulmus climbed to his feet and approached the bundle. He scooped it up in his arms and unwrapped the cloth. Inside, he found a healthy, grey eyed, White Blood baby. "What are we going to do with you now?" he said to the child, their future now so uncertain. "Acernis," he called out, "You seem to have a way with babies, take this child to Magpie Gorge, first thing in the morning and wait for us there."

"As you wish Mentoris," he responded, just as he had always done, for as long as he knew Ulmus.

"I told you, I am not your Mentoris anymore."

Acernis just smiled, accepting the bundle into his own arms. "It seems I am to take you home," he explained softly to the child, "back to Magpie Gorge."

Chapter Seven

5,261 days before the eclipse.

Dance, music, and laughter reverberated throughout Falcon Hall. Orange Bloods and White Bloods intimately embraced on the top floor, while the floors below were filled with stories of previous conquests. On the ground floor, gathered around the fire stone pits, they danced and sang, as the musicians played on.

Agapeta stood at the Lapsae balcony. "Brothers. Sisters. Falcons and Sparrows," she declared. The laughter and dancing stopped momentarily, as everyone turned to listen. "Tonight we drink, tonight we dance and tonight we laugh, for soon our great leader, Leanorus, severs his blood bond to the gods." She paused and smiled in his direction before continuing, "And I say to the gods, good luck trying to bring him to heel." Those gathered below laughed while raising a cup in Leanorus's direction.

Leanorus struggled to his feet from his position, nestled down between a group of White Blood women. "Thank you, all of you," he paused, "tomorrow may I wake with a sore head, full stomach and a satisfaction only a woman can bring me," he chuckled. "Well do not just stand around looking at me, drink, dance, celebrate my last mortal night!" he commanded, as he sat back down among the women.

Vesnus, seated to the left of his mentor and leader, took a sip of wine, before a White Blood girl snatched the cup from his hands, giggling and beckoning him to follow her. He raised his hands in dismay at her actions, before shaking his head at her. She shrugged her shoulders and moved on to the next man.

"I hope you are not planning on being like this the whole night," Leanorus taunted.

Vesnus smiled back at his mentor, "Forgiveness Mentoris."

"Bah!" Leanorus dismissed his apology. "Seems you have an admirer," he said, pointing across the crowded room. Vesnus peered through the figures dancing in the light of the fire to see Mania staring back at him. "Do not let me down this time," Leanorus jested playfully. Vesnus smiled to his mentor before getting to his feet. Leanorus tried to raise a cup to his pupil, before being swallowed up in the horde of women, begging for his attention.

Vesnus made his way through the crowd to the spot where Mania stood, but she wasn't anywhere to be seen. Keen not to dishonour his friend again, Vesnus glanced around the room, looking for her. Eventually, he spotted her smiling suggestively from the far end of the hall, peering around the end of one of the stair cases, that led to the floor above.

He returned a look of confusion. She beckoned him to her. He made his way through the dancers, musicians and drinkers. As he drew closer to her position, she giggled and ran up the stairs, where she waited, lent against a pillar.

He felt the adrenaline beginning to take control over his legs, then his breathing, arms and finally his thoughts, as he gave chase. Mania, always a few steps ahead, led him along the first floor to the next set of stairs. The pair climbed up through the hall, until they were both now at the top. With no more stairs to climb he drew closer, as for once she stood still, smiling, waiting for him. She was finally cornered. Invigorated by the chase, she remained composed, as her prize approached. She held her breath, as he placed his hands on her hips and lent in to her. Vesnus closed his eyes, expecting his lips to meet hers.

Mania slipped from his grasp and bolted through a door, giggling. He followed her out on to the balcony overlooking the towering, Falcon Island Camp, and the bay at its heels, as the sun set on the horizon.

"Now you definitely have nowhere left to run," he laughed. She stepped up on to the railing without taking her eyes off his. "What are you doing?" he shouted with concern, as she leapt with poise and grace from the balcony to the one below.

"Vesnus," she called out softly, beckoning him to follow her.

"The things I do to please my Mentoris!" he muttered to himself, as he leapt from the balcony, catching the railing below.

She giggled as he pulled himself up. As he'd come to expect, she ran through the door back into the hall, to the Lapsae balcony. He sighed before walking through the doorway in pursuit.

Once again, he found himself alone. Leanorus saw his pupil now stood above him, and returned a look of confusion. Vesnus shrugged his shoulders while raising his hands. Leanorus tilted his head to his right, gesturing that Mania went through the door into his office. Vesnus mouthed to his mentor, "But she keeps running."

"Follow her!" he mouthed back, knowing neither could hear the other over the celebrations in the hall. Vesnus sighed before heading through the door into Leanorus's office, expecting the now seemingly pointless and tiresome pursuit to continue.

Inside the office, he was unexpectedly greeted by Agapeta, screaming at Mania for disturbing her. Vesnus looked at the desk, where countless scrolls lay disturbed, before Agapeta noticing another intruder, began to berate Vesnus too. Mania took this opportunity to run down the stairs and back out on to the ground floor of the hall. Before

Vesnus could give much thought to what Agapeta was actually doing in Leanorus's office, Mania called out to him. Grateful to be relieved from Agapeta's scolding, he willingly followed.

"I beg your forgiveness. I did not know Agapeta would be in the office," Mania explained, taking Vesnus by the arm, before leading him down to the chamber below the hall. She worked her way through the statues of their ancestors, through to a dark, quiet corner. She caught her breath before apologising again.

He placed his hands on her hips. This time she looked up at him, biting her lip before leaning in to him. Their warmth now shared. Their bodies finally at rest together. She took a deep breath, breathing in his aroma before wrapping her arms around his waist. Their breathing slowed. She reached up to kiss his lips; he reciprocated, bowing his head ready to embrace her.

"Interfectorem albi sanguinibus," Claricius declared, reading aloud the inscription on a statue near the pair. They both returned a cold glare at the unwanted disruption.

Vesnus sighed, "What do you want Claricius?"

"Oh nothing Vesnus," he said callously, "I was just admiring the efforts of our ancestors. You know they repelled revolutions? Tore down our enemies and brought peace to Rytus, so that we may live the comfortable life that we do?"

"Can you not admire the ancestors over there?" Mania replied coldly, releasing her grip on Vesnus.

"Just thought you might wish to discuss this further Mania, perhaps just the two of us?" Claricius sneered.

Mania scoffed at the ridiculous suggestion, "Can you not see that we are busy?"

Hurt by her cold refusal, Claricius dismissed himself from the chamber, and returned to the hall upstairs.

"There is something about him that makes my skin crawl," Mania explained, watching him leave.

"Forget him," Vesnus replied.

Mania smiled up at Vesnus as they resumed their embrace, both now filled with lust for one another. Their lips finally met in a flurry of passionate desire, hidden away from all but the cold stone eyes of their ancestors, who maintained their watch, unmoved by the young lovers.

Vesnus raised Mania up in his powerful arms. Filled with a surge of lust, he pressed his body against hers, pinning her to the wall. He ran his fingers through her hair as she gasped with pleasure.

"MANIA!" Agapeta screamed, charging across the chamber.

"Mother!" Mania replied, pushing Vesnus back, who just as surprised, lowered Mania to the floor. He turned to face Agapeta, who slapped him clean across the face.

"Get out of my sight child!" she demanded.

"But," Mania replied, fearful of her mother.

"I said GET OUT!" Agapeta screamed.

As instructed, Mania adjusted her tunic, before running out of the chamber. She pushed Claricius aside as he stood watching, gleaming with pride at the bottom of the stairs.

"And you Claricius!" Agapeta shouted, pointing at the door, while remaining riveted on Vesnus. With the smile wiped clear from Claricius's face, he too did as instructed, and reluctantly made his way back up the stairs.

"I..." Vesnus spluttered.

"How dare you?" Agapeta demanded.

"Excuse me?" he replied.

"She is MY DAUGHTER. The only mortal embodiment I have left of the man I loved."

"But..." again he tried to respond, before being coldly shut down by Agapeta, as her vivid orange eyes narrowed and her lips became pert with rage. "It was harmless fun," he replied, pleading for a moment of sanity.

"FUN?" she screeched, her hand now firmly around Vesnus's neck, her furious face pressed against his. "And what of the blood debt?" she demanded.

"I do not understand?" he replied.

"Of course you do not! You do not understand how the world really works. No, you like the rest; you listen to the lies of the Raven and his pathetic attendants."

Agapeta paused, his familiar scent igniting her memories. The warmth of his skin, reminding her of a touch so sorely missed, as his breathing grew laboured. She looked at the terror in his eyes, as anger turned to remembrance. She released her grip. She took a step back and a deep breath.

"I lost her father to the gods and their greed for blood," she explained, turning away. "She is innocent to the true ways of the world; I cannot let her know what true pain really feels like. To be forced to watch, as the only man who ever understood her, is torn apart as the crowds cheer." She paused as the emotional pain welled inside, her left hand now cradling her chest. "Every agonising cry of pain, every tear of flesh, met with a roar of approval from the crowds. Cheering, clapping, laughing, as he lay in a pool of his own blood and flesh. Only once did he break his gaze on Mania, as she lay in my arms, just a bundle, just a child, just once to close his eyes for the last time." Her stone like resolve broken, as a single tear rolled down her cheek. She turned back to Vesnus. "I will not let you, or anyone else do that to her, do you understand?"

"Yes Domina," he said, bowing his head respectfully.

Agapeta wiped the tear from her cheek, as the candles flickered in the stone cold chamber. The two Orange Bloods stood silently, as laughter permeated the room from the hall upstairs. Agapeta glared at the young Orange

Blood, as her thoughts turned from reflection, to her duties at hand.

She paused to compose herself before turning to leave. The remnants of dust and debris that littered the floor, crunched under foot as she approached the door. She stepped out, only to be interrupted by a White Blood with a letter. "Again?" she asked angrily, before snatching the letter. She read it, then screwed it up in her hand. She turned her head slightly, "I need you and Claricius to travel into the village, to collect a debt."

"Why Claricius?" Vesnus sneered.

She ignored his question. "Do not judge their debt. Grant them dignity in your mercy," she requested before leaving.

Vesnus stood quietly deliberating his feelings. He turned to the closest statue, reached his hand out, and felt the cold gritty stone beneath his fingertips. He looked to his ancestors for guidance. They remained silent as they always did, their gaze unmoved, unbroken. Vesnus adjusted his tunic and left the chamber.

Inside Leanorus's office, he was greeted by the cold stares of Agapeta and Claricius. "Make this quick," she demanded, while explaining to them both the finer details of the debt to be collected. Mania watched from the first floor, with growing sadness, as both men made their way out of the hall unnoticed by the revellers.

Vesnus collected his bow, quiver and blades from the stores.

"Why do you need that?" Claricius asked, pointing to the bow.

"Go prepared, come back victorious," Vesnus replied.

"He is just a farmer," Claricius sneered, picking up only his blades and a torch, which he lit before heading out.

The two men followed the stone path leading from Falcon Hall, at the top of the hill, down to the village of Falcon Reach. Shrouded in darkness, the village was an abrupt contrast to the hall. The silence of the night was pierced only by the sounds of the dogs howling, standing guard over the fields and livestock, as their masters slept. The smell of manure and the stagnant water in the swamps, impregnated the cold air. The unlit wooden homes of the White Bloods, perched on wooden stilts in the swamps, swayed and creaked, as a cold wind howled down the narrow alleyways. Claricius scoffed with contempt at the squalid conditions.

"They do not live like this through choice brother," Vesnus remarked.

Claricius rolled his eyes before pointing in to the distance, "This way!"

They continued deeper into the maze of homes, each identical to the last; a deliberate reminder to the White

Bloods, that they are no different to each other, in the eyes of the Imperators.

"Here," Claricius declared, handing the torch to Vesnus, before preparing to force open the rotten wooden door, that did little to protect those inside from the elements. Vesnus stopped him, handed the torch back, and simply lifted the door out of the way, before gesturing to Claricius to proceed.

Inside the tiny room, slept six White Bloods, with their handful of possessions and tools, with little room left for cooking or living. The smell of rot and damp was almost over powering. Claricius took a deep breath in anticipation of waking the exhausted White Bloods from their sleep. Vesnus raised his hand to silence him, before pointing to a couple lying together on the floor. Between them lay a carefully wrapped bundle, a baby. This was the debt that Agapeta had referred to. The laws of Rytus were very clear; a blood debt had to be paid.

Vesnus crept over to the couple and tried to wake them. Only the man woke from his deep sleep. Startled by the two Orange Blood Falcons standing before him, he quickly got to his feet. Vesnus gestured to the man to head outside. The man obliged and led the two Falcons out on to the frozen fields, away from the homes of his fellow White Bloods.

"I know what we have done," the man explained.

"Then you know why we are here?" Claricius replied.

"Yes," the man said, looking up at the night sky.

"Your child, a girl or a boy?" Vesnus asked.

"A boy," the man replied.

"Then it is his mother's mortal body that we must offer to the gods," Claricius declared.

"NO!" pleaded the man, "Please. I beg of you, do not take my wife."

"It is law," Claricius said callously.

"The gods will have their blood. What difference does it make if it is mine or hers? She is sick, her blood bond will be severed in just a few days' time. I beg of you, let her spend those last few days with our son. Please!" he dropped to his knees, begging for their mercy.

"Very well," replied Vesnus.

"You cannot," declared Claricius, "the law states..."

"The law states that a blood debt must be paid, just as the man said."

"When Agapeta hears of this!" Claricius barked.

"Agapeta? Leanorus is not lost to the gods yet. He is still our leader. I answer only to him!" Vesnus angrily replied.

"I will have no part in this deceitful violation, and I will make sure Agapeta is well aware of your actions."

"Run to Agapeta, just as you did before," Vesnus remarked spitefully.

The rage boiled over inside Claricius, who lashed out at his blood brother. Vesnus instinctively grabbed the fist heading in his direction, and used it to push Claricius off his feet on to the floor. He landed in a frozen puddle of mud, breaking the thin ice.

Claricius looked up at Vesnus and hissed, "Traitorous vermin!" Vesnus offered to help his brother up. Claricius smacked the helping hand away and struggled to his feet, slipping in the mud and ice. He eventually stood up, wiped the mud from his face, and began making his way back towards the hall.

Vesnus turned and helped the cowering White Blood man up, from his knees. "I will grant your request," he said, placing his hand on the man's shoulders to comfort him. "Do you wish to say goodbye to your wife first?"

"No," replied the man confidently, "let her sleep. I will see her again soon in just a few days."

"Very well, perhaps we should go somewhere..." before Vesnus could finish his sentence, the silence around the two men was shattered by the savage sound of a rogue dog, tearing into flesh. The screams of Claricius, as he frantically tried to fight off the beast, echoed off the distant buildings.

Vesnus handed the torch to the White Blood man, removed the bow from his own back, and collected an arrow from his quiver. He steadied his bow, before correcting for the cold wind. Meanwhile, Claricius tried in vain to reach for his blades, as the dog tore down on the flesh and bone of his flailing arms. He panicked and attempted to protect his face, but in doing so revealed to the animal his neck. The dog guided by its own instincts, took the opportunity and launched for the exposed target.

Just as Claricius realised his mistake, he heard the unmistakable whistle of the arrow, as it pierced the air; striking the animal straight through the chest, into the heart. The beast fell silently to the floor.

As Claricius looked back, there stood his blood brother, his saviour. Bow in hand, a guardian figure, illuminated in the pitch black of the frozen fields. Claricius struggled to his feet, before clumsily staggering back towards the hall.

Vesnus collected the debt.

Vesnus carefully cleaned the blood from his arrow and blades, before putting them, with his bow, back in their respective places in the store. He placed his hand on the well-worn wooden handle of the doors to the hall. He paused to compose what he would say, when confronted by Agapeta and her pet Claricius. He took a deep breath and opened the door.

Inside, a handful of Orange Bloods staggered around looking for another drinking companion, while White Bloods

100

began tidying up the hall. Dotted around the room were a few heaps of sleeping Orange Bloods, and snoring could be clearly heard from the higher floors. Not the welcome Vesnus had feared, but certainly a preferred one.

He made his way up to Leanorus's office, where he found White Bloods busily tidying up, while Agapeta inspected a scroll on the desk. "Is it done?" she asked, without looking up.

"Yes," he replied.

"And what happened to Claricius?" she asked, now looking at Vesnus.

"I assumed he had returned to the hall Domina," he explained.

"Oh he did, but he will not talk to anyone. He is covered in his own blood, and his clothes are torn to pieces. Was this by your hand?"

"No Domina, he was attacked."

"By whom?" she asked.

He thought for a moment. If he told the truth, then Claricius was sure to become a laughing stock. Torn to pieces by a farmer's dog; hardly a desired legend. "I could not see Domina," he replied. Agapeta could sense he was lying, but it was getting late, and she didn't really care. She dismissed Vesnus before returning to her work.

He calculated he could probably get in a few hours of sleep, before having to head out again for practice in the morning. He made his way to the stairs, in search of a free bed.

"Vesnus," a hushed voice from one of the side rooms called out, "come here." He followed the sound of the voice, to find Leanorus and a few of the other more senior Orange Bloods gathered. "Is she still in my office?" Leanorus asked quietly.

"Agapeta?"

Leanorus nodded.

"Yes Mentoris," replied Vesnus.

"I am not even dead and she has already laid claim to my office," he said, shaking his head.

Vesnus noticed the hundred or so letters scattered on the table in the middle of the room. "These are the same letters Agapeta receives? I recognise the symbol," he said, as he picked one up to inspect it.

"Very good Vesnus, they are," Leanorus responded.

"There must be over a hundred here."

Leanorus nodded, "They are debt letters, demanding the repayment of old debts to the gods."

"Who is sending them?"

"We do not know, but we have our suspicions. We believe it may be a zealot, trying to appease the gods, for the fall of Ravenstone," Leanorus explained, "look." He passed one in particular to Vesnus.

"This has your name on it, Mentoris" he replied.

Leanorus nodded again before dismissing the others from the room.

"Vesnus, brother; I do not know what will happen in the next few days but I fear for the future of the Falcons. I fear for the future of Rytus. I cannot explain it, but I think the gods are plotting, moving into position to turn our world upside down."

Vesnus looked at the floor, "Yes Mentoris."

"Or perhaps I am just a cynical fool?" Leanorus laughed. "I have just one favour to ask of you brother."

Vesnus looked up at his mentor and friend, "Anything, whatever your wish, I will grant it."

"Careful brother, do not make promises that are beyond your power as a mortal," Leanorus said with a smile. "No, when it is time to sever my bond," he said, while pointing to the letter in Vesnus's hand, "I want it to be you."

"Me?" he asked.

"I trust you the most," Leanorus replied, offering his hand out to Vesnus.

The two men shook. "Yes Mentoris, it will be an honour."

"Thank you. I did not want it to be left to someone, who could not even fight off a farmer's dog," he said with a wink.

Chapter Eight

1,001,570 days after the eclipse.

"Sorry I am late," Max announced, as he closed the classroom door shut. He turned around to find his seat but the room wasn't laid out as it usually was. The scratching of pens on paper ceased and the room fell deathly silent. Everyone had stopped work to look up at Max, even the teacher glared straight at him. Max looked around, these were seniors in their purple jumpers and not his class mates. This wasn't in fact his class at all. His throat became torrid. The sound of his own heartbeat grew louder. He took a moment to think before silently opening the door again and leaving. As the door closed shut behind him, he checked the number on the door, 'ROOM 107.' He had the correct room, but where were his classmates?

The shrill tone of the morning break alarm woke Max from his confusion, he wasn't late at all. He'd just interrupted an earlier class; his history lesson was after break. The horror of having to see the same teacher again in just fifteen minutes sent a shiver down his spine. How utterly embarrassing, he thought, as the corridor filled with children of all ages rushing for the playground.

Reluctantly Max followed the crowds outside. Some of the children played games in their thick winter coats, while others sat on the walls chatting. He hated break times, lunch times, and after school clubs. He was happiest in his own world with only himself for company.

Desperate to escape it all, he made his way towards a quiet spot around the corner, away from the other children, somewhere he'd be left alone. The ground beneath his feet began to squelch in the dirt, releasing a familiar earthy smell. The mud was slippy but it didn't matter. Max sat down using his school bag as a mat. He took solace in the fact the next lesson was, at least, one he looked forward to, even if the teacher was present at the most embarrassing moment of Max's school life, so far.

Taking care not to fall off, he pulled a sketch book from his bag, as well as the tiny nub of a pencil he kept exclusively for drawing. The sketch book was bursting at the seams with images and cuttings. A couple of the pages fell out on to the floor. Max picked them up, and carefully wiped the muddy marks off with his jumper.

He flicked through the drawings, every single one of them was a recollection of what he saw in Rytus. The girl in rags standing in the collapsed room, reaching out; out to Max, no-one else; just the two of them. Sometimes the backgrounds would change, or the lighting. Sometimes Max would draw himself as an adult, sometimes he'd draw, only to screw it up, and throw it away.

Eventually he found the last blank sheet. He began to furiously sketch, just as he had done countless times before. He could draw her in less than a minute now, he'd had that much practice at it.

He pondered for a moment, perhaps this time he'll draw in that idiot in the Raven's mask. Maybe this time, he'll draw the girl punching that idiot right in his stupid face, he thought, smiling to himself, imagining how funny that would've been to see.

The light dimmed, as three shadowy figures appeared on his page, blocking out the sun. He looked up as three of the vilest boys in the school glared down at him.

"What are you doing there? Writing another stupid poem about that ghost you think you saw?" taunted one of the boys while the other two laughed.

"I don't think I saw her; I *know* I saw her!" Max replied adamantly. All three boys laughed and pointed at Max.

One of the boys to Max's right, snatched the book from his hands, spilling a large number of the pages. Another of the boys stomped the pages into the mud, while laughing callously. The third boy snatched the book from the first, spilling yet more pages. "What do we have here?" he said with a malicious tone, "Surprise, surprise, it's sketches of your imaginary girlfriend." He watched Max's eyes well up with tears, as he took each sheet and tore it up in front of him. Max lent forward from his seated position, his knees sinking into the mud, clutching and grabbing at the torn pages while the boys continued to laugh. One of the boys grabbed Max's bag and proceeded to empty its contents into the mud.

"Why? Why are you doing this to me?" Max pleaded.

"Because you're a Demi Blood, that's why," the boy coldly replied.

Content with the misery inflicted, the boys left. Max clung tightly on to the pages he had managed to save, as the bell rang to signify the end of break time. He collected his belongings from the slimy mud, put them into his ruined bag, and stuffed all the pages he could collect, back into the front pocket. He looked down at his trousers and shoes thick with mud. He immediately knew he would be in trouble with Mother later. He tried to brush it off, but only succeeded in rubbing it in.

With a heavy heart, he made his way back into the school. He stopped at the door to the classroom to let out a heavy sigh, before walking in. Hopefully this time he'd got it right, and no further embarrassment would befall him today at least, he hoped. As soon as he opened the door, the children in the front row began to point and laugh. His teacher tutted loudly, and walked to the door to stop Max in his tracks.

"Go to the toilets and wash yourself off. You are not coming into my classroom again looking like that," he said, pointing down the corridor. The teacher peered out of the doorway, and saw the muddy trail Max had left, "And you can spend your lunch hour cleaning the halls too." The rest of the children in the class giggled as the teacher closed the door on Max.

The sound of the furthest tap dripping, echoed around the cold blue room, designated as the boy's Year Seven toilets. As the cold water rinsed away the mud, the familiar earthy smell returned. It was a welcome change to the smell of the cheap disinfectant that seemed to cling to every surface. He cleaned himself off as best he could, in the tiny sinks, using the budget paper towels that seemingly refused to absorb any liquid.

He found a seat at the back of the classroom and dumped his bag on the floor at his feet. The two boys seated near Max giggled, as he pulled out his muddy pencil case and wet exercise book. A heavy text book was slammed down in front of Max. "Page 71," the teacher demanded.

No matter how hard Max tried, he could not make a legible mark on the wet paper of his exercise book. In the end he gave up, and began instead to drift back to Rytus, back to his happy place. Who was the girl he saw? Could she see him? If so, how? he wondered.

"MAX!" the teacher demanded, "Who did I just say led the troops in 1627?" Max frowned, searching his mind for the answer, he glanced at his text book, which he had failed to open. The rest of the class began to laugh. "Shut up!" barked the teacher, quickly losing his patience, "Well Max?"

"Er? Henry, the, er? Fourth?" The teacher slammed his own text book down on the desk, causing the boy sat there to jump. Max looked down at his hands and clenched them tightly.

"Page 104, please Max, NOW!"

He opened the text book and began scanning the page.

"Harry Goodiers, Red Blood, born in Crooksby, Leicestershire Sep 1591, son of the minor gentleman..."

The teacher turned back to the board and continued his lesson. Max tried to concentrate on the text book, but instead he found his mind began to wonder back to Rytus. He refocused and looked down at the text book. He realised to his horror that his absent mind had sketched the girl in the margin. He tried in vain to rub it out, but his muddy eraser only smudged the graphite. His heart began to race, and his mouth felt dry, as his breathing intensified. Dread permeated his body. He looked up mouth open, eyes wide.

"Sir! Sir!" the boy next to him shouted out, with his hand raised in the air.

"Yes Bellbury?" the teacher responded.

"Max has drawn in the text book, Sir!" the boy declared, with a big grin on his face. Max sunk down in his seat, as the inevitable unfolded around him.

The Headmaster's office lay in the oldest part of the school, off a corridor lined from floor to ceiling with wooden panelling. The wide corridors, high ceilings and adult sized chairs, made Max feel very small, as he waited for the arrival of his parents.

A telephone could be heard ringing in the office down the corridor, while the school's secretary quickly dashed in her high heels from the break room to answer it.

Mother was first to arrive, tottering along in her high heels and fur coat. She stopped and tutted at Max, for the state of his clothes, before carrying on to the office. Eventually Father appeared in his grey suit. He didn't even look at Max. Instead he strode past without as much as a sideward glance.

Max could hear the muffled dull tones of the headmaster through the wall, followed by concern from Mother and short precise answers from Father. Swinging his legs back and forth between the chair legs, soon grew tiresome, and Max resorted to doing what he did best, daydreaming.

The cleaner flicked off the light switch for the corridor, waking Max from his fantasy, before heading down the stairs to the reception area. Now entirely alone and just a few steps from a dark and empty school, Max finally felt at ease.

A girl giggled. He turned to see, but the corridor remained dark and empty. Another giggle. Max jumped down from the seat and began to follow the sound. The giggling grew louder as he turned the corner. There, sure enough, at the end, as he'd dreamt so many times before; there she was, the girl in rags from Rytus. He hesitated at first, perhaps it was a cruel trick, he thought.

She stretched out her arm as she always did, only this time, she beckoned him forward. Max checked back towards the offices. The corridor still lay pitch black, filled with only emptiness and boredom. The only thing it led to, was a telling off and a scolding. After carefully weighing up his options, he proceeded towards the girl.

She continued to giggle as they began to play a game of tag. She would run on ahead and Max would try and catch her. At first he walked, but soon he was running and then sprinting, following the light of her smile. Occasionally she'd look back to make sure he was keeping up.

He found himself on the ground floor, out of breath. He stopped for a moment before running on to catch up. He turned the corner and ran straight into Father. "Where have you been?" Father said angrily, "It doesn't matter. Get upstairs now; we've been looking for you." He grabbed Max tightly by the arm, and began marching him off. Max looked back to see the girl fade into memory, just as she always did.

Outside the office, Mother and the headmaster waited for the return of Father, with Max tightly in tow. Father plonked a frightened Max down in front of the pair, before they all marched into the office.

Inside, everyone found their seats quickly, except for Max, who slowly walked into the cheerless office matching the décor of the corridors. The three adults watched Max intently as he made his way around the edge of the office, to the only free chair on the far side of his parents. He climbed up onto the seat as the headmaster leant forward over his large wooden desk.

"We have been talking Max," the headmaster explained, glaring over his glasses, "we think you may be happier at a state school. We feel you don't belong here, anymore." Max looked at the disappointment in Mother's eyes, before looking at the floor. "To be honest Max," he said with emphasis on his name, "I see your future as being very bleak in general. Unless you get your act together, straighten up and work hard, I don't see much of a future for you at all." The headmaster lent back in his chair, as Mother and Father pleaded for a change of heart.

Max's attention turned to the window behind the headmaster; he watched the lights in the car park flicker and dance in the wind. Only two cars were left, Father's and the other, he assumed, belonged to the headmaster. It wasn't long before his imagination took over. Soon the lights began to sway more heavily, before breaking free of their metal bonds. They began to swirl in random directions as twenty or so children dressed in rags, began to dance and play around the two cars. The children formed a circle, revealing a figure stood in the middle, waving at Max.

"Snap out of it Max, we're leaving!" Father barked grabbing his arm. He tried in vain to see out of the window but Father's grip only grew tighter.

Mother thanked the headmaster for his time before closing the door behind them. She made her way out to the car while Father squared Max up. "Do you understand how much trouble we went through to get you into a good school like this? Do you comprehend for one moment what we have had to give up to get you here?" his face now red with rage. Max began to withdraw in fear, only for Father to stand him up again and continue shouting at him.

The headmaster appeared at the door, coughing loudly. Father apologised and took Max by the arm down to the ground floor. "Just you wait until we get home, then you'll understand the pain we've been through for you."

Chapter Nine

5,260 days before the eclipse.

Magpie Hall lay in darkness. The dust and debris lay scattered on the floor. Acernis looked at the splintered wood and torn scrolls. His thoughts turned to the day he first arrived at the hall. The first time he met Ulmus and the wonderful things he taught him. He remembered vividly the first time a White Blood child was presented to him. The cut was deep and bloodied. His mother was frantic with concern and desperate for Acernis's help. With Ulmus at his side, he healed the wound. The look of gratitude in the mother's eyes, never left Acernis. Whenever he felt alone or in need, he would simply remember her smile.

His reminiscing turned to the task he had been assigned, to take the new child to Magpie Gorge. Acernis knelt down and grabbed a length of green woven fabric from the floor. He used it as a sling and wrapped it around his shoulders and back. He put on his green paenula and collected the child from the White Blood Nutrix.

He turned back to the door of the great hall, and took one last look at the place he'd called home since he came of age. With a heavy heart he carefully opened the hinged door, trying not to disturb the broken one, that had been propped in place. It served as a poignant reminder of why they were no longer welcome here anymore. Acernis couldn't help but feel guilty for what he had done. It was true he had saved Decimus's life, but at what cost? Just as carefully, he closed the door, and made his way out into the deep snow.

The grounds of the palace lay quiet and still, as if even the white stones themselves were sleeping. Only a handful of Red Guards patrolled the grounds, while most of Rytus slept soundly. Keen to avoid any confrontations, Acernis made his way hastily towards the stairs. A Red Blood, positioned on the top step, placed his pilum into Acernis's path.

"Going somewhere in a hurry Pica?" he asked.

Thinking on his feet Acernis replied quickly, "I am to head into the City to collect supplies."

"Odd time of day to be heading to the city, what with the sun yet to rise; do you not think?" the guard said smugly. Acernis laughed nervously before ducking under the pilum, and continuing down the stairs.

The guard laughed callously, "Run Pica, run while you still can, three days left lad, three days!" Acernis raced from the bottom of the steps and across the bridge. He ran past the old Magpie Tree and in to White City.

In the marketplace, White Bloods were stirring, preparing to set up their stalls. Walking quickly, keeping his head down, Acernis hurried east past the circus. Inside he could hear the horses whinnying, snorting and pawing at the ground beneath their heavy hooves, as they waited impatiently for their morning feed.

He drew closer to the Eastern Gate leading out of the city. Here the houses began to thin out, allowing a damp mist to hang at his feet. The cold started to creep up on Acernis, no longer held back by the high walled, grey stone and wooden homes of the White Bloods. He wrapped his paenula tighter around his precious cargo before stepping up his pace.

The gates were still closed when Acernis approached. A thick layer of frost lay undisturbed. He reluctantly put his hand against the ice cold metal of the handle. It was stiff but it turned. The door weighed down by the snow and icy water, was difficult to push open. Acernis strained, before managing to open the door, just enough to slip through.

Outside the city's walls, lay the Eastern Stables of White City, where Acernis hoped to find a Green Blood's horse. He approached the door of the stable master, raised his hand to knock, but paused; unsure whether he would be welcomed this early in the day.

"Can I help you?" a voice asked.

Acernis turned around to see a beautiful White Blood woman, with long flowing white hair. She stood in the paddock looking puzzled.

"I need to get to Magpie Gorge," he explained.

"You better come in then," she replied pointing to the door into the stable.

"Have you ridden before?" she asked, looking at Acernis's strangely bulging paenula.

"Once or twice, well, just once really, the day I left Magpie Gorge," he replied a little sheepishly.

Unable to take her eyes off this peculiar shaped man stood before her, she suggested, "You will need a Green Blood's horse."

"Erm? Yes, please, I think so," he said with uncertainty.

"I think I have one that could work with you, given the right encouragement," she said with a sly smile. She left the stables to fetch the chosen horse from the paddock. Acernis turned to peruse the stable only to be greeted with the glare of three Red Blood horses. He instinctively looked away.

"Pica!" she called out to Acernis, "Come see." She held on to the reins with a gleaming smile, as her eyes filled with pride. The radiant large white horse stood proudly to attention. The light gleaming off the magnificent creature, cut through the early morning air, like a brightly burning lantern. Its mane and tail were a swirling mix of ebony and emerald, identical in colour to Acernis's own hair. As he approached, the green Ivy pattern, engrained in its flesh from the brow to each foot, began to glow brighter.

He reached out his hand and placed it on the neck of the horse, feeling his way down the silky hair coat. Inside, he felt his soul at ease with the green aura of the horse. Acernis wasn't really sure how he was going to mount this enormous animal though. Eventually, with a little help from the White Blood woman, he managed to climb up. He got himself settled, just as the sun began to break on the horizon. "Take care of her," she said, waving him through the gate. Acernis smiled back, thanked her and trotted out on to the path to Magpie Gorge.

The city's walls disappeared into the distance behind him, as he made his way across the various narrow bridges and stone roads. The smell of stagnant water from the swamps filled the air, leaving Acernis with a bitter taste in his mouth. He carefully folded back the woven fabric, and checked on the child, who was thankfully still sleeping soundly.

The horse stopped. She stood rigidly still, with her head raised high, before letting out a loud snort. Acernis could sense that something had startled her. He looked around for any unsettling signs. Nothing. Suddenly the horse dropped her head and charged forward. The rapid clapping of her metal shoes against the stones, echoed loudly about the trees lining the route. Alongside, the undergrowth began to twitch, as three grey wolves came into view. Acernis clung on tightly to the reins as the wolves gave chase. The snorts of the galloping horse soon became drowned out by the snarls of the wolves, and the sound of their gnashing teeth. With the wolves snapping at her heels, the horse valiantly rode on.

A single wolf stood poised in the road ahead. His long tail and thick silver fur quivered in the breeze, as he maintained a cold watch on the approaching horse. On spotting the wolf, the horse came to an abrupt halt.

The wolves circled Acernis. Their muzzles foamed with excitement and their teeth were bared as a warning. The horse looked around desperately for an escape. She had to run, she had to go. She reared up, throwing Acernis from the saddle. He threw his arms tightly around the child in his care, and landed with a thump. The horse bolted through the pack, kicking out at her pursuers. The three grey wolves chased after her. Only the silver wolf remained.

Acernis turned to face the beast. The silver wolf glared back. His ears were pricked forward and he showed little sign of aggression. Instead, the wolf seemed merely curious. He sniffed the air as his green eyes flashed across Acernis. He dropped his head and gingerly approached the man. Acernis, concerned for the child, remained still, until the wolf began sniffing and pawing at his paenula.

Cautiously, Acernis pushed the wolf's face away from the child. The wolf stepped sideways and approached again. Acernis, using more force, pushed the wolf back. The wolf persisted.

Acernis sat up. He cradled the child with his right arm while trying to push back the wolf with the other. His fur was thick, with coarse long hairs protecting the soft undercoat, but it did little to disguise the wolf's malnourished frame. Acernis stroked the animal's side, feeling his protruding ribs, as he attempted to connect with the wolf's aura.

A deep growl resounded from the wolf's muzzle, as he withdrew into a defensive pose. Acernis held his breath. He had never seen another soul react in this way. Never before had there been a refusal to the initial bond.

The sound of paws crunching through the snow resounded through the trees, as the three grey wolves returned. The chase had been exhausting, and they had returned defeated. Their stomachs too, clung desperately to their malnourished frames. Their ribs were apparent. They licked at the silver wolf's muzzle before trotting back into the woods. The silver wolf looked once more at Acernis, before following the others. Acernis scrambled to his feet, and left with little other choice, continued his journey on foot.

The sun broke through the clouds, as it lifted from its slumber into the sky above; casting rays of light on to the hillsides around the swamps. Acernis scanned the unusually barren lands that lay before him, as a collection of black and white feathers fluttered in the wind, catching his attention.

The brittle twigs and branches snapped loudly underfoot, as Acernis left the road to investigate. He steadied himself against the arid bark of a nearby tree before kneeling down. The collection of black and white feathers bore no cuts, and the body remained free of bloodied wounds. The talons were tightly curled and the beak lay devoid of pigment. Acernis collected a few of the feathers to take with him to Magpie Gorge, to ascertain the cause of death, before climbing to his feet.

Acernis stood opened mouthed as the feathers flittered from his grasp. Before him lay only horror, bathed in the fiery orange glow of the rising sun. Before him lay what he could only assume was a sign from the gods themselves. Before him, among the dried up brittle husks of the spruce trees, scattered across the barren dirt, lay a myriad of lifeless and tattered magpies. The cruel wind twisted about their inert bodies, carrying with it more frayed and torn feathers.

Of the once abundant forests east of Rytus, nothing grew, nothing moved and nothing made a sound; except

Acernis's footsteps tapping against the flag stones, as he cautiously joined the road again. He raced along the road to the foot of Magpie Hill Camp. The steep hill was a struggle, as the icy atmosphere tore into his lungs, but he was determined, he needed answers.

As he drew nearer to the gorge, he heard the familiar sound of a horse whinnying. He looked up from his frozen fingers to see his Green Blood horse waiting patiently. He felt relieved to see her again. Had she not drawn the wolves away, they surely would have torn them both to pieces, he thought. He took a moment to catch his breath before he opened the paddock and secured her safely inside.

He placed his hands on the weak wooden fence, that stood between him and a 600 foot fall to the bottom, and couldn't help but marvel at the gorge below. In the gorge lay the homes of over 300 White Bloods, their children, and their Green Blood students. Spread across five floors, each home had been hand carved out of the towering rock face, linked by a series of narrow wooden platforms and bridges.

He opened the door to the staircase and made his way down, treading carefully in the poor light. He continued down to the bottom of the gorge, where Green Bloods sat eagerly listening to their tutors. From the very youngest all the way through to their coming of age; classes of children lined the path through the gorge. Some learnt to brew medicines from Ra and Glukoriza; while others learnt surgical procedures using scalpels, drills and forceps. Cages to hold curious animals were chiselled into the rock face, while unusual plants and trees grew from gardens perched on stone ledges. In the middle lay a circle consisting of seats cut from the gorge itself. In the centre of which, stood a wooden table and lectern, where a master spoke out to his pupils.

"Acernis, my dear friend!" called out the master, upon sighting his former pupil, "what an honour it is to see you again." He stood with arms outstretched as a smile widened across his face. Acernis, a little embarrassed to be called out in front of the children, approached gingerly before embracing his former master, with care not to crush the precious child in his care.

"Little Picas gather around, gather around," the master called out. "This is Acernis, the man I told you about," he said, still grinning.

"Lychnus, you told them about me?" Acernis asked with concern.

"Only about your triumphs my dearest friend," Lychnus said, before noticing the peculiar shape of his paenula. "Have you come seeking a cure for your disfigurement?" he asked discreetly.

Acernis laughed, "No, I bring a child from the gods." He carefully unwrapped the woven fabric, and gently lifted the child out before presenting him to Lychnus.

"A White Blood? Why do you bring us a White Blood? Is he sick?" Lychnus asked, taking the child from Acernis.

"Patience friend," he replied, gently steadying Lychnus's arm, "no, I am afraid I come bearing some unsettling news." Lychnus stared at Acernis, fearful of the next words to fall from the young man's mouth. "Perhaps we can talk in your insula?" Acernis suggested, while gesturing towards the children intently listening to every word.

Lychnus nodded and turned back to the children, "Little Picas I want you to practice your subigebant umbrarum while we are gone. I will return and I will ask Acernis here to decide a winner!" he said with a smile.

"Subigebant umbrarum?" asked Acernis, as he wrapped the woven fabric back around the White Blood child, "I thought that was banned under the new laws?"

"It is, but by the time the Red Bloods have made it down that narrow staircase, clunging and clanging as they go, we have already retreated," he jested. "They have not caught us yet!"

Lychnus opened the door in to his insula, before signalling his friend to enter first. He lit a ditch of tarred fluid, causing a bright green flame to race around the room, flooding it with a warm flickering light. "Please," he said, pointing to one of two chairs positioned at the table. Acernis obliged with the request as both men sat down.

"Brother," Acernis declared as he lent forward, "I have been sent to warn you, but I fear that on my journey, I saw a sign from the gods themselves. A sight that filled me with dread."

"Warn me?" Lychnus responded.

"Yes, by order of Ulmus," Acernis explained.

"Go on," Lychnus replied as he leant in closer, while Acernis calmly explained everything that had happened at Magpie Hall.

Taking a moment to process all that he had just been told, Lychnus lent back in his chair, and tapped his index finger against his lip. "So they are all coming here? Including Ulmus?" he paused. "And Cinis?" he asked with a concerned tone. "Please, not Cinis too?" he said shaking his head. Acernis simply nodded. Lychnus rose from his chair, and placed his arm on the cold stone wall, before resting his head.

"And what of your journey?" Lychnus asked with a concerned tone, "You spoke of a sign from the gods?"

"Yes. I saw the trees stripped of their greenery. I saw the ground barren of life and I saw magpies, too many to count. Dead. As far as the eye could see," Acernis explained with growing distress.

Lychnus sighed loudly. "The Codex Vitae has failed," he responded with a defeated resonance. "I had hoped to find a solution before alerting the Pica Dominus. However, it seems the gods grow increasingly cruel."

"Life does not return?" Acernis asked.

"It is far worse than we could have ever feared," Lychnus replied sitting back down. "All of the animals starve before they can create new life."

"That would explain the weakened wolves," Acernis retorted.

"All have suffered," Lychnus replied. "We too are running out of food. The adults hardly eat at all now. They save what they can for the children. It is unsustainable and it is spreading!"

"Spreading?" Acernis asked.

"Yes, from the east. I fear it will not be long before it reaches Magpie Gorge, and destroys everything that we have ever held of value. I also fear it will not be long before it spreads to White city and beyond; until all of Rytus is consumed." Lychnus explained.

"Forgive me friend, I was not aware. I will return to White City at once, and I will tell them of what I have seen," he replied as he rose to his feet.

"Nonsense," Lychnus replied. "It has been so long since we last spoke, we have much to discuss. You can return to the city in the morning."

Chapter Ten

5,260 days before the eclipse.

Sunlight began to flood Falcon Hall. Inside, the White Bloods busied themselves clearing away the remains of the night before. They collected up the broken fixtures, including lamps and decorative plates, before setting the furniture back in position. In his office, Leanorus tidied away the mess left by Agapeta. He collected up the scrolls, putting them back in their rightful places, and returned the room to the condition he had inherited it in. He walked to the plaque he had given pride of place on the wall, and carefully lifted the bow held there, from its torpidity. He inspected the limbs before grasping it firmly. He turned to the window and tensed the bow. He lined up the sight with a tree in the distance as the smile grew larger on his face. He felt like a child again, his mind now vividly re-living the memories. His first kill, his first kiss, his first love, they all came flooding back.

A knock at the door. Leanorus turned to see a White Blood stood patiently in the doorway. She let out an almighty scream upon seeing her master with bow aimed squarely at her, before running from the room. Leanorus lowered his bow, "Oh concacavi," he said cussing himself before heading out in search of the terrified girl.

On the top floor, Vesnus carefully stepped over his fellow Orange Bloods, sprawled about the place, as he made his way quietly to the stairs. Those that were awake cursed the quantities of wine they had drunk the night before, almost as much as they cursed the cockerels crowing at the new dawn in the distance. Vesnus made his way down to the ground floor, just in time to hear a scream, followed by the White Blood girl running from Leanorus's office. Vesnus sprinted over.

"What has happened?" Vesnus asked.

"Did you see a girl come this way?" Leanorus replied, still bow in hand.

"Er? I did, but..." Vesnus responded staring at the old bow, before meeting his mentor's glare.

"I did not mean to scare the poor thing," Leanorus explained dropping his shoulders accompanied with a heavy sigh. He stood quietly contemplating the thoughts swelling in his mind before turning to face Vesnus.

"It's odd..." Leanorus commented, "...I know in my heart that I do not want to leave this place." He paused looking around the room, "But, it seems brother, that the gods must have their blood." Leanorus looked unusually sober and sedate. He placed his hand on the shoulder of Vesnus and smiled. "Though I am gladdened that it will be by your hand, friend," Leanorus said reassured, reminding Vesnus of his promise the night before.

Vesnus smiled, "It will be a great honour, Mentoris."

"Oh! Before I forget," Leanorus declared, "another letter has arrived for Agapeta. I managed to intercept it this time," he said with a sly smile. "I want you to go to Raven's Edge Camp, find this Ericus..." he said, pointing to the name on the letter, "...and discover Agapeta's part in all of this," he explained, pushing the letter into Vesnus's hand. "This may be my last chance to save the Falcons."

"Yes Mentoris," Vesnus agreed, "once my chores are complete."

Leanorus nodded in agreement and excused himself back to his office. Vesnus made his way towards the wooden door at the far end of the hall. He opened the door and trotted down the stone steps into the hall's kitchens. The smell of hot oats and water being prepared by the White Bloods filled the room, as the steam from the boiling water heated it to an almost unbearable temperature. The White Bloods wiped their brows as they stirred the large clay pots.

Vesnus carefully felt his way along the bottom of the wall, before tugging at something small, stuck between the wooden planks. He struggled for a little while longer before freeing a dead mouse from the trap. A White Blood girl recoiled in horror as Vesnus threw the shrivelled mouse into the air, before catching it with his other hand. He returned a smile to the girl, and left through the second door.

He stepped out of the kitchens, into the deep snow, and made his way towards the aviary, positioned on the westerly face of the hall. He lifted the clasp on the door and ducked inside. Twenty or so falcons called out at the intruder. Vesnus approached one in particular, opened his hand and offered the dead mouse. The bird snatched the gift and using her talons, tore into it, before consuming it. "Good morning to you too Velox," Vesnus jested, as he stroked the bird with his index finger, being careful to avoid a nip from her sharp beak. He picked up a thick leather gauntlet and placed it on his left hand, before collecting Velox from her perch.

Together they made their way out into the snow, away from the towering walls of the hall, out in to the frozen lands. Velox excitedly began to flap her wings in anticipation as Vesnus approached the centre of the field. He raised Velox into the air on his left hand before releasing her jesses.

She stretched out her wings and leapt from the gauntlet, swooping downward, before quickly gaining height and speed. She climbed into the morning sky, riding the breeze from the ocean as it rolled in. Her eyes scanned the horizon looking for her prey, her silhouette unmistakable against the rising sun. Vesnus watched Velox as she raced across the sky, making the most of the limited freedom she was afforded by her master.

In the distance a flock of sparrow birds shot up into the air, scattering in all directions. Vesnus whistled to Velox, but she was already well aware the game had started. She banked into a tight turn and gave chase. The flock began to thin out as Velox singled out her victim. She swooped to the left, as the sparrow dropped downward. She banked again and reached out with her talons. She collided into the sparrow. The pair tumbled towards the frozen ground as a trail of feathers fluttered in their wake. Vesnus held his breath. Another turn before she spread her wings, cutting her rapid descent into a graceful glide. Effortlessly, she gained height again as she tore into her catch. Vesnus admired her grace as much as he envied her agility, though the thought of a lifetime of being locked in an aviary, sent a shiver down his spine.

The clanging of metal armour interrupted the more familiar sounds of the morning, as Vesnus's attention was drawn by the troop of Red Bloods, marching with haste along the stone road towards Falcon Hall. Vesnus called to Velox, who obediently returned to her master, having now finished her meagre meal. The pair quickly made their way back across the fields without drawing the attention of the Red Bloods. He quietly snuck back up to the aviary; returning Velox to her favourite perch, before returning to the kitchens.

Inside, White Bloods began to ascend the stairs to the great hall, being careful not to spill a drop of the breakfast they had been preparing since dawn. Vesnus carefully pushed past, hoping to beat the Red Bloods to the front door.

"Leanorus!" Vesnus called out as he tumbled into the hall. He sprinted across the table that had been set up in the middle, towards Leanorus's office, scattering bowls and tableware in all directions. Intrigued by the commotion Leanorus began to descend the stairs from his office into the hall. Before Vesnus could explain, there came a thunderous knock at the door, shaking the dust from the wooden frame with every strike.

"Red Bloods," Vesnus declared, pointing at the door.

"Red Bloods? Here? They have no right to be in Falcon Reach, what could they possibly want?" Leanorus questioned, while making his way over to the door. Everyone but Vesnus backed away, unsure of what was about to happen.

Leanorus carefully inched open the door, only to be sent falling backwards as the Red Bloods burst into the hall uninvited. Vesnus ran to Leanorus's aid as the 12 Red Bloods marched in, in a two wide formation. Their red tunics, bronze cuirasses and silver helmets were barely visible behind their enormous wooden red shields, bearing the sigil of the Red Eagle. Orange Bloods and White Bloods looked on as the spectacle unravelled before them.

"How dare you?" Vesnus barked before being interrupted.

"I present forth the arrest warrant for Marius Albus Coquus," the Red Blood at the head of the troop bellowed, as he unravelled his scroll.

"You have no jurisdiction in Falcon Reach," Leanorus snapped angrily, as he found his feet.

Unmoved, the troop leader continued, "For the murder of a Red Blood."

The sound of gasps echoed about the hall. Faces began to appear over the balconies, while braver Orange Bloods began to swarm the ground floor. Immensely outnumbered and unsettled, the Red Bloods shuffled slightly before slapping the butts of their shields against the floor, like frightened rabbits stamping their feet to warn predators and rivals. The head of the troop remained unmoved, "He is to report immediately to White City to appear before the Blue Bloods."

Not to be intimidated, Leanorus squared up to the troop leader, his vivid orange eyes burning deep into the glare of the Red Blood. "Not while I still draw breath," he sneered.

The hall fell silent as the two men refused to back down.

The sound of a wooden bowl, filled with hot water and oats, clattering to the ground, broke the tension. A White Blood man then leapt across the table, disappearing into the crowd.

"Detain that man!" the Red Blood troop leader commanded, pointing in the man's direction. The two Red Bloods directly behind him, raised their swords and took a step forward, as instructed. Immediately, all the Orange and White Bloods on the ground floor took a step closer to the Red Bloods, containing them more tightly.

"Are you prepared to die for a White Blood?" the troop leader barked at Leanorus, with a growl and raised sword.

"I am prepared to defend the laws of this land, even if they must first be washed with red blood," he sneered back.

"I knew you would be trouble. CONSTITUO!" The Red Blood leader screamed as the men behind him slapped their shields to the floor. They took a crouched position and held their swords so as to protrude from the formation.

The Leader placed his sword to a yet unmoved Leanorus's throat. "AGGREDIOR!" he commanded to his Red Bloods. The troop moved forward, one step at a time, in the direction of the man who ran. They slapped their shields against the floor before taking another step forward, pushing those in their path aside. The leader remained transfixed on Leanorus, sword still pressed to his throat.

Orange and White Bloods began to pelt the troop with anything to hand. A shower of shoes, chairs, bedding and personal belongings, rained down against the bright red shields. They spat and hurled abuse at the troop who, instead, continued to slap their shields and grunt with each step taken across the hall.

"Stand down!" Agapeta called from the Lapsae balcony, with Leanorus's ceremonial bow in hand, charged with an arrow and her aim firmly fixed on the Red Blood leader. The Red Blood leader snorted dismissively into Leanorus's face, continuing to stand his ground.

"I said STAND DOWN!" Agapeta called out again, as Claricius joined her side with bow and arrow sighted at the Red Blood Leader.

The Red Blood leader let out an almighty laugh before pressing the sword further into Leanorus's skin, causing orange blood to seep down the edge of the blade.

"This is your FINAL warning!" Agapeta shouted, as more than a hundred Orange Bloods positioned their bows over the balconies of the hall, and took aim at the Red Blood leader. He looked up at the arrows trained on his position, as a bead of sweat trickled down his face.

"SUBSISTO!" the Red Blood leader called out, raising his hand. The troop halted. He lowered his sword and took a step back from Leanorus.

"I, Leanorus Aurantiac Falco, Pater Familias, Lapsae Falco, leader of the Orange Bloods and father of Falcon Reach, alone decide this man's fate," Leanorus bellowed, his voice echoing around the hall. "Bring him to me."

As instructed, Orange and White Bloods began to shuffle around, until the man was thrust before Leanorus. The Red Blood leader stepped forward to take the man, only to be greeted by the sound of a hundred bowstrings tightening. He stepped back. The man knelt at Leanorus's feet.

"You are accused of murder," Leanorus stated, staring into the man's nervous grey eyes. "An act that not only brings shame upon you, but all of us gathered here." The man closed his eyes as a tear fell, pooling on the floor.

"What awaits him at White City?" Leanorus asked, addressing the Red Blood leader.

"A trial by the Blue Bloods, to determine his guilt," the leader replied, devoid of any emotion.

"Very well. My Falcons will escort this man to see that his trial is fair and just," Leanorus declared summoning Vesnus, Claricius and Placidus to step forward.

The Red Blood leader sighed, "If it will put an end to this madness..."

"This is not madness, this is law!" Leanorus snapped.

"FORAS," the leader barked, signalling the troop to stand down, and head towards the door. They each began to file out. Orange Bloods and White Bloods immediately reinstated their barrage of abusive words and projectiles. The leader opened his arm to indicate the accused to follow next. Claricius barged past, followed by Placidus then the accused man.

Vesnus stepped forward to follow, but felt a hand grab his arm. "See that he gets a fair trial," Leanorus pleaded, "but do not forget your promise to me." Vesnus nodded and followed the man out. The Red Blood leader slammed the door behind him, as he followed up the rear of the group.

The three Orange Bloods collected their blades and bows. The group then made their way out of the grounds of Falcon Hall, along the stone road to White City. The path led them around the Dying Woods, named for both its purpose and its appearance.

Along the way, birds began calling out in the crisp cold air, as the barren trees creaked and groaned with the breeze. Vesnus tried to break the rhythmical clanging of the armour and shields of the Red Bloods by faltering his step, but no matter how hard he tried, he always found himself stepping in time with the Red Bloods.

Vesnus quickly became distracted as the rustling of leafs trailing them grew louder. He was confident they were being followed. The sound of a twig snapping resounded about the trees. The group halted as the Red Bloods drew their swords. A small, brown fox jumped from the overgrowth, running to the feet of Placidus.

"Not now Liquens," Placidus pleaded, "I will play with you later. I promise."

The Red Blood leader callously scoffed as he returned his sword, "You Orange Bloods and your pets." Placidus ignored the remark.

The group resumed their march for White City as the fox continued to follow them. He followed all the way along the road to the Western Gate.

"Stay!" Placidus commanded halting his march.

The fox tilted his head before continuing to follow Placidus towards the gate.

"No," Placidus commanded, "stay!"

Bemused, the fox sat down and waited.

Red Bloods positioned at the gates glared at the group as they passed into White City. A dishevelled White Blood girl approached, lifting an empty bowl to Claricius, who pushed her away.

"Get lost," Claricius sneered. Vesnus watched with sadness, as the girl stepped back, before realising that another ten or so Red Bloods from the gate, had joined the back of the group.

The sound of the Red Blood's armour echoed off the tall buildings of the city, as White Bloods began to spill out on to the streets, to see the group pass. They reached Sparrow Bridge and continued to march on. The tone of their stamping feet changed slightly against the melting snow on the smooth white stone. The three outnumbered Orange Bloods looked to the Blue Palace on the right as the troop turned left towards the Red Barracks. Vesnus and Placidus exchanged worried looks. Claricius remained smug, his confidence in his own abilities and his animosity towards the White Bloods, clouding his judgement.

The group carried on through the barracks, before taking one last turn towards the small bridge, to the fighting pit of White City. The Orange Bloods were immediately commanded to stop. The accused man was then ripped from the group and marched across the bridge.

"But I am to ensure a fair trial," Vesnus insisted, as his voice became drowned out by the furore.

A large Red Blood towering over the Orange Bloods, sneered at the three men, "Beat it little Falcons, fly back to your little wooden cage."

The Red Blood troop leader laughed as Vesnus and Placidus hopelessly outnumbered, reluctantly withdrew. Claricius peered through the siege of Red Bloods as the accused man in the pit, now with his hands bound behind his back, was forced down on to his knees; before he himself was pushed back to join the other two men. He huffed loudly at the contempt of the Red Bloods before unwillingly joining his fellow blood brothers.

"What will we do now?" Placidus asked.

"Why bother? He is just a White Blood," Claricius said dismissively.

Vesnus took a moment to think, before running back through the Red Barracks, back towards the Blue Palace.

"Oh for the love of Pluto," Placidus said rolling his eyes before running to catch up, as Claricius unenthusiastically followed.

Vesnus ran back across Sparrow Bridge, progressing quickly through the swarming crowd as the other two struggled to keep him in sight. He raced along the stone street before taking a sharp turn down a narrow alleyway between two armourers. Darting up the steep incline and the occasional jagged stone step, he made his way to the top of the fighting pit.

White Bloods continued to pour in, onto the cold stone steps that re-commissioned the pit as an amphitheatre for such occasions. White Bloods from the palace stood patiently in the Swan's Nest overlooking the pit. Red Bloods stood to attention at strategic positions while others patrolled through the crowds. Two held the accused man in position with their swords pressed firmly against the back of his neck.

"What kind of trial needs this many Red Bloods?" Placidus asked, resting his hand on Vesnus's shoulder.

"Something does not feel right," Vesnus replied.

The chatter of the crowd hushed, as Tiberius stood up from his seat in the Swans Nest, adorned in his shining legate uniform. "My citizens of Rytus," he bellowed, whipping the crowd into a frenzy of applause and cheers. Tiberius lapped up the admiration of the crowd before continuing. "Citizens, I present before you, Marius Albus Coquus," he said, pointing to the accused man. "He stands before you accused of murdering a Red Blood." The cheers of the crowd turned to boos and jeers as the accused man remained unmoved. Tiberius muted the crowd before continuing. "Pray tell Marius, how do you stand before the gods?" he asked, raising an eyebrow.

"Nocens," replied the accused man.

"Do you hear that? He pleads guilty before the gods!" Tiberius laughed as the crowd began to cheer loudly. "Do you wish to beg forgiveness from the gods before I pass judgement, vermin?" he continued mockingly.

"Yes Imperator," the accused man spluttered.

"What? I cannot hear you," Tiberius laughed. "Well?" he said coldly.

"Yes imperator," the accused man repeated.

Tiberius unable to hear the man, raised his hands and shrugged his shoulders. The Red Blood stood at the accused man's side, nodded to Tiberius.

"Very well then," Tiberius said, a little annoyed.

The accused man looked up, his face pale, as tears cascaded down his cheeks. "He had to die. He took the woman I love, my wife. He took her away from me and he forced her to do..." he paused as the disgust welled up inside, "...he forced her to do unspeakable things. He tore her to pieces and returned her to me a shadow of herself, and..." Tiberius looked on slightly taken a back as the crowd fell silent. "...she returned with child. He sentenced her to death," he screamed, arms outstretched. "The gods must have their blood, and I gave them his instead," he explained with heartfelt sincerity before he fell to the ground, sobbing into the frozen dirt.

A slow hand clap broke the silence as Tiberius acrimoniously applauded the man. All those gathered, with the exception of the three Orange Bloods, turned to face Tiberius as he began to bellow with laughter, before them themselves joined in laughing and pointing at the accused man.

"That, White Blood, is a great story. However, it is far from the truth," Tiberius declared. The accused man looked up from the dirt in dismay. "For you see, I have a witness. He states that you were in fact caught stealing bread,"

Tiberius loudly declared as the crowd brought his every word.

"No!" the accused man cried out.

"You were caught stealing bread, and in an attempt to escape justice you stabbed a Red Blood, as he tried..." Tiberius continued, before being interrupted.

"NO!" the accused man screamed out.

"You stabbed the Red Blood as he tried to detain you, as confirmed by Ericus," Tiberius continued, raising his voice above the desperate pleas of the accused man.

"Ericus? That name..." Vesnus said bewildered.

"You killed the Red Blood, and what is worse, you were the one who butchered your wife." Tiberius blared out.

"This is not a trial," Vesnus commented.

"NO!" the accused man continued to plead.

"This is an execution!" Vesnus declared.

"You were the one who forced yourself upon your wife. You were the one who sentenced her to death." Tiberius continued, shouting over the cheers of the crowd and the pleas of the accused man. "Bring her in!" Tiberius instructed, pointing to the Red Bloods by the pit's gate.

As commanded two Red Bloods hurriedly brought in a terrified White Blood woman, her face and arms covered in bruises and her arms bound behind her back.

"Why?" The accused man pleaded.

145

"You, Marius, are GUILTY of murder," Tiberius roared, "and you, Hatia, bore a son. The gods must have their blood. Therefore, I, Tiberius Hyacintho Olor, Imperator and Legate of the Red Bloods, sentence you both to die, like the animals you are!" he said cruelly.

"I have to stop this," Vesnus declared, taking a step towards the pit.

"How?" Placidus asked grabbing his arm, "How, exactly? We are outnumbered by Red Bloods and who knows how many riled up White Bloods. And let us not forget Tiberius, stood right there!"

The Red Bloods began to leave the pit, but not before forcing the terrified White Blood woman onto her knees. The gates to the pit were sealed behind the last Red Blood, and a cage wheeled into position by a smaller gate. The cheers of the crowd drowned out the sobbing of the two White Bloods on their knees, as the man shuffled towards his wife. He leant into her as she nestled her head into his shoulder. The wolves in the cage were further agitated as the Red Bloods banged on the side, while continuing to rile up the hungry beasts.

"Incipio!" Tiberius commanded.

"I am so sorry that I could not save you," Marius whispered.

The two White Bloods looked sincerely into each other's eyes as the gate on the cage was lifted. The pounding of the wolves' paws on the frozen ground seemed so distant; as were the growls and snarls as they gnashed their serrated teeth. The rapid intakes of breath as the wolves sprinted across the pit, now faded into insignificance. It took but a moment for the animals to clear the short distance, but to Marius and Hatia, it seemed almost a lifetime. A smile appeared on her face as the wolves drew closer, and, although he knew a painful death loomed behind her, he felt entirely at peace.

"I cannot stand here and watch," Vesnus said with disgust before leaving.

As the three Orange Bloods made their way from the pit; the sounds of wolves tearing into flesh, accompanied with the cheers of the crowds emanating from the pit, turned Vesnus's stomach with every step. The three men made their way down into the street, before taking a moment to compose their thoughts.

"Ericus?" Placidus enquired.

"What?" Vesnus replied.

"Ericus, you mentioned that name back there," Placidus responded.

Vesnus still shocked and disgusted took a few moments to think. He then pulled the letter out from under a strap on his leather armour.

"A blood debt letter?" Placidus asked, snatching it.

"Where did you find that?" Claricius asked, suddenly interested.

"It is of no matter," Vesnus said dismissively.

"Well, let us go find out what really happened," Placidus declared excitedly, as he began to head back towards the gate, "let us go find the truth!" Immediately he walked straight into a temple attendant, who, unknowingly to the men, had been listening in to the conversation. "Oh by the gods, I am so sorry," he said apologetically, as he picked up the young woman from the floor. Her beautiful white temple palla now dirtied, filled Placidus with an enormous degree of guilt. He tried to brush the dirt away, only making the situation more awkward, for all involved. Realising, eventually, he let the young woman continue.

"Hey!" he called out, realising the letter was now absent from his grasp. He turned around sharply to confront the young temple attendant, but instead he was greeted by hordes of White Bloods spilling from the pit, having satisfied their blood lust. There was no sign of the young woman anywhere.

The sound of wares from a market stall crashing to the ground drew the attention of everyone including Vesnus and Placidus, as Claricius ran with haste away from the other two, knocking the stall over.

"Oh no you do not brother," Vesnus called out before giving chase, "not this time!"

Chapter Eleven

5,260 days before the eclipse.

The smell of searing flesh filled the air, as the successful new Red Bloods were each branded with the sigil of the red eagle. The grunts of Velius, and the muffled groans of discomfort from all but Aulus and Darius, echoed around the Red Barracks. Their resolve remained strong, even as the red hot kiss of the iron boiled and blistered their skin.

The cool clean water of the baths offered welcome relief, as they washed the blood and dirt from their brandished bodies. The bitter taste of victory in the trials lingered on their lips before pooling and falling to the ground, splashing on the cold stone floor.

The men lined up before Publius, who in turn, handed them each an unworn tunic and a single pair of shoes. The coarse woollen garment was itchy and heavy. The shoes offered little protection from the elements. With them though came a sense of pride, knowing that each of the New Bloods had earned their right to wear the fundamentals of a Red Blood's uniform.

"What of our armour?" asked Velius egotistically.

Publius glared at the upstart before responding coldly, "You are to collect them from the armourer in White

City." He paused to contemplate the cruel idea swelling in his mind, smiled and continued, "Velius, I have a special task for you."

Thrilled at being singled out for a mission of seemingly great importance, Velius grinned with pride as Publius commanded the pompous Red Blood to await his return. Publius ducked out of the room momentarily before returning, carrying the large steel plated cuirass from the hall of honours.

"You will carry this to the armourers, have it cleaned and then, only then, collect your armour before returning with both. Do I make myself clear?" Publius commanded. Velius looked at the enormous and intricate metal mass with horror as Publius unceremoniously dumped it upon him. "A word of advice brothers," Publius explained as he turned to face the remaining five men, "first one to get to the armourers usually gets the better gear."

Publius let out an almighty laugh as the men raced out of the barracks, followed eventually by a heavily laden Velius cursing every god he knew the name of.

The sound of leather sandals sloshing in the melting snow resounded from the walls of the palace, as the young men jostled for position over Sparrow Bridge, and into White City. Their progress was unexpectedly halted, as the streets around the armourers began to overflow with White Bloods, each trying desperately to reach the spectators entrance to the fighting pit, before an execution taking place there ended. The hum and excitement of the gathered crowd almost drowned out the desperate pleas of a man in the pit, before the sound of booing and hissing filled the district. Undeterred, Aulus and Darius pushed on, scrambling and struggling their way through the determined citizens.

Darius was first to reach the armourers, closely followed by Aulus and the other men, with no sign of Velius. The smell of steel being worked in the furnace flooded out onto the street, interrupted occasionally by the smell of fresh leather being tanned. The men excitedly entered the armourer's workshop. Two waiting White Bloods collected Darius and took him to be fitted in a back room, while the armourer looked Aulus up and down, tutted, inhaled loudly, then screwed his face up in contemplation.

"Should fit," he muttered to himself, before turning to the racks of armour proudly displayed behind him, his large hands stained with the cuts and scars that came with crafting and repairing armour. Though he most likely possessed the strength of a bear, he handled each piece of armour with the same care a mother would handle a new born child. He picked up a bronze chest plate and carefully placed it down on the counter before Aulus.

Aulus couldn't help but admire the intricate detail and pattern cut into the piece, before noticing the repairs to the area designed to protect a Red Blood's heart.

"What happened?" he asked respectfully, pointing to the repair.

The armourer placed his large hands over the plate before looking up at Aulus, "Wolf got 'im." Not being one for idle chat, the armourer turned again, collected a selection of cuirasses, and secured the chest plate into position. He carried the armour over and lifted it above Aulus's head. He lowered it on to Aulus's shoulders. The weight took him by surprise; he had to quickly readjust his stance before the armourer could begin strapping the armour together.

An enormous sense of pride began to swell inside Aulus, as the armourer continued to suit up the young Red Blood. His greaves glinted in the light, as the intricately decorated metal plates, still warm from the armourer's touch, fell into their rightful places. The red protective strips above his thigh trickled into position, as the bronze cuirass shimmered with confidence for its new owner, with every breath Aulus took. My very own armour, he thought, as a sly smile appeared on his face. The final piece, the helmet, was lovingly presented by the armourer, just as Velius burst in through the door.

Velius panted trying to catch his breath before dumping the prized metal work at the feet of the armourer.

Aulus saw the anger seething inside the furious White Blood, and decided instead to quickly take the helmet and beat a sharp retreat out of the workshop.

Aulus stepped out into the street, his new armour singing his every step with a clap of metal. "Finally!" he declared loudly, throwing his arms open.

Darius, who had been waiting for his Blood Brother outside, laughed before patting Aulus on the back, "Indeed brother." Both men chuckled as the sound of the armourer roaring at Velius, spilled out from the workshop behind them; before beginning their short journey back to the Red Barracks.

With the execution now apparently over, citizens began to swarm the streets again. Only this time the two Red Bloods did not have to struggle through the crowds. In their shining armour, the White Bloods parted instinctively, like prey wary of a predator passing through the flock. And though the armour was heavy, both men stood taller than they had ever done before, their pride seeing them tower over the citizens of Rytus. Both men felt entirely at home, like they truly belonged for once. Not of White City though, or their hometown. No, now they were Red Bloods of Rytus, now they belonged anywhere and everywhere. The entire known world was home to the two towering Blood Brothers of Rytus, Darius and Aulus.

"Welcome home," Publius said warmly upon their return, beckoning the men back into the barracks. "Good fit, good choice," he said congratulating them on their new armour.

Eventually Velius joined the men. His armour was slightly too big for his frame and his helmet bore the scars of many battles won, but many more that had been lost. The very sight of him caused Publius to snigger, as he tried to hold back the laughter.

Gurgana, a middle ranking Red Blood, announced her arrival into the room with a cough, causing Publius to turn in her direction.

"I beg forgiveness, Tiberius approaches," she said, respectful of her rank.

Publius nodded in acknowledgment and stood up. "Go find some free bunks," he commanded, "and stay out of the way of the Old Bloods." He promptly left the room.

Aulus and the men approached the dormitory. Instantly they felt unwelcome, unwanted and exposed, even in their new armour. The eyes of each of the Old Bloods glared straight through each of them. Even Velius felt uneasy.

Aulus sighed and moved into the room, accepting that this was most likely going to be the only reception they would receive until they had proven themselves. The others followed, staring at the heels of Aulus. It felt like walking into the den of a pack of angry wolves, still chewing on the bones of their last meal.

Eventually, the New Bloods each found space that incurred the least amount of grunts and snarls from the Old Bloods. They began to settle in as best they could. Aulus deduced the dormitory's atmosphere most likely hung at the end of a delicate thread, one provocation could see the room explode. He decided it would probably be wise to make sure he wasn't in the room at the time.

Velius dropped his helmet. The loud and unwelcomed noise of metal on stone caused every pair of eyes in the room to look in his direction. Accompanied by the unequivocal sound of steel rolling along the gritty stone floor, it rolled under his bunk, past the chests, and into the right foot of Gaius.

Gaius looked down, then glared up at Velius, before picking up the helmet. His cold stare and horrific scar filled Velius with terror. He froze to the spot as Gaius rose from his seated position. The room fell silent with anticipation, as each foot step taken by Gaius echoed against the cold stone walls. Velius's red eyes grew wide, as Gaius strode up to the frightened New Blood. Gaius thrust the helmet into Velius's lap, knocking the wind out of him.

"Be more careful," he sneered, with a threatening tone.

Velius, flustered and unnerved, nodded in agreement. Gaius turned and made his way back to his bunk. Before Velius could burst into tears, Publius entered the room.

"Gaius, Varia..." he bellowed. "Tiberius wishes to go in to White City. I need you to escort him."

"As you command," they replied.

"I beg forgiveness," Acacia interrupted. "Perhaps I may be permitted to join too?"

"Very well," Publius replied, "Take Acacia, and er?" He scanned around the room, "You there!" He said pointing at Aulus.

"Aulus," he replied respectfully.

"Yes, take Acacia and Aulus with you. It will do well for them to learn alongside the Old Bloods," Publius explained.

Gaius and Varia both raised their eyebrows with scepticism before nodding in agreement.

"Very good," Publius said, as he clasped his hands together. "Suit up."

"Brother, we have only been here a day, and already you are to escort a Blue Blood," Darius said congratulating his friend.

"You best not slow me down boy," Gaius growled.

Disturbed by Gaius but still brimming with pride inside, Aulus followed the others out of the barracks. Tiberius waited impatiently in the square at the foot of the

Blue Palace, in his brightly polished armour and red tunic, arms folded and pouting.

"Finally. I wish to travel to the Eastern district. Let us move out," he said, irritated.

Tiberius immediately led the troop out across Sparrow Bridge into White City, followed by Gaius and Varia, with their bright red distinctive transverse crested helmets. Behind them marched Acacia and Aulus with their plain, undecorated helmets, more befitting of their ranks.

Any White Bloods unwilling or unable to move out of the way fast enough, were forcefully moved by Gaius's and Varia's pilums, as Tiberius relentlessly marched on. The troop pushed through the marketplace, taking a tight turn; where they were greeted by an overturned cart, blocking the street.

Tiberius burst into a fit of rage, cursing any White Blood in the immediate vicinity. "Move this cart at once!" he barked.

"Forgiveness Imperator," Acacia interrupted, "I know of a quicker way around."

Tiberius nodded as Acacia took the lead. The troop turned around, and continued back along the main street from the Palace towards Red Hell Gate. They marched past the shops and homes of shocked and confused White Bloods, heading further South into the deepening snow.

"Are you sure this route is correct?" Tiberius questioned.

"Yes, Imperator," she replied.

The grey stone and spruce insulas of the White Bloods towered above them to the right, while to their left stood the rotten hovels of the Ruinae. Acacia turned, eventually leading them to a dead end.

"You have led us astray. I will see that you are duly punished for wasting my time," Tiberius barked.

"CLOSE RANKS!" Varia cried out.

Tiberius looked around in dismay, as a crowd of hooded White Bloods surrounded the troop.

"Back away!" Tiberius instructed. The hooded White Bloods continued to close in on the troop.

"I said BACK AWAY!" Tiberius snarled. "I AM TIBERIUS HYACINTHO OLOR, IMPERATOR AND LEGATE OF THE RED BLOODS, AND I INSTRUCT YOU TO STAND DOWN!"

One of the hooded White Bloods launched for Varia who instinctively and precisely struck back knocking him off his feet. "BACK AWAY!" she instructed.

Another of the hooded White Bloods drew a short blade from under his toga and lunged for Tiberius. Gaius grabbed the man by the arm and broke it over his knee. The hooded White Blood riled in pain on the floor.

"Imperator, we are outnumbered. We need to get you to safety, NOW!" Varia cried out.

"Yes," Tiberius said, nodding in agreement.

"The grain store over there!" Acacia called out.

The troop formed around Tiberius, moving the Blue Blood toward the safety of the store, while keeping the White Bloods at bay. Soon pebbles, rocks and anything of considerable weight began to rain down on the troop. Without their shields, the troop were vulnerable.

"Tiberius must die!" shouted a hooded White Blood.

"He dishonours his vows to the gods," another shouted out.

The barrage of projectiles and accusations endured, as the Red Bloods continued to fight back the baying White Bloods.

Eventually they reached the store. Varia was just able to open the door enough to squeeze Tiberius and Aulus inside before slamming it shut. Varia turned back to ensure the White Bloods could not follow. All colour drained from her face as Gaius stood before her, his hand firmly clasped around his own throat. He stared back, as the blood began to spurt and pool between his fingers. He dropped to his knees revealing behind him the hooded White Bloods, and Acacia, blade in hand.

"You! You did this! Why?" Varia gasped.

Acacia stepped forward. "I seek a higher order," she whispered callously in Varia's ear.

A cold and unfamiliar pain washed over Varia, the sting of betrayal all too real, as Acacia's blade ripped into her abdomen. The red blood gushed down the steel blade to Acacia's hand, before dripping into the crisp white snow below.

Varia's crested helmet dropped silently alongside Gaius's motionless body. Varia had just enough strength to look Acacia in the eye one last time, before falling into the snow herself.

Inside the poorly lit grain store, unaware of events outside, Tiberius and Aulus caught their breath.

"Your rank?" Tiberius demanded.

"Decem, Imperator," Aulus replied.

Tiberius sighed, "Can you fight?"

"I have been well trained, Imperator," Aulus responded.

"Let us hope that is enough to get us out of here alive," Tiberius grumbled. "Where are the others?"

"I am afraid, my dear Imperator, oh great idolatrous one, that they can no longer help you," a voice from the corner of the room called out.

"Who speaks?" Tiberius replied, squinting in the poor light, "state your title."

The hooded White Blood man stepped forward, "My title?" he laughed. "My title is insignificant compared to your heinous crimes against the gods; crimes for which you must pay."

"How dare you threaten a Blue Blood?" Tiberius snarled. "I am your Imperator and you will do as you are commanded."

"Oh but you are wrong. For you see, I am doing as I am commanded. It is just that you are not *my* Imperator," the hooded White Blood responded, as another stepped forward from the shadows, followed by three more.

"Stop this nonsense immediately," Tiberius demanded.

"The gods must have their blood," the hooded White Blood declared, as he drew a blade, launching for Tiberius.

Chapter Twelve

5,260 days before the eclipse.

"Forgiveness Dominus, a letter has arrived for your attention," Aegle explained timidly. Marcus stopped eating, sighed loudly and beckoned her forward. She placed the letter on the table in front of him before turning to leave.

"Thank you," he said respectfully.

She paused momentarily, pondering whether to respond. To ask, to question, why had he embraced Acquilina? Marcus could sense her hesitation and sat silently, anticipating her companionship. She dismissed her thoughts and left.

Disappointed, and feeling lonelier than he had ever felt in nearly two lifetimes, he dropped his shoulders. He sat quietly for a moment, deliberating his purpose, before picking up the letter. The unbroken seal of the blue swan, narrowed the suspected patrons down from the citizens that could write, to the four Blue Bloods capable of sending a letter from the Palace with the seal still intact. He broke the seal and read the short and precise note:

Raven,

I seek another meeting, in private. I will be waiting today, in the usual place. Your discretion is, as ever, appreciated.

- Blue Swan

Marcus sat back in his chair, contemplating the letter. As the note indicated, this was not the first time he had been summoned by the Blue Swan. Duty and law dictated that the Raven could not refuse the request, however, if he were to ignore it, how could the Blue Swan bring it up without prompting further questions? The older Blue Bloods continue to grow suspicious of the Raven's power, keeping the younger ones on side could help move plans along, he thought. He mulled it over while finishing his meal. Marcus then tossed the letter into a lit torch, collected his purple paenula, and made his way up the stairs into the temple.

The temple was a stark contrast to the dreary winter's day outside. Every corner was lit up with the warm glow of purple candles. White Bloods were occupied, decorating the normally plain white stone walls with brightly coloured fabrics and sweet smelling displays of iris and lilac. They smiled as they worked, chatted happily and laughed loudly. Children giggled and ran through the temple, carrying more flowers and fabrics for their guardians. Marcus noted how happy everyone was; even his attendants who were giving water to the White Bloods, were doing so with broad smiles.

He took a deep breath and for once, no longer the focus of attention, he watched everyone else. He hadn't heard laughter echo around the temple for such a long time. He took great comfort knowing that everything that was here, was here because of him. The White Bloods were, at least for the moment, free of worry, free to laugh, free to live. Marcus had every intention of keeping it that way.

His thoughts were only interrupted by a small boy running straight into his side. The boy realising who he had just bumped in to, looked up, his eyes filled with terror. A young White Blood man came running over.

"I beg forgiveness Raven," his head bowed and his arms wrapped tightly around the boy.

"Please, do not fear me friend," Marcus replied softly.

The young father looked up confused, his eyes darting from side to side.

"The boy, he has no shoes?" Marcus enquired.

"Forgiveness, I do not understand," The man replied, before he quickly collected up the boy and moved away, to the edge of the temple. Before Marcus could question why the man was so afraid, his attendant, Aellae, approached.

"The citizens await your arrival Dominus," she remarked, passing a lit purple candle to Marcus.

Marcus took one look back at the man and the shoe-less child before nodding in agreement. He pulled up his hood, accepted the gift of light and followed his ten attendants out of the temple. They made their way along the corridor and down the white stone steps to the street. Carefully they stepped out into the slushy snow.

Men and women stood silently, as the white hooded attendants and the purple hooded Raven paraded by. The group contradicted the grey stone walls of the towering insulas, their brilliance reflected against the pallas and togas of the White Bloods; like a drop of purity in an endless sea of grey.

Marcus looked at the citizens lining the route. Their faces looked withered and tired. Their bodies more akin to skeletons dressed in scarred and dirtied skin. They were cold but they had not given up hope. He could see it in their eyes. He gripped the candle tightly, it's warmth appreciated, despite the smoke from the wick.

The marketplace fell respectfully silent as the group entered. The attendants filed up the stairs of the wooden platform, before taking their positions at the back. Marcus walked to the front.

"Citizens of Rytus," Marcus called out, "Red Bloods, Orange Bloods, Green Bloods and White Bloods. Winter can be cold, winter can be cruel, and winter can feel relentless. We gather here today to banish winter from our hearts, to share joy, to celebrate and give thanks to the gods. They have given us the ground in which we grow our crops, the rain that keeps them watered, and the seed that we will sow in the spring. As a mark of respect for one another, I ask of you now, to share the gifts that you have brought, as we share this gift from our beloved Imperators."

Marcus turned to the waiting White Bloods from the palace, expecting them to be carrying the traditional large sack of grain. Instead they were empty handed, eyes fixed on the ground at their feet. Marcus turned to his attendants, who in reply shrugged their shoulders.

"Where is the grain?" Marcus asked quietly, trying not to alert the waiting crowd.

"I beg forgiveness Raven, the Imperators said they will no longer share their food with the White Bloods," came the fearful response.

"WHAT?" Marcus shrieked. Stunned, he contemplated how best to handle the situation, anxious to avoid a riot.

"Erm?" he hesitated, "It would appear there has been a slight delay in the gift from our devoted Imperators." The crowd began to mutter and rumble with quiet insinuation and suggestion. "No matter friends, I am sure we will not let this oversight ruin the occasion," he said a little disdainfully. Aware the crowd were getting restless, he continued on quickly, "Let the gift giving commence!"

Soon the grumbles of accusation turned to gleeful chatter, as citizens began uniting and giving what little they had. Farmers from Falcon Reach shared the handful of extra yields from their crops. Butchers shared small offerings of meat, and fruit pickers shared anything that had not already rotted. Even the wine makers were able to gift small quantities.

"Excellent," Marcus declared, "let the feasting and games begin."

The citizens sat down at the long tables laid out in the marketplace. The cruelty of the Blue Bloods long forgotten, as the men, women, and children burst into song. Marcus descended the stairs of the platform, and offered his blessings to the tables of revellers. They in turn thanked him for his continued guidance and support.

Satisfied that the festival period was now well underway, Marcus signalled to his attendants. They descended the stairs and led Marcus back to the temple.

"Should we prepare your bath Dominus?" Aellae asked, as they entered the temple. Marcus did not respond. He did not lower his hood. He instead walked straight past and down to his own private quarters.

Unable to contain his anger any longer, he picked up a bronze plate and threw it across the room. It clattered against the stone walls before coming to rest on the floor.

168

Unsatisfied, Marcus picked up a chair and smashed it against the wall, as he roared out in frustration.

"HOW DARE THEY?" he boomed, before smashing up the case containing his large collection of scrolls. The anger throbbed and burned deep inside his core, until he was left panting for air. His hands trembled and his mind grew clouded. He had to lean against the wall to catch his breath.

The pain began to subside, and his vision grew clearer, so much so that he noticed the remnants of the letter from the Blue Swan in the torch beside him. A sly smile appeared before giving way to a rancorous laugh. With a wild idea alight in his mind, he stood up straight, composed himself and walked to the smashed scroll case. He searched among the broken wood and scattered scrolls before collecting one in particular. He picked up the bronze plate and moved to the middle of the room. He drew the purple aura into his hands and began to read the scroll aloud.

Marcus's resolve remained strong, his purple eyes darting across the words, his voice cutting into the infinite void of his lonely quarters. A cold wind of change flooded into the chamber, as the torch on the wall flickered, before bursting into a new brighter origin of light. The flame reached upward, licking at the ceiling before being entirely extinguished. Lifted by the wind, the lingering hot embers swirled and danced. They rose from the torch and entwined around Marcus like purple stars in the night's sky. It only took a handful of the ashes to ignite the woollen garments, and soon Marcus was engulfed in a scorching purple flame. His purple paenula was reduced to the colour of ash, his hair was singed of its purple tipped hue. His eyes were drained of colour and his fingertips grew white and pale.

The flame promptly died away, plunging the room into darkness. Benevolently the torch reignited. Disguise achieved, Marcus left the chamber and made his way towards the Blue Palace.

He hurried across Sparrow Bridge unhindered, but was stopped at the steps into the palace.

"Palace is closed today White Blood," snapped the guard.

"How can it be closed?" Marcus replied perplexed.

"Tita is not allowing anybody in or out, now get lost," the guard barked.

Infuriated by the guard's pompous attitude, Marcus crossed back over Sparrow Bridge, grumbling and muttering to himself. It was imperative he met with the Blue Swan, if he was to set his ingenious plan into motion. He paced the street scratching his head, before remembering a previous encounter. The Blue Swan had ordered Marcus to leave the palace via a secret passage, that led to the mines below

Sparrow Cave Camp. Once inside, he would be free to roam unquestioned, and could simply leave through the passage again. Thrilled with his own ingenuity, Marcus sprinted through the streets, and out of the Western gate.

Outside of the city, a grey mule and cart waited unattended. Marcus thanked the gods for their assistance and drove out along the road, away from White City.

Once over the first bridge, Marcus pulled over. If he was to get passed the guards and into the mines below, he would need to convince them he was there for a reason. He searched his mind. A delivery! he thought. Of what though? he wondered. It did not matter; he just needed to pretend he had something important. He collected up the fabric covering and spread it across the empty cart. It sagged in the middle and would not fool even the most stupid of Red Bloods. He pondered his predicament before collecting up heaps of snow from the side of the road. He piled it up high in the cart before covering it over.

The mule plodded along honourably as the cart rocked and creaked down the coarse stone road. They crossed over the second bridge and took a right. The camp rose up from the mountains like a series of grey tombs jutting out of the snow. Access was only possible by the steep path that lay before them.

"Sorry girl," he said apologetically to the mule, before driving on.

Equally determined the mule fought on, her steady hooves finding purchase in the cracks of the stone. Slowly and carefully they climbed up.

The relentless wind howled through the mountains, bringing with it the stinging pain on freezing bare skin. Marcus pulled his hood as far forward as he could, his freezing hands almost frozen white. His teeth chattered and his legs ached, as the cold encroached into the muscle and bone.

"Halt!" the Red Guard at the gate commanded.

"Tita has sent me," Marcus replied.

"Tita sent you?" the guard questioned, as he looked around Marcus at the full cart. He looked Marcus squarely in the eyes. "What is in the cart?" he asked, suspicious.

"A gift, for your seniors, for Saturnalia," Marcus replied, his confidence diminishing quickly. The guard stood silently for a moment, thinking.

"Show me what is in the cart," he demanded.

"I am to show it only to your seniors, those were Tita's orders," Marcus replied, growing increasingly nervous.

The Red Blood drew his blade, "This does not sound like something Tita would do? Show me what is in the cart, now!"

"Or, I could turn around. Return to the Blue Palace and inform Tita that you would not receive her warm gesture. That you turned it away, doubting her kindness."

The guard's red eyes grew large. He nervously cleared his throat and turned to the gate keeper, "Let him through." He stepped closer to Marcus, "You will not tell Tita what I said? Will you?" he said quietly. Marcus smiled and nodded before driving the mule forward.

Inside, the camp was practically deserted. Only two Red Bloods were positioned by the doors of the great hall. The handful of others stood huddled around a fire pit, trying desperately to warm their hands. No-one paid any attention to the White Blood and his mule.

It had been a long time since the mines below the camp hummed with activity. Only a few White Bloods were spared occasionally to search out the cavernous void for any hidden deposits. Mindful to avoid any more questioning though, Marcus collected a lit torch and quietly made his way down the stairs into the cavern.

The cavern had been strategically hollowed out to create dormitories, kitchens and even a temple for the workers. Back when the mines were rich with minerals, roughly three hundred White Bloods called this cavern home. Now every foot step echoed around the empty hall, as the smell of sulphur and exhausted torches filled the air.

The sound of iron on stone was all but a distant memory now.

He remembered the route he had taken to escape the palace and made his way back along the tunnel. At the end, he found himself stood at the neck of a vast network of caves. The ground in front of him dropped off into a seemingly bottomless pit of darkness. Above him the rock face towered into the heart of the mountains above. Regardless of his intended route, his only option was to cross the old wooden bridge, that joined the tunnel to the caves on the other side. He was sure the bridge didn't look this dilapidated the last time he was here.

Nonetheless, Marcus held his breath, and gingerly stepped out onto the ancient wooden bridge. He paused. The bridge held. He exhaled and stepped forward. This time the bridge creaked. He froze, his heart racing. The creaking halted. He stepped forward, the bridge swayed to the right before coming to a rest. Marcus continued on.

About a third of the way across, the sound of a loud crack, followed by a long and excruciating creak, echoed around the vast expanse. He turned to look behind him, just as the wooden supports groaned, twisted, and began to collapse in to the void below. Marcus ran. He ran as fast as he could, dodging the wooden planks as they began to splinter in his path. The bridge fell from under him, as he made a final leap towards the ledge.

He landed clumsily, his waist colliding against the jagged rocks of the ledge. He scrambled up just in time to see the bridge disappear out of sight behind him. He picked up his torch and examined the gap. A collection of rickety and unstable support beams jutting out of the rock face, were all that remained of the bridge now. Marcus sat down for a moment to catch his breath, before continuing on.

He reached the end of the passage, and emerged into the kitchens of the Blue Palace. The smell of exotic and delicious food being prepared exclusively for the Blue Bloods, filled the air. He could only begin to imagine what it tasted like. Carefully, he closed the door behind him and dusted himself down.

Now free to roam the palace grounds, Marcus made his way to the designated meeting spot, the Blue Temple. He found a spot in the shadows and settled down, waiting for the Blue Swan to arrive. From the temple, White City seemed so magical. The snow topped rooves of the tall White Blood homes; the theatre to the left, the circus in the distance, and the Raven's temple, his temple, standing taller than any other building in Rytus; rising from the city, a monument to salvation, to hope and to the freedom craved by so many, glistened in the sunlight.

"Are you here?" A voice suddenly whispered.

Marcus turned around to see Lucius, the Blue Blood, calling out.

"I am here, Blue Swan," Marcus replied.

"Show your face so I know it is not another of mother's cruel tricks."

Marcus stepped forward.

"Oh, you are wearing a, er? disguise," Lucius replied a little shocked. "It is you though, I mean you are the, er? Raven?"

"Yes Imperator," Marcus replied respectfully.

"Ah, wonderful! Would not want one of mother's White Bloods to hear what I am about to tell you," Lucius said with a mischievous smile. "I need your help Raven. I need you to kill Servius."

"Excuse me?" Marcus replied, stunned.

"You know, killed, dead, in the afterlife. Revoke his life."

"I cannot just take a life," Marcus retorted.

"Oh but you must. For you see, I have been planning it for a while now. With Tiberius out of the way, only Servius can stop me. I will marry mother, instead of my sister Quinta, and there will be no-one to challenge me, or my judgment..."

Marcus lost for words, continued to stare at Lucius.

"...though I do suppose it may be an issue with Quinta's Decem Dies Mille ceremony tomorrow, it does not leave a lot of time." Lucius continued on, now mumbling to himself.

"Tiberius out of the way?" Marcus questioned.

"Hhhmmm?"

"You said, with Tiberius out of the way," Marcus reasserted.

"Oh yes," Lucius chuckled to himself, "I have arranged for him to a have a little accident in the Ruinae. Quite clever of me really."

"What have you done?" Marcus asked in dismay.

"Oh it was very easy, I found some fanatics of yours. Confirmed their appetite for White Blood flesh, and then promised them all sorts. They agreed to sort it out for me," Lucius explained smugly.

Marcus sighed heavily, while stroking his forehead to ease the pain of trying to process everything that Lucius had done.

"I do not know what to..." Marcus paused, another idea forming in his mind. He tapped his lip with his finger and began to pace the temple.

"What are you doing?" Lucius asked.

"Shush, I am thinking," Marcus replied. "Quinta's Decem Dies Mille ceremony is tomorrow."

"I just said that, but I do not see..."

"That does not give us a lot of time," he explained. "I accept your proposal, my Imperator," He said, bowing to

177

Lucius. "Your actions make my job very difficult Blue Swan, so I will need your help."

"Very well..." Lucius agreed, a little suspicious of Marcus's intentions.

"I will give you a vile from my more personal collection. One drop will aid digestion, two will ease tension, three or four will aid sleep but five will lead to an unpleasant death," Marcus explained. "Give just five drops to Servius, no more, no less," Marcus looked to Lucius to judge whether he truly understood his instructions, before continuing. "However, you do leave me with a problem. A blood debt must be paid on his death, as well as Tiberius's. I will not have time to request favour with the gods. Therefore, you will have to provide me with two Blue Blood children."

"How do I...?" Lucius asked puzzled.

"Before Quinta's Decem Dies Mille ceremony, you will see that a Blue Blood child is promised to the gods. Do I make myself clear?"

"I er? Think so," Lucius replied. "But Quinta...?"

"Do as I have instructed and Quinta will not be of any further concern to you." Marcus said, getting a little frustrated. "Now with that settled, you can walk with me to my temple." Marcus instructed, his latest plan now in motion.

"Why?" Lucius questioned.

Marcus raised an eyebrow, "I will give you the vile, to avoid it falling into the wrong hands. Also the grounds are closed to anyone wishing to enter or leave; and my planned exit route is... no longer an option."

Lucius smiled "Bah!" he exclaimed dismissively. "Mother is in the city, and Servius lounges around like a wounded old lion waiting to die. So I am in charge now, and I have to confess, I rather like it."

Chapter Thirteen

5,260 days before the eclipse.

"Shush. Shush, little one," Petrina whispered as she rocked Dianus gently in her arms. It was of no use, he continued to cry. "You will wake father and father needs his rest now, little sparrow," she spoke softly, in the vain hope that it might calm the child. Despite her best efforts Alpheaus appeared at the doorway.

"He is hungry and you need your sleep," he said. "I will fetch a Nutrix, then when I return you can sleep," he instructed.

"I will go get a Nutrix while you rest with Dianus," she replied, concerned for her father's wellbeing.

"I suppose you are right," he agreed reluctantly. "Here, take this. It should be enough," he said, pushing a small coin purse into Petrina's hands. "While you are gone, I will prepare us a morning meal," he said with a smile.

"I do not think that is possible father," she replied anxiously. "We have not a crumb in the entire insula," she explained.

Alpheaus thought for a moment before taking a few more coins from a hole in the wall. "Take these, they are our last coins. Spend them wisely and bring back food for yourself," he instructed.

"But..." she replied.

"Now, go on get out of here before I find the strength to descend those stairs myself," he replied with a tender tone.

She made her way towards the door, turned to her father, and smiled as reassuringly as she could, before leaving as instructed. She descended the stairs and made her way out onto the street. Outside, the smell of fires burning in the courtyards, and fresh bread being baked in the bakeries, danced and lingered in the air. Her father's talk of food made Petrina realise just how hungry she was. Her priorities remained unchanged though, without a Nutrix, Dianus would die. She pulled up her hood, and made her way out to the Nutrices quarters in the Western district of White City.

Hundreds of White Bloods swarmed the streets. Traders carried stock to their shops below the insulas. Tailors repaired clothing. Blacksmiths worked the forges and farmers began making their way to the market. Petrina had to watch her step to make sure she wasn't barged out the way by a careless White Blood, or worst still, crossing the path of a Red Blood.

In the marketplace, the celebrations for Saturnalia had begun, led by the Raven, with the exchanging of food and small gifts between more fortunate White Bloods. She watched as the butchers shared slithers of mutton. The very thought of tasting meat again made her stomach growl loudly. In the corners, older White Bloods played a game of twelve lines, in celebration of the relaxation of gambling laws through Saturnalia. The sound of laughter and song filled the air, as the troubles of the past were drowned out. She was pleased to see her fellow White Bloods so happy for once, despite her growing hunger pangs.

She worked her way along the crowded streets, eventually arriving at the Nutrices quarters. She opened the door to be greeted by an administrator working at a desk.

"And what do you want?" he enquired callously.

"I seek a Nutrix," she replied.

"It will cost you coin," he explained, raising an eyebrow.

Petrina emptied the coins out into her hand and counted the cold metal pieces.

"They are twenty denarii," he said, counting the coins in her hand quicker.

"But..." she spluttered.

"Do you want a Nutrix or not?" he said heartlessly.

"Well, yes..." she tried to explain.

He beckoned Petrina over to his desk before snatching the coins from her hands.

"Very well," he explained arrogantly, while scribbling in a ledger, "a Nutrix will be sent to your home later this afternoon." He paused, "Which is where?"

"In the Eastern district..."

"The Eastern district?" he interrupted rudely. "Well the transport alone will cost you more than twenty denarii."

"But you have taken all that I have," she said tearfully.

"Very well, be gone with you," he instructed.

"But..."

"I said, be gone."

Hesitantly, Petrina left the quarters and began to head back out onto the street. Does that mean a Nutrix is coming or not? she wondered. And what am I to do about getting food? she questioned, becoming increasingly distressed. She decided to head back to the marketplace; perhaps a more fortunate White Blood would take pity on her.

"You looking for trouble girl?" a voice boomed as Petrina clattered straight into a Red Blood.

"I beg forgiveness," she squeaked, before running away from the towering, furious man.

She sought refuge in an alleyway. Hungry, frightened and desperate, she felt a void of hopelessness opening up inside. She wanted to scream out or burst into tears. She couldn't really tell which would bring her the least amount of unwanted attention.

Behind her, the sound of a man choking and gasping for air, echoed around the oddly deserted street. She turned to see a young White Blood man, just around the corner, drop to his knees grasping tightly at his neck. The scratches from his finger nails were so deep that white blood began to seep out. He slumped on to the stones of the street.

Petrina ran over to the man, hopeful that she could in some way assist. As she turned the corner, she saw a second figure running away. She grasped the hand of the White Blood man but there was no pulse. Petrina ran back to the Red Blood she had bumped in to. He had already moved on and was nowhere to be seen. A little distance down the street, Petrina spotted an Orange Blood.

"Please, you have to help me," she cried out to the Orange Blood.

"Clear off child, I am busy," he replied coldly.

"But..." she tried.

"I said clear off," he barked.

There must be more Red Bloods nearby, she thought. She began to run along the streets, looking down each and every alleyway, until she spotted a lone Red Blood.

"I need your help," she panted.

"I have no time for your games White Blood," he responded.

"But a man needs help," she explained.

"Is he someone important?" he asked.

"I do not know," she replied.

"Is he a Red Blood or a Blue Blood?" he asked.

"Well, no he is a White Blood," she responded.

"Then no, he is not important and you are wasting my time," he responded.

"But..."

"You are wasting my time," he maintained coldly, standing over her.

Terrified of the callous Red Blood, Petrina returned to the White Blood, only to find he was gone. Instead, in his place lay the start of a streak of white blood, trailing into a covered courtyard nearby. Curious, Petrina followed the trail.

Inside the courtyard, a troop of Red Bloods stood to attention. The White Blood man lay in a heap at the feet of a Blue Blood. Petrina quickly ducked down behind a large flower bed, for fear of being spotted.

"We caught the White Blood who stole from your kitchens, Imperatrix," a Red Blood reported.

"Good," Tita responded, looking at the dead man, "I do not want these vermin to think they can just take what they want from us." She snorted at the White Blood man before turning her nose up in disgust. "Make an example of the body, string it up or something." The Red Blood nodded.

185

"What of the stolen bread Imperatrix?" he asked.

"Oh," she responded, "I do not want it, not now a filthy White Blood has had his hands all over it. Throw it to the rats."

Petrina watched in disbelief as the Red Blood cast the bread into the courtyard. Tita and her Red Bloods left. Petrina saw her chance. She charged out from her hiding spot, and ran straight for the discarded bread.

"Hey you!" a Red Blood called out.

Petrina froze, her heart pumping rapidly.

"Drop that!" he demanded.

She thought for a moment, before running as fast as she could out of the courtyard. Two Red Bloods charged after her.

Petrina ran through the alleyway, darted across the street and into a shop. She hurdled the counter before racing out through the back door. She could hear the clatter of the Red Blood's armour behind her with every step she took. She charged down the street, past the latrines and scampered into the southern tip of the Ruinae.

"Hey! Watch it!" A White Blood called out as Petrina navigated the nest of homes stacked on top of each other.

"Come back here!" a voice demanded as she cleared another few tight turns. She reached the end of the street, before jumping on to the roof of one of the homes. With nowhere else left to run, she dropped down into the mass of brambles and weeds, that occupied the small space between the homes and the city's walls.

"This way!" a Red Blood called out.

Sure she was going to be caught, she held her breath and remained as still as possible.

The clatter of the Red Blood's armour faded into the distance. Petrina untangled herself from the brambles and squeezed out of the tiny gap between the walls, into a small courtyard. She brushed off some of the dirt and took a bite of the bread. She savoured the taste. It was so fresh, and not lumpy like the bread she was used to. It tasted heavenly. She began to laugh and smile at her achievements, just as the bitter sting of the cuts from the brambles began to bite. She inspected her legs, arms, and palla, torn to bits and soaked in white blood.

"Please," a weak voice called out.

Petrina looked up as a small group of young and dishevelled children began to form around her.

"We are so hungry," they cried.

Petrina looked at the bread in her hand, there was barely enough to share between herself and her father, let alone this growing horde of hungry children. She pondered it for a moment trying to decide what her father would do in this situation.

"Here, this is for you," she declared, as she divided up the bread.

Chapter Fourteen

5,260 days before the eclipse.

"Hail Quinta," greeted the White Blood tutor.

"Praeceptor," came the pretentious reply, as Quinta entered the Blue Blood's study.

"I was just discussing the history of Rytus with your younger sisters," the tutor declared, hoping for a response.

"How we landed at Ravenstone and lived on the mountain and the gods got angry and swallowed up the city and everyone died and..." Numeria explained excitedly.

"Not everybody died, you idiot," Spuria barked back rudely.

"Indeed Spuria," the tutor responded, "but it is not befitting of a lady of your standing to call your sister, and fellow Cesar, an idiot." Numeria stuck her tongue out at her sister while the White Blood tutor tried desperately to restore order.

"Why is Quinta here?" Numeria asked, "She is not going to be a Cesar after her Decem Dies Mille ceremony tomorrow..."

"It is punishment for not being old enough to travel into the city with Mother yet," Quinta spat bitterly.

"Knowledge is not punishment," the tutor replied, "it can give us the wisdom to lead, to guide and to prevent the gods from swallowing us all up. Is that not right Numeria?" Spuria and Numeria both burst into a fit of giggles.

"Well, this is enlightening," Quinta replied sarcastically, as she sat down.

"Now that Quinta is here, perhaps she can tell us why we must obey the blood bond?" the tutor requested.

"No," Quinta replied firmly.

"Why not?" The tutor enquired.

"You are questioning me?" Quinta snarled back, "Tomorrow I will be your Imperatrix! You cannot make demands of me. I am no longer a child. You are the tutor. You explain to these two fatuus children what it all means."

Shocked and taken aback, the tutor sat silently for a moment.

"It is, the, er?," the tutor spluttered.

"Well?" Quinta demanded.

"It is a promise to the gods, that we will share the delicate balance that keeps Rytus strong," the tutor explained.

"I have no patience for this," Quinta declared before storming off.

Relieved, the tutor declined to stop her from leaving.

"She is just like mother," Numeria retorted. Spuria giggled and the tutor smiled.

"You do realise that once she is an Imperatrix, Quinta will become your mother. Lucius will be your father.

Tita and Tiberius will become your grandparents..." the tutor continued.

The protesting and giggles faded into the distance, as Quinta made her way to the palace's formal gardens overlooking White City.

"Once I am Imperatrix, I will see that White Blood thrown to the wolves," Quinta muttered to herself as she paced the gardens.

"There is more to being a Blue Blood than having the people you dislike thrown to the mercy of wild animals," Servius explained as he emerged from the shadows.

"Forgiveness grandfather, I did not know you were in the gardens," Quinta replied respectfully.

"What troubles you child? Why are you not in your lessons?" He asked. Quinta shrugged her shoulders before bowing her head. "You will be an Imperatrix tomorrow, surely that is reason enough to be happy?" He suggested with a smile.

"What is the point of being an Imperatrix if I am not allowed to do as I wish?" she replied.

Servius thought for a moment before answering with a proposition. "Come, let us go to the Necropolis. I wish to show you something."

Enthused at the idea of being allowed out of the palace and out of White City again, Quinta accepted.

"First we must disguise ourselves, we would not want your mother finding out, now would we?" Servius said with a wink and a smile.

The pair made their way into the White Blood quarters, where they picked up a grey palla for Quinta, and a grey toga for Servius. They pulled up their hoods, and made their way towards the stairs that led out of the palace grounds.

"Halt!" a Red Blood demanded, "No-one is to leave the palace."

"On whose orders?" Servius sneered.

"Tita's," the Red Blood responded.

"That woman!" Servius muttered before revealing his true identity to the guards.

"Forgiveness," the Red Blood replied respectfully. Servius nodded in gratitude, before ushering Quinta through unrecognised. The two made their way down the stairs, across Sparrow Bridge, and in to White City.

Amongst the White Bloods the pair were unidentifiable. Certainly, to the White Bloods, there seemed no reason to give the pair priority footing. Servius and Quinta were forced instead to push their way through the bustling throng. A sharp jab in his side from a stray elbow finally convinced Servius to change the intended route.

"This way," he explained, pointing to the street on the left, opposite the Raven's Temple. They boldly fought their way through and into the relative calm of the side street. Quinta gazed back at the temple where she saw Lucius stood on the steps. He talked with a hooded man before accepting a vile. Quinta continued to stare, as Lucius turned and began making his way down the steps. He looked up, and straight away, spotted the unmistakable bright blue eyes of Quinta, glaring back at him. Surprised and alarmed, she gasped before returning to Servius's side.

"We will take a right at the theatre. That will lead us towards the Eastern Gate," he explained.

Quinta had never been down this street before. The homes here were much smaller, older, and more dilapidated, than the ones she had seen previously. The smell of damp, mould, and stale water, was almost overpowering. Sick and weak White Bloods, who were forced to rely on their relatives, were sporadically laid out on the floor. They begged the pair for food, causing Quinta to recoil in horror.

"Tell me child," Servius questioned on spotting Quinta's reaction, "Why do you think the gods gave Rytus the gift of the White Bloods?"

"To serve us," she replied coldly.

He chuckled before responding. "No, and you would be a fool to think that."

Quinta, unappreciative of being called a fool, stopped and glared at him.

"Like us," he explained, "they live only to serve themselves."

"I do not understand," she replied, before walking on.

"Why does the tailor make the men togas for winter?" he asked.

"So that they do not get cold," she replied.

"Wrong again," Servius replied, accompanied with another chuckle. "The tailor wants to make sure his family can eat. To do this he must buy food with coins. To get coins he must sell clothes. To sell clothes he must make what people need. And what do we need in winter?"

"Togas," Quinta responded.

"Exactly," he said, smiling at Quinta. "The White Bloods do not want to serve us anymore than you want to serve them, we must work together."

"Get off me," a voice behind Quinta and Servius called out as the White Bloods swarmed Lucius, halting his attempts to quietly follow the pair.

"It seems we are not alone," Servius jested. "Let us see if your brother has learnt anything of humility, or whether he is as deluded as my dear daughter Tita," he suggested, before gesturing Quinta to carry on ahead of him. Lucius was left behind to find his own way out of the growing crowd.

Quinta and Servius, being tailed by Lucius, made their way through the streets before arriving at the Eastern

Gate. Quinta and Servius made their way out of the city unhindered, as Lucius was once again swarmed.

"Seems he has not learnt a thing," Servius laughed, leaving the Red Bloods positioned on the gate to defend Lucius.

The air outside the city hung heavy with a dense and unrelenting fog, slithering in from the swamps. Quickly the pair raced on to the Necropolis. Servius promptly unlocked the gate and guided Quinta through. They cleared the yard swiftly and disappeared into the walled tomb of their ancestors. They shook the damp from their clothes and began lighting the torches.

Quinta stood silently and respectfully, as Servius approached the urn of his beloved Decima. He sighed heavily before stroking the cold, smooth surface of the porcelain. He bowed his head and closed his eyes, as the memories that pained him most, deluged his mind.

"Do not make the same mistakes I have made, Quinta," Servius pleaded. "I failed Decima. I failed Tita, Tiberius and Lucius. I was too concerned with my own pride that I failed to see what they had become. And with that, I have failed you!"

Quinta approached Servius, and although hesitantly, placed her arm around the mournful shadow of her grandfather.

"I have lived a life of regret," he explained, straightening up and standing tall again. "Yet I may still have time to save Rytus," he proclaimed.

"What do you mean, grandfather?" Quinta asked.

"Darkness conquers our enemies and soon it will sail for our shores," he explained, rejecting Quinta's comfort, choosing instead to pace the tomb.

"You are not making any sense," Quinta explained.

"Tita places too much faith in the gods. Tiberius craves for the flesh of the White Bloods with such veracity, he has been likened to an animal. And Lucius..." he paused, "Lucius remains the epitome for selfish greed and the lust for power..."

"I would not say it was lust, more a desire to have what is rightfully mine," Lucius declared, as he slithered into the tomb like a snake cornering a pair of startled mice.

"You have no place being here," Servius snarled, "not after what you did to Decima."

A look of confusion befell Quinta's face, as Lucius, with eyes narrowed, drew closer to Servius.

"Get out!" Servius bellowed, "You have desecrated this place with your filthy footsteps. You have brought shame on all of us. GET OUT!"

"I simply did what needed to be done," Lucius explained as he began to circle his grandfather.

"Then you leave me with no choice," Servius barked, as he raised his hand to Lucius.

"I would not be so quick to do that, if I were you," Lucius explained callously, as the troop of Red Bloods from the Eastern Gate entered. "Restrain him!" Lucius commanded.

Before Servius could protest, the Red Bloods apprehended him and forced him to his knees.

"What are you doing?" Quinta demanded.

"I will deal with you next," Lucius barked.

Lucius made his way over to the stone table at the end of the room, and collected a cup. He tipped out the last few drops of remnant wine from Decima's funeral, and produced the vile that Quinta observed him collect from the man at the temple.

"What is that?" Quinta demanded.

"Just something to help Servius sleep," Lucius explained. "I am afraid dear sister, he has gone quite mad," Lucius sneered. "I bet he told you the story of the tailor and his togas. Has it not occurred to you dear Grandfather, that if we let the White Bloods think for themselves, let them question their duties, that those idiotic White Bloods might decide that they do not need us around, and that we might just GO COLD AND DIE?" He bellowed towards Servius.

"You have lost your mind," Servius gasped.

"Now, let me remember," Lucius conjectured. "One drop to aid digestion," a single drop fell from the vile, into the cup. "Two to ease tension," he added another drop. "Three to aid sleep," he muttered, before emptying the entire vile into the cup. "Oops," he said unconvincingly.

"You vile, vicious spawn of Orcus," Servius snarled.

"Silence him!" Lucius commanded.

Servius looked up in fear at the Red Bloods towering over him, as the largest of the troop drew his blade.

"NO!" Quinta cried out, running to Servius's aid.

"If Quinta is to become my wife, it is about time she learnt her place," Lucius sneered, directing another Red Blood to seize her.

The Red Blood towering over Servius flipped his sword over and using the butt, demolished Servius's jaw with one almighty blow. Servius cried out in agony as the pain shattered through his bones. Blue blood dripped from Servius's splintered face as he began to writhe in excruciating pain.

"NO! You monster!" Quinta cried.

Lucius strode confidently across the room before pressing the cup into what remained of Servius's lip. Servius continued to groan in torment as Lucius tipped the contents of the cup in to his mouth. With all the strength Servius could muster, he cursed Lucius.

Servius fell to the floor in a heap. Quinta filled with despair, cried out. Her mournful wails echoed off the cold stone walls of the tomb. Lucius dismissed the Red Bloods from the tomb, and ordered them to watch over the entrance, to make sure he was not disturbed. He turned to Quinta, and with a fiendish grin etched into his face, he approached her. "And now dear little sister," he said belittlingly, "time to honour my obligations."

Chapter Fifteen

1,003,186 days after the eclipse.

Max cradled his right arm. The cast was heavy and cumbersome. He had hoped to gain more signatures and messages of support. Instead the plaster remained bare, but for a few sympathetic remarks and one crudely drawn image. He struggled with the weight of his heavy back pack, which seemed possessed with a desperate desire to slide down his left arm. The unforgiving crowd blocking the hallway, jostled Max aside, as he tried desperately to protect his arm. Eventually, he made his way with the others out of the school and into the playground at the front.

Coaches and buses lined the driveway, waiting for their precocious cargo. No-one was waiting for Max. He would have been surprised if anyone was. He zipped up his coat as best he could, and began making his way to the pedestrian exit. He waited patiently at the crossing as a large car approached. As he had predicted, the car did not stop for Max, instead it sped up and deliberately aimed for the puddle at Max's feet. His resolve held strong as the icy cold water drenched his clothes. The mud dribbled down his black trousers before splashing on to his shoes. His father had always told him that any sign of weakness was pathetic, and not a characteristic he cared for; so with that in mind, Max continued across the road unbroken.

The taunts from those yet to board their rides home were merciless and cruel. "Filthy Demi Blood!" they shouted mockingly. Although Max was fairly new to the school, it hadn't taken long for his heritage, or rather, lack of, to be cascaded through the ranks. He was shunned by his peers and disregarded by his teachers. His talents and abilities pushed aside because he lacked a pure blood line. What other choice did he have? Father was determined that Max would finish school with the connections and benefits he never had. Failure was not an option.

Max continued out of the school grounds and down the narrow alleyway towards the city centre. The ground was carpeted in a beautiful collage of the reds and oranges of autumn. The mossy walls glistened with droplets of water, reflecting the dusky rays of the sun. Despite the overwhelming smell of rotting foliage and animal excrement, it served as a welcome change to the harsh and unforgiving reality of every day at school, and every night at home.

He continued on for half a mile or so, before the smell of cigarette smoke charged the air around him. The smell grew stronger as he neared a side road. As Max turned the corner he was confronted by the sight and smells of a group of older boys from the school.

"You!" One of the boys said, pointing at Max, "you're that boy the juniors are talking about. The Demi Blood. Aren't you?"

The rest of the group turned to face Max, their minds apparently void of any possibility of thinking, if their expressions were anything to go by, Max surmised.

"Well?" The boy demanded as the rest continued to stare, jaws wide open, eyes staring into a distant space. It was a wonder they weren't dribbling.

"I guess so," Max replied dismissively.

"Smoke?" The boy asked, holding out a packet of cigarettes.

Max approached the group, cautious that it may yet still be a trick. It wouldn't be out of place for boys from his year to be waiting around the corner to strike.

The boy took a cigarette out of the pack, lit it from his own and handed it to Max. Smoking wasn't new to Max; he had tried a few of his father's while grounded at home. However, being invited by a group to join in any activity, was entirely new to him. Still unsure of the group's intention, Max cautiously accepted the cigarette. Sure that the other boys were poised at any moment to strike, his brain ordered adrenaline to be coursed into his blood stream. Soon he would need to run or fight, his muscles had to be ready.

He gauged the faces of those around him. He wasn't sure they even knew where they were, let alone who he was.

"Ignore them," the boy explained, "they're on," he thought for a moment, "they're on something a little stronger." He winked before encouraging Max to continue.

With no sign of the other boys, and eager not to ruin the only congenial encounter he'd had since moving to the school, Max inhaled. Max wasn't entirely sure if it was the adrenaline pulsing through his entire body, or the toxins from the cigarette, but he felt a great weight lift from his shoulders.

The boy smiled at Max, "Name's Peter, you're in Year 9 right?"

Max nodded.

"Max, isn't it?" Peter asked.

Max nodded again.

"Don't say much do you?" Peter chuckled, before noticing Max's arm hidden in his coat. "What happened?"

"Er?" Max looked down at his arm. Unable to tell the truth for fear of reprisal. He had to think quickly on the spot. "I, er? Fell over," he muttered unconvincingly.

"And your trousers? Was it those idiots in your year?" Peter asked as he bunched his hand into a fist before pounding it into his other hand. "They're all a bunch of snobby, stuck up, snooty, good for nothings. Without their parents they'd be lucky to be sweeping the streets. Not an ounce of common sense between the lot of them."

A police siren warbled in the distance.

"Time to move fellas," Peter cried out to the boys gathered. Max readjusted his back pack before offering his unfinished cigarette back to Peter.

Peter smiled and dismissed the offer, "I'll see you around, Max." He then began pushing the other boys in various directions before waving good bye. "Come on you morons, get moving! Bunch of dead heads."

Max crossed the street and continued on his path home. He arrived at the corner of his street before finishing his cigarette. He extinguished it by throwing it on the floor, smearing it across the pavement with his shoe, and kicking it into the gutter.

"You're late..." Mother barked, "... and look at your clothes!" She gasped in horror before taking a few steps back, "and you stink!" She grabbed the perfumed spray on the side and squirted it directly at Max. "Go upstairs now, have a shower. Leave your clothes on the floor in the bathroom, I will deal with them," she said, still repulsed. In the front room, Father remained unmoved, the TV blaring away loudly. "Go on, dinner will be ready soon," Mother insisted.

Once clean, Max returned to the sanctuary that was his room. His walls were adorned with posters, drawings and images of crested Red Guards, archers, and countless sketches of the girl from Rytus. He picked up his headphones and plugged them into his computer. He booted up the old machine and tapped his fingers on the desk impatiently, as it slowly cranked into life. After a few uttered threats of permanent dismemberment, Max was finally able to load up the music player and a browser. The worn keys tapped away as Max continued his research into the known history of Rytus.

He was already familiar with the social structure and the well-known myths. Now he was more interested in the unsolved mysteries, the unexplainable, and the downright weird. He was a little uncoordinated with the mouse in his left hand instead of his right, but otherwise his progress remained unhindered.

Habitually, he visited the virtual world he had been creating when his time allowed. He had invested hours. Rows of houses neatly arranged, the occasional decorative item, and a statue to motivate his virtual settlers. In Max's world everyone was happy, no-one went without and everything was perfect.

The screen went blank, the music faded away. Max looked up at Father towering over him, his face red, his eyes narrowed. Father was furious. Max removed his headphones.

"Your mother has been calling you for ten minutes," he bellowed. "I work hard to give you the life I never had. And this is how you repay us?" he spat, as he forced the words out. "Your mother cries at the table while you sit here playing games. You assured me this machine would be used for homework. Do you know how much trouble I had to go through to get this for you? No! Of course you don't." He picked up the keyboard and pulled it as far as the cables would allow, before slamming it against the desk. The plastic keys shattered against the hard wood. Max, terrified, shielded his face. Father threw the remains of the keyboard back on the desk before marching Max downstairs into the kitchen.

The table had been cleared except for one plate. Max collected a knife and fork from the drawer and sat down to eat. The food was cold and tasteless, but it didn't matter to Max. It had been nearly twenty-four hours since he last ate, as punishment for Father having to drive him to the hospital. He was ready to eat just about anything. Even Mother's cooking. He struggled to cut the slab of white meat on his plate, whatever it was, before eventually finishing. He stood up from the table and washed up.

As Max struggled to dry the plate with one hand, he heard Mother whispering in the pantry. Curious as to why

Mother was in there, and why she was whispering to herself, Max crept closer to listen in.

"You know I can't just leave. I know. I don't think he means to hurt me... I know. I will. As soon as the time is right. I don't know when," she whispered, as it became apparent she was talking to someone on the phone.

Max began to question himself. What did Mother mean? Had missing dinner really hurt Mother so much? Why was she talking of leaving? "I have to go in case he hears me, I love you too." Max quickly put his plate away and ran upstairs before Mother could emerge.

He collected the broken keys and pushed as many as he could back into the keyboard. It didn't really matter where they went, they were so well worn it made little difference. He rebooted the machine and began searching the internet again for stories of Rytus.

1,003,187 days after the eclipse.

"Rumour has it, that you were seen smoking with the senior boys yesterday." Max was trapped, as the group of vile boys in his year pushed him into the corner of the playground. "I don't remember allowing you to talk to the seniors," the largest and most unpleasant boy remarked. "Perhaps it's time to put you back in your place, Demi Blood!" He pushed Max into the wall and took hold of Max's left arm. "You belong to me, not the seniors. Do I make myself clear?" he barked into Max's face.

Unsure whether it had been the chance meeting of Peter the day before, or perhaps hearing that Mother was so upset with him that she wanted to leave, but for whatever reason, Max decided to take Father's example for a change. His blood began to pulsate with rage, his eyes narrowed, his mind became silent. Today he would not run. Today he would fight.

Max defied the boy's grip and rotated his own arm. With his palm facing upward, he gripped the boy's arm tightly. He yanked the boy downward while bending his leg. The boy's forehead and nose cracked against Max's knee. Shocked, the boy remained silent as he stood him up again. Max drew his left arm back, and with the bottled rage of nearly nine years of constant abuse, he smashed his fist straight into the boy's nose. The boy staggered back, perhaps expecting support from his friends. Instead they glared at his nose as it began to drip with red and white blood. The group recoiled in horror.

"You're a Demi Blood too," they began to call out.

The boy looked Max squarely in the eyes, before falling backwards, flat on to his back. The group descended quickly into a squabble as they began to question their loyalties. No-one paid any attention to Max. He remained silent, captivated by the boy lying on the floor.

"What is going on here?" a teacher demanded.

The group scattered like frightened rabbits, leaving Max to explain the situation. The teacher looked at the boy on the floor. "About time," he muttered under his breath before turning to face Max. "Head teacher's office, NOW!" he commanded.

Well-rehearsed with the routine, Max waited silently for the arrival of his parents. He peered out of the glass doors of the reception hall, to see the rain thundering down outside. Father arrived first, and as per usual, ignored Max entirely. Mother was different this time. She walked by without saying a word. She didn't stride in confidently like she normally would. She lowered her umbrella, her face obscured by her large sunglasses, and shook the rainwater on to the mat.

"SUSPENDED!" Father bellowed, as he gripped the steering wheel with increasing force on the ride home.

Mother stared silently out of the windscreen. Her giant sunglasses did little to hide the enormous bruise around her right eye, now visible from Max's position in the back seat. Max also thought it best not to respond.

He cleared the condensation from the side window and peered out into the rainy suburbs. They passed the spot where he had met Peter the day before, but there was no sign of him today. Max figured he probably didn't want to be stood out in the rain.

Father pulled up on the drive, his face still bright red and ready to burst. He practically punched open the front door before slamming it back against the wall of the hallway. Mother and Max disembarked and made their way into the house a safe distance behind him.

Without needing to be prompted, Max made his way straight up to his room. He sat on his bed admiring the big bruise now forming on his knee, it even resembled the shape of the boy's face. The matching set on his knuckles were also coming through clearly. Downstairs he could hear both Mother and Father screaming at each other. Rather than risk the computer being smashed to pieces, he chose instead to pull out his sketch book, and do what he always did when he needed to escape. With the girl from Rytus he was safe. He was in control. No-one else was there to tell him what he could and couldn't do.

The rough texture of the paper alone reminded Max of his safe place. He tried to grip the pencil with his right hand. Trying to move his thumb induced a crippling pain throughout his arm. He hadn't attempted to draw with his left hand before but he was pleasantly surprised by the results. He sketched furiously. Max was free to roam anywhere he could draw. The insulas rose out of the paper, towering into the realms of the gods, as the White Bloods busied themselves in the streets. He drew the Blue Palace and imagined what it would have been like to live there. He drew great long tables for feasting. He topped them with exotic foods and decorated them with beautiful flowers and foliage.

Max became further immersed in his drawing, as he drew the charging horses in the circus, sprinting across the sand in front of the cheering crowd. He drew White Bloods debating in the forums. He drew the busy marketplace as the citizens traded their wares. He drew the funeral processions of the Blue Bloods that he had read about. The actors and musicians followed with smiles adorned on their faces. The Red Bloods protected the people and the people were happy.

The bedroom door flung open, smashing against the wall. Mother tugged desperately at Father's arm, "No! Please!" she cried out.

Max shrunk into the corner of his bedroom, as Father marched in, and began to systematically destroy everything Max had ever cared about. He tore the posters, drawings and sketches from the walls. He picked up the computer and hurled it to the floor.

"GET OUT OF MY HOUSE!" he bellowed fiercely.

"NO! He is only a child!" Mother pleaded.

Father shoved her away. She hit her head against the door frame and slumped to the floor.

"Mother!" Max cried out.

"GET OUT!" Father screamed.

"Where will I go?" Max implored.

"I do not care. I will not have you ruining your mother's name in every school in this city. I have had enough." Father raised his hand again to Max.

Max grabbed his father's arm and instinctively thrashed it against the edge of the bed frame.

"You vile piece of..." Father cried out as he knelt in agony.

Without hesitation Max picked up the chair from his desk and smashed it over Father's back. Father fell silently in a heap on the floor at the base of the bed.

"Mother wake up!" Max begged as he ran to her side.

Drowsily Mother looked up at Max, then at Father.

"What did you do?" She asked.

"We need to go, NOW!" Max explained.

She nodded and Max helped her to her feet. They left everything behind.

"I know where we can go," Mother explained as she started up the car. Her bright blue eyes were almost drowning in tears, a stark contrast to the smile growing across her face.

Chapter Sixteen

5,260 days before the eclipse.

"What happened?" Publius asked as Aulus and Acacia raced into the Red Barracks, breathless and sweating. "Where are the others?" he demanded.

Tiberius staggered in behind them, clutching at a wound in his side.

"Fetch a medicus now!" Publius barked. "Imperator, you must sit," he insisted, as he guided Tiberius to a nearby bench. A White Blood ran from the barracks towards the Green Blood's Magpie Hall, while another kindly offered Tiberius a cup of water. He snatched it from her hands and quickly gulped it down.

"Where are Gaius and Varia?" Publius queried.

Acacia looked dolefully at Publius before shaking her head.

"White Bloods!" Tiberius blurted out having now finished his drink. "Tried to kill me..." He continued before snarling at the White Blood girl who tried to retrieve the cup, "... cornered me. If it was not for this brave young Red Blood, I would surely have perished." Tiberius explained, as he pointed at Acacia.

"What happened brother?" Darius asked, alerted by the commotion, as he entered the room.

Aulus removed his helmet and wiped the sweat from his brow.

"We were cornered in the Ruinae by zealots," he explained.

"What?" Darius demanded.

"The path was blocked, we went around. We were cornered. They tried to kill us. Varia, Gaius..." Aulus had to stop to catch his breath.

"Acacia, Aulus, wait here. I wish to speak to you after I have seen that Tiberius is attended to," Publius instructed.

"Yes Dominus," they each responded, as Publius escorted Tiberius out of the room, into the senior's quarters.

Acacia turned to Aulus. She glared into his red eyes. Without saying a word, Aulus could feel it, Acacia was stalking her prey. She was sizing him up. The two young Red Bloods continued to glare at one another before Darius managed to snap Aulus out of his apparent trance.

"What of the others? The seniors? Where are they?" he asked.

"Dead," Aulus replied, as he watched Acacia walk by.

"What? How?" Darius persisted.

"I do not know," Aulus explained, as he finally turned to face his friend.

"But..." Darius pleaded for answers.

"Did you see that?" Aulus asked.

"What?" Darius responded.

"The way Acacia looked at me then."

"Argh!" Darius cried out in frustration, "For once forget about who you are going to bed next and TELL ME WHAT HAPPENED."

"What? No, I meant..."

"Acacia, Aulus, here NOW!" Publius commanded on re-entering the room. He took the two young Red Bloods into the corridor outside the senior's quarters, and began to press them both for answers.

"Where are Gaius and Varia?" He demanded.

"They are dead, Dominus," Acacia answered.

"How?"

"We were overpowered. The White Bloods struck them down," Acacia began to elaborate.

"Where are they now?" Publius asked.

"In the Ruinae, at the doors to the large grain store," Aulus responded.

"This does not make any sense," Publius declared, "stay here."

Publius left the corridor and made his way into the main living quarters of the barracks. He ordered every Red Blood in the room to suit up, before commanding them to head straight to the Ruinae, to retrieve the two lost Red Bloods. "Spare no-one, bring them home," he declared before returning to Acacia and Aulus. "Acacia, Tiberius

215

states that you saved him," she nodded. "Good, Aulus you are dismissed."

Aulus, disappointed that his efforts, for now at least, were being overlooked, nodded before moving out to clean up. He removed his armour and carefully placed it in the racks. Deflecting a blade in the grain store had left him with a deep wound in the palm of his left hand. He gathered some discarded fabric from the bottom of the rack and made his way to the baths. The icy cold water came as a shock to his muscles, but helped to numb the pain in his hand quickly.

He cleaned out the wound as best he could, the events at the grain store still running through his mind, before leaving the waters and drying off. He then bound his hand using the fabric he had acquired. He made his way to his bed and sat down. Why had Acacia stared at him like that? How did the White Bloods overpower and kill two skilled Red Bloods? So many questions now clouded his mind.

"...and then this Red Blood storms into the store," Tiberius bellowed out from the senior's quarters. Aulus couldn't help but listen in.

"She saved my life and I want her duly rewarded," he demanded.

"But I cannot simply..." Publius tried to explain.

"Nonsense, I am the legate. You will do as I have commanded of you."

A stray footstep behind him caused Aulus to turn, just as Acacia approached. She froze. Aulus rose from his seated position and squared up to her. Unknown to Aulus, she slipped the blade into the ruffles of her tunic, before concealing it under her arm. Their eyes met. Acacia stared upward, her red lips slightly parted. Aulus unsure what Acacia truly wanted of him, raised his arm, and placed his hand on her left shoulder.

"You did well," he said reassuringly.

Acacia panicked, afraid he would discover the concealed blade. She dropped her shoulders to dismiss Aulus's touch and ran from the room.

The sound of Red Blood armour clanging and clashing together, echoed off the walls as the troop returned. Aulus threw on his tunic and ran to the entrance to greet them.

In the background, White City lay silent. A dense mist clung to the buildings, pierced only by the silhouettes of the marching troop returning home. Their heads bowed and their hearts heavy.

Benedicta led the way, as her red crested helmet and shining bronze armour sliced through the gloom. Behind her marched Velius, his battered and ill-fitting armour almost melded with the bitter despair emanating from the troop. White Bloods who had gathered in the street to see what was happening, dispersed to the edges of the road. They held back their children and stood silently, respectfully. Even the birds remained silent. All except a single eagle perched on the precipice of a White Blood insula, who cried out loudly.

Aulus moved aside as the troop entered the barracks, he felt a bitter sadness penetrate his core as they passed by. Benedicta removed her helmet as she passed over the threshold. Velius passed by, followed by Darius carrying Varia's helmet. The red crest now tattered and plucked bare in places, and the once gleaming helmet now stained with red blood, was a disparaging tribute to its owner lost to the gods.

Behind them came the rest of the Red and White Bloods sent to help. Two powerful Red Bloods carried in their arms the naked bodies of Varia and Gaius, stripped of their armour and clothes.

Publius entered the dormitory with Tiberius in tow. They both stood in silence as the two lifeless bodies were carried to the Eagle's shrine.

The large and powerful Red Bloods lovingly lowered their brother and sister to the floor. They laid them out reverently, as the others gathered around them. Benedicta took the helmet from Darius and placed it on the floor by

Varia. A cold breeze rushed in from the direction of the fighting pit, ruffling Gaius's hair as he lay motionless on the floor. Though the Red Bloods were familiar with losing brothers and sisters in battle, this felt somehow different. Each person gathered stood silently as they searched inside their own mind for the answers to a question they didn't understand.

"Fetch an attendant," Publius barked, commanding a White Blood, who without hesitation, immediately left for the Raven's temple.

The crowd parted as Publius approached. He knelt down at the side of Gaius and Varia. He considered all of the Red Bloods to be his children, his responsibility and his friends. He closed his eyes for a moment to fight back his emotions before scanning over their inert bodies. He placed his hand on Varia's forehead. It was icy cold. He sighed heavily, as he continued to fight back any sign of what he perceived to be a weakness.

"They earned the right to call themselves Red Bloods in the Eagle Blood Arena. I will see that they are reunited with the gods there," Publius declared solemnly. "Benedicta, please see that they are clothed," he requested. "See that the horses are prepared for our journey," he said, instructing a White Blood, as he rose to his feet. "Ceremonial dress," he commanded to the other Red Bloods, "we are going home."

Publius approached Tiberius, who had been waiting patiently at the back of the group. "I will do as you have commanded of me my Imperator, but first I must see to my own kind," he explained.

"Very well," Tiberius said in agreement, his firmness apparently a little less wintery towards Publius, "but on your return you are to report to me immediately. Do you understand?"

"Yes Imperator," Publius acknowledged while bowing his head respectfully.

Tiberius turned his back on Publius and marched out of the barracks, with his arms folded and his nose turned up.

With an attendant from the Raven's temple in tow, the large group snaked out of White City. They stopped at the Eastern Stables to collect horses, and a carriage to carry Varia and Gaius.

The sound of the horse's shoes on the stone road, and the monotonous tone of the iron clad wheels of the carriage, echoed in time with the metallic cacophony of the Red Blood's armour. Together they marched through the parcel of land that separated the Blue Mountains from the Red Hell desert.

They made their way through Falcon Reach, passed the stilted homes. In the frozen fields White Blood children played in the freezing fog, while the farmer's dogs yapped and barked with excitement, as they attempted to join in the games.

White Bloods tended to the cattle and sheep in the fields, before stopping to watch the torches of the carriage glide along the viaduct over the swamps. It was unusual, but still spectacular, to see the Red Bloods in ceremonial dress, marching. Their brightly polished armour, red crested helmets and bright red shields glistened through the bleakness, aided in part by the occasional ray of sunlight breaking through the mist. The straight road ahead of them disappeared into the distance, as the group marched onwards to Eagle Blood Shores.

The glow of the thousand or so candles in the Invictus Temple in the distance, penetrated the haze as they approached the outskirts of the village. The sound of Invictus steel being worked in the forges resounded about the steep hillsides surrounding the arena. The normally bustling market hall fell silent as the troop marched into the city. Word spread quickly. Soon White Bloods and young Red Bloods began to flood into the streets to see the unusual procession pass by.

At the end of the road the group turned right before passing through the entrance to the ancient arena, traditionally reserved for young Red Bloods preparing to prove their worth in battle. The carriage waited on the road as the group filed into the courtyard. In the rock face, an ancient shrine to the god of war, Mars, stood mutely. Countless pools and trails of wax, from the candles that once burned there, were now sprinkled with snow. White Bloods broke away from the group and dusted the snow away, before lighting them once more.

Publius ordered everyone to halt. Eight Red Bloods formed up either side of the entrance. Publius looked on from the far end of the courtyard, as the carriage pulled away. In its wake stood the large and powerful Red Bloods, carrying the bodies of Gaius and Varia. The White Bloods retreated to the shadows as the Red Bloods stood in formation, their chests proudly forward, the base of their shields resting on the floor.

The two burdened Red Bloods passed through the courtyard to meet Publius. They followed him into the cavernous room in the far corner and carefully made their way down the staircase carved out of the rock, being careful not to lose their footing. They climbed down several flights of stairs before emerging into the crater, said to have been formed in the heart of the mountain by a stray lightning bolt from the god, Jupiter.

Gaius and Varia were some of the last Red Bloods to prove their worth in the arena. Now it lay under a thick covering of snow, mud and debris. The crunch of every foot step in the snow echoed loudly against the imposing and magnificent walls of the arena.

A large number of White Bloods appeared from the staircase carrying with them kindling and wood. They cleared away the snow and built two pyres. Publius continued to maintain his frost like resolve as the two Red Bloods lowered Gaius and Varia on to the pyres. The attendant from the Raven's temple entered the arena and sprinkled the two lost Red Bloods with bone dust, salt and sage. With heavy hearts the group left the arena and made their way back up the staircase to the courtyard.

The Eagle Blood Arena began to shimmer with sunlight as the fog began to lift. The gods seemingly keen to watch proceedings, cleared the mist from the skies. Red Bloods and White Bloods alike began to fill every level of the spectator's enclaves; with some having to descend five flights of stairs to find a suitable spot to pay their respects.

Publius approached the railings protecting him from a fatal fall to the arena below him. With earnest, he glanced down to the pyres and the lone White Blood stood with torch in hand.

"Brothers, sisters," he bellowed, his voice echoing around the crater, "it is with great sorrow that we must allow Gaius and Varia to pass to the afterlife. Take solace knowing that they earned the right to call themselves Red Bloods with honour and dignity. In life they were valiant, brave and righteous. In death they shall rise in the fields of Elysium, at the side of Mars. There they will continue their fight for justice, they will fight for what is right and they will fight for us here in Rytus. Remember them fondly. Remember them wisely. Remember them."

He looked upwards to see young White Blood children laid on their bellies, their faces glancing over the ledge to the arena below. He paused for a moment. He had little time left before his blood bond was to be severed. Was this enough time to save Rytus for all the children, regardless of their blood gens? he wondered. Would disobeying Tiberius bring them a better future, or would it just end his days early? He scanned the gathered Red Bloods. Would obeying Tiberius bring them salvation from the gods? he pondered. Or would things just continue as they always have done, regardless of the decisions he made? What was his purpose, if he could not prevent the deaths of those in his care, had he failed them? Unable to silence his own mind, he signalled to the White Blood below, who lit the pyres.

The flames quickly took hold of the kindling, which cracked and hissed. The snow nearby began to melt as the smoke began to rise, filling the skies with the unmistakable scent of the funeral pyres.

Aulus looked on. He too was filled with guilt. Was there more he could have done? Could he have fought harder, stronger or better to save them? Maybe if he had stayed at their side instead of protecting Tiberius, just perhaps he could have saved Gaius and Varia? he thought. The guilt began to burn fiercely in his chest as the two Red Bloods were consumed in the flames below. His mouth felt dry, as the crackling of the wood resounded from the cold stone walls of the arena.

All stood in silence, all stood respectfully.

"I have to talk to you," Darius whispered. Aulus looked back at Darius, nodded and followed him outside. Acacia took note of the two men leaving, as did Publius.

Outside, in the shadows of a villa, Darius began to explain his concerns. "When we went to find Gaius and Varia, it was deserted. Not even the rats were scuttling around and they love grain stores," he proclaimed. "There was blood on the floor, everywhere," he said excitedly.

"I know," Aulus replied, still racked with guilt.

"But," Darius continued, "It was red."

Aulus returned a look of confusion.

"Those that attacked you and Tiberius were not White Bloods brother," Darius explained, "They were Red Bloods."

"What?" Aulus replied.

"I found this," Darius said, as he pulled a piece of clothing from under his armour.

"This is just like the cloaks they were wearing," Aulus declared.

"I found it, discarded behind the grain store. Look!" Darius said, pointing to the garment in his hand.

"Red blood?" Aulus asked puzzled.

"Exactly," Darius declared.

"Perhaps it was from Varia, or Gaius?" Aulus questioned.

"Perhaps, but then why is it red here, here where the garment is torn, presumably from Acacia's blade?" Darius posed.

"Why would our own kind attack us?" Aulus asked.

"I do not know brother, but we were watched while we were there," Darius explained.

"By who?" Aulus asked.

"I saw their eyes, their grey eyes, watching from the shadows," Darius explained.

"You are to return immediately," interrupted Benedicta, "Publius has something important to announce."

Dutifully, the two men ceased their discussion and followed Benedicta back inside, where the Red Bloods had gathered around Publius.

"Brothers, sisters, friends," he proclaimed, "I wish to announce my successor.

Chapter Seventeen

5,260 days before the eclipse.

The wailing of the hungry Dianus echoed loudly around the insulas. Petrina stopped, glanced upwards to the dark clouds above, and contemplated what she would tell her father. She placed her hand on the cold handle of the door, and reluctantly pushed it open.

Slowly she climbed the stairs, past the slightly larger and more spacious homes of the marginally better off White Bloods, up to the top floor. A man stood in the doorway of the neighbouring home. He watched Petrina closely as she tried to avoid eye contact with him. Her emotions were now torn between a quick escape from him, and having to explain why she was returning empty handed to her father. Unsure of the man's intentions, she chose the latter and quickly disappeared behind the door to her home.

Inside, Alpheaus stared out of the narrow window overlooking the insula opposite. The daylight cast an unflattering image of her father, his collar bone prominent. His face withered and thin. Petrina hadn't noticed before just how ill he looked. She tried to close the door as quietly as possible so as to not disturb him, hoping that the wailing of Dianus would disguise her return.

Perhaps she could run and hide in the bedroom, she thought, this might give her time to think, to work out what to tell Alpheaus. With the top two floors of the insula being made entirely of wood, which tended to warp in the wet winter months, the door dropped, colliding loudly with the wooden floor.

Petrina gasped and bit her lip before turning to face Alpheaus. Slowly he broke his gaze and turned his head to face her. A cold wind blustered through the window, knocking snow from the ledge onto his shoulder. He smiled weakly at her before looking down at the discontented Dianus. Alpheaus's fingers began to shake violently as he tried to comfort the boy. Annoyed that his body no longer seemed to be at his command, he cursed his fingers before looking back up at Petrina.

"You are cold," she said rushing to his side, "you must move away from the window." He looked up at Petrina, but his eyes didn't seem to focus on her at all.

"You are icy cold," Petrina declared with concern. She took Dianus and wrapped him in her tattered palla before placing him on the floor, then led her father to the bedroom. She guided him to the bed. He sat down then lay on his side. He curled up, his knuckles now neatly tucked under his chin. Petrina pulled the old, frayed blanket up over her father and gently stroked his cheek. He looked up at her, whispered, "Thank you," and closed his eyes. She leant forward and kissed his forehead, before returning to Dianus.

Her stomach rumbled loudly. She felt the guilt of that mouthful of bread. They were in the grip of winter with the spring not due for months. What were they going to do? Everything seemed utterly hopeless as Petrina embraced tiny Dianus in her arms. She rocked back and forth on the cold floor to try and distract herself and Dianus from the agony inside. The howling wind made her tears bitingly cold against her skin. With nothing else left to try, she began to sing to Dianus.

"Fly above the clouds,

Fly little sparrow,

Fly high into the sky,

Fly as straight as the arrow.

Do not tumble,

Do not fall,

Do not be afraid,

The gods welcome us all."

Perhaps too weak to continue crying, or hopefully soothed by the sound of Petrina's singing, Dianus fell asleep. Petrina continued to rock him, until she too, felt her eye lids feel heavy.

5,259 days before the eclipse.

The warm winter sun rose from the east, bathing the room in a golden glow. Petrina woke suddenly. Her arms were empty. Baby Dianus was gone. She sat up, the sun now shone directly into her eyes. In front of her, she could make out two silhouettes seated by the table. She rubbed her eyes and ducked out of the direct sun light. At the table sat Alpheaus and the stranger from next door.

"Petrina," her father called out weakly, "this is Otho."

The man looked over to Petrina and smiled sincerely.

"He has given us food..." Alpheaus tried to explain before coughing loudly. Instinctively Petrina rushed to her father's side.

"I will be alright," he said reassuringly, whilst taking Petrina's hand.

"Where is Dianus?" Petrina asked, slightly fearful of the answer.

"He is with my wife, Laelia," Otho explained.

Petrina turned to her father. "Have you traded him?" she asked in dismay.

"No," Otho laughed, "see..." he called out to Laelia who obediently entered the room. In her arms she cradled Dianus as he fed from her breast. She smiled at Petrina before standing alongside Otho.

"Please," Otho said, as he pointed to the bowl of oats and water on the table, "for you!"

Petrina hesitated. Perhaps her mistrust of her neighbour had been misplaced after all. Too hungry now to refuse, she picked up the bowl and retreated back to the spot where she had spent the night.

"What do you say friend?" Otho asked Alpheaus.

Alpheaus thought for a moment before responding, he stroked his wispy beard and lent back in his chair. Although invigorated by the meal so generously provided, he was still desperately sick and weak.

"You could take Petrina," he replied, "She is still a child by law, but she is wise beyond her years."

The three White Bloods turned to Petrina, the sunlight indulging her long white hair in a celestial glow. Petrina looked up from her bowl, as the three White Bloods stared at her, apparently in awe.

"Are you sure?" Otho asked.

"I will only slow you down. I must return to my work if I am in any hope of bringing in coins to support my family," Alpheaus explained. "I will stay behind and care for Dianus," he declared.

"You should be resting," Laelia instructed, "I will care for you and Dianus while the others head to Falcon Reach."

"That does not seem like a fair deal for you," Alpheaus replied.

"The Blue Bloods in their palace, prepare to feast in celebration of the Decem Dies Mille ceremony, while hard working White Bloods starve in the streets below. The gods do not care for fairness anymore," she declared with bitterness.

"Then it is settled," Otho declared, clasping his hands together. "We leave immediately."

Petrina stepped out into the street where she joined twenty or so men. She could only assume that every family in the insula had sent at least one of their own.

"To Falcon Reach," Otho cried out, taking the role of leader.

The crowd of men and Petrina, turned towards the Eastern gate, and made their way along the road. The group quickly drew the attention of the Red Bloods stationed around the city as they passed by.

"Why are we going to Falcon Reach?" Petrina asked the man next to her.

He sighed before responding, "We are going to get bread, stupid."

"I am not stupid," Petrina replied.

He huffed, "There is a bakery in Falcon Reach and word is they still have grain. We are going to that bakery."

"Oh," Petrina replied, wondering if Otho realised she didn't have any coin to purchase anything.

"Halt," the Red Blood on the gate commanded. "Where are you all going?" she asked, suspicious of the group's intentions.

"To Falcon Reach, to buy bread," Otho responded.

The Red Blood looked into Otho's eyes, mulled over his intentions in her mind, before permitting the group to proceed out of the city. Content that they were no longer the city's problem, the Red Bloods that had been tailing the group dispersed back to their patrols.

Petrina had never been out of the city before. Her daily chores mostly involved fetching fabric for her father to make in to togas. She therefore decided it wise to stick closely to the group, rather than risk getting lost. The group continued along the road and over a bridge. To their right the Dying Woods stretched into the distance, to their left the seemingly endless barren fields of Falcon Reach. The homes strutting out of the swamps on stilts seemed smaller than she had imagined they would be from the tales and songs. Ahead of them smoke rose from the rooftops, as the smell of bread being baked filled the air.

The group followed the road before turning into a nest of identical homes. They twisted and turned through the narrow alleyways until the bakery came into view. With it came the unwelcome sight of a large group already waiting. Clearly they weren't the only ones to hear the good news.

"I hope they do not run out," a man in the group declared.

Still unsure whether to tell Otho she was penniless, Petrina remained silent, as the group joined the back of the queue. Ahead of them White Bloods talked loudly, discussing the cold, their hunger and their displeasure with the Blue Bloods.

"I hear they feast on three kinds of meat," one declared.

"They send the Red Bloods out across the ocean to bring back exotic foods," another joined in.

"I saw them throw good food to the dogs," another said.

A pair of Red Bloods entered the square outside the bakery. Instantly all talk stopped. The White Bloods stood in silence as the Red Bloods eyed the waiting crowd. The men in Petrina's group began to tense their fists. They glared back at the Red Bloods with narrowed eyes. The adrenaline coursing through their bodies began to tense their muscles. Their blood began to drain from their extremities to the safety of their inner core.

The wind rushed down the narrow alleyways, whistling as it went by. One of the Red Bloods stepped forward. The snow below his feet crunched loudly. His metal sword chirped with a metallic ring as it collided against his bronze armour. The second Red Blood stepped forward, his beautifully decorated metal greaves ringing with every footstep.

Petrina brushed the hair from in front of her face, only for the wind to blow it back. The less confrontational White Bloods looked solemnly at their feet in the snow. The more confident ones stood tall and watched from the corner of their eye, as the Red Bloods paced the queue.

Without warning, one of the Red Bloods grabbed a young White Blood man by the scruff of his neck, and pressed his face into the man's. The strip of metal protecting the Red Blood's nose remained the only thing between the pair.

"Looking for trouble?" The Red Blood growled.

"No... I er?..." The White Blood man stuttered.

Otho had to hold back one of the men in the group as he attempted to lunge for the Red Blood, just a few spaces ahead. It was noted by the second Red Blood, who squared up to Otho. He used his chest armour to thrust Otho into the man he had held back. The first Red Blood dropped the young man and drew his gladius sword before marching over to Otho.

The Red Blood thrust the tip of the sword under Otho's chin. He forced Otho's head up. The Red Blood glared furiously. His face, now red with rage, almost blended perfectly with his red lacerna.

"Perhaps you and your friend here would like to settle this?" he barked, spitting into Otho's face as he spoke, "No?"

The Red Blood dropped Otho, stepped back from the group and threw out his arms as he addressed the crowd.

"My blood brother and sister were betrayed by your kind, cowering behind hoods. They died a dishonourable death at the hands of pathetic White Bloods; White Bloods like you all," he bellowed, pointing is sword towards the crowd. "Perhaps you think you can kill us too?" He paused, waiting for a response. The crowd shifted nervously but no-one responded.

"Where are your hooded murderers now?" He demanded, his face getting redder with every word. "Bring them to me!" he called out.

He raised his arms higher, dropped his gladius sword and dagger into the snow, as he roared in frustration. His chest pulsated with every intake of breath as the wind thrashed his lacerna, causing it to flail behind him. "NO-ONE?" He cried out. The crowd remained silent.

He waited. Then picked up his sword and dagger from the snow and put them back in their rightful place. The second Red Blood joined his side as the first addressed the White Bloods again, "You can hide like vermin in the crowd, but you cannot hide from the gods," he declared. "The gods will have their blood. I guarantee that!" he roared.

236

The two Red Bloods marched towards the bakery, pushing aside anyone in their way. The crowd began to murmur and cry out with frustration as the two men charged inside.

Outside, the panicked crowd lurched forward as the scramble to grab what was left began. Those at the back began pushing those in front forward. A large woman behind Petrina fell to the floor knocking Petrina off her feet. Another man lost his footing and stood directly on Petrina's left hand. Her cries of pain were muffled as another White Blood fell. She had to turn her face to avoid his hips crashing down on to her cheek.

The cold snow on her back began to drench her clothes as the bodies blocked out the light above her. In total darkness with the crushing weight on her chest, and the icy cold embrace of the snow, Petrina panicked. She tried again to call out. The constriction prevented her lungs from filling as they emptied with every exhale. Her thoughts turned to her father and little Dianus. She would never see them again. She began to drift out of consciousness.

A tugging sensation on her arm caused her to focus again. It achieved little else. She was well and truly trapped. An opening appeared in the dark void. Light flooded in, followed by the silhouette of a face. Otho smiled as he laid eyes on Petrina. The men helped the fallen White Bloods to their feet as Otho pulled a relieved Petrina up on to hers.

"I thought you were lost to the gods for a moment there," he said with a relieved smile.

Only Otho, a few of his group and the fallen White Bloods remained, stood in the slushy snow where Petrina had fallen. She looked at the bakery, it was now swarming with White Bloods, desperately fighting to snatch what they could.

The fighting halted. The crowd parted. The two Red Bloods emerged. Their satchels brimmed with bread. The crowd gazed in disbelief as the Red Bloods marched on with complete disregard for the White Bloods.

The baker appeared at the doorway and shrugged his shoulders to indicate they had taken all that he had left. The White Bloods began to cry out, shouting and heckling the Red Bloods. Frustrated they began to grab at anything they could to hurl at the pair.

The Red Bloods laughed at the pathetic amounts of snow that began to fall on them. The occasional snow ball glanced past their faces, or bounced off their armour. The larger Red Blood removed some bread from his satchel. He raised it to his mouth and took a large and animalistic bite. He laughed as the crumbs fell into the snow below. He hurled the satchel before him and positioned it on the floor. He sat down behind the freshly baked bread, and continued to eat his fill in front of the desperate White Bloods. The second Red Blood looked back, smiled and continued on his way, disappearing down an alleyway.

The crowd surrounded the lone Red Blood. He discarded some bread into the snow callously. A young White Blood grabbed at it. The Red Blood knocked him back with the butt of his gladius sword and laughed loudly.

A White Blood woman ran from the crowd and snatched the soggy bread. The Red Blood struck her down with the blade of the sword. She fell into the snow.

"Monster!" A man yelled out from the crowd.

The Red Blood glared back.

Two men ran from the crowd, grabbed his right arm and pulled the Red Blood downward. The Red Blood swung his left arm at the pair, missing one, hitting the other in the side of the head. The man dropped into the snow. The other clung on. Another man leapt on to the Red Blood's back. He grasped hold of the Red Blood's lacerna, causing the pin to press into his throat. The Red Blood reached up with his left arm to grab the man. A woman leapt from the crowd and grabbed it.

White Bloods began to pile on to the Red Blood. One drew the gladius sword and attempted to wound him. The weight of the sword threw him off balance. He dropped the sword into the snow. A woman grabbed the dagger from the Red Blood's belt.

The Red Blood looked up as the woman loomed over him. She raised the dagger in her arms and brought it crashing down into his mouth. With furious vigour she withdrew the dagger and stabbed him again and again. Red blood splattered her brow as she tore into him. The Red Blood slumped to the floor.

Two men grabbed at the satchel. A third man swiped the first clean across the face. He dropped to the floor. A woman tugged at the satchel. Another beat her back. Hands began tearing into the fabric as hungry and desperate White Bloods fought fiercely.

Seeing her chance, Petrina darted into the fray. She dodged and eluded the scrapping White Bloods. She ducked through the legs of a man, as he took a swipe at a larger woman, just as a loaf dropped in front of her. Petrina grabbed the loaf. A swift and agonising kick to the cheek saw her drop it. She looked up as the man reached down to grab the bread. Petrina's mouth began to fill with the bitter taste of blood.

Petrina spat the blood from her mouth. She watched the snow melt as the blood began to pool, revealing the earlier discarded bread. Quickly, she dug around in the snow and found a few more pieces. She hurriedly gathered them up in her tunic and clambered to her feet. She barged her way through the crowd as others began to give chase.

"Over here!" Otho cried out, waving to her.

Petrina charged towards Otho. A hand grabbed her arm. She dodged left. The hand lost its grip.

"Quick!" Otho called out, "Go! Run! Run as fast as you can."

Petrina, as instructed, ran as fast as she could. She ran past Otho, heading back through the maze of homes.

Behind her, Otho and his men slowed down the pursuing crowd. He swung for another man before crying out to Petrina, as she disappeared into the alleyway, "The gods will have their fill of blood today, tell Laelia I do not intend to join them!"

Petrina glanced back just in time to see Otho drop to his knees, clutching his chest.

Chapter Eighteen

5,259 days before the eclipse.

"Back so soon?" The White Blood woman in the paddock asked.

Acernis, too concerned with reporting to his seniors, simply nodded.

"How was she?" The woman asked.

Acernis furrowed his brow.

"The horse," she clarified.

"Oh!" Acernis responded. "Very good, no trouble at all," he replied, afraid to mention the wolves on the way to Magpie Gorge.

"Let me help you," she proclaimed, moving forward to assist him.

"Thank you," he said sincerely, as he climbed down from the enormous horse. He returned her smile before looking awkwardly at the floor. A moment of silence passed. Both were unsure how to continue or end the conversation without offending the other.

"I should..." Acernis began to explain, "I should probably get going."

"Of course," she responded dutifully.

He backed away, straight into the side of a Red Blood's horse.

"Sorry," he said apologetically, turning towards the horse.

The woman giggled.

Acernis turned back, unsure what had truly washed over him. Whatever it was, her smile seemed beautiful. Her cheeks, her eyes, her hair were perfect. He stood silently, lost for words.

"You were going?" she laughed.

"By the gods, you are right. I must go," he declared.

She waved Acernis on his way as he ran from the paddock to the Eastern Gate. She wrapped her arms around herself and imagined what it would have been like to embrace the shy Green Blood man. Hopefully, if the gods were kind, she may find out one day. Even though she knew the law would not allow it, the very thought alone made her smile though.

Acernis fought his way along the crowded street, past the circus before turning towards the grounds of the palace. A procession of White Bloods bearing exotic flowers, lavish banners and intricate fabrics blocked Acernis's path. He ducked and bolted through the bearers before coming face to face with an extravagant display of blue winter lilies. The succulent pollen made Acernis sneeze, much to the displeasure of the White Blood holding the arrangement.

Acernis had not long passed the Raven's Temple before the scent in the air changed dramatically, from the exquisite scent of the flowers, to one of burning dried animal skin.

"The scrolls!" he cried out, looking at the plume of smoke billowing from Magpie Hall.

With haste, he charged through the crowds, causing great discontent among the normally patient White Bloods. He shoved his way across Sparrow Bridge to the steps of the Blue Palace.

"Slow down Pica," a Red Blood warned.

Regardless, Acernis bounded up the stairs and entered the garden terraces. He raced down the maeniana to Magpie Hall. A team of White Bloods groaned and strained as they attempted to lift the large wooden door back into position, the smoke still billowing from the room. Acernis quickly darted under the ladder and into the hall.

Inside, the smell of soot accompanied by thick black smoke, stifled the air. Acernis, short of breath, coughed and spluttered. Cinis looked up from the glowing embers, her face smouldering with a crooked smile and narrowed eyes.

"You have returned!" Ulmus declared with arms outstretch, as he entered the hall from a side room. "By the gods woman," he declared, directed at Cinis, "you will be the death of us." Ulmus coughed, as he walked to greet Acernis.

"What has happened?" Acernis asked.

"Cursed woman would rather burn all that we have, than leave it to the Blue Blood's care," Ulmus explained. "Though, it might have been possible to simply carry it to Magpie Gorge," he shouted towards Cinis.

She raised her hand and dismissed his suggestion.

"It would be a great weight to burden," Acernis commented.

"I suppose you are both right," Ulmus sighed. "Tell me, why have you returned?" Ulmus asked. "Where is the child?"

"The child is safe," Acernis explained, "but I must talk with you immediately. It is of great importance."

"Very well," Ulmus said placing his hand on Acernis's shoulder, "I could do with the fresh air," he said, raising his voice.

The cruel smile extended across Cinis's face, but otherwise she remained unmoved.

The two men left the hall and made their way back along the walled maeniana. "I have seen with my own eyes," Acernis explained, "the plants and animals are dying."

"But the Codex Vitae?" Ulmus queried.

Acernis shook his head.

"This is troubling indeed," Ulmus proclaimed.

"Forgive me Pica," a young White Blood called out as she attempted to navigate around the two men, while carrying a neatly folded banner. Ulmus and Acernis jumped out of the way as more White Bloods began to swarm the immediate area. Acernis looked to Ulmus for an explanation.

"Quinta's Decem Dies Mille ceremony," he replied with disdain.

The courtyards and gardens were awash with colour. Long plumes of peacock feathers, arranged delicately with blue and gold winter flowers, perched on plinths. Cooks from the kitchen paraded the courtyards with neatly arranged meats and fruits, dressed with exotic sauces and shaped like temples, a circus and a bulla. Banners featuring the sigil of the Blue Bloods were strung up on the white marble walls of the palace. Not a single White Blood rested as they rushed to meet the demands of their master.

"You there!" Tita cried out, pointing in the direction of the two men.

Ulmus and Acernis, confused, glared back.

"You! The Green Bloods. Why are you just standing there? Should you not be leaving already? And what is that dreadful smell?" She glanced over to Magpie Hall. "By Orcus!" she shrieked. "Fatuss, what are you doing to our hall?"

Tita marched past the pair, elbows bent, fists bunched tightly.

"I do not think it wise to be around when Cinis and Tita clash," Ulmus jested, "let us find the others. I suggest we start with the kitchens."

The two men turned and made their way to the relative sanctuary of the White Blood quarters. Just as Ulmus had predicted, they found two Green Bloods pinching scraps of exotic food. Seniorem distracted the White Bloods, while Iuniperorum pilfered a slither of meat from one of the delicate displays.

"Brothers," Ulmus called out. "There is something we must discuss. Perhaps we should adjourn to the Magpie Tree?" Ulmus jested.

"Lead on," Seniorem responded as he sneaked some of the stolen meat into his mouth.

"The Codex Vitae no longer wills the plants and animals to reproduce east of Magpie Gorge," Acernis explained upon reaching the tree. "And it is spreading westward. If we do not stop it, it will consume us all."

"You have seen evidence of this?" Iuniperorum asked.

"I have. I have also heard the stories from the seniors and citizens of the gorge. The adults starve. The children go hungry. It is unstoppable," Acernis declared.

The group furrowed their brows and contemplated a response.

"We must call the Green Bloods to order," Iuniperorum demanded.

"I agree," Ulmus replied.

"How?" asked Seniorem.

"With the call of the Magpie," Ulmus answered. "Watch."

Iuniperorum and Ulmus gestured for the younger Green Bloods to stand back as they stepped up to the tree. The two senior Green Bloods placed their hands upon the trunk. They closed their eyes, took a deep breath and began to chant.

"Deos, audi nos," They called out. "Vocare picae," they chanted.

Starting from the roots, a green aura pulsated beneath the bark with each chant, upward towards the leafy canopy. The evergreen leaves of the Magpie Tree began to glimmer and radiate with the brilliant green, pulsating aura. The ancient tree was once again awake. It was ready to listen.

"Clama ad eos," the Green Bloods demanded.

The aura began to radiate into the atmosphere creating a swirling cloud of pulsating green droplets. The droplets swirled around the tree, trapped in a whirlwind. They began to crash into one another, until they formed the shape of magpies. They raced around the canopy, increasing in speed and altitude. Soon the magpies flew clear of the tree and began to form a tight column.

The column of magpies drew tighter until, they themselves, began to form the image of a much larger magpie. The large green magpie effigy rose high into the winter's sky. With an almost deafening caw, the effigy cried out. In doing so the green aura dispersed like a shockwave.

All citizens of Rytus saw the light race through the sky, as far as Eagle Blood Shores in the south. Instinctively the Green Bloods of Rytus knew exactly what they were required to do.

The tree fell back into silence once more, as Iuniperorum and Ulmus withdrew their touch.

"What will happen now?" Seniorem enquired.

"They will come," Ulmus responded.

As morning turned to afternoon, the shadow of the tree began to fill with Green Bloods, drawn by the light.

"We cannot remain here," Iuniperorum declared.

"And we cannot return to the hall," Ulmus replied. "It is uninhabitable.

"Then we must find sanctuary elsewhere," Iuniperorum demanded.

Ulmus thought for a moment, where could so many Green Bloods be addressed and the situation resolved? He tapped his foot as he thought, and chewed his bottom lip.

"The theatre!" he cried out. "We should go to the theatre. It is not far from here. We can address our blood brothers and sisters appropriately there."

"Agreed," Iuniperorum responded with a nod.

Leading the way, Ulmus led the growing group through the streets of White City to the theatre. Never before had so many Green Bloods filed through the streets. White Bloods gathered at the edges and looked on at the spectacle. Children pointed before asking their guardians a barrage of questions. Red Bloods disregarded the dishonoured blood gens as they passed by. Orange Bloods changed their intended paths to avoid the group and the attendants of the Raven's Temple watched on from the steps.

The Green Bloods entered the theatre unhindered. The senior Green Bloods gathered on the stage, as more Green Bloods continued to file in. Acernis remained at his mentor's side, eager to be on hand if he could help.

Ulmus addressed the crowd and explained all that Acernis had told him, including the stories he had been told.

"This is blasphemy!" cried out a member of the crowd.

"Nonsense, this is the fault of our leaders," another shouted, as he rose to his feet.

The debate quickly descended into bickering and blame.

"Please," exclaimed Ulmus, "Brothers, Sisters!" he shouted, both arms raised in the air.

Eventually the crowd simmered down again.

"The trees and the animals are dying. It is coming here. We cannot ignore it. We must decide on action, now!" Ulmus cried out.

The crowd began to murmur until another Green Blood shouted out, "We must inform the Blue Bloods."

"Yes, they are our Imperators," another proclaimed.

"They will know what to do," the crowd began to cry out.

Ulmus turned to Acernis and Iuniperorum for guidance. Acernis shrugged his shoulders. A look of bewilderment befell Iuniperorum's face.

"Very well," Ulmus declared. "We will seek the guidance of the Blue Bloods."

The crowd erupted into loud debate and discussion as Ulmus and the other seniors descended from the stage.

"I will go," Acernis offered. "This is my doing."

"Nonsense," Ulmus said dismissively. "We will all go."

Leaving the noisy Green Bloods behind in the theatre, the seniors made their way out to the Blue Palace.

"Two days left," the Red Guard positioned at the bottom of the stairs sneered. Unruffled, the Green Bloods continued their charge.

In the courtyards and gardens, the preparations for Quinta's Decem Dies Mille ceremony were almost complete. Only a few finishing touches were being made as Tita watched proceedings from the steps of the private Blue Blood quarters. The thought of having to face her again, almost turned Ulmus a new shade of green. Acernis however, rather more fortunate with his dealings with Tita, took the lead.

The group gingerly approached the steps and halted respectfully at the bottom. Tita turned up her nose, looked away and responded coldly.

"Now what?" she demanded.

"We have troubling news from the east Imperatrix," Iuniperorum explained, his head bowed.

"It will have to wait; can you not see we are busy?" she replied furiously.

"Please, I beg your forgiveness," Ulmus responded sheepishly. "But..."

"Are you deaf?" She replied coldly.

Stunned and taken aback, the two senior Green Bloods retreated backwards. Acernis stepped forward onto the first step. Tita could not ignore this blatant act of disrespectful behaviour. She swung around and glared at the Green Bloods before her.

"How dare you?" She shrieked.

"The Codex Vitae is dead. The plants and animals are dead. Soon death will consume us all!" Acernis quickly responded.

The seniors held their breath in anticipation of Tita's furious response. She narrowed her eyes and scowled at Acernis. She descended the steps until she stood just one above him. She studied his appearance before staring into his green eyes. She turned her head from side to side, trying to remember why this particular Green Blood felt so oddly familiar. Unable to make the connection she drew back.

"You have seen this with your own eyes?" She asked the seniors, unable to break her gaze on Acernis.

"Acernis has," Ulmus responded, gesturing towards the younger Green Blood.

"Acernis?" She replied, trying to remind herself of the name. She flexed her brow and raised her right hand, her palm poised to touch Acernis's cheek.

"The White Bloods of Magpie Gorge verge on starvation," Iuniperorum explained, snapping Tita from her spell.

"White Bloods?" Tita snarled, "You defy the gods with your interference. Now you come to me for help?"

She took a step backwards, ascending the stairs.

"You fix this!" She commanded, "You caused this. You enraged the gods. Now your people will pay for your crimes. Their blood is on your hands."

She turned her back to the Green Bloods and charged up the stairs again.

"But, Imperatrix..." Ulmus pleaded.

"I gave you, for reasons which escape me now, good will. And now you return to the palace. On the day of my daughter's Decem Dies Mille ceremony? And demand what exactly?" She shouted down to the cowering group.

"We must send them food," Acernis explained.

Tita dealt Acernis a deathly glare.

"You!" She screamed. "It was you! You were the one who deceived me."

"Over 600 White Bloods and Green Bloods call Magpie Gorge home, you cannot just let them die," Acernis cried out, stepping up.

"Guards!" Tita cried out, leaning fearfully against the railing behind her.

"The blood of the innocent will wash across these lands. Death approaches from the east. It WILL consume us all," he called out, drawing closer.

"GUARDS!" Tita screeched.

"Acernis!" Ulmus pleaded.

Seven Red Bloods swarmed the group. The seniors did not resist.

"Even the Blue Bloods cannot escape this!" Acernis cried out.

"Back down!" A Red Blood instructed, grabbing Acernis by his paenula.

"Rytus will fall," Acernis shouted, now just a few paces from a panicked Tita.

Two large Red Bloods grabbed Acernis. One placed his large arm around Acernis's chest, the other around his waist. With ease, the two Red Bloods lifted Acernis from the floor and began to descend the steps.

"Your actions today, will decide if Rytus rises or falls," Acernis called out, resisting the Red Bloods.

"Quiet, you," a Red Blood instructed while placing his hand over Acernis's mouth. He continued to struggle as the Red Bloods carried him down the steps.

"Their blood will be on your hands," Tita called out as she stepped forward from the railing. She watched with growing confidence as the guards pushed the senior Green Bloods away, while the muffled protests of Acernis were contained.

Maintaining a safe distance from the group, she edged closer to the steps. She waited until her guards had cleared considerable ground, before calling out to the Green Bloods. "You are banished from White City! You and all your kind. You are to return to Magpie Gorge and never step foot in this city AGAIN!"

Chapter Nineteen

5,259 days before the eclipse.

"Dominus," Aegle dutifully announced, "as requested." She stood with her left arm outstretched. A White Blood woman dressed in a grey toga brushed past Aegle.

"Thank you," Marcus responded before accepting the prostitute into his private quarters. "That will be all," he said, dismissing Aegle.

Relieved, Aegle left. Marcus watched her ascend the stairs before turning to face the other woman.

The prostitute smiled suggestively before letting the toga slip from her left shoulder. Marcus sat down. The woman twirled in the centre of the room. She dropped her toga lower on her left shoulder before dropping it on her right. Marcus continued to watch intently as the woman let the toga fall to the floor. She giggled and approached him.

She placed her left arm on his right shoulder. Her long white hair draped across him as she leant into him. Marcus looked up at the White Blood woman, as she lowered herself on to his lap. She stared into his purple eyes and smiled.

He lifted his right hand and ran the back of his fingers down her cheek. He pressed his index finger to her lower lip and drew her lip forward. He lent forward and kissed her softly.

His desire extinguished. He withdrew. A horrified look flashed across her face. He dropped his hand and stared into her grey eyes. He could kiss a hundred White Blood girls and never recreate the moment when he first kissed *her*. He faded out of focus and remembered *her* touch. The smell of *her* skin, the feelings *she* and only *she* could conjure inside of him.

Furious at being unable to satisfy the longing within, Marcus grabbed the prostitute by the throat. He rose to his feet. The terrified woman tried to cry out in fear. Marcus tightened his grip. Lost to the gods and irreplaceable, no prostitute could possibly come close to *her*. What was he thinking?

The woman kicked out trying to loosen his grip.

Her screams as the flames took hold, the sound of the masonry and heavy wooden beams cracking, buckling and falling to the floor. The unmistakable sound of the Red Blood's armour as they barricaded the door to prevent escape. The orders of a Blue Blood to seal them in. The agony of the unrelenting heat.

The prostitute clawed desperately at Marcus's hand.

He tried everything in his power to save *her*, but he could not fight back the flames. He could not save *her*.

22,414 days before the eclipse.

Half a lifetime separated them when they first met. As soon as he laid eyes on her he knew she was the one. An unexplored world formed the backdrop, the skies sprinkled with the light of the gods, and at the altar, there she stood.

Every day he would climb the mountain to see her. He would bring offerings for the gods. She would smile politely at him, just as she did the others who brought her gifts. He never gave up.

Each day, as he toiled in the mines to the east, he would think of her. He practiced what to say. How to gaze at her and imagined her response. He would collect his wage and head to the trader's market to spend it all on her. It wasn't until he broke into a large vein of amethyst, that he had the most wonderful of ideas. He chipped away a tiny piece of the precious purple stone and carefully hid it so that the guards would not find it on him.

Over time, he carefully worked the stone into a pendent. He saved his wages for seven weeks and purchased a delicate silver chain to hang it. Terrified of refusal and potentially being ousted to the guards, he hid the necklace with a simple note among his usual offerings, and presented it at the temple.

That night he prayed to the gods, that they would just this once, allow her to break away from the strict decrees, and just this one time, notice him.

The next morning, terrified of failure, he nervously worked the mines. Paranoid of the guards and whether they knew what he had done, he lay low. As the sun set he grew confident that he had yet to be discovered. He quickly left the mines and made his way home to collect more offerings. Nervously he climbed the steps of the mountain side. Quietly he joined the back of the queue for the temple. Each step closer sent his heart racing into a fit. Sure that his heart couldn't beat any faster, he cautiously approached the temple.

Afraid to look up, he presented his offerings while remaining focused on the base of the altar.

"Thank you," she whispered softly.

Unable to refuse curiosity, he looked up. Before his eyes hung the pendent. Its glorious purple light, infused with her immortal spirit, blossomed brightly. He gazed up into her intense purple eyes and became utterly lost. She returned a sincere smile of gratitude. With no one left in the temple to disturb them, she leant down and gently whispered into his ear.

"Gaia," she uttered, "my name is Gaia."

That night they lay together in the grass, on the mountainside, under the stars. They chatted for hours. She had been raised to be fearful of others, to serve only the gods, to never know the warmth of friendship. He explained the life of a White Blood, how they would work hard under the commands of the Blue Bloods. How he longed for the freedom to explore the lands, to feel the soft sands of the south and to see the towering trees to the far east.

They paused. Each found themselves helplessly lost in one another. Forbidden by the gods, illegal in the laws of the lands, she drew closer and kissed his lips. Nothing else mattered in the whole known world. For that brief moment they were both content. They were both happy. Their desires were silenced. Their responsibilities quashed. Their mortal spirits entwined.

A broad smile grew on both their faces as she withdrew. Overjoyed, she giggled and jumped to her feet. She glanced back at him before running home. He continued to lie in the grass, staring at the stars, savouring the moment.

Night after night they continued to meet, hidden from prying eyes. They embraced in distant fields, hidden in the canopy of the trees or in the caves in the cove. They travelled anywhere and everywhere, eager to satisfy their curiosity, until they happened upon a large network of caves. Hidden at the base of the Blue Mountains, behind the plateau where the Magpie Hall perched, it was a secret that only they knew about.

She led the way, her arm outstretched behind her. His hand tightly bound to hers. Confident they were alone, they held each other tightly. Passionately they embraced one another. Guided by his hand she lay on the floor. He ran his hand along her side before loosening her palla. She gazed into his glistening grey eyes as he began to undress her.

Against everything they had ever been taught, they became one. Unable to contain their passion, their groans of delight echoed around the cavernous network of caves. Exhausted but satisfied, he lay at her side.

Often absent from their duties, the pair frequently escaped to the cave in the Blue Mountains. Until the gods saw fit that Gaia should bear a child. Afraid of the consequences and terrified of the purists, the pair ran away together. Time passed quickly and soon Gaia was gripped in the miracle of child birth. She cried out in agony, her screams of anguish echoing through the sanctuary. He never left her side. He held on to her as tightly as he could, fearful of ever letting go. He guided her through the suffering and pain, speaking softly. Eventually Gaia's screams were echoed by the cries of a child. Exhausted, Gaia smiled as he lovingly presented the child to her.

"He is beautiful," she remarked.

"He takes after you," he retorted with a smile.

The pair drew together, cradling their forbidden miracle.

With an almighty roar the ground around them began to shake violently. He quickly rushed to his feet and ran to the entrance. A powerful shock wave emanating from Ravenstone, threw him to the ground. A colossal cloud of thick black smoke rose in to the sky, like a series of monstrous demons being released from the fiery confines of the mountain.

Unknown to the couple, on the western side of Ravenstone, the ground beneath the city began to tumble into the ocean below. A cascade of molten rock, accompanied with the homes and lives of nearly 200 White Bloods, fell from the mountain side.

Trees were stripped of their bark before being dragged by their roots. The deer that called the forest home were pulled by their hooves into the murky waters. Children and adults alike struggled for anything to save them, as the ground below them opened up. Homes were torn to pieces, masonry crumbled and fires ignited throughout the city, as white hot magma poured out of the mountain side.

A deadly mix of poisonous gas and steam bellowed into the air, choking all in its path. The ocean surged westwards as nearly a third of Ravenstone disappeared into the grasp of Orcus.

The skies in all directions turned to a despairing mix of burning ash and steam. Within just a few moments what remained of the western side of the mountain now lay buried under several feet of suffocating ash.

The couple looked on in horror as the birds of Rytus were instantaneously silenced. The insects synonymous with summer were vaporised in the hot clouds, leaving the screams of the thousand citizens of Ravenstone as all that remained.

The eastern side of Ravenstone collapsed into a fiery crater. Homes were torn from their foundations before tumbling out of control in to the magma below. The bodies of every blood gens burned furiously as they too fell into the pit.

A choking combination of ash and pumice stone, began to rain down on the couple, forcing them back into the safety of the cave. They retreated as far back as they could. The whistles and screams of the fiery boulders landing outside the entrance, resounded about the walls of the cave. He clung on tightly to her, shielding their child, as the gods tore Ravenstone to pieces.

Days passed before the couple could leave the safety of the cave. Outside, the landscape was unrecognisable. Where dense forests once stood, all that remained now were the bare trunks of the trees. The lake at the foot of the cave was littered with broken branches and burnt logs. The water was black like tar and clouded too heavily to see through at any depth. Doubting that the gods had been left with no other choice but to punish Rytus for their sins, the couple retreated deeper into the caves.

Desperate to save Rytus from further repercussions, she sealed them inside using a large boulder that had rained down from the mountain. Using her powers, gifted from the gods, Gaia crafted ten White Blood attendants to serve and protect their precious child. Together they toiled day and night to carve a temple to the gods, inside the Blue Mountains, where they would spend the remainder of their days begging for forgiveness.

To the east, Gaia planted a garden using a slither of light in the rock face, to feed the hungry plants. South of the garden a stair case was cut into the rock, ascending to the gods on top of the life giving Blue Waterfalls. There Gaia and her attendants carved out a second temple, where a thousand candles burnt brightly, in memory of the lives lost.

He devoted his time to raising their son. Unlike his parents the child was half caste, most evident in his eyes; one purple, one white. The child possessed some of his mother's powers, but not all. He was weaker than her, but as strong as his father.

As the days turned to night inside the temple beneath the mountains, Gaia began to resent the child. In him she saw the burning fires consuming the citizens of Ravenstone. Within his heart she was sure screamed the souls of a thousand women and children falling to their death. Every sound he made began to sound like the muffled screams of the men and women sucked into the cold grasp of the ocean. He became to her, a symbol of every sin she had ever committed. Every vow she had made to the gods, broken in a moment of raw lust.

She grew cold towards the child. She could no longer look upon him. She instead began to throw herself into her rituals. She spent every waking moment begging for forgiveness from the gods. She punished herself in the hopes that they would forgive her and all that she had done. She starved herself. She beat herself. She cast her hands into the hot embers. She bathed in icy cold water. She tried anything and everything. No matter how much she pleaded, she could not banish the screams from her nightmares. There became only one course of action, only one way to banish the nightmares. The child had to die.

As the father and child slept peacefully, she entered the room. With blade raised she struck out. Instinctively, he awoke and seized her hand, protecting the child. With a fiery determination burning in her eyes, she fought back. Her madness weakened her, but she still remained an even match for the White Blood man. He fought as best as he could, torn between the only woman he had ever loved and their only child.

Inside the child, he could see a brighter flame burning, a desire for truth and justice. Innocent to the lies of the gods and free to live a life absent of the torment she would inflict on them both if given the chance. Inspired, he began to overpower her. Her powers were now a muddle in her mind. Her purpose murky. Her only clear intention now was to end the agony tearing her apart inside. Desperately they both fought for what they truly believed was the right thing to do.

A mistake. She fell to her knees. He dealt the blow. She dropped to the floor and drifted out of consciousness. Unable to let her deliver the child to the gods and with a heavy heart, he dragged her into another room, and sealed shut the door behind him as he left.

With bear like strength he broke the seal on the cave and stepped out into the sun's fading light, the child in his arms. He turned as the ten attendants squinted in the twilight. Unable to justify his actions to them and unsure of their allegiances, he sealed the cave again.

Unfamiliar with the light of the full moon, the man struggled on through the mountains. Being sure to avoid the city growing below the newly built palace, he stumbled on until he found a clearing in the Dying Woods. Using rocks from the nearby river and kindling from the woods, he built them a fire and together they spent the night under the stars.

The morning sun was unforgiving, his eyes, now more attuned to the dimly lit cave, struggled to focus. Unsure how he would raise the child, alone and effectively blind, the man had no choice but to secure a future for his son.

Before the cocks crowed in the village, he snuck down to a well-kept White Blood's home, and placed the child on the ground outside. He retreated to a safe distance and watched with anticipation as the White Bloods began to stir.

A door opened and out stepped a young White Blood woman. She glanced down at the child at her feet. She looked around for his family before carefully lifting the child in to her arms. She checked again before smiling at the child before her. She admired his unusual eyes, surely a gift from the gods she thought. She stroked his cheek which made him giggle. She clutched him tightly and went back inside.

Satisfied that the child would be safe from Gaia and her attendants, the father turned to leave. "Remember all that I have taught you son. Be forgiving, be kind and be true to yourself, Marcus."

5,259 days before the eclipse.

Marcus looked down at the prostitute now lying motionless on the floor. He dropped to his knees.

"No!" He cried out, "No! This is not how it was meant to be."

Furiously he raised his hands in frustration and let out an almighty roar. He fell to the floor, curled up at her side and sobbed uncontrollably.

His tears dried and soon he began to focus on the wall of names. A thousand reasons why what happened at Ravenstone was not his fault. A thousand wrongs to be righted. A thousand blood debts to be taken, in exchange for the thousand that died at Ravenstone. Retribution would be paid.

He climbed to his feet and approached the wall. He placed his forehead against the cold stone. What if the gods were right? What if that blood was on his hands? Tormented he clawed at the wall. Pale purple blood began to seep from his fingertips as he tried in vain to extinguish the names.

He turned his back to the wall and threw himself against it.

"How can I be true to myself if I do not truly know who I am?" he cried out. His breathing intensified as he searched his mind for the answers.

"I beg your forgiveness Dominus," Adreana interrupted. Marcus turned sharply to face her. "It is time..."

Chapter Twenty

5,259 days before the eclipse.

Quinta lay tightly in a ball, sobbing on the marble floor of her quarters. Her tears pooling beneath her, the sleeve of her palla soaked through. Her hair no longer neatly braided, her makeup smeared and her will broken.

"Quinta?" Braria called out as she approached the young Blue Blood with care. "What has happened?" she asked as she gingerly knelt at the side of the once fiery girl. She carefully grasped a lock of Quinta's hair, moved it to the side and then, breaking the most basic of rules, placed the palm of her hand on Quinta's back. Quinta flinched. Braria withdrew immediately, awaiting a scolding. Quinta snivelled, but no scolding followed. Braria brushed the hair from Quinta's face and stared with concern.

Reluctantly, Quinta opened her blood shot, tearful eyes. Her focus pinned entirely to the grey eyes of Braria. Quinta sniffed loudly before wiping her nose on her wet sleeve. No words needed to be exchanged, immediately Braria knew something terrible had befallen the once confident Blue Blood. The young girl so sure in her own abilities and the future that lay before her, was now a closely guarded entanglement of mutilated clothes and a shattered spirit.

No longer afraid, Braria placed her right arm into the tight bundle and with the love of a mother she helped her up. Quinta stumbled clumsily to her feet. She clung on tightly before staring upward at Braria. Here there was a love she had never seen before. No expectations. No demands. No pomp or circumstance, just genuine concern for her wellbeing.

Braria and the girl both happened to glance upon the highly polished metal surface of the mirror in the corner. Quinta broke away from Braria's grasp and approached it. She reached out and touched her fingertips to the cold metal. Her focus changed to the girl before her. The girl who normally stood before her was brave, beautiful and elegant. Not the mangled mess that now presented itself. The dried blood on her lip, the graze across her chest and the stranger in the mirror, none of it made any sense.

"Today is my Decem Dies Mille ceremony," Quinta remarked still transfixed on the mirror. "Today I become an Imperatrix..." she paused, as she inspected the girl before her more closely, "today, I become a..." she stopped.

"A woman?" Braria responded.

Quinta looked down at the floor, a mixture of confusion and guilt choking her words, clouding her mind. To run away now would mean running as far as she could, and never being allowed to return to Rytus. Staying would mean facing her fears, facing him.

271

Braria approached Quinta. They both stared at the girl in the mirror, before Braria responded calmly, "We must prepare." Unsure and afraid, Quinta agreed.

Quinta clung on to what remained of her tunic as Braria lifted the mudded and torn grey palla from Quinta's shoulders. The once soft wool, pulled and tattered, now felt coarse to the touch. Braria released Quinta's hair from its knotted and tangled braids. Quinta removed her tunic and lowered herself silently into the warm water of the bath. Braria entered the water and approached her master. She ran Quinta's hair through her finger tips as she worked free the mud and grit.

The touch of Braria's hand on her skin turned to the forceful grasp of Lucius. The sound of droplets of water falling into the water echoed into the whispers of Lucius in her ear. The water cruelly reflected only Lucius's face. Terrified, Quinta quickly abandoned the bath.

The water dripped from her fingertips as she stood naked before the gods. Her breathing quickened. Her heart raced. Her thoughts now lost in a flurry of nightmarish memories before the glint of the mirror caught her attention again. She drew closer. There, within it, stood a new Quinta, devoid of the embellishments of the Blue Bloods. Bereft of the innocence her childhood had afforded her. Here was Quinta, the woman.

The heavy red drapes fluttered as nine White Bloods entered Quinta's room. Just as they had done every day of their lives, they set about preparing the Blue Blood for her day ahead. To their surprise Quinta did not object as they pulled and pushed her into position. Silently, Quinta maintained her stone like resolve, occasionally glancing up at the mirror as the transformation drew to its conclusion. Relieved, all the White Bloods dutifully left, including Braria.

The stranger in the mirror, complete with swan fibula, an intricate embellishment of everything a new Imperatrix was expected to be, glared back. On the table nearby, the woollen dolls of Quinta's childhood looked on. Their expressions unchanged. Their purpose lost to the relentless appetite of time. She picked up the oldest of them. It had been a gift from her father. Night and day she would use it to practice the routine of her Decem Dies Mille ceremony. As her collection of dolls grew she would practice the roles of everyone that would be there on the day. From the Raven's attendants in their long white pallas to the waiting citizens, eager to see their new Imperatrix, they all knew their place.

The unwelcome call of the buccina horn resounded from the courtyard, through the corridors, and into Quinta's room. It was time.

Quinta solemnly gathered up her dolls, took a deep breath and vacated the quarters of her childhood. She followed the corridor to the shrine of Decem Dies Mille. One by one she placed the woollen dolls into the fire. Mutely she watched the faces of the dolls disappear into the flames before being consumed entirely. Perhaps there was still time to run?

The call of the second buccina echoed through the palace. Quinta sighed heavily. She closed her eyes, drew her hood and bowed her head. She thought silently for a moment before staring one last time into the flames. Time had been so cruelly snatched from her grasp. There remained only one option now; resolution.

In the corridor ahead waited her ten attendants, each brimming with pride. Braria smiled encouragingly as they each began to whisper blessings upon the new woman that stood respectably before them. The third buccina resounded.

Bravely, Quinta stepped out. The courtyards rejoiced with the laughter of the Blue Blood children at play, the music from the citharas of the musicians and the footsteps of the White Bloods as they danced along duly.

The fourth and final buccina sounded. Laughter, song and dance were replaced with hushed chatter and the shuffling of feet as the citizens made their way to their allocated positions.

Quinta wrapped her arms tightly around her chest and stepped forward. In front of her lay a clear and direct path to the Blue Temple; the steps lined with Red Bloods, standing proudly to attention. To her left, White Bloods from the palace peered through the parade trying to catch a glimpse of proceedings. The privileged citizens of Rytus filled the courtyards and gardens to her right, only interrupted by the occasional table of fruit and plates of meat. Around them, towers of neatly arranged flowers and on the walls of the palace, banners fluttered in the breeze.

A deep breath and a step forward, the soles of her shoes tapping gently against the white stone floors. The door behind her slammed shut. She looked up. All eyes were on her.

She took a sharp intake of breath. Everything she had ever done, everything that had been in her control, led to this moment. She stepped forward. The long blue train of her palla dragged along behind her, pulling her backwards slightly. She glanced upwards. Carefully she climbed the first step. Confronting Lucius now would be impossible. She moved up to the third step. What would Tita think if she knew what he had done? The fourth step. What would Tiberius think of his precious little blue flower, its petals torn from the stem? A sniffle to her right, Quinta glanced sideward to look at the Red Blood, who maintained his position. Remembering her own etiquette, she dropped her arms to her side and continued her climb to the Blue Temple.

The crowds swarmed behind her as she made her way up the steps. Citizens clambered for a good position to watch proceedings as Quinta's world became entirely desolate.

A raven, with little care for pomp and circumstance, called out as it swooped overhead. Quinta watched for a moment as it climbed higher into the skies. Free to travel with the winds, it darted across the thermals before riding the breeze, heading to distant lands.

Quinta wondered what it would be like to join the birds; to fly away and never return. To decide freely where her future lay, to travel and watch the citizens toil below. Anything but be a puppet to a fate already played out in the generations before her.

Near the top of the steps, selected members of the Green, Red and Orange Bloods waited patiently. Respectfully they parted to allow Quinta to proceed through.

Inside the temple, at the altar, awaiting her arrival stood the most senior of the Raven's ten attendants. Hood drawn, scroll in hand and head bowed ceremoniously. Behind her, stood six other attendants, hands clasped, hoods drawn and heads bowed.

With poignancy, Quinta crossed the threshold and entered the Blue Temple. Hesitantly she proceeded past the waiting entourage. The eyes of Tita and Tiberius felt as though they had burned almost instantly through her synthetic shroud. Quinta chose instead to remain transfixed on the ground beneath their feet. She paused momentarily at the empty position reserved for Servius, and wondered if he had yet been discovered.

As per tradition, her brother stood next in the line. His pristine toga was a distant disparity from the demons he concealed beneath it. Quinta glanced upwards. His smug face served only as a painful and unwelcome reminder of the anguish he had inflicted upon her. Her stomach turned. She felt dirty, uneasy and disgusted.

Tormented by the revulsion welling inside her and the traditions that had been laid in stone thousands of generations before hers, Quinta turned away from Lucius and focused instead on the waiting White Blood attendant before her. Respectfully Quinta removed her hood and advanced up the five small steps of the altar before kneeling in front of the attendant.

The temple fell entirely silent, interrupted only occasionally by the wind chimes joyfully resounding in the breeze.

"I, Achillea, child of the Raven, asks who is presented to the gods this day?" the attendant called out reading aloud from the scroll.

"I am Quinta Hyacintho Olor, daughter of Tiberius and Tita, sister of..." she hesitated. His name felt like poison on her tongue, "...Lucius."

"Quinta Hyacintho Olor, daughter of Tiberius and Tita and sister of Lucius, you kneel before the gods today to ask for permission to rule these lands. To stand at the side of our Imperators and call yourself equal in their image. To guide and protect the White Bloods, to lead and make use of the Orange, Red and Green Bloods for the prosperity of Rytus and her citizens of all true blood gens."

"I do in honour of the gods," Quinta responded duly.

"Rise before them, accept their gifts and make solemn your vow," the attendant commanded.

Quinta as instructed rose to her feet. Achillea gestured to the first two attendants behind her. They stepped forward and presented a ceremonial jug of water.

"Quinta Hyacintho Olor, do you accept this gift from the goddess Venus?"

"I accept."

The two attendants poured the water from the jug into the waiting hands of Quinta.

"Just as Venus gave life to Aeneas she granted on to us the gift of life through the offering of water. Use the power within it to grant the citizens the right of cleanliness and clear sight. May your abstinence through your innocence be rewarded and with it, in time, bear a new pure blood child of Rytus."

Quinta drank from her hands. The two attendants returned to their previous positions.

"Do you, Quinta Hyacintho Olor, accept this gift from the goddess Bellona?"

"I accept."

Two attendants stepped forward carrying with them two lamps. The first attendant poured oil from the unlit lamp onto Quinta's hands. The second attendant used the second lamp to light the oil. Quinta watched in awe as the flame flickered and danced in her palm.

"May Bellona's flame burn brightly within you at all times. May its guidance bring you the tenacity and bravery required to lead Rytus in times of victory and war. May your endurance shine through even the darkest of storms."

Quinta felt the heat of the flame begin to fade as the oil became almost entirely exhausted.

"Do you accept this gift from the goddess Minerva?"

"I accept."

Achillea raised her right hand and drew it rapidly across the flame, instantly extinguishing it. The smoke, caught in the wake, drifted to Quinta's right, following the line taken by the attendant's hand. Unannounced, a gentle breeze ebbed in to the temple, contesting the smoke's path.

The smoke changed direction creating a stir before Quinta's eyes.

"Let Minerva's wisdom guide you, let caution and judgment protect you and the citizens of Rytus. Let prudence and sanity be the winds that guide your decisions, wherever they may take you."

Quinta watched the breeze carry the smoke upwards.

"And do you Quinta Hyacintho Olor, pledge yourself wholly to the gods and goddesses in all their forms?"

"I do."

"To obey their commands, to honour their wishes and seek their guidance at all times?"

"I do."

"To protect Rytus and all true blood gens in times of wealth and in times of poverty?"

"I do."

"To stand united at the side of Lucius, to serve the gods undivided and bring forth a child of pure blood?"

Quinta turned to look at Lucius grinning behind her. She paused for a moment. Could she truly say no? Did she really have a choice?

"I do," she replied.

"Then accept this gift from Vesta," Achillea commanded as she scattered soil into Quinta's palms.

"May the ground beneath your feet serve as a reminder of your vows to the gods and their promise to keep you safe in return for your betrothal. May your obligations guide you in your journey. May the gods bless you and your union with Lucius." Achillea gestured towards Lucius, before bowing her head respectfully.

"I call now upon the Raven to bless and sanctify this union before the gods, may his guiding hand confirm the true will of Quinta," Achillea announced, hand now outstretched towards the entrance to the temple.

On cue the Raven entered. With hood drawn and voice silenced, he marched quickly across the marble floor. Each footstep resounded loudly from the walls as he made his way to the altar. Those gathered bowed their heads respectfully as the Raven passed, all except Lucius who couldn't help but smirk.

The Raven paused behind Quinta. Achillea bowed respectfully to her master, who in return acknowledged her with a nod.

"I present before you Marcus Pupura Corvus, the will of the gods and protector of the citizens of Rytus," announced Achillea.

Quinta rose from her knees and turned to face the Raven before bowing.

"Marcus Pupura Corvus, do you decree Quinta is of pure blood?"

Marcus approached Quinta. He raised his right hand and placed his palm on her forehead. He inhaled loudly and

281

closed his eyes. He remained motionless for just a moment before nodding in agreement.

"Marcus Pupura Corvus, do you decree Quinta is due the title of Imperatrix of Rytus?"

Marcus nodded.

"Marcus Pupura Corvus, do you decree Quinta is true to her vows?"

Marcus remained unmoved.

Achillea waited a moment before repeating herself.

"Marcus Pupura Corvus, do you decree Quinta is true to her vows?"

Marcus opened his eyes and removed his hand.

Achillea looked around nervously as the crowd began to stir.

"Marcus Pupura Corvus, do you decree Quinta is true to her vows?"

Marcus turned and began to leave. Quinta remained motionless.

"Dominus?" Achillea called out in desperation.

Furious, Tita stepped forward to confront the Raven but Tiberius held her back. Lucius began to laugh loudly as the crowd erupted in to accusations and conjecture. The Raven disappeared into the emotional crowd as Achillea looked to her blood sisters for guidance.

"She is unfit!" a voice cried out from the crowd.

"This is an outrage," another called out.

"Remove the impure."

"Cast her out."

"SILENCE! ALL OF YOU!" Tita demanded furiously.

It made little difference as the voices of the crowd only strengthened inside and outside the temple. Soon Tita became entirely drowned out.

The crowd outside the temple grew restless and lurched forward. The Red Bloods fought back, parting the way for the Blue Bloods to escape. While Tita and Tiberius's guards protected their masters, Quinta saw her chance. She gathered up her palla and ran for the steps.

Chapter Twenty-One

5,259 days before the eclipse.

"What do you think Ericus actually meant?" Placidus asked as the small boat carrying the three Orange Bloods drew closer to the shoreline.

"When?" Vesnus responded.

"When he spluttered about the 'Pact of Ravenstone'?" Placidus replied.

"Oh, you mean when he was trying to explain his actions, right before *somebody* silenced him?" Vesnus responded sarcastically, hinting towards Claricius. Claricius snorted dismissively before leaping from the boat into the shallow water.

"If we stopped to listen to all the nonsense that falls from the lips of the dying, then our work would never be done," Claricius responded.

"Have you no compassion brother?" Placidus asked.

"No curiosity?" Vesnus pried, hoping to provoke a response.

Claricius ignored the pair and collected the rope from the small wooden jetty. Vesnus and Placidus jumped from the boat, and pushed it just out of reach of Claricius. Claricius glared at the pair before treading deeper into the cold water of the bay. He struggled as the bottom of the boat began to drag against the rocks and sand, but persisted until the boat was close enough for the rope to reach. He tied the boat up before joining the others.

The trio made their way across the bridge over the river and followed the road through the Dying Woods. Waiting patiently at the side of the road was Liquens, the little brown fox.

"How does he do that?" Placidus remarked with a smile.

"What?" Claricius responded unimpressed.

"No matter where I go, or where I have been, I know I am home because Liquens is here to greet me."

Vesnus and Claricius exchanged sceptical looks as Placidus bent down to pet Liquens. The fox reared up and nuzzled Placidus's hand.

"Who is a clever little fox?" Placidus babbled.

"Behold the mighty Orange Blood assassin! Tremble before the man and his clever little fox," Claricius retorted, causing Vesnus to snigger.

"Bah!" Placidus responded, dismissing the pair.

The three Orange Bloods and Liquens, followed the stone road through the Dying Woods. The road led them across the viaduct over the valley and trees, before reaching Falcon Hall. They cleaned their blades and replaced their bows in their respective places in the stores, before making their way inside the hall.

Inside, Mania stood patiently waiting for their return.

"I must speak with you," she said, approaching Vesnus.

Claricius let out a quiet growl of discontent while Placidus smirked. Vesnus nodded to Mania in agreement and followed her to a quiet corner.

"I am worried," she explained, her hands cusped and her eyes fixed firmly on Vesnus.

"About?" he responded.

"Leanorus and Mother have not returned."

"From where?"

"Another of those letters arrived and they both left immediately for Magpie Gorge. I do not know why they went, but they have not returned and I am worried," she responded nervously.

"They are the two best Orange Bloods in the whole of Rytus. I am sure they are fine," he replied placing his hand on her shoulder to reassure her.

"In my dreams I saw two mighty falcons lose their way and fall from the skies. They were torn apart by the sparrows before burning in a purple flame. Something is wrong," she explained, "I know it."

Vesnus placed the palm of his hand against her cheek. She closed her eyes and immersed herself in the warmth and comfort of his touch. She opened her eyes, placed her hand over his and looked up into his vivid orange eyes.

"Please, find them. Bring them home," she pleaded.

Vesnus thought for a moment.

"Very well," he replied. "I will need Velox. She can search from the skies while Placidus and I search on foot. We will find them and we will bring them home. I promise."

"Thank you," she responded reassured.

Vesnus went immediately in search of his friend.

"Brother!" Vesnus exclaimed as he landed his hand heavily on Placidus's shoulder. "We are to go to Magpie Gorge."

"Why?" Placidus asked.

"I will explain on the way."

"Lead on brother!" Placidus declared as Claricius continued to growl with the ferocity of a wolf pup.

Vesnus collected Velox from the aviary while Placidus collected their bows, quivers and blades. Liquens, not one for being left out, joined the group, and the two Orange Bloods, falcon and fox, left for Magpie Gorge.

"Going through White City will take too long. I fear we do not have the time to spare. We shall travel across the Red Hell." Vesnus explained.

"Very well," Placidus replied.

They travelled along the road, passing the homes of the White Bloods standing above the swamps, to the bridge south of Falcon Reach. Velox flapped her wings impatiently, which made Liquens excitedly race around the legs of the two Orange Bloods.

The wooden sign dictating the way creaked and groaned as the wind whistled down the road towards the group. Velox attempted to leap from Vesnus's hand but he had a firm hold of her jesses. Frustrated, she flapped wildly.

"Patience friend, you will fly soon enough," he said in an attempt to reassure the bird. Encouragingly she calmed down, as the group made their way east, entering the Red Hell.

The road across the red desert was only accessible during the colder months. It stretched from the walls of White City in the north to the land between Falcon Reach and Eagle Blood shores in the west, to Magpie Gorge in the east. The great sand dunes ascended high into the sky and dwarfed even the tallest temples and camps of Rytus. A place of exile, it was renowned for the many lost souls who had been devoured by the fiery sand. Only the desperate dared to cross it during the hotter summer days and only the foolish dared to stray from the road.

As promised, Vesnus released Velox, who without hesitation, soared into the sky. Liquens ran along behind, chasing her shadow, darting across the sands, looking back occasionally to make sure he didn't lose sight of Placidus.

The two men and their companions followed the road as it led around the dunes, eventually turning on to the narrower seldom used path to Magpie Gorge. The dunes began to reduce in height until they disappeared into the lakes east of White City. They continued to follow the path through to the swamps until they were able to cut across to the main road. Keen to keep Velox on hand, Vesnus called her back as Liquens happily trotted along at the heels of Placidus.

They followed the road south and climbed the hill to Magpie Gorge. Vesnus noted the sun sitting low on the horizon before turning into the secretive world of the Green Bloods.

The gorge was alive with the sound of chatter and debate. Children could be heard playing along the narrow walkways, while White Bloods attempted to navigate their way around them. At the bottom of the gorge, Green Bloods chanted their lessons back to their White Blood tutors, while older Green Bloods practiced their knowledge on the hillside.

Vesnus peered into the village in search of his mentor, but the clusters of tightly knitted walkways and bridges made it almost impossible to see. Knowing that Leanorus was familiar with Velox and would know that Vesnus was in the area, Vesnus released her. She swooped down between the wooden passages and disappeared into the gorge.

"Do you think they are down there?" Placidus asked as he peered over the fence.

"I do not know brother, they have been gone for far longer than expected," Vesnus responded.

"They are probably back at the hall, laughing at us now," Placidus suggested with a smile.

"I hope you are right brother."

Velox returned to her master's gauntlet and began preening her feathers. Vesnus could only wait and see if his mentor emerged from the chasm below.

"We could go down there and look," Placidus suggested. "But then I suppose, we are better to wait here so we do not pass them. It is like an ant's nest down there."

Before Vesnus could respond the doors to the only stair case into or out of the gorge opened. Vesnus straightened up and approached the door to greet his mentor.

Two young White Bloods passed by heading for the hillside. Vesnus felt dejected. Where were Leanorus and Agapeta?

"You there," Placidus called out to the White Bloods, "We are looking for two Orange Bloods."

"Well," one of the White Bloods responded, "I have seen two Orange Bloods."

"Where?" Vesnus replied with interest.

"Well, *you* are two Orange Bloods."

Agitated, Placidus lunged forward at the White Bloods. Vesnus held him back.

"A man and a woman. They came here and have not returned. I must find them," Vesnus explained.

"A man and a woman came by yesterday, before sunset. Spoke to a hooded man. Said they were going to Magpie Hill Camp," the other White Blood responded.

"And they were Orange Bloods?" Vesnus queried.

"They looked like Orange Bloods, with their orange hair, bow, quivers and blades."

"Yeah, they looked like you two," the first White Blood added.

Vesnus, Placidus, Velox and Liquens raced back along the road and made their way north to Magpie Hill Camp.

Against the twilight sky, the camp looked eerily deserted. Something did not feel right. Vesnus slowed the group and began to approach the camp with hesitation.

Liquens dropped his ears flat and lowered his head. Velox cried out, her screech dissipating into the cold stone walls of the camp. The two Orange Bloods tried to comfort their companions but it was impossible to disguise their own reservations.

The stables at the base of the camp were unmanned. Two horses whinnied loudly before snorting and pawing at the ground. Velox extended her wings and scanned her surroundings.

The lamps on the gatehouse flickered in the cold breeze. The absence of the chatter and commands of the Red Bloods that guarded the camp was almost deafening. The oddly barren trees made for a discouraging backdrop to the foreboding camp, as the group cautiously climbed the steps.

Velox began to peck and claw at Vesnus's gauntlet, before crying out and trying in vain to fly to freedom. Vesnus decided it would be wiser to let her go. He could collect her on the way out, besides she would be of little use in the narrow courtyards and halls of the camp. He released her jesses and without hesitation she darted straight for the safety of a nearby tree.

"You can wait here too if you like," Placidus suggested to Liquens.

Liquens looked up at Placidus before peering past him to the camp.

"Very well," he replied, grateful of the companionship, "you may follow."

The trio continued to the gatehouse and unhindered, entered the courtyard. A fire smouldered in the centre, the smoke rising into the night's sky. Someone had been here recently. They were clearly not alone.

Together they explored the camp. Each room brimmed with the belongings of the Red Bloods. Half eaten food lay cold and stale on the tables. Most of the weapons lay undisturbed in their racks, and the armour remained neatly arranged in the dormitories. Only the sound of the wind whistling through the cracks in the walls accompanied the group, as they tried to piece together the whereabouts of their missing blood gens. Unable to find the answers they needed, the trio headed back into the central courtyard.

Liquens began to sniff the air, his ears pinned back. His rear legs grew tense as he anticipated the moment he'd have to run. He began to bark alerting the others. Vesnus and Placidus looked about the courtyard, searching the shadows. Liquens began to snarl and lower himself closer to the ground.

"Stand down Falcons," a voice called out from the darkness.

"Who speaks?" Vesnus responded.

"You are outnumbered, drop your weapons," the voice demanded.

"Show yourself" Placidus cried out.

"Do as we say and you will be spared."

293

"We mean no harm. We are looking for two lost Orange Bloods. We are not here to fight," Vesnus explained.

"Then you are to be lost too," a second voice proclaimed.

Thirteen large White Bloods armed with swords, their faces and clothes stained with red blood, emerged from the shadows and surrounded the group. Liquens began to hiss and growl before retreating between Placidus's feet.

The White Bloods started to circle the group, snarling and snapping at the trapped Orange Bloods.

"We just want to find our blood brother and sister, we do not want to cause any trouble," Vesnus insisted.

"Let me reunite you," one of the White Bloods jested as he launched for Placidus with his sword.

Vesnus knew their bows were unsuitable at short range but their blades were small and agile. They could be used for close combat. However, any attempt to counteract an attack of this nature would have to be precise and quick.

Vesnus reached for his blade and threw it at Placidus's attacker. The blade spun through the air before piercing the left eye of the aggressor. He grabbed at the wound, screaming in agony. He dropped to his knees and keeled over, as blood began to pour from his eye socket.

A second White Blood grabbed Vesnus from behind, placing a choking hold across his neck. Vesnus grabbed at the White Blood's arm. Placidus grabbed his own blade and thrust it into the attacker's stomach. He withdrew the blade and struck again. The man fell to the floor.

A third and fourth White Blood launched for Placidus, while a fifth and sixth grabbed Vesnus. Liquens with all his might bit down hard on the ankle of the third White Blood. The woman retracted and shook Liquens fee from her leg. Placidus ducked under the fourth White Blood, and thrust his blade into the chest of the White Blood woman.

Vesnus kicked out at the man in front of him, delivering a winding blow that left the assailant breathless. Vesnus grabbed the shoulders of the man behind him and threw him over the top of his head, causing the man to land squarely on the breathless man. The pair collapsed to the floor.

Placidus kicked the fourth White Blood in the back with the sole of his shoe. A loud cracking noise emanated about the courtyard as the man cried out in pain. He dropped to his knees, clutching at his back.

Another White Blood lunged for Vesnus, picking him up by his waist. He charged Vesnus into the stone wall behind the two Orange Bloods, winding Vesnus. While the White Blood held on tightly, another White Blood raised his sword to strike Vesnus's throat.

Vesnus looked at the blade as it loomed before him, the steel glinting in the moonlight, when in its reflection he saw a familiar shadow. Velox struck the White Blood in the face, slicing the flesh with her talons. She pecked at his eyes while disorientating the man with her flapping wings. He dropped the sword and staggered backwards. The other White Blood turned to see his compatriot drop to the floor, his eyes now just pools of white blood. Vesnus seeing his opportunity, struck the back of the White Blood's head with his fist, rendering the man unconscious.

Another two White Bloods grabbed at Placidus. Liquens leapt on to the unconscious body of a fallen White Blood and sprung upward. He grasped the face of Placidus's attacker and bit down hard on to his nose. The White Blood desperately tried to remove Liquens, who continued to scratch, claw and bite down as hard as he could.

Vesnus gasped as he tried to catch back his breath. He looked up just as the other White Blood drew his sword and prepared to strike Placidus. Vesnus drew his bow and an arrow. He had no time to aim. He fired. The arrow whistled through the air before striking the White Blood in his right arm. The White Blood cried out in pain, dropping the sword. A second arrow whistled through the air and struck the White Blood between the eyes, instantly silencing him. He dropped to the floor.

The three remaining White Bloods remained unnerved. The largest signalled the other two to advance on Placidus while he made for Vesnus.

Placidus drew his second blade and cleanly sliced the throat of the approaching White Blood. As he dropped to the floor, Liquens bounded across and leapt for the other White Blood. The White Blood raised his sword. Liquens yelped. The White Blood then struck at Placidus, cutting into his left arm.

Enraged, Placidus launched his blade into the abdomen of the White Blood. He stabbed him with vigour, withdrew the blade and stabbed him three more times, grunting with every blow. The White Blood dropped to the floor, revealing to Placidus the sight of Liquens lying motionless on the floor.

Vesnus drew another arrow and fired it at the large White Blood man closing in on him. The arrow struck the monstrous man in his left shoulder. He reached across with his large right paw and snapped the shaft of the arrow. He chuckled as his cumbersome feet crashed against the flag stone. Each footstep echoed around the courtyard, as the beast of a man lumbered towards Vesnus.

Vesnus fumbled around for his blade as the monstrous man drew his sword into the air above his head. The thought of slicing the Orange Blood clean down the middle grew into a large obnoxious grin. He laughed as he prepared to bring the sword crashing down through Vesnus.

The arrow whistled across the courtyard. The iron head sliced into the flesh at the base of the man's skull before cracking open the bone and tissue within. The arrow head penetrated the man's spinal cord with ease, severing the delicate network of fibre before punching through the trachea. The arrow head came to rest with the tip pressing against the front of the man's throat.

Vesnus looked on in dismay as the man dropped the sword behind him and began clutching at the protruding tip. His cries for help curdled in the blood that began to flow from his mouth. With the grin firmly wiped clean from his face, he looked to Vesnus for an explanation before collapsing to the floor.

Placidus stood silently in the man's wake, his arms by his side, bow in hand and his head hung low. He turned to face the spot where Liquens now lay. The cruel wind ruffled his luxurious fur, and his velvet black ears lay at rest. Placidus dropped to his knees and gingerly placed his hand on the little fox's side. Liquens opened his eyes and looked up at Placidus. His tail twitched at the sight of his friend at his side. "Thank you," Placidus whispered as he stroked Liquens side. Tears began to well in the Orange Blood's eyes as he continued to comfort his wounded companion.

Vesnus felt a great sense of guilt at the sight of his blood brother, the man he had dragged along with him seemingly for no reason at all. They had yet to find Leanorus or Agapeta and now Liquens lay wounded on the floor. Where would they go from here? What would they do now? he asked himself.

The screech of Velox echoed about the courtyard. Vesnus turned to see her standing on the threshold of an open doorway. Vesnus approached with curiosity, only for Velox to take flight through the doorway, disappearing inside. Vesnus gave chase.

He followed Velox down the narrow staircase, with only the sound of the flapping of her wings and the screech of her call to guide him. He collected a torch from the bottom of the stairwell and followed the sound of Velox as she cried out to him. Together they navigated the cavernous network of prison cells and torture chambers until he finally caught up with her.

She stopped and began to hop impatiently by a door. Vesnus approached cautiously. He presented the torch forward to light the way, revealing the trail of orange blood leading to the man heaped in a pile in the corner of the dank cell. Terrified at what he may find, Vesnus drew closer. The man lay face down in a pool of orange blood, his clothes torn, ripped and beaten. Vesnus reluctantly reached out and rolled the man over. It was Leanorus.

Vesnus was overcome with horror. Here was his mentor, the man who had taught him everything he had ever known; from his values and morals to his fighting techniques and prowess. The man who towered above all others, who stood for justice and righteousness, now lay battered and beaten in a pool of his own blood before him.

Leanorus coughed and spluttered.

"Mentoris!" Vesnus cried out.

Leanorus looked up and on seeing Vesnus managed to muster a weak smile.

"We must get you back to Falcon Hall immediately," Vesnus declared. He lifted Leanorus's arm over his head, supported his weight and attempted to guide his mentor out of the cell.

"Please," Leanorus whimpered, "put me back down."

Conflicted but obliged, Vesnus complied and gently placed his mentor back on the floor.

"We were tricked," Leanorus struggled to explain.

"Please Mentoris, you are weak, you need a Green Blood."

Leanorus dismissed Vesnus's concerns with a weak wave of his hand. "We were tricked, led here under false pretences..." he coughed. "I failed her. I should have been more aware. I should have seen it coming."

"We must get you a medicus!" Vesnus affirmed.

"The girl, her daughter," Leanorus spluttered.

"Mania?"

Leanorus nodded, "Tell her I am sorry."

"Mentoris?" Vesnus begged.

"Please, your promise," Leanorus muttered.

Vesnus leant in closer to hear.

"Let me die by your hand, as per your promise to me. Not by those brutes."

Vesnus looked at the desperation in his friend's eyes. He nodded and drew his blade. Vesnus collected the debt.

Chapter Twenty-Two

1,004,647 days after the eclipse.

He raced along the pavement, dodging lampposts, sandwich boards and shocked on lookers. His black hoodie, baseball cap and cheap gold chains were typical of the companions he now considered friends and allies. His cheap white trainers squeaked against the flag stones of the pavement, as the plastic bag secreted under his arm rustled against the poor quality plastic fibres of his hoodie.

"Come back here!" the shopkeeper called out.

His athletic figure allowed the young man to sprint faster and further than his overweight pursuer with ease, aided in part by the adrenalin induce by the chase. He looked back as the shopkeeper stopped, placed his hands on his thighs and began to pant with exhaustion. The young man smirked before colliding into a waiting figure.

The figure wasn't taller or wider than him, but his body armour, helmet, tools and defensive weapons made the figure appear so. His hi-vis badge and radio were synonymic with his trade and bore instant recognition to the young man. He abandoned his escape and stepped back.

"Well Max," the figure boomed, "looks like you've got some explaining to do, again." Max dropped his head, admitting defeat, and complied with the instructions of the policeman.

"Back again are we Max?" the desk sergeant enquired rhetorically, his red eyes glaring at Max.

"Yes sir," The arresting officer responded, "apprehended with stolen goods, sir."

The desk sergeant tapped away at his keyboard, before directing the officer to take Max to the cells. "C6," he instructed.

"Come along son," the arresting officer directed, as he turned Max to face the corridor to his right.

The arresting officer patted Max down while two others stood with arms folded in the background. The cell door was opened and Max was led inside. Max sat down on the hard wooden bench as the heavy metal door was slammed shut.

The grey breeze block and flickering fluorescent light cared as much for Max as he did of them. Behind a low wall there was a toilet and in the corner, behind a wire cage, was a CCTV camera. The smell of disinfectant was almost overpowering and the pale blue blanket on the bench was stiff and harsh to the touch. Max could only assume that it had been washed so many times on a high temperature setting that it probably didn't resemble the original colour at all.

Max looked at his fists as the anger inside began to well. He cried out in frustration before striking the wall to his right. He punched the wall again and again but the anger didn't fade.

"Stop that," a voice at the door commanded before the hatch was slammed shut again. Max recoiled and looked at his knuckles, now bloodied and bruised like so many times before.

The light from the tiny window, at the top of the wall furthest from the door, grew dimmer before turning to the artificial incandescent glow of the street lamps outside. Max paced the room. He felt it was inhumane to keep an animal in these conditions, so how was it fit to keep a human here? Max hadn't done anything that bad; he'd just taken a few packs of crisps and gum, and a magazine for Mother. So why were they holding him for so long? They hadn't held him for this long before.

The hours began to drag as Max grew increasingly impatient. He approached the door and tried to listen for signs of life. Perhaps they'd gone home and forgotten about him? he thought.

"I didn't do nothing," a voice called out from another cell.

"I don't feel so good," another cried.

None of the usual footsteps that paced the corridor could be heard, perhaps they really had gone? Max tried to lie down on the wooden bench but resorted to positioning himself in the corner. He placed the scratchy blanket over his legs and tried to at least get some rest.

"Max?" the voice at the door called out. "Max, I'm the welfare officer, and we're going to come in. OK?" Max couldn't be bothered to respond.

A pair of red eyes appeared at the hatch, they scanned the room and the hatch slammed shut again. The lock unlatched and the metal door swung open. One officer, unarmed, well kept, walked in, followed by two others with pepper spray and batons attached to their belts. The unarmed officer cautiously approached.

"Max?" he asked.

Max looked up and grunted.

"Max, I'm the welfare officer and I'd like to talk to you if that's OK?"

Max rolled his eyes, lifted his legs back onto the bench and turned away from the welfare officer. The officer maintained a neutral expression. This kind of reception was to be expected, Max wasn't unique or special in this aspect.

"Now Max," he said with a patient tone, "this is the third time this has happened. You'll be legally an adult soon. Do you not think that there's a better future for you out there?" Max knew he didn't have to respond to the officer, not under these conditions. He wasn't on trial.

The officer sighed. "Well, we will call your mother. Tell her that you are here again. She can come and pick you up. OK Max?"

Max stared at the wall. The officer tutted and reluctantly left. "Damned Demi Blood," one of the officers sneered as they followed the welfare officer out. The door slammed shut. Max was alone again and he was glad of it.

1,004,648 days after the eclipse.

The light at the window changed to the red glow of dawn. The cell door swung open, waking Max from his uncomfortable sleep.

"Come on," the officer instructed, "out!"

Max yawned, stretched and slowly got to his feet. The waiting officer grew impatient and demanded that Max hurry up. Intentionally, Max dragged his feet as he walked as slowly as he could, from his cell to the sergeant's desk. The officer knew it was more trouble than it was worth to physically push Max, so decided instead to resort to growling quietly under his breath while making pushing motions behind the infuriating child. Max took the time to prepare what he would tell Mother, a few apologies and promises should take that worried look off her face again.

"Hello son," a familiar voice called out.

Max looked up in horror. There was Father.

He looked to the officers for clarity, an explanation, even an apology, something to explain this. The sergeant stared down his nose at Max, as he stood stunned in the middle of the room.

"Perhaps you can set the boy straight, before it's too late," the sergeant suggested to Father.

"Thank you," Father responded before extending his arm towards Max, beckoning him to come along. Lost for the words to protest, Max did as he was instructed and walked with Father.

Outside the police station, Father led Max to an expensive, silver sports car. Max stopped.

"Get in, son," Father instructed, as he unlocked the vehicle.

Confused and overwhelmed, Max obliged.

A blip of the throttle accompanied by a loud exhaust note, signalled the start of the engine, as Father put on his driving gloves.

This man looked like Father and spoke with his voice, but didn't act like he had done in the past, before Mother and Max had to run. Who was this stranger? More importantly, where was Mother?

Father sighed and turned to Max, "You can't go on like this Max. I realise I haven't been a good father to you..."

Max turned to face the side window.

"...I just," he paused, trying to think of how to phrase the words, "I know you're better than this. Don't turn out like me. Don't be the failure that I became."

"Failure?" Max yelled as he turned to face Father. "Looks like you're doing pretty well for yourself."

"This?" Father asked gesturing to the steering wheel. "I'm up to my eye balls in debt to pay for it. I come home to an empty house I can't afford. I eat microwave meals for one. I go to bed without my wife. I wake up without my son. I'd call that a failure. Wouldn't you?" he said as he began to raise his voice.

Max turned back to the window.

"Look," Father pleaded with a calmer but disenchanted tone, "I've spoken to Mr Crimpstone..."

"WHAT?" Max screeched.

"...and I've managed to convince him not to press charges."

"YOU SPOKE TO THE SHOPKEEPER?" Max shouted in disbelief.

"Just you and your mother come home..." Father pleaded.

"Are you being serious?"

"...and I'm sure we can sort this all out."

"I'm getting out" Max declared.

"What? No!" Father demanded. Max released his seatbelt and got out of the car. "Come back here!" Father cried out, lowering the side window. Max drew up his hood and started walking home. Father got out of the car and threw up his hands in dismay.

"FINE!" Father bellowed, "I am NEVER bailing you out again. YOU ARE ON YOUR OWN!" Max stuck his middle finger up at Father and continued his march home.

After a couple of miles, Max realised he wasn't too far from his grandmother's house. She always had a keen interest in his welfare, and was always so amazed by the things he could do with his phone. She would welcome him with open arms, a hot cup of tea and some of those chocolate biscuits she used to get in just for him. She had all the time in the world for Max and was always proud of everything he had achieved. He turned off the main road and began making his way to her street.

He opened the old wooden gate, lowered his hood and trotted down the path to her front door. Hopefully he wasn't too early. He didn't want her to have to get up just for him. He knocked on the door and waited patiently. She was taking a little longer than usual, but perhaps she had to get dressed first? He knocked again. It was too early for her to have gone out to the shops, he thought. He peered through the letterbox. Something didn't feel right.

He searched through the bushes for the piece of red string, and used it to pull out a plastic bag. He opened it and removed the spare key. He unlocked the porch door and peeled back the corner of the carpet to reveal another key. Grandmother was always so afraid of being locked out without a phone, that she had to use this elaborate scheme of hiding keys in secret places.

Max tried to open the door, but it was stiff and difficult to push. He pressed his shoulder against the door and forced it open. He slipped inside and let go of the door, causing it to slam shut. He looked down and there was Grandmother, lying unconscious behind the front door.

He immediately knelt down at her side and tried to wake her, "Grandmother! Grandmother!" he cried. He gently shook her, but she wasn't coming around. He felt for a pulse. She was alive. Max jumped to his feet and ran straight for the phone.

"Ambulance please," he responded calmly. "My Grandmother. She's unconscious. She's on the floor. Please, you have to help her!"

Max listened carefully to the instructions he was given. The phone line wasn't long enough to carry the phone over to her, so he had to put the phone on the side and return to her. He carefully rolled her on to her side and placed her in the recovery position, just as he had been shown how to at school. She let out a quiet groan.

"It's OK grandmother, an ambulance is coming. You will be OK," he explained, hoping to reassure her.

The wait felt almost endless, but swiftly the ambulance arrived. Max took a step back and let the paramedics do what they needed to do. The paramedics agreed to let Max ride with them, and they set off for the nearest hospital. The ride to the hospital was disorientating. Soon Max wasn't even entirely sure they were still in the same city. The siren wailed against the parked cars as the blue lights reflected from the windows and shop fronts.

Grandmother was pale and weak. The paramedics had placed a mask on her face and various leads for a monitor on her chest. A bump in the road made her hand fall from the side of the trolley. Max lent forward and lovingly held it tightly. The paramedic stopped for just a moment to glance at the boy, with his black hoodie, fake gold chains and tears in his eyes.

Though the ambulance had stopped, the doors remained closed for a considerable time. Eventually the ambulance moved up again and the doors were quietly opened. The paramedics wheeled Grandmother out of the ambulance and into the Accident and Emergency department.

Bays were separated by long green curtains, while machines beeped and churned away in the background. Staff raced around and porters wheeled patients along the corridors. Children sat fidgeting in wheelchairs, while concerned parents held on tightly to the handles. Two police officers stood waiting outside one bay, while a snowboarder was carried in to another on a stretcher.

Max followed Grandmother's trolley into an empty bay. He stared silently as the paramedics transferred her onto the bed before leaving. She and the girl from Rytus, were the only people in the whole world who had ever noticed Max existed. Everyone else had always been too busy with their own lives and matters to give him any notice; or worse still, ridiculed and tormented him. It didn't matter what Max had done or not done, she was always there to listen. Even if she didn't mean it, she was always so convincing with her awe at the things Max had achieved. She adored his drawings and always complimented his fascination with history. It always felt, no matter what, that for once, he had someone on his side.

The bay burst into life as nurses swarmed Grandmother. A doctor arrived and began examining her. Max, wanting to give her the best possible chance, slowly backed out of the bay.

His phone began to buzz in his pocket. Fearing being scolded for having a phone on in the hospital, he made his way out, following the exit signs. The buzzing stopped, long before Max had managed to work his way out of the maze of corridors, where he found himself in the waiting room.

"Max!" Mother cried out, phone in hand, as she raced across to greet him. She flung her arms around him and hugged him tightly.

Hours passed before a green eyed nurse called for them from the reception desk. She led the two to a quiet side room. Mother wept uncontrollably as she broke the news. She then excused herself and left Max and Mother to console one another.

Max glanced out of the small tinted window into the waiting room. There stood Father, alone. He had finally heard about his mother and made it to the hospital. Mother looked up and watched Father sit down in the waiting room.

"I think it is time I told you the truth. It is what she would have wanted," Mother explained as she held tightly to Max's hands. She looked into Max's Demi Blood eyes as tears began to well in hers. She lent in closer and took a deep breath. "That man," she said pointing to the waiting room, "is not your father."

Chapter Twenty-Three

5,259 days before the eclipse.

"Get away from me!" Quinta demanded.

"What are you doing?" Braria asked.

"Do not question me, White Blood," Quinta snapped back.

"But..." Braria enquired, placing her hand on Quinta's wrist.

"I said get away from me!" Quinta screeched, snatching her hand away. "I should have you thrown to the wolves and torn limb from limb for even speaking to me."

Braria remained at the heel of Quinta's shadow as she paced her room. Quinta turned sharply and glared at the concerned White Blood.

"Do you have any idea what it is like to have your entire fate decided for you? To be cast into a role you did not ask for? To be pulled and torn and ripped apart until you become what is expected of you?" Quinta drew closer to Braria, maintaining her glare.

"From the moment I was born I was expected to conform. I cannot be myself. I cannot be different. I have to be who I am expected to be. I cannot do what I want. I cannot think what I want. And now! And now?" Quinta threw her hands up before slumping into a chair. "And now the gods have spoken." She grasped her forehead, trying to decipher the events at the Blue Temple. "And now I will never be an Imperatrix." Cautiously Braria approached as tears began to well in Quinta's eyes.

"He knew," Quinta sighed.

"Who?"

"The Raven. He knew."

"I do not understand..."

"Lucius!" Quinta exclaimed, sitting upright.

Before Quinta could explain anything to Braria, the thunderous steps of Tita and her guards resounded along the corridor. Tita held up her hand signalling the guards to hold position before barging into Quinta's room.

"GET OUT!" Tita bellowed, instructing Braria to leave at once.

Like a frightened pup, Braria ducked out of the room and wriggled through Tita's unhelpful guards, who were blocking the way.

"YOU!" Tita cried, her face contorted with fury, her finger pointed squarely at Quinta. "You have brought shame upon our family. You have condemned us all in the eyes of the gods!"

"But, I..."

"We are Blue Bloods. We are leaders, we are powerful, we rule the people and all of Rytus will bow to us."

"You do not understand," Quinta said, pleading with Tita to listen.

"We will have redemption before the gods. You will be made an example of, for the citizens and for Rytus!" Tita barked.

Quinta fell to her knees and grovelled before Tita.

"Please! Mother!" she begged.

Tita took a step back, away from Quinta.

"Detain this animal!" Tita demanded, signalling her guards.

Quinta crawled closer to Tita and grasped tightly to her mother's palla. She looked up at the cold, stone-like figure before her, "Please!"

Tita maintained her resolve, folded her arms and turned away.

Quinta sobbed uncontrollably as the guards entered the room.

"Mother! Please!"

Two of the guards approached Quinta and lifted her to her feet. Quinta held on to her mother's palla tightly. "No! Mother!" she screamed as the guards pulled Quinta away. Quinta held on with all her might as a guard threw her over his shoulder. Tita grabbed her palla and tugged it free of Quinta's waning grasp. Quinta screamed and kicked as hard as she could. It made little difference to Tita, Quinta felt her own heart shatter.

Quinta wept desperately as the guard carried her from the Cesar's Quarters, towards the small prison carved into the rock below the palace, usually reserved for White Bloods awaiting trial. Onlookers stopped what they were doing to watch, as the bizarre sight passed by. Braria, who had taken refuge in the gardens, ran towards Quinta, only to be stopped by the guards. Solemnly the group marched down the stairs.

Each step jarred Quinta's soul. Her family had betrayed her. The people who were meant to keep her safe from harm, had now sentenced her to death. Her brother had marked her. Her mother refused to forgive her. Now she would die, to please the gods; to please Tita.

The prison consisted of a small room, brimmed with tiny cages. It was unlit, unforgiving and unkept. The stone walls were wet, green and mossy. The bars of the cages were rusty. The straw spread about the floor was black and decaying. The smell of urine permeated the tiny room. Tita's guards prised open one of the cages and placed Quinta inside. The poignancy was not lost on the Red Bloods as they locked the cage and left without saying a word. Inaudible to the palace above and in total darkness, Quinta curled up into a ball and howled in despair. There was nothing else to do, except wait to die.

"Quinta," a voice whispered. She recoiled in horror, searching the darkness for the source. It had to be the wind, she hoped.

"Do not be afraid my child," the voice whispered.

Quinta held her breath. A thousand purple candles ignited instantaneously, bathing the prison in a warm purple glow. Quinta gasped in amazement. The Raven smiled with a mischievous grin. Quinta desperately scrambled to a far corner of the cage.

"You!" She hissed. "You condemned me! You are the reason I am to die!"

"On the contrary," the Raven suggested. "This is Tita's interpretation of the will of the gods. I am here to offer you redemption and with it, your salvation."

He placed his hand through the bars, and offered his open palm to Quinta. She examined the man before her. His hooded paenula concealed most of his face, but his purple eyes were inescapable. She felt immediately drawn to him. He leant in closer, stroking her cheek softly. Quinta felt her heart flutter. Her lips began to tremble with anticipation. She tried to fight it. Her breathing slowed. She could not escape his gaze.

It was however his actions, or rather, lack of, that had turned Tita against her own daughter. For that reason alone, Quinta withdrew further into the corner, as far away from the Raven's hand as physically possible in the tiny cage.

Disparaged, the Raven withdrew. He stared at his palm and thought silently for a moment before sitting down on the damp stone floor. Quinta felt uneasy as the Raven continued to stare at her. Realising how unsettling his actions were becoming, he broke his gaze and stared at the floor.

"I can free you," he declared, maintaining his focus on the floor.

"Free me? From this cage?"

"Yes, on one condition."

Quinta remained silent.

"I will free you, on the condition that you will travel to my temple with me. And there you will remain, until you have repented your sins before the gods."

"So I will swap one prison for another?" Quinta replied, frustrated.

"You will have the freedom afforded to my attendants."

"And what happens when I have repented my sins? What will happen to me then?"

"I will set you free," the Raven declared, looking up at Quinta to judge her response.

"And what of Tita? She will never allow such a thing," Quinta remarked.

"Come with me and you will never need fear Tita again."

Never fear Tita again? How could that truly be possible? She had little regard for the Raven's status in Rytus, let alone simply allowing him to free her godforsaken daughter from the vengeful death she probably had planned for her. Only in the afterlife could Quinta hope to no longer live in fear. Perhaps this is what the Raven meant? Either way, she surmised she had little choice in her own demise. Agreeing to the Raven's demands did come with the pleasure of denying Tita one last victory over her. What did she truly have to lose?

"And what of my child?" Quinta asked.

Shock washed over the Raven's face.

"You know you are with child?" he asked.

"Well, that is why you marked me as impure? Is it not?"

He paused before responding.

"I will raise her as one of my attendants. She will live in the sanctuary of the temple, protected by the gods."

"She?" Quinta asked with a curious smile.

"Yes," the Raven nodded, as a shy smile broke through his otherwise composed demeanour.

Refusing the Raven would spell the end for both Quinta and her unborn daughter. Accepting would perhaps, at least, wipe that smug smile of Tita's face for a while.

Whatever he had planned for her, it was the only chance her unborn daughter would get.

"I accept," Quinta declared.

The Raven leapt to his feet as the candles extinguished entirely, sinking the prison back in to total darkness.

Quinta looked around frantically. Only silence accompanied the emptiness of the bleak room. Her heart sank. A cruel trick of the mind perhaps? Quinta's head and shoulders dropped as despair set in. She began to sob as the last of her hope dissipated into the darkness.

Without warning, a slither of light penetrated the gloom, as in the Raven's place, now stood a single purple candle, its flame dancing wildly in the breeze ebbing in from beneath the prison's door.

"Follow the light," the voice whispered.

Hesitant of the true origins of the vision, Quinta gingerly shuffled forward. She reached out to place her hands on the bars of the cage. She fell forward. Quinta landed heavily on the palms of her hands. Where had the bars gone? she wondered. Before she could contemplate it further, a second purple candle illuminated the prison door.

Perhaps it was all just a conjugation of her mind, a dream by chance? Regardless, she did as instructed and approached the light. Cautiously she pushed on the door handle. It turned freely. She opened the door and stepped out.

A third candle ignited, piercing the pitch dark of the night sky; then a fourth, fifth, sixth... illuminating the way forward. Invigorated by hope, Quinta walked quickly, before running, then sprinting along the edge of the lake that separated the palace from the city. She raced past the Red Barracks and followed the light to the bridge. She looked back as the candles behind her burnt out as she passed by.

A buccina resounded from the steps of the palace, alerting the guard. A second and third buccina sounded off as the alarm was raised.

The Raven looked on from the balcony of his temple as Quinta scampered across the bridge and into the fighting pit. Raised voices clung to her heels as she cleared the sandy arena. She clattered to a halt at the towering stone wall before her. Designed to keep the wild animals from leaping from the pit, Quinta was now trapped.

The footsteps of the Red Bloods echoed along the walls of the palace, growing louder as they drew nearer. Quinta looked around desperately, searching for the next candle.

There, on the top row!

She ran to the large section of tree trunk used by the Red Bloods to train. With enormous ferocity and determination, she hauled the cumbersome trunk to the edge of the pit. She clawed her way up and on to the splintered trunk, leaving behind a trail of blue blood. She pulled herself on to the first row of seats.

Nearly exhausted, Quinta climbed the rows before following the candles to the street west of the fighting pit. The Raven returned inside the temple to prepare for her arrival.

Quinta paused momentarily to catch her breath. She looked at her torn and ragged hands, dripping with blood. The next series of candles ignited. Drained, but determined, Quinta followed the light to the discreet door of the attendant's quarters.

She placed her hand on the door and took a deep breath.

"Stop!" a voice demanded.

Quinta turned sharply in its direction.

Aegle, one of the Raven's attendants, stood before her, clutching a grey palla.

"Please," Aegle pleaded, "do not do this."

Quinta, shocked, removed her hand from the door.

"He speaks of freedom, but you will never be free. You will not be safe here. You will not be safe in this city."

"I do not understand..." Quinta responded.

"We do not have much time. Take this palla. Take it and run!"

"Where will I go?"

"The Dying Woods."

"I do not know how to get..."

"Follow the road west. Hidden from sight is the home of a Green Blood. I know her well; she will protect you. She will see that you are safe from harm, and safe from him."

The moonlight caught Aegle's eyes as she leant forward to present the palla. Her green and grey eyes were a whole new phenomenon to Quinta. She had heard stories of the Demi Bloods, but had also been led to believe they had been wiped out in the holy war; and any subsequent incarnations had been hunted like wild animals by the purists, in the names of the gods.

Dumbfounded, Quinta accepted the palla. Aegle tried to fasten the palla, but without the pin it was difficult to keep it together. Aegle tutted loudly before spotting the swan fibula clinging by a thread to Quinta's tunic.

"The gods favour us!" She declared excitedly, before fixing the palla from the back, so as to hide the grandeur of the fibula from prying eyes.

"Over here, I have found blood!" A Red Blood exclaimed loudly in the fighting pit.

"May the gods bless you," Aegle said, blessing Quinta. "Now, run!"

Quinta drew up her hood and sprinted in to the maze of White Blood insulas, heading for the Western Gate.

Quinta slowed her pace as she approached the gate to avoid alerting the guards. She made sure her face and blooded hands were concealed.

"Hey! You!" the guard on the gate called out pointing towards Quinta. Certain she could not out run the guard she maintained her stance and continued towards the gate.

"You there! Stop! I want to talk to you!" the guard persisted.

Nervously Quinta began to tremble with fear.

The guard approached.

Quinta closed her eyes and held her breath.

The guard marched towards her, brushed past her and confronted the man behind, "I know you! You are a wanted man!"

Relieved, Quinta pushed on and ran from the city.

Outside the city's walls, the air seemed colder and more unforgiving. Deep snow lay undisturbed at the side of the road. The sky, lit up with the burning effigies of the gods, rolled on, uninterrupted to the horizon. Quinta was free, but she was alone.

Following Aegle's advice, she followed the road west. She crossed a bridge and was immediately presented with a fork in the road. To Quinta's left the road disappeared in a straight line into the distance to Eagle Blood Shores, to her right, the Blue Mountains, and ahead stood trees, a lot of trees.

"Hidden from sight?" Quinta remarked on the advice from Aegle, "How am I meant to find it, if it is hidden from sight?" Hesitantly, Quinta stepped into the woods.

She marched on as the undergrowth grew thicker. Her palla dragged behind her, along the fallen branches and thorn bushes until it became snagged, as she entered a snowy clearing. Quinta bent down and carefully freed the fabric from the branches.

The silence of the desolate woods was shattered by the howl of a wolf nearby. Quinta turned quickly. She could not see the wolf. Cautiously, she stood up.

A snarl to her left, a growl to her right. She was not alone anymore.

Her instincts told her to run, but she was tired and afraid. She remained motionless.

A flash of fangs in the moonlight. The glimmer of red eyes, focused on her every move. With their powerful hind legs and agile paws, the wolves quickly surrounded her.

Quinta held her breath.

A black wolf approached, teeth bared. Two more appeared following in the footsteps of the first. Ears pinned back, head lowered, muscles poised to pounce. All they needed now was for Quinta to turn and run.

Quinta turned and leapt into a sprint, the wolves gave chase.

With ease they kept at her heels, almost at a trot. The black alpha wolf led the pack, and any wolf that dared to snap at Quinta's heels was immediately warned off. Their prey was still a threat. They would have to chase her until she tired too much to fight back. Besides, he was enjoying the chase.

Quinta glanced back as the alpha closed in. A fallen branch lay ahead. Quinta turned too late to see it. She tripped and fell into the snow.

The alpha leapt on to her back, biting and clawing, anything to draw her attention. She only needed to turn her head slightly to allow the others a clean shot at her neck.

Her arms flayed as she struggled to defend herself from the alpha. She screamed, turned her head and struck the alpha on the side of his muzzle.

The waiting wolf launched, seizing her neck in his razor sharp teeth, dragging her on to her back. The agony of the punctures, although significant, was inconsequential to the pressure of the jaws clamping down on her, as she collapsed into the melting snow. The remaining wolves tore into her, ripping flesh from bone.

As the snarls of the wolves drowned out all other sound, Quinta looked up at the assortment of matted wolf fur and blue blood. She felt her blood trickle down her arms as the stale breath of the wolves bore down on her. Quinta lost consciousness.

Chapter Twenty-Four

"Anything?" Laelia asked.

Alpheaus, glanced out of the window before shaking his head. Laelia placed her hand over her heart, sighed mournfully and stared into Dianus's eyes. Dianus, cradled in her arm, looked up at her before letting out a gentle giggle which made Laelia smile again.

"I am sorry," Petrina said, sat on the hard wooden floor.

"Nonsense child," Laelia responded, "you brought us much needed food. I am sure Otho will return shortly and he will regale us with tales of his adventures, as he always does." Laelia placed her hand on Petrina's shoulder and smiled reassuringly.

Laboured footsteps thumped against the steps leading up to the top floor. "Otho!" Laelia declared excitedly, handing Dianus to Petrina. Laelia threw open the door and approached the stairs to greet her husband. The sight horrified her, made her stomach turn and her legs feel weak. Otho staggered towards her, his face and body a contorted mess of dried white blood, bruising and deep wounds. Celsus, one of the men from the group, supported

Otho's weight. He too bore the wounds of the fight, but he had fared much better than his friend. Laelia stood aghast as the two men made it through the open door and into Alpheaus's insula.

"Please, here..." Alpheaus gestured towards a chair.

Celsus carefully lowered his friend before seating himself down on the floor, exhausted. Petrina gave Dianus back to Laelia and collected two cups from the table. She left the room to collect water.

"Otho?" Laelia pleaded, "What happened?"

Celsus wiped his own face with the back of his hand before responding. "Damned Red Bloods..." he paused to catch his breath again, "...slaughtered the lot of them, we only just made it out alive. Unlucky nothus!"

Shocked, Laelia turned to Alpheaus for help.

"He needs a medicus," Alpheaus reasoned.

"You will be lucky to find one of late," Laelia explained.

Alpheaus tried to respond but was held back by a fierce coughing fit.

"It is you who needs the medicus friend," Celsus remarked.

Alpheaus braced himself against the wall before bringing his fit under control. "There is a Green Blood that owes me favour..." he coughed. "He may be able to help. He resides in the Ruinae. I will fetch him."

"You are in no fit state to leave the insula," Laelia replied.

"She is right," Celsus remarked. "I will go."

"He will not know you," Alpheaus spluttered.

"No, but he will know me," Petrina declared as she re-entered the room.

Petrina handed a cup of water to Celsus and one to Laelia for Otho.

"No!" Alpheaus demanded. "I will not send you to the Ruinae."

Celsus took a sip of water before passing it to Alpheaus. Alpheaus, unable to continue talking for a moment, stopped to take a sip from the cup.

"I can go with him," Petrina declared, pointing to Celsus, afraid to explain that she had already been there just two days before.

Alpheaus banged the cup down on the table, startling Laelia. "I will not allow it!"

Otho began to cough and splutter as blood began to fill his lungs.

"He needs Ferox, or he will die!" Petrina shouted.

"Please," Laelia begged.

Alpheaus looked at Celsus and sighed, "You promise no harm will come to her?"

"Promise."

Alpheaus searched desperately for another solution, another answer, but his efforts were in vain.

"Very well..." he conceded.

Petrina smiled broadly.

"...you are not to leave his side," Alpheaus declared to Petrina, pointing towards Celsus.

"I will keep her safe," Celsus pledged. "Now, where in the Ruinae are we to find this Ferox?"

Petrina and Celsus made their way down the stairs and out into the street.

"What is your name?" Petrina asked.

"Celsus. Yours?"

"Petrina."

"Oh," Celsus responded, not entirely sure how to maintain a conversation with a girl Petrina's age. "Your dad..."

"Alpheaus."

"Oh, I see," he replied lumberingly. "Unusual to see a Father and Daughter," he jested. Petrina did not respond. Keen to ease the awkward tension, Celsus gestured for Petrina to lead the way. Petrina accepted.

The smell of faeces hung heavy in the air, along with the smell of damp and rotting wood. It was not how she remembered it. Petrina felt afraid but Celsus strode in like he was home.

"Now, Alpheaus was a bit sketchy on this part," Celsus said.

"Perhaps we should ask for directions," Petrina suggested.

"Not wise little sparrow. If you want to keep your guts inside you, it is probably best we do not speak to anyone."

The very idea made Petrina hold tightly onto her stomach.

They began working their way along the alleyways, stepping carefully over the unconscious drunks strewn across them.

"Stick close girl, 'lot of thieves and murderers here..." Petrina held tightly onto Celsus's arm, as a man muttering to himself barged past. "...and those of ill mind," Celsus concluded. They turned a corner and entered into a small courtyard. Dotted around the edges were women wearing togas.

"Why do these women wear togas?" Petrina enquired.

"They are whores," Celsus explained. "Wait here."

"But..."

"I will return shortly."

Petrina felt very afraid and lost. She had no idea where she was, or how to get home.

"Oh, here is a pretty one," a drunken man blurted as he wobbled towards Petrina.

Heeding Celsus's advice, Petrina remained silent, held tightly onto her stomach and attempted to avoid eye contact.

"Playing hard to get are we?" the drunk jested. "Here, let me just..." he placed his hand on Petrina's leg. Petrina froze. The drunken man began to run his hand further up.

"Back off!" Celsus demanded, charging back towards Petrina.

"I saw her first!" remarked the drunk.

"I said, BACK OFF!" Celsus bellowed, pushing the drunken man away from Petrina. He stumbled and fell to the floor, cursing Celsus.

"Come, this way," Celsus explained, clutching Petrina tightly. They made their way out of the courtyard and into an alleyway.

"I should not have left your side," Celsus asked. "Are you alright?"

Petrina nodded and wiped away a tear.

"I am sorry. I will never leave your side again."

Petrina tried to smile.

"Come, I have directions, the sooner we find this Ferox, the sooner we can leave," Celsus declared.

Celsus led Petrina through the alleyway until they entered a larger courtyard. "There," he said, gesturing towards a large wooden building on the other side.

"Just as father described," Petrina said enthused, "with the drawing of Fecunditas above the door."

Petrina stepped forward, Celsus stopped her.

"You see that man?" Celsus asked.

"The one sat on the steps?" Petrina replied.

"Know why he waits?" Celsus challenged.

"No."

"He is an Orange Blood; he is waiting for a target."

"A target?"

"Right now, inside, someone is spending their last day having the time of their life," Celsus jested.

"Well, if it is his last day, why is the Orange Blood waiting for him?"

"Who do you think makes sure it is his last day?"

"The Raven?"

"Oh sweet innocent child," Celsus smiled.

They made their way across the courtyard and entered the large wooden building.

"Hail Dominus," a woman dressed in a toga greeted. "Oh," she said spotting Petrina, "you are here looking for the Domina." Before Celsus or Petrina could explain, she called back towards the administrator seated in a room at the back, "Another one for you."

"Another? Domina simply cannot afford to keep buying these girls. It is getting out of hand. Can they not sell her to the farms instead?" he shouted back.

"Forgiveness," Celsus said, bowing to the whore. "We are looking for a Green Blood called Ferox." The woman stared back blankly, shrugged her shoulders and walked off.

Celsus looked at Petrina, "Now what?"

"Ask him," Petrina suggested, pointing towards the room at the back.

Gingerly Celsus approached the source of the voice. Petrina stayed close to his heel, she felt uneasy. The excited screams were frightening, and the whole establishment smelt musky.

"Forgiveness," Celsus said interrupting the administrator.

"What?" he barked back.

"I er..."

"I do not have all day. Do you not see that we are busy?" he said, pointing to the giggling women leading men through the building to private rooms.

"We are looking for a Green Blood called Ferox..."

"People come here to forget who they are. Not to be reminded by a White Blood who lost a fight and his little girl."

"But I..."

"If you are not paying get out!" the administrator barked.

"I just..."

"I said GET OUT!"

The administrator stood up and slammed the door in Celsus's face.

"I think that went quite well," Celsus said jokingly.

Petrina did not laugh.

"You seek Ferox?" a voice behind them enquired.

"Yes," Celsus responded as he turned to face the woman.

She held out her hand and gestured for coin.

Celsus sighed before unbuttoning his paenula. He reached under his tunic and began to fiddle with something hidden inside. He continued to struggle for a little while longer before producing a coin purse. The woman looked where Celsus had been fiddling and began withdrawing.

"Ten denarii," Celsus declared forcing the coins in to her hand.

She returned a look of disgust.

"Twenty denarii?" Celsus asked, producing more coin.

"Thirty," the woman insisted.

"THIRTY?" Celsus turned and quietly counted the coin he had left.

"Twenty-five," he said with a big grin on his face.

"Twenty-seven," she demanded.

"Fine, twenty-seven," he sighed, placing all of his coins and his coin purse into her waiting hand.

"Ferox, the Green Blood. He has gone to the Raven's Temple, to..." she paused trying to think how best to phrase it, "... to repent." She snatched shut her hand and sauntered off into another room, closing the door behind her.

"The Raven's Temple? Well we know where that is!" Celsus said optimistically.

"But where are we now?" Petrina responded.

"Ah..."

The pair stepped out of the malodorous lupanarium, into the sunlit courtyard. It took more than a moment for their eyes to adjust.

"The Orange Blood? He will know how to get out of the Ruinae," Petrina suggested, pointing to the man still sat on the steps. Celsus nodded and the pair approached.

"The Raven's Temple?" The Orange Blood replied, "Follow the babies!" he said, as he pointed to one of the temple's attendants placing neatly wrapped bundles into a hand cart.

"Babies?" Petrina queried.

A White Blood stepped out of the lupanarium, nearly colliding with the group. He too struggled to adjust to the contrasting light.

"Excuse me," the Orange Blood said apologetically to Petrina and Celsus, as he stood up and stepped past them. He approached the White Blood man.

"Filbertus?" the Orange Blood enquired.

The man nodded.

"Good," the Orange Blood declared drawing his blade.

"To the temple," Celsus declared pushing Petrina away from the soon to be bloodied scene.

The pair followed the attendant and her cart, until they were clear of the Ruinae.

"I doubt we have much time," Celsus observed.

"Let us hurry," Petrina replied as she broke into a sprint.

They raced through the bustling streets straight to the steps of the temple. There, they were greeted by a crowd of citizens seeking the Raven's guidance.

"How will we ever find Ferox now?" Petrina asked. Celsus took her hand and led Petrina past those waiting on the steps and made for the temple.

"Stop!" an attendant from the temple demanded. "The Raven is not to be disturbed on this day."

"I beg your forgiveness," Celsus requested, "We do not seek the Raven."

The attendant raised her eyebrow, "Then, do tell, why you are here?"

"We seek a Green Blood, a friend."

"This is not a social hall. This is a temple; it is a place of worship," she barked blocking their path.

Celsus growled with frustration before turning back.

"What will we do now?" Petrina asked.

"I do not know," Celsus responded, sitting down on the steps.

"We could return to father, ask him for..."

"Alpheaus?" Celsus rebuffed, his words catching the attention of a mysterious man lurking in the shadows. "Alpheaus is stubborn and foolish."

"Take that back at once!" Petrina demanded.

"Forgiveness child, I am tired. It has been a long day."

"Petrina?" the man in the shadows enquired. "Is that truly you?"

Petrina spun around to face the man, "Ferox?"

The man withdrew his hood and stepped out of the shadows. His face was ragged and scarred, his voice hoarse and raspy. He walked with a limp, and looked weak and malnourished.

"Ferox?" Celsus asked, hopeful there had been a misunderstanding.

Ferox ignored Celsus and instead chose to concentrate solely on Petrina. "You have grown so tall," he commented.

Petrina smiled.

"What of your father?" he asked.

"He is sick, but he will not accept my help," Petrina explained.

"Then your friend is right, he is as stubborn and as foolish now as the day I first met him," he replied with a sly smile in Celsus's direction. "Now tell me child, who were you looking for?"

Ferox listened with great interest as Petrina explained everything that had happened at the bakery, and everything that had happened since.

"And this man carried Otho all the way back from Falcon Reach?" he asked, gesturing to Celsus. Petrina nodded. "Truly a friend to cherish," Ferox surmised. "It is true, I do owe Alpheaus my life and he must truly wish to help this Otho if he sent you, his dear Petrina, into the Ruinae to look for me..." he paused, stroking his stubbly beard, "...very well. I will do what I can."

Petrina leapt for joy. Celsus slowly rose to his feet, a little anxious of the frail Green Blood's power. The trio descended the steps of the temple and joined the hum of the streets below.

"APAGE!" A Red Blood called out as he charged through the crowd.

Ferox drew up his hood and stepped sideward, into the shadows of the tall insulas. Petrina, taking his lead, also stepped aside.

"Damned Red Bloods," Celsus muttered as the Red Blood brushed past. Normally the Red Blood would have stopped to confront the cocky White Blood, this time however, he continued on with haste.

The commotion and chatter grew louder as the trio approached Petrina's home. As they turned the final corner they were forced to stop immediately.

Five Red Bloods stood watch at the door to the insula, while White Bloods stood just out of reach cursed, spat and jeered.

"Nothus!" They cried.

"Murderers!" They sneered.

Petrina began to fight her way through the crowds, only for Celsus to grab her and pull her back.

"What are you doing?" he queried.

"Father..." she cried.

"Have you lost your mind?" Celsus asked with concern.

Without warning, the doors to the insula swung open. Four Red Bloods stepped out, clutching tightly to Otho and Alpheaus.

"FATHER!" Petrina cried out, as she tried to jostle her way through the crowd.

"NO!" Celsus shouted grabbing Petrina tightly by the arm.

"But I..."

"NO!" he demanded, pulling her in tightly.

Otho's feet dragged against the flag stone, his head unsupported. It was impossible to tell if he was conscious from their position behind the crowds. Alpheaus's face was bloodied and swollen, but he was able to walk, slowly.

The crowd surged forward to challenge the Red Bloods.

"STAY BACK!" the Red Bloods commanded.

"Let me go!" Petrina cried out.

"Be quiet girl," Ferox demanded. "You will see us taken too."

"I do not care, let me go!" she demanded.

Ferox glared at Celsus to shut her up. Petrina kicked out as Celsus held on tightly, lifting her from the floor; her screams muffled by his hand.

The Red Bloods formed a defensive line as the crowd surged again. Celsus was knocked off balance and Petrina managed to work her way free of his grasp. She leapt forward. Ferox reached out and grabbed her hand.

"We are White Bloods!" the crowd began to chant. "We are strength! We are the people!" they screamed, as they began pelting the Red Bloods with rocks.

Ferox grasped tightly to Petrina. She immediately froze as his aura began to take control over hers. He closed his eyes and she went limp.

The crowd surged forward again. The Red Bloods drew their gladius swords.

"Take her," Ferox cried out to Celsus, his eyes still tightly closed, as the trauma of Petrina's earlier years began to fill his mind.

The crowd rushed backwards, knocking Petrina into the waiting arms of Celsus. Ferox fell back with the crowd, losing his grip on Petrina. She awoke.

The Red Bloods charged the crowd, slicing any citizen foolishly close.

Ferox staggered back towards them, as the Red Bloods drew dangerously near. Petrina opened her mouth to scream as Ferox grasped the two White Bloods. He pushed them both back against the insula. With just seconds to spare Ferox closed his eyes, "Vanesco!" The trio disappeared into the shadows.

Petrina sobbed quietly, as the Red Bloods struck down the White Bloods who weren't quick enough to get away. Ferox remained focused on his quiet chanting, while Celsus felt only guilt.

Satisfied, the Red Bloods returned to the street outside the insula, dragging Otho away. Ferox broke his trance, and the trio stepped out from the shadows, gingerly.

Petrina watched helplessly, clinging to the paenula of Celsus, as the Red Bloods ordered Alpheaus to walk on. Dragging his feet and with his head hung low, Alpheaus obeyed their commands. "Father," she sobbed, as Ferox tried to comfort the young girl. Petrina felt heartbroken, as her father disappeared into the sea of Red Bloods, fearing that she may never see him again.

Chapter Twenty-Five

5,258 days before the eclipse.

"Where is Quinta?" Marcus muttered impatiently as he paced back and forth. "My instructions were clear. Her salvation lies here, with me."

Aegle maintained her silence as she continued to scrub the floor.

Marcus slammed his fists down on the table, startling Aegle. "They must have captured her," he declared. Aegle turned her head away from Marcus and smiled smugly.

Marcus roared with frustration, "They continue to mock me, reducing my propositions to nothing but ash and cinder." He smashed his fists against the stone wall of his quarters. "How much longer am I to wait before they are to answer for their crimes?"

He turned from the wall and cried out loudly as the resentment continued to build inside. "I will go to the palace. I will confront Tita!"

Aegle dropped the scrubbing brush, the smile now absent from her face.

"I have toiled for too long to allow this to slip through my fingers now," Marcus declared, as he collected his paenula.

A look of horror radiated from Aegle's face. If Marcus found out what she had done, he surely would have no choice but to cast her far from Rytus. She jumped to her feet.

Marcus charged for the steps to the temple above. Aegle opened her mouth to speak. She hadn't spoken out of turn for days, not since Marcus had embraced Acquilina. She paused. Speaking now could draw suspicion; raise questions that she could not answer. She stepped back. Better to let him go now and use the time he was absent to plan her escape, she thought.

Marcus ascended the stairs, putting on his paenula as he climbed the steps. He had no time to stop. Adelia, on spotting her master, ran to his side.

"I am to go to the palace," Marcus proclaimed, as he marched on.

"Forgiveness Dominus, a large crowd has gathered to seek your council. May I suggest it unwise to leave by the front?" Adelia suggested dutifully.

Marcus nodded in agreement, "Thank you." He turned on his heels, his purple paenula splaying out as he turned. He raced into the attendant's quarters and reached for the modest door out on to the street. He turned the handle and stepped out.

Making his way through the marketplace mid-morning would be unfavourable. The hum of citizens going about their daily business would halt. Each would stop to seek his council or to wish blessings on their misfortune. Marcus was angry. He wanted to confront Tita, now! He turned east and climbed the steps to the fighting pit instead. He stepped out on to the top row of seats and sprinted down towards the pit. He jumped down into the wet sand and turned to face the gated entrance.

He stomped through the pit and passed the gate. He strode across the bridge, his arms bent at the elbow, into the grounds of the Red Barracks. Inside, a handful of Red Bloods rose from their seated position to watch the Raven march past.

Marcus hurried along to the steps of the palace. With no direct orders from Tita to guide them, the Red Bloods allowed him to pass through unchallenged. He bolted up the stairs and made his way into the grounds. Marcus turned towards the quarters of the Imperators.

"To think I was beginning to doubt the gods," Lucius cried out, his hands clasped tightly together.

Marcus stopped and turned to face Lucius.

"You received the summons!" Lucius declared excitedly.

Marcus glared back, confused.

"To speak with Tita?"

What summons? Marcus had not received any notes from the palace for two days, or anyone else, now he came to think about it.

"She will not speak with anyone," Lucius explained. "She will only speak to you, she sent for you."

"Yes," Marcus responded, still a little bewildered, "that is why I am here."

"Please," Lucius beckoned, his arm outstretched to indicate the way.

Marcus followed Lucius to the chamber below the quarters of the Imperators. Two Red Bloods stood guard, making Marcus nervous of Tita's true intent. Lucius glared at the Red Bloods, as he waited for the door to be opened. Lucius stepped forward to proceed, only to be stopped by the Red Bloods. Lucius stepped back. Marcus stepped forward and entered the chamber.

Inside, Tita sat silently and alone at the end of a large table. The door was slammed shut behind him. Tita looked up. Her eyes were blood shot. She looked like she had not slept in days.

"Praise be to the gods," she declared with relief. "Please, sit!" she requested, pointing to the chair nearest to her.

Marcus looked around the room. It didn't seem to be a trap. There didn't appear to be any Red Bloods waiting behind the columns or in the shadows. As best he could tell, it was just the two of them. He approached the chair, pulled it back and sat down facing Tita.

She sighed heavily. "I have failed you and I have failed Rytus," she said solemnly.

Who was this woman sat before Marcus? She wasn't the terrifying Blue Blood who'd normally scream her demands in his face. She wasn't the strong and remarkable reflection of the epitome of a Blue Blood. His anger almost dissipated momentarily. Here was Tita, just as afraid and vulnerable as the gods had initially intended. He respectfully clasped his hands together and placed them on his lap. Unsure how to respond and keen to hear Tita's thoughts, he sat silently, listening.

"I tried to remain strong. I suspended my selfish wants and desires. I raised my children in the ways of old. I respected my position; for the good of Rytus, no matter the cost," she explained, as she dropped her head and the tears began to fall. "I did everything that was expected of me. I have lived by the code. I have done everything that has been demanded of me," she declared, as her tone became angrier. "The gods in return hold Servius in eternal slumber. My husband abandons the grounds of the palace to lie with the whores of the Ruinae. My son has no respect for the code, or the citizens of Rytus. And my daughter..." she paused, her tone changing to one of despair, "...my daughter will never be an Imperatrix." She stopped and looked to Marcus as he looked solemnly at the floor. "You had to do what is expected of you, expected of all of us," she declared, rising to her feet. "And now the gods have snatched her from my grasp," she proclaimed walking past the back of Marcus's chair.

From her grasp? Then she does not have Quinta? Marcus surmised.

Tita turned to face the wall behind Marcus, "Why do the gods continue to punish us?" She walked back towards her own chair. "Continue to punish me?" She spun on the spot and dropped to her knees before Marcus. She placed her hands on his, and looked up at him, her eyes continuing to well with tears.

"I offered them my own daughter, only for her to be cruelly snatched away. Tell me Raven, PLEASE! What more do the gods want of me?" she pleaded.

Marcus was stunned. He had no idea how to respond to her. This was not why he had come to the palace at all. His heart began to race. He became tense, withdrawing his hands from Tita's.

Tita looked down, realising what she had done. She quickly withdrew her hands to her chest and rose to her feet.

"I beg forgiveness," she requested, returning to her chair.

Marcus rose from his seat. It was evident Tita did not know where Quinta was, and time was slipping away.

Marcus began to leave but paused. Tita was weak and desperate. Forging an alliance now could prove useful when the time came to strike. He placed his hand on her shoulder.

"Before the dawn there must be darkness. Before the flower there must be dirt. Before the feast there must be slaughter." He removed his hand and approached the door, "Retribution will claim the unjust. The righteous will rise to the new day. You have my word."

Tita watched silently as Marcus left, the door closing softly behind him.

"What did she say?" Lucius demanded.

"I must return to the temple with great haste," Marcus explained, leaving Lucius to flounder in his wake. He charged through the grounds and descended the steps. With no time to confront the crowds, he raced back past the Red Barracks and over the bridge. Keen to not have to scramble up the walls of the pit, he made his way up the steps to the Swan's Nest and bolted to the edge of the platform. He leapt from the white marble precipice and landed gracefully on the middle row of the seats of the fighting pit below. He hurried down the steps on the far side and towards the discreet door to his attendant's quarters.

He stopped. Something on the door caught his attention. He leant in closer. It was blood, blue blood. A faint hand print now became evident, someone had tried to wipe it off, but it was there, just. Quinta had been here! She had made it to the door. But where was she now? he wondered.

Marcus closed his eyes and placed his finger tips on the bloodied hand print. His mind screamed with a thousand images of the events that unfolded, all at once. Marcus staggered back from the door. He caught his breath and approached the door again. He placed his hand on the hand print and closed his eyes.

Instantly, Marcus was immersed in the moment. There stood Quinta, talking to a woman. Marcus gasped. It was one of his attendants, though he couldn't make out which one. Quinta accepted a grey palla, the attendant fastened it using Quinta's swan fibula. The Dying Woods? What lay in the Dying Woods? The moment became sketchy and disconnected. The moment flashed forward to the howls of wolves, Quinta's screams and the tearing of flesh.

Marcus recoiled. His heart racing, he stood breathless. He had been betrayed. His heart sank. He needed confirmation. He opened the door and stepped inside. He ran down the steps to his quarters and flung open the hangings over the wall of names. He grabbed a torch and started searching the wall.

"No!" he cried out, running his fingers over the stone. "NO!" he screamed as Quinta's name began to turn to sand beneath his fingertips. He raised his fists in anger before slamming them against the almost barren spot where her name was once solidly set. His plans in ruins, his trust betrayed. He raised his hands in the air and screamed furiously.

Quinta was to give him a pure blood child which, despite the powers he had been gifted and those that he had taught himself, was something he could never hope to achieve again in his lifetime. Obtaining Decimus had taken nearly all he had, and now to fulfil the expectations of the citizens of Rytus, he would have to find a child to take Quinta's place.

His legs went weak. He quickly sat down on the floor. He brought his knees to his chest and sat silently, alone in his quarters. This could be his downfall, everything that he had planned, everything he had worked for, destroyed.

"No!" he declared, "I will not fail *her*." He rose to his feet. In defiance, he strode over to the wall, collected a jagged rock from the floor and began scratching in a name. "We have sacrificed too much to give up now, I will finish this," he declared before drawing the hangings closed.

He confidently climbed the stairs from his quarters and grasped Aegle by her shoulder. "It is time," he declared. She froze. "It is time for the cutting," Marcus concluded.

"As you wish Dominus," she responded dutifully.

Marcus returned to his quarters. Aegle sighed with relief before summoning the other attendants. They extinguished the candles in the temple, dismissed the waiting crowds and filed into Marcus's quarters.

Marcus collected a battered chunk of wood from the corner of his room, before settling down in a chair. His attendants circled around him, preparing a fluid of Tyrian purple, while others worked together to sharpen a small blade. Marcus lent back in the chair, tilting his head as far back as he could. He stared at the ceiling, clutched tightly to the wood, and entered a trance like state.

Two of his attendants placed their hands on his head, holding it tightly in position. Another held open his left eyelid, while a fourth approached with the sharpened blade. A fifth and sixth stood close by with the prepared Tyrian fluid. Another pair held down his hands and legs to prevent him kicking or striking out. The remaining pair stood by with cloths to soak up the blood and straps to tie Marcus down if required.

Marcus took a deep breath. "Begin," he commanded.

He flinched as the sharpened blade cut into the scar tissue around his iris. The attendant held her nerve as she followed the scar around a quarter of the circumference. Another stepped forward, and using a highly polished strip of wood, guided a few drops of the Tyrian fluid into Marcus's open eye.

Marcus squeezed the battered wood in his hand tightly, as he grunted in pain. The Tyrian fluid penetrated his fading-grey iris, turning it intensely purple. And though the ceremony had rendered him in time, totally blind in that eye, it did not stop the pain. An attendant stepped forward and with care, soaked up any remaining fluid before sealing the wound again with the embers of the tip of a burning wick. Marcus continued to grunt in pain as his attendants washed away any remaining debris with cold water.

They released their master and stepped back. Marcus remained in the chair, frozen in the same position. Breathing heavily, cursing the gods. The attendants collected up their paraphernalia and retreated.

Aegle was the last to leave. She looked back at her master. Though she had great conviction in her actions, she could not help but feel remorse. He had taken her in when no-one else would, and in a moment of jealousy she had betrayed his trust.

Marcus, sensing Aegle's lingering presence, turned his head in her direction. She raised her head to meet his gaze. The recognition was instant. The vision at the door, the attendant that had betrayed him; It was her! It was Aegle! Her eyes were unmistakable. No other in his care had eyes like hers.

"You," he cried out, still weakened by the cutting ceremony.

Aegle stood in silence, convulsed by her own guilt.

"Why?" he asked, turning towards her, falling from the chair.

Aegle turned and ran from his quarters.

"WHY?" he screamed, as he clambered to his feet and gave chase.

Aegle charged for the steps pushing the other attendants out of her path. Marcus came charging after her. She reached the top of the temple's steps before Marcus caught her. He leapt into the air, crashing into her. She tumbled down the first flight of steps, landing in a heap.

Marcus climbed to his feet. In the street below, citizens stopped to observe the commotion. Keen to contain the situation, Marcus descended the steps and collected up Aegle. The onlookers stood dumbstruck, including the two Red Bloods who had been patrolling the street. Marcus's steps cut loudly through the silence, as he ascended the steps of the temple, carrying Aegle back inside.

The two Red Bloods exchanged glances, "What was that about?" one asked.

"I do not know, brother," the other responded as he began to head up the steps to investigate.

The attendants looked on with concern as Marcus carried Aegle to the back of the temple, to the attendant's quarters. He carried her into the centre of the large dormitory, and placed her down carefully on the table in the middle. He sighed heavily and stroked her forehead, torn by the deep seated affection he held for her and the bitter sting of betrayal.

Aegle awoke, and upon sighting Marcus stood over her, let out a blood curdling scream. Alerted, the Red Blood ran into the temple and followed the sound of her screams and protests.

"You there," the Red Blood called out directed at Marcus.

Marcus spun around, "How dare you?" he sneered.

The attendants backed away to the edges of the room, as Aegle lay screaming in fear on the table.

"What have you done to her?"

"This is of no business to you, Red Blood," Marcus scoffed.

"Let her go!"

"Get out!" Marcus demanded.

"No!" the Red Blood declared defiantly, drawing his gladius.

Marcus dropped his hands and stood up straight, "You will do as I command!"

"She needs help," the Red Blood declared as he stepped left, trying to step around Marcus.

"Then you leave me with no choice," Marcus condemned.

Marcus charged for the Red Blood. Not expecting the Raven to resort to physical violence, the Red Blood was caught off guard, sending him and Marcus flying backwards down the three steps to the bunks below. The Red Blood clattered onto the floor, his gladius resounding against the stone as it fell from his grasp. Without thinking it through properly, Marcus swung for the Red Blood, smashing his knuckles against the Red Blood's cold metal helmet.

"Concacavi!" Marcus cried out clutching his bloodied fist.

The Red Blood jumped to his feet, collected Marcus by his waist and charged him back against the marble wall. Marcus gasped as the air escaped his lungs, winding him.

Marcus, learning from his previous mistake, ripped the Red Blood's helmet off and used it to clout the Red Blood across the face. The Red Blood staggered backwards. He reached out to his right and collected one of the attendant's cooking pots. He threw it at Marcus. Marcus ducked. The pot smashed against the white marble.

Marcus gathered his breath and raced back towards the middle of the room, passed the Red Blood, and collected the gladius sword from the floor. The Red Blood turned towards Marcus and extended his hand, commanding Marcus to halt. Marcus charged at the Red Blood, sword poised. The Red Blood rebuffed the sword's cut with his thick leather cuffs, pushing Marcus back against the table. The final heavy blow caused the Red Blood to drop to his knees.

Marcus raised the sword to deliver the fatal hit, "You should not have meddled with the affairs of the temple."

Marcus felt the cold blade slice into the core of his back. He tensed up. The pain scattered quickly as anger overwhelmed him. He brought the sword crashing down. The blade smashed into the Red Blood's skull. Red blood sprayed on to Marcus's paenula as the Red Blood fell backwards. He clattered against the floor, as a gush of red blood pooled about his head, collecting on the white marble floor.

Marcus turned towards Aegle, the sharpened blade still dripping with purple blood, firmly in her hand. "I have shown you nothing but kindness," he remarked. "Why have you betrayed me again?" he pleaded.

Aegle still lay on the table, open mouthed, staring up at her master. "My life has been nothing but torment," she cried, snatching the gladius from Marcus. She climbed to her knees, positioning the tip at Marcus's throat. "You talk of freedom, but I will never be truly free. But by this sword..." she quickly withdrew the gladius and spun the sword around.

"NO!" Marcus screamed, as he tried to stop her.

With conviction, she thrust the sword into her own chest. "...I will be free at last."

Chapter Twenty-Six

5,258 days before the eclipse.

"Bloody idiot," Velius muttered, removing his helmet as he entered the Red Barracks. No-one paid him any attention. Instead, Velius marched straight up to Publius. "Arminius has deserted his patrol," he reported smugly.

Publius sighed. He placed down the sword he was inspecting and turned to face Velius. "Yes?" he asked, having not listened to Velius properly.

"Arminius has deserted his patrol," he repeated, the smile growing rapidly across his face.

"So why are you telling me?" Publius responded coldly.

Velius looked surprised.

"Go and find him," Publius commanded with a condescending tone.

"Well I know where he is," Velius replied much to Publius's disapproval. "I am not going in there to get him though."

Publius rose from his seat and stood towering over Velius. "Are you disobeying a command?" he bellowed.

Velius stepped back, his bottom lip trembling. "He went into the Raven's Temple and ...." He snivelled.

"Go, find him and bring him back here to me!" Publius demanded.

"But..."

"GET OUT!" Publius barked.

Velius ran out of the barracks, almost bursting into tears as he went.

"Aulus, Darius, go hold his hand," Publius commanded pointing towards the door, before sitting back down and picking up the sword again.

"Wait up," Darius cried out, as they gave chase.

"I do not need your help," Velius sneered, as the two Red Bloods caught up with him.

"You have no choice brother, Publius commanded we accompany you," Darius jested, landing his hand on Velius's shoulder, causing Velius to scoff with disapproval.

"Lead on brother," Aulus requested, arm outstretched ahead.

Velius scowled at the pair and continued on towards the Raven's Temple.

"In there," Velius explained, pointing up the steps to the doors.

"Very well," Darius commented before trotting up the steps.

"Wait!" Velius cried out, "You cannot just go in there."

"Why not?" Aulus asked running up the first few steps.

"The Raven could be in there," Velius responded.

"And?" Darius pried.

Velius stuttered as he began to resemble an embarrassed toddler.

"Come along brother," Darius cried out, waving his arm to encourage Velius. Velius looked back towards the barracks, before hesitantly following the two blood brothers up the steps. The stories he had been told as a child terrified him; the hooded man in the purple paenula, deciding who would live and who would die; taking life and granting it in the same breath. His powers were mysterious and the White Bloods who raised Velius were deathly afraid of him.

Darius knocked confidently on the large wooden door.

Inside, footsteps echoed loudly as an attendant approached. The door creaked on its hinges before a woman, in a white hooded palla, appeared in the narrow gap.

"Yes?" She demanded.

"Blessings be upon you," Darius replied, trying on his best charm. Aulus couldn't help but laugh. "My brothers and I are looking for..." he turned to Velius.

"Arminius," Velius responded sheepishly, refusing to make eye contact with the temple's attendant.

"...Arminius. We have been summoned to return him at once to the Red Barracks," Darius explained, giving the largest, most coquettish smile he could muster.

"The Red Blood that barged in here in the middle of a ceremony? Distracting the Raven from his work, as he tried to save a woman overcome with madness? Risking enraging the gods and disturbing our prayers?" she barked back.

Darius turned to Velius for the answer. Velius nodded in agreement.

"Yes, that would be the one," Darius replied.

"He is no longer here," she explained. "The Raven charged him with the duty of returning a thief to the Ruinae." She abruptly retreated back into the temple, slamming shut the door behind her.

"Thank you," Darius shouted sincerly through the door, the flirtatious smile still evident on his face.

"To the Ruinae then," Aulus declared, leading the way down the steps.

"But..." Velius muttered.

"Come along Velius," Darius commanded.

The trio made their way into the outskirts of the Ruinae, looking for clues, looking for Arminius. Velius tried to ask the White Bloods for assistance, but instinctively they backed away at first sight. Like sharks swimming through a school of fish, the Red Bloods were kept at a safe distance at all times. All eyes were on them.

"This is hopeless," Velius muttered. "We will never find him. The White Bloods are of no help at all."

"We could ask in there," Darius suggested, pointing towards a tavern jutting out from the collection of hovels.

"Do you think that wise brother?" Aulus asked.

Darius shrugged his shoulders, "Perhaps they saw something?"

The trio approached with caution. Darius placed his hand on the door.

"Wait," Velius demanded, transfixed on a dark alleyway to the side.

Darius and Aulus exchanged confused glances. Darius removed his hand from the door. Velius cautiously entered the alleyway. Something had caught his eye; something metallic, something bright among the mud and dirt of the Ruinae. A helmet! Velius bent down and collected it up. It had a large dent in the side and red blood splattered about the back of it.

"I have found something," he called out. Darius and Aulus approached.

366

"What is it?" Darius asked.

"His helmet," Velius responded.

Velius looked further up the alley. There, at the end, lay a Red Blood still in his armour, dumped in a heap. Velius drew nearer. Arminius lay face down in the dirt. His armour scuffed and bloodied. Velius rolled him over to make sure it was truly him.

"BY THE GODS!" Velius screeched. His stomach turned at the sight. He looked away and vomited.

Aulus approached gingerly. Arminius was barely recognisable. His face was a mangled mess of flesh and bone. Blood was scattered about his tormented face and his skull had been caved in by a heavy blow.

The three Red Bloods stood silently. As the very sombre realisation that he was truly dead, sunk in; even the gods themselves could not fix this mortal vessel.

Aulus removed his own red lacerna and respectfully, with the help of Darius, wrapped it around Arminius. Aulus lifted Arminius from the ground and with respect, carried him from the Ruinae. Darius and Velius followed silently, while Velius carried Arminius's helmet.

Aulus's footsteps echoed through the barracks, as they made their way through to the Eagle's shrine. Publius sighed with growing despair. Aulus carefully lowered Arminius to the floor before the shrine. Velius placed

Arminius's helmet at his side. The three stood in silence. Red Bloods were meant to die for honour, before the gods, to keep the peace and to secure the future of Rytus. They were not meant to be butchered in the streets of the Ruinae.

"Where did you find him?" Publius asked earnestly.

Aulus explained all that they had found, along with showing Publius the extent of Arminius's injuries.

"To lose a Red Blood to the thieves, beggars and cowards of the Ruinae is insult enough. To lose three demands immediate action," Publius declared, his face growing red with anger.

Publius pointed to the remaining Red Bloods resting in the barracks, "Brothers, sisters, for too long now we have suffered at the hands of these outcasts. For too long they have disobeyed the laws of this land. For too long they have begged, stolen and pillaged. They have taken from us. They have taken our brothers and sister. They have taken our own blood. Suit up!" He commanded, "It is time to collect what is rightfully ours!"

With the ferocity of an enraged bull, Publius led the Red Bloods on a march towards the Ruinae. The metal tips of their pilums crashed against the stone, their metal armour sang the chorus and their chants filled the air, as they marched. "INVICTUS!" they cried.

"Halt," Publius commanded as they reached the desolate outskirts.

The Ruinae stood oddly quiet before them. The drunks had been cleared away. The thieves that prowled the streets had vanished. The whores had retreated and the children stayed behind closed doors. Only the howling wind greeted their arrival.

The dank alleyways were too narrow to allow the Red Bloods to march in formation. Instead they had to form a line of single file, each following the one before, led by Publius. Keeping close, they snaked through the Ruinae, to the spot where Arminius had been found.

"Here?" Publius asked. Aulus and Velius nodded.

"Aulus, Velius, you are to stay with me. The rest of you wait here, I have questions for these vermin," Publius commanded. The three Red Bloods entered the tavern nearby, while the others took up defensive positions outside.

Inside, the smell of stale wine, stagnant water and vomit permeated from the walls. The tavern fell deathly silent. All eyes focused on the towering Red Blood stood in the door way. His crested helmet, adorned with red ostrich feathers, his highly polished silver armour and arms bulging with both muscle and scars in equal quantity, was a sight to behold. His overwhelming presence was neatly presented against the backdrop of the red lacerna hanging from his

369

shoulders. In his wake stood the two young Red Bloods, the larger, a near mirror image of Publius as if he had been cast from the same clay. The other was a smaller, weaker pup, in ill-fitting armour, afraid to make eye contact with anyone.

Publius scanned the hostile tavern. No-one now dared to catch his gaze. They looked at their cups, feet, hands, anything but Publius. No-one, that was, except for a Green Blood, giggling to himself in the corner.

The three Red Bloods approached the Green Blood's table.

"Do tell friend," Publius taunted. "Why are you laughing?" he said, slamming his fist down on the table.

The Green Blood fell back into his chair, startled.

"You are drunk," Publius declared with disgust.

"That I am," the Green Blood replied, struggling to sit back up, spilling his coins on to the table.

"Good, then you will talk," Publius declared, sitting down on the chair opposite. While their leader and mentor sat, Aulus and Velius remained standing behind. Publius watched the Green Blood slowly count out his remaining coins before spotting one marked with the stains of red blood.

"Where did you find this?" Publius demanded, picking up the coin.

The Green Blood looked up at Publius, his green eyes stained yellow with excessive drinking. He picked up his drink and gulped down the last remnants of the wine before slamming the empty cup back on the table.

"Where did you find this one?" Publius repeated, holding the stained coin between his index finger and thumb.

The Green Blood stared at his empty cup. Publius instructed Velius to fetch more wine. Velius nodded dutifully and lifted a jug from the next table. He began to empty the contents into the cup. His hand shook with fear, spilling some of the wine on to the table.

Publius grabbed Velius by his cuff, "Enough."

"Now tell me," Publius sneered at the Green Blood, "who has the blood of my brothers and sister on their hands?"

"Well," The Green Blood slurred, "the answers you seek are not here in this tavern. All you have here are thieves, beggars and cowards," his emphasis on the last word, combined with his glare at Velius, was not lost on the young Red Blood.

"Then tell me where," Publius ordered, getting impatient.

"Go to the Lena," The Green Blood garbled.

"The madame of the whores? Why?"

"It is her duty to know who is coming and going from the Ruinae. Who comes, who goes, who owes. She knows it all. She will have the answers you seek." He took another gulp of wine before slamming the empty cup down again. "That is where I got the coin." Velius leant forward to top up the cup. Publius stopped him, signalling no more.

The Green Blood looked solemnly at his still empty cup, "You will have to go without me." He paused to belch. "I am no longer welcome there." The Green Blood collapsed onto the table before drifting into a deep sleep.

Publius stood up and turned to leave. He came immediately face to face with a White Blood his own height and stature.

"You are not welcome here," the man insisted.

Publius signalled to the other two to head out.

"You are not welcome in our home," the White Blood scoffed.

Publius squared up to the man. "Home?" He laughed. "You mean this stinking cesspool of filth, decay and waste?"

The White Blood snarled, bearing his teeth. Undeterred, Publius pushed the man aside and followed the other two out on to the street.

Outside, the men followed Publius through the alleyways to the lupanarium. This time Publius signalled for five Red Bloods to join him, including Aulus and Darius. Velius, relieved, remained outside with the others. As the troop entered, Aulus felt a shoulder brush against his own. He looked to his right where a young Orange Blood woman now stood. She smiled. Aulus, lost in her vivid orange eyes, couldn't help but smile back.

"You are looking for me?" Nox, the Lena of the establishment declared, stood in the middle of the hall, arms folded, awaiting their arrival. White Blood whores and their patrons peered from behind the stained drapes, as Publius demanded answers to his questions.

"I fear you are mistaken," Nox replied.

"NO!" Publius shouted. "Their blood was spilt in the Ruinae. I will have what is owed to me!"

"You have no jurisdiction here!" She screamed back. "We are well within our licence as, granted by Tiberius himself. You cannot do anything to us."

Enraged, Publius commanded the Red Bloods to search every room until they had their answers.

"You cannot just do as you please," Nox insisted.

Publius dismissed her protests and ordered his troop to advance.

The Red Bloods began searching the rooms, looking for anything that might indicate who was responsible for the deaths of Gaius, Varia and Arminius. Half naked patrons and scantily clad whores were pushed aside, some thrown from their beds before scattering in all directions.

Publius continued to glare at Nox, when from the back of the establishment came an excited cry, "I have found something!"

Darius and Aulus stood in the administrator's office, pointing to a small handful of coins scattered with red blood. The administrator cowered in the corner.

"Dominus, I have found this," another Red Blood explained as he entered the room carrying a bronze chest plate.

"Gaius's!" Publius gasped, carefully accepting the armour. He looked mournfully at the chest plate, placing his hand over the heart. "Dear friend," he whispered to himself.

"Tear this place apart!" he commanded, marching back into the main hall, "I want everything that is ours returned. You will have some explaining to do before the Blue Bloods," Publius declared, finger pointed squarely at Nox.

"Do you not see?" She shouted back in defiance, "Tiberius and the other Blue Bloods do not care for you or your kind. They do not even respect your traditions. They make you fight in the fighting pit, instead of earning your honour in the Eagle Arena. Why are you so blinded?"

"We are Red Bloods, we are strength. We are guided not by our own desires but by those of our leaders. We fight for what is right. We fight for Rytus. We do not question. We do what is required. Silence her," Publius commanded,

374

directing two Red Bloods to lock her away in the administrator's office. "Detain any others who question us," he instructed.

"Dominus!" A voice called out, "I fear you may wish to see this with your own eyes."

Publius followed the voice outside, to a tiny courtyard with towering high walls. Cowering at its edges lay women, hooded. They sobbed and pleaded for mercy.

"Look," the Red Blood explained, pointing to one woman in particular.

Publius approached. She held tightly to a bundle of cloth. Publius knelt before her. She sobbed but did not stop Publius, as he removed part of the coverings to reveal two shimmering red eyes.

"A child?" Publius asked, almost stunned, "I do not understand."

He looked up. The mother's eyes too were unmistakably red.

"How can this be?" he queried.

Publius looked around him at the women and their children. From White, Red, Green and Orange, not just pure bloods, but Demi Bloods too, they all glared back, terrified.

"Dominus," the Red Blood at the door insisted.

"Yes," Publius responded, climbing back on to his feet. Publius took one more look back into the courtyard before closing shut the door behind him. He returned to the main hall where his Red Bloods were waiting. They stood proudly around the horde of stolen treasures they had recovered.

"Fetch the rest of the men, I have some questions for the Lena," he declared.

Aulus and Darius flung open the doors. The sight of what they saw, froze them rigidly to the spot. Publius, sensing something was wrong, spun on the spot to face the door.

His footsteps echoed about the courtyard as he stepped out, followed by the five Red Bloods he had taken with him into the lupanarium.

Roughly forty dishevelled citizens stood watching from the edges, while ten hooded White Bloods stood towering over Publius's ten Red Bloods, knelt on the floor in a circle. Their arms held above their heads, while they looked down at the floor. The Red Blood's swords were now in the hands of the hooded White Bloods, with the tips resting at the bases of the Red Blood's necks.

"Please, friend," one of the White Bloods taunted, while gesturing with a Red Blood's sword, "Join your brothers and sisters."

Outnumbered, Publius raised his hands above his head and followed the instructions of the hooded White Blood leader. He stepped into the middle of his Red Bloods, but refused to kneel. Aulus and Darius, along with the other three Red Bloods followed their leader to the centre of the circle.

"You should have not strayed into the Ruinae," a familiar voice called out from behind the hood. "Now you and your men will pay for your arrogance."

"Remove your hood, fight like a warrior, not a coward," Publius demanded.

"Very well," the hooded man responded, removing his hood.

Publius recognised him straight away. He was the man who had confronted him in the tavern.

"You!" Publius responded in dismay. The man smiled in return. "My men have earned the right to fight with honour and dignity. Why do you believe the gods have granted you the same freedoms?" he demanded.

"Why are you so blinded?" the man asked, shaking his head.

Publius instinctively turned to the lupanarium to see Nox now stood at the doorway, watching with a sly smile on her face.

"You will pay for your crimes!" Publius declared, drawing his gladius.

Immediately, as if on cue, the blood stained coins in Publius's pouch and those carried by the five Red Bloods, began to effervesce with green gas. The air became toxic.

Aulus and Darius gasped desperately, Publius coughed loudly. The Five Red Bloods dropped to their knees weakened by the gas. Publius dropped to his left knee.

"NO!" He screamed, fighting back. He struggled to his feet and lunged forward towards the White Blood man.

"All you had to do was name Acacia as your successor, and none of this would have been necessary," the White Blood man sneered, unaffected by the gas.

Publius fell forward, dropping his sword and landing his hand on the man's shoulder. His face contorted, his veins turning green.

"The sins of your kind, the betrayal of Ravenstone, all those who are guilty of sin will face judgement," the White Blood declared loudly.

As ordered, the remaining hooded White Bloods struck at the Red Bloods knelt before them. Aulus looked at the coins in his hand as they bubbled and dribbled through his fingers, pooling in the cracks of the floor. The screams of his fellow Red Bloods were silenced by the gurgle of fluids filling their airways, as they were slaughtered like animals. The sound of metal slicing through flesh, the splash of blood and muscle torn from bones plunging to the floor; the taste of blood in his own mouth, accompanied with a metallic copper taste, none of it seemed real, it couldn't be, it had to be a nightmare. Powerless, he fell to the floor. The weight of his slain brothers and sisters pinned him to the spot, as they fell on top of him. Darius staggered free from the poison's grasp, and grabbed Aulus's arm. He tried desperately to drag him clear.

"Go," Aulus gasped, directing Darius to run while he could.

"No, brother!" Darius pleaded.

"Go!" Aulus spluttered.

Velius cried out as his own sword sliced into his cheek. Darius looked back to Aulus before catching Velius. With a tug to his right, Darius was able to save Velius, and amid the commotion, dragged him into a side alley.

The gathered White Bloods laughed and cheered as the Red Bloods were dismembered. The now suddenly sober Green Blood from the tavern smiled callously as their screams were drowned out by the enthused crowd.

Aulus tried again to escape, he pushed upward with his powerful arms and glanced over to the spot where Publius once stood.

"No!" Aulus gasped, as he was forced back down to the floor. The weight of those above him rendered him breathless, as Publius's head was thrust into the air on the end of his own sword. Aulus tried once more to free himself, he was trapped. With his breath escaping, the commotion around him fell silent, his sight faded and his body became still.

Chapter Twenty-Seven

5,258 days before the eclipse.

"We are Orange Bloods. We are swift. We are precision. We serve Rytus and all her citizens," Pius, a senior Orange Blood declared.

Dutifully the White Bloods gathered in their positions with torches, ready to light the kindling of the pyre.

"He shared freely his wisdom. He taught many of us gathered here the skills and knowledge we cherish. He was unlike any leader before," Pius continued solemnly. "Though his mortal body will be returned to the soil, may the gods grant his soul passage to the fields of Elysium."

Briana stepped forward and placed a single denarius on Leanorus's breathless lips.

"May this coin grant you passage to the afterlife," she declared before placing another coin at the side of Leanorus. "May this coin see that you are able to grant passage for our lost sister, Agapeta." She stepped back.

Those gathered bowed their heads momentarily as a mark of respect. The White Bloods carrying the torches stepped forward and lit the pyre. The flames took hold quickly.

Vesnus watched as his mentor was rapidly seized by the flames. On the other side of the burning pyre stood

Claricius, his face glowing with the light of the fire, his scowl intensifying as the flames flickered. Vesnus did not care. He shifted his focus away from Claricius and back towards his mentor. The flames turned Leanorus's body smoky black before the pyre began to shift, lowering Leanorus into the smouldering pit below. Vesnus had never felt so alone before.

Vesnus felt a warm and gentle hand embrace his own, clasping tightly. He looked right to the tearful Mania stood alongside. Vesnus squeezed her hand back. The two stood silently, watching the flames. The others began to depart the small peninsula, making their way back towards the hall.

Claricius glanced back towards the silhouettes of Vesnus and Mania, hands held tightly together. He scoffed loudly, partly to annoy Placidus alongside him as they walked. Placidus did not care. He ignored Claricius and climbed the steps in total silence. This served only to further irritate Claricius, who in retaliation, pushed Placidus aside and raced up the steps back to the hall.

"I am sorry that I could not find her," Vesnus commented solemnly.

Mania released his hand. "I know," she replied wistfully. "I just..." she paused trying to hold back the tears. "The things I said to her," she explained, woefully sobbing. Vesnus placed his hand on her shoulder to comfort her.

Mania instead turned and ran back towards the hall, her face in her hands.

Vesnus stared into the flames. So many questions to ask, so much he did not understand. Now his mentor was gone, who could he ask? Mournfully, Vesnus joined the others and ascended the steps back from the bay to the hall.

Vesnus stopped at the door to the hall. What would life be like now he was on his own? He knew this day was coming, but he had never planned for it to start under these circumstances. Hesitantly Vesnus opened the door and stepped inside.

"Claricius wishes to see you in the office," a White Blood reported.

What right had Claricius to demand his counsel? he pondered. Driven by curiosity, Vesnus made his way to the office.

"Good," Claricius declared upon sighting him. "A debt letter has arrived."

"Let me see it," Vesnus demanded reaching forward.

Claricius pulled it away. "You are to travel to the village and..."

"You are telling me what to do?" Vesnus asked, astounded.

"The others are busy, I have been asked to make sure the debts do not fall behind," Claricius explained pompously.

"Why you?"

"Because I am better than you!" Claricius sneered.

Vesnus glared back, his eyes narrowed.

"Be careful brother," Vesnus warned, "you are beginning to forget yourself."

Claricius turned up his nose, waving the debt letter in Vesnus's direction. Vesnus snatched the letter and left.

"Pompous, arrogant weasel, just once I would like to take him into the practice yard and run an arrow straight through his tiny little..."

"Another debt letter?" Mania asked, waiting patiently.

"Yes," Vesnus replied, halting his rant.

"May I see?"

Vesnus handed the letter over.

"It is just like the one mother received," she declared. "Look," she said, pointing to the claw symbol. "It is unlike the original letters. It is more crudely drawn. And look..." she began smudging the symbol with the palm of her hand, "it wipes off. The others were sealed in ink."

"You are saying this and the one before were not written by the same hand as those before them?"

Mania shrugged her shoulders, "Perhaps."

"Who is it for?" She asked handing back the letter.

Vesnus opened it, "It is for..." He froze. "I must go at once!" Mania grabbed Vesnus by his arm. Vesnus turned to face her.

"Thank you for going to look for her," she said with gratitude.

Vesnus tried to smile reassuringly but inside he felt only guilt. Perhaps if he had travelled faster, refused to chase Claricius or let Ericus go, perhaps he could have saved Agapeta, perhaps he could have given his mentor the dignified death he deserved? Vesnus blankly returned her gaze as she looked up at him with affection. He had to look away, he felt he had let her down. Mania released her grip and let him go.

Vesnus made his way down into Falcon Reach as the White Bloods slept. He knew exactly where he was going. His swift footsteps whispered across the wooden decking which linked the tiny hovels together. His orange birrus muffled the sound of his wooden bow and leather quiver as they clapped together. He charged through the alleyways, twisting and turning like Velox riding the air currents. He raced on, deep in to the nest of the oldest buildings in the village.

He skidded to a halt. Vesnus looked up at the home before him. It seemed so much smaller than he
384

remembered. He placed his hand on the door as the memories of his childhood flooded his conscience. He took a deep breath and gingerly opened the door, stepping softly inside.

"I was beginning to believe you were not coming," declared the woman knelt before her shrine to Juno and Pluto, her back to Vesnus.

Vesnus stood speechless. Could it truly be her? he wondered. He held his breath in anticipation. She rose to her feet and turned to face him. Their eyes met. Suddenly half a lifetime apart became meaningless.

"Vesnus!" she gleefully declared.

She leapt across the small room and wrapped her arms tightly around his waist. The pain of recent events evaporated instantly. He embraced her closely, pulling her in tightly.

"I prayed to the gods that they would send you," she explained, joyfully staring up at him with tearful grey eyes.

"And now I am here," he replied softly. He rested his head against hers, running his fingers through her long white hair. Her warmth and tenderness matched no other. He finally felt complete.

Her diligence and obedience had seen the gods reward her, granting her the one final wish she truly desired above all else. She breathed in his aroma and closed her eyes as she became almost overwhelmed with tears of joy.

"You have grown so much," she whispered.

"As have you," he replied.

She inhaled deeply before stepping back. Vesnus reluctantly released his grasp.

"Look at you," she said in awe.

Vesnus smiled, throwing open his arms in an awkward pose.

"I have missed you," she said with sincerity.

"I have missed you too, Isebella," he replied stepping forward.

She looked up, her lips slightly parted. She lifted her right arm and placed her hand tenderly on his chest.

"Has my last day already ended? Am I in the plain of Asphodel?" she jested, feeling the delicate leather of his armour beneath his birrus.

Vesnus laughed tenderly. "No," he whispered, before removing his birrus and gently collecting her hand in his.

She guided their hands upward, resting her hand on his cheek. He closed his eyes. There was so much they had both shared before he had been sent away. So much energy flowed between them. Their attraction to one another was undeniable but so was the law. His passion was hungry for a taste of her. He had to resist. If they were discovered, he'd be banished from Rytus until the end of time.

Would the gods allow her just one moment of pleasure in exchange for a lifetime of servitude? Perhaps, somehow, she could experience her Asphodel without damming his mortal soul for eternity. Her breathing intensified.

They had obeyed the law diligently, if they gave in now, then surely a lifetime of abstinence had to bring favour with the gods? he reasoned. He kissed her hand tenderly. He felt the urge intensify. She felt her body quiver.

How could they deny a passion that felt so right? He had fought his desires for her from the day he met her, until the day he came of age. She had obeyed her seniors and had never visited Falcon Hall to see him. Yet through it all, they had never forgotten one another.

"To Tartarus with the gods," he muttered, leaning forward.

Vesnus met Isebella's lips fervidly. She reciprocated, running her fingertips through his hair. He placed his hand on the small of her back, pulling her into his body tightly.

She led Vesnus to the corner of the room, to a pile of furs on the floor. He carefully removed his bow and quiver, placing them gently on the ground. She helped him remove his leather body armour. He softly kissed her neck as she unbuttoned her tunic. It fluttered to the floor. Vesnus let out a quiet moan of admiration, ripping off his tunic as he dropped to his knees before her.

He placed his hands on her hips. She closed her eyes and gasped softly as Vesnus positioned his lips just below

387

her belly button. He kissed her softly as he moved downward. Forced to brace against the wall beside her, her gasps turn to moans of delight, his cool breath provoking a new and elicit pleasure against her wet skin.

She knelt down in the furs, placing her finger under his chin. She guided him forward as she leant backwards. He placed his hands either side of her. She exhaled loudly as he kissed her stomach, before guiding his tongue up from her naval, inducing a deep rooted passionate tremble in her delicate skin.

Her ecstasy became uncontrollable. She cried out with fervour at each powerful thrust from Vesnus, as he gripped her passionately. Vesnus's conviction turned to exhilaration.

She drew his blade. Vesnus's body convulsed. He was now gripped by the rigidity of mortal euphoria. He groaned loudly as he tried to regain control of his own body. He could only watch as she lifted the blade high.

Weakened, he fell to her side.

"I can see the plain of Asphodel," she exclaimed with a smile.

Vesnus scrambled to his knees.

"Thank you," she gasped, the blade embedded in her chest.

Vesnus tried to stagger to his feet, before falling backwards on to the floor. He watched as her life ebbed away, pooling at her side. What had she done? Her debt was due, but this was never the intent.

Anxious, upset and confused, Vesnus quickly gathered up his belongings. He hurriedly dressed, put on his armour and collected his bow and quiver. Tormented by the decisions he had made, he ran from her home and fell into the alleyway outside. His mind was now a deafening commotion of agonising confrontation of his own beliefs. His stomach felt violently disturbed. Uncontrollably, he vomited in the street.

He needed to think. He needed to go, anywhere. He stumbled down the steps at the end of the alleyway and fell into the sandy soil below. He crawled towards the bay and collapsed into the salty water.

The pain and confusion began to propagate into anger. Vesnus wiped the sandy water from his face and climbed to his feet.

"She knew of my feelings," he growled. "That was my blade, my debt, she had no right to take it from me!"

His heavy footsteps sunk into the shore as he marched back towards her home, keen to protect his reputation and to retrieve his blade. His arms were rigid, his face screwed up tightly and his brow furrowed.

He made his way along the alleyway and turned towards the door. He lifted his hand and reached for the handle.

A voice called out from inside, "By the gods!"

Vesnus halted.

"By Pluto, what has happened?" the voice cried.

Vesnus withdrew his hand. The thought of explaining why the woman he had been banished from ever seeing again, now lay naked with his blade embedded in her chest, sent a shiver through his core. While he could explain the debt owed, there was little he could do to explain his methods. He contained his rage and retreated.

The commotion building at Falcon Hall was audible from the edges of the village. Vesnus continued with caution. Keen to not draw attention to himself, he quietly approached the stores to return his bow and quiver. Vesnus opened the door, startling Placidus. Placidus hurriedly tried to hide a collection of cloths in the corner. But upon realising who had entered; Placidus stood up and moved away from the bundle. The events in Falcon Reach were momentarily pushed from his mind, as Vesnus approached.

The orange fur overflowed from the cloth and the white tip of the tail was a stark contrast to the dusty wooden floor of the stores. Liquens the fox met Vesnus's gaze with a weak stare.

Vesnus, reminded by the events at Magpie Hill camp, struggled to shake the torment of the passing of his mentor. The moans of pain as he lay dying on the cold floor of the camp, the pleading for mercy, it had cut deep. He had carried out his last request and kept his promise, but now he felt empty inside. He would not wish this hollow feeling on anyone, especially not his friend. The friend who unquestioning, followed Vesnus to the camp, the friend who fought at his side, and the friend who's companion now lay dying on the floor of the stores. Vesnus watched Liquens close his eyes. His breathing was laboured and the cloth was soaked with orange blood.

"Is he safe here?" Vesnus asked.

"What else could I do?" Placidus responded. "I could not leave him in the woods. He is too weak. He would surely die. I owe him my life. I cannot allow his to simply slip away."

Without saying a word, Vesnus left the stores and made his way out. Placidus did as best he could to make Liquens more comfortable, offering him some water.

Vesnus returned. In his hand he had a rabbit, held proudly aloft.

"Thank you brother," Placidus replied collecting the rabbit. He picked up his blade and began cutting through the white blood and flesh. Vesnus watched as Placidus offered the meat to Liquens. The weak fox lifted his head and licked gently at the warm meat.

"May the gods bless you with good fortune," Vesnus offered reassuringly. Knowing that Placidus would do all he could to look after the little fox, Vesnus decided it best to leave him be. He knew little of their habits, but Placidus had studied them well from a young age. Liquens would be in safe hands.

Vesnus left the stores and quietly entered the hall. Crowds of Orange Bloods and White Bloods had gathered. The language was fierce, their words were cutting and their jeers were vile.

"This is an outrage," they declared.

Vesnus merged into the crowd drawing his hood, fearing that word of Isebella's discovery had already reached the hall.

"Brothers, sisters," a familiar voice cried out from the Lapsae balcony.

Vesnus stopped and turned to face Claricius as he addressed the crowds.

"Leanorus is dead," he said with a vulgar smile.

"Merda!" a man in the crowd cried out.

"With Agapeta absent from her duties," he said with a sneer, "I am forced to make the most solemn of decrees. I Claricius Aurantiac Falco..."

"Cūlus," Another man cried.

"...doth decree that I am to bare her duties as leader of the Furtim Falco," Claricius declared.

The crowd grew increasingly hostile, as the shouting continued to intensify.

"As the new Dominus of the dark claws, it is with great honour I am to announce Leanorus's successor," Claricius called out, signalling to the door from the office.

Vesnus stood in stunned silence. Time seemed to slow as Mania walked along the balcony above him. Why was Mania there? What was going on? he tried desperately to figure it out.

"Brothers, Sisters and Friends," she said addressing the crowd. "I bring you worrying news." Vesnus held his breath, fearing his banishment. "I have discovered that our dearly departed Leanorus and Agapeta were led to their deaths on false pretences."

The crowd turned to hushed debate and speculation.

"And I know who it was who led them there," she declared, her eyes wide and her finger pointed into the crowd below.

Vesnus stared with anticipation toward Mania. Finally, he would have a name. Finally, he would know who was responsible for the betrayal of his mentor.

"It was Vesnus!" she cried.

Chapter Twenty-Eight

5,258 days before the eclipse.

Acernis waited in the shadows induced by the flickering torches positioned on the doorways of the insulas. He looked up to the maeniana in the Blue Palace's grounds as the Green Bloods began to file out of Magpie Hall, carrying with them their belongings.

A single Red Blood approached. Acernis quietly stepped back against the wall of an insula. The Red Blood continued on his way, unaware of the Green Blood lurking in the shadows. Acernis waited for the Red Blood to march out of ear shot, before bolting across the street. He ducked into a doorway closer to the bridge.

He scanned the palace. Three Red Bloods stood watch at the top of the garden walls. One was positioned guarding the steps and one patrolled along the edge of the Blue Lake. It had taken him over a day just to sneak back into White City undetected. Even with the unusually reduced guard, approaching Sparrow Bridge now was out of the question. He would be spotted. He had to wait.

The light emanating from the lamps held by the Green Bloods, stalked the dispirited Picas, as they made their way out of the grounds. Their heads hung low and their footsteps were heavy. Together they marched onwards, descending each step slowly and begrudgingly. Ulmus carried with him a large collection of the scrolls he had manage to save from Cinis's purge. As he reached the bottom, a scroll fell from his grasp and plunged to the floor. Unable to contain himself any longer, Acernis stepped out of the shadows and raced towards the bridge to assist his mentor.

In his haste, Acernis failed to spot the other Red Blood patrolling the streets and clattered straight into her. To steady himself Acernis reached out, finding only the bare wrist of the Red Blood for purchase. He grasped tightly, to stop himself from falling. The pair froze.

The Red Blood stood entranced as Acernis became gripped by his gift. He felt the adrenaline of the fighting pit surge through her body. The deluge of emotion triggered by her first kill and the bitter sting of resentment. He felt the anger well as a Blue Blood, now stood before her, refused to send the guard to look for someone she respected and held dear. Her mentor! They would have revenge. The vision began to fade.

The two figures dropped to their knees. The Red Blood grew breathless. Acernis awoke. He had little time before the Red Blood's unconscious body would clatter against the stones, alerting the others nearby. He guided the Red Blood gently down to the floor before breaking the bond. The Red Blood began to stir. Acernis took his leave, heading back into the shadows.

With more care, Acernis stayed in the darkness, working his way gingerly towards Ulmus. He glanced back as the Red Blood climbed to her feet, dazed and confused.

Ulmus began to cross the bridge heading towards Acernis. Time was fleeting. The Red Blood rubbed her eyes before scanning the area for an explanation. Acernis's heart began to race. If he ran too soon he would be spotted by the stationed Red Bloods. If he left it too late he would be spotted by an increasingly displeased Red Blood, just a few paces away. The footsteps of the Green Bloods grew louder, drawing the Red Blood's attention. Acernis was out of time.

The head of the Red Blood, watching the bridge from the garden's walls, dropped. The night had taken its toll on the tired guard, he was fighting to stay awake. Acernis saw his chance. He leapt from the shadows. Charging quickly, he bolted across the flagstones and disappeared into the marching crowd of Green Bloods.

The dazed Red Blood looked towards the spot where Acernis had been stood, the sudden motion catching her eye. She peered into the darkness but saw nothing. Unable to surmise what had happened, she furrowed her brow and continued on her way. Acernis caught his breath. He was safe for now.

His thoughts turned to the vision. Revenge? he pondered. Against whom? Acernis watched the Red Blood cross the street, joining two others near the Magpie Tree. Acernis, caught up in curiosity, abandoned his pursuit of Ulmus and focused instead on the Red Bloods.

Eager to discover more, Acernis turned around and made his way to the other side of the street. He jumped down from the flagstone, into the sandy edges of the lake. The Green Bloods continued their march onward as Acernis ducked down under Sparrow Bridge. With his knees in the sodden mud, he crawled forward towards the Tree. Cautiously, he peered around the bridge's foundations and listened in.

"Now is the time to strike," the smallest of the Red Bloods remarked.

"They continue to mock us. Every word is another stake in the heart of the Red Bloods," the second commented.

"What of the guard?" the third asked.

"They have been commanded to stand watch over the palace in place of our missing brothers and sisters," the second sneered.

"And their quarters?" the third asked.

"Unguarded," the first replied.

"Very well, Acacia. I will see us into the grounds," the third declared.

"And I will see that the path is clear," the second declared.

"And I shall bring the Sword of Ravenstone. What was once a symbol of hope, will now serve as a reminder of the vows they have betrayed," Acacia cried out with an agitated tone.

The three Red Bloods stopped suddenly and turned towards the bridge.

"You there! Green Blood!" the third bellowed.

Acernis held his breath.

"Lost?" the second taunted.

Acernis kept rigidly still.

"Perhaps the butt of my sword will help you find your tongue," Acacia jeered.

"Forgiveness," a voice from the bridge called out followed by the gentle patter of footsteps sprinting into the distance.

The three Red Bloods laughed callously.

"Calm yourself sister," the third commanded. "We will have our justice. It is time to remind the Blue Bloods of their vows. It is time to send a message. It is time to kill Tita."

Acernis gasped, returning to the shadows of the bridge. He waited cautiously for the footsteps of the Red Bloods to fade, before emerging back on to the street. He charged towards the marching Green Bloods and jostled his way through.

"Mentoris!" he cried out.

Ulmus stopped and turned to face Acernis. "My dear boy!" he called out joyfully. "I thought you had been thrown out of the city?" he said.

"I must talk with you," Acernis insisted.

"Well, we have a long walk ahead of us..." Ulmus jested as he tipped some of the scrolls into Acernis's arms.

"I beg forgiveness Mentoris, but this is a matter of great urgency," Acernis explained as he carefully re-positioned the scrolls.

"Very well," Ulmus replied, slightly jarred by Acernis's tone. "What is it that is so important?"

"The Red Bloods move to kill Tita," Acernis reported.

"Good," Ulmus replied coldly.

"Mentoris!" Acernis gasped.

"Bah," Ulmus said dismissively as Cinis sniggered. "Why should we care?"

"But Mentoris?" Acernis challenged.

"What?" Ulmus responded.

"We need to save her," Acernis insisted.

"Why?" Ulmus asked.

"Because it is the right thing to do."

"The right thing to do? That has never bothered the Blue Bloods, so why should we save them?" Ulmus objected defiantly.

"Because," Acernis halted his march, "we are not Blue Bloods."

Ulmus stopped and turned to face Acernis.

"We are Green Bloods. We believe in the Codex Vitae. We heal the sick. We heal the wounded. We do whatever we must to protect all the citizens of Rytus, including the Blue Bloods. And right now, Tita needs us," Acernis declared.

Ulmus glared at Acernis.

"She had you marched out of the city!" Ulmus cried out. "She kicked us out of our own Magpie Hall. She has banished us all from the city until the end of time!" he bellowed. "By the gods themselves, why would you want to save her?" he protested. The rage on Ulmus's face was apparent. His teeth bared like a wolf preparing to strike.

Acernis met Ulmus's glare and replied, "Because I have seen into Tita's soul. She is as afraid as we are!"

Ulmus stood silently, his face still contorted with rage before exploding into a fit. The scrolls clattered to the floor as Ulmus swung his arms about wildly like a disgruntled toddler. Ulmus turned from Acernis and muttered his displeasure before sighing loudly. He turned back towards Acernis.

"How much time do we have?" Ulmus asked still irritated.

Acernis explained everything that the Red Bloods had said. Ulmus pulled Iuniperorum aside and instructed the other Green Bloods to continue to Magpie Gorge, where they would meet them in the morning.

"The good news is," Ulmus explained to Iuniperorum, "her quarters remain unguarded. The bad news is; her guards are positioned around the grounds of the palace."

Iuniperorum shrugged his shoulders and replied, "well, if it were easy, it would not be fun."

"Sparrow Bridge is being watched. May I suggest we take a trip to the fighting pit?" Ulmus suggested with a cheeky smile.

The three Green Bloods, sticking to the shadows, snuck quietly to the steps of the fighting pit. Once inside they made their way along the top of the pit. Iuniperorum and Acernis leapt from the top row and scrambled up the side of the Swan's Nest. Ulmus leapt but misjudged the ledge, falling backwards. Acernis quickly grabbed his mentor's wrist and pulled him up with the help of Iuniperorum. They raced down the steps of the Swan's Nest and gathered in the shadows of the gate to the bridge across the lake surrounding the palace. Iuniperorum peered around the corner and scanned the area for Red Bloods.

A lone Red Blood marched along the corridor of the Red Barracks bordering the edge of the lake. Iuniperorum pointed to the Red Blood and signalled for Acernis and Ulmus to wait. Silently, Iuniperorum crept across the bridge and approached the Red Blood from behind. He reached up and placed his hand across the Red Blood's eyes. He placed his other arm around the Red Blood's waist and caught him as he fell under Iuniperorum's control. Iuniperorum guided the Red Blood quietly down to the floor and signalled to the waiting Green Bloods to advance. Acernis and Ulmus crept across the bridge and joined Iuniperorum as he moved the unconscious Red Blood into a doorway.

"How long will he be out?" Acernis asked.

"Long enough," Iuniperorum replied.

The three men snuck along the corridor and halted before entering the square at the foot of the steps to the palace.

"I see two on the steps," said Ulmus.

"And one on the maeniana above us," Iuniperorum added. "Wait until he turns, then head over there," he said pointing to the door of the prison situated below the maeniana. "Stick to the shadows," he instructed before stepping out.

"Wait..." Ulmus pleaded.

Iuniperorum strolled across the square heading towards the steps. The two Red Bloods standing guard straightened up and glared at the cocky Green Blood.

"Halt," the Red Blood commanded.

"Oh hey, look what we have here then," Iuniperorum slurred. "Two more shiny eagles," he jested pretending to be drunk. "I wager that *you* cannot out-drink me either!"

"You are to leave White City at once," the Red Bloods warned.

"I am going to bed," Iuniperorum continued, pretending to wobble.

The two Red Bloods exchanged unimpressed glances.

Meanwhile the guard on the maeniana above reached Magpie Hall at the end and turned around.

"Go!" Ulmus declared.

The two Green Bloods crept along the edge of the square. Keeping to the shadows just as Iuniperorum had said. They reached the door to the prison and held their breath.

"This is not your home anymore," the Red Blood explained, talking slowly so Iuniperorum understood.

"Go to Magpie Gorge," the other insisted.

"Silly shiny eagles, I live in the hole, not a gorge. No wait, hall, not hole," Iuniperorum giggled before trying to push past.

Quietly, Acernis and Ulmus kept close to the wall, working their way across, nearer to Iuniperorum.

Losing their patience, the Red Bloods drew their gladius swords.

"Oh," Iuniperorum replied spotting the swords. "They are big!"

The Red Bloods sighed loudly, put their swords back, turned Iuniperorum around and pushed him away. He used the opportunity to check on the position of the guard patrolling above. The guard was just about to reach the other end of his patrol route, he needed more time. Iuniperorum signalled discreetly to the waiting Green Bloods to hold their positions.

"I remember now," Iuniperorum declared, turning back to face the Red Bloods. The two guards rolled their eyes. "I have to go to the gorge," Iuniperorum declared. The Red Bloods glared at him. "That is west of here. No, east. No west," he muttered to himself. He turned around to check on the guard. Just a little longer and the trap could be sprung.

"Where am I?" Iuniperorum asked with a drunken smile, as he turned back to face the guards.

One of the Red Bloods, taking pity on the fool, began explaining the route out of the city to the gorge. Iuniperorum looked puzzled.

"I see," Iuniperorum responded once the Red Blood had finished. Iuniperorum took one last look at the patrolling guard and turned to face sparrow bridge. He wobbled towards the bridge before staggering left and falling face first into the sandy shore. The two Red Bloods sighed and stepped down from the steps.

"Come on you," the sympathetic Red Blood declared as he approached Iuniperorum.

Ulmus grabbed the first Red Blood and silently bought him down to the floor, unconscious. Acernis reached up to grab the second. The Red Blood heard the approaching footsteps and turned around. Acernis stopped dead. At first the Red Blood was confused and then angry. He opened his mouth to raise the alarm. Iuniperorum grabbed his wrist and bought the Red Blood silently under control. The three men dragged the Red Bloods out of sight and retreated to the shadows of the steps.

"That was close," Iuniperorum whispered, as they listened out for any signs of the alarm being raised. Acernis breathed a sigh of relief as only the rhythmic sound of the patrolling Red Bloods resounded from the white marble of the palace. The three men crept up the steps and halted before the top.

"How many?" Iuniperorum asked.

"I can only make out one at the top of the next set of steps. There may be more but I cannot see." Ulmus explained as he peered around the corner.

Iuniperorum crept back down the steps, watched for the patrolling Red Blood, and dashed out. He collected a rock from the shore of the lake and made his way back up the steps to meet the others. He aimed into the gardens above and threw the rock. It travelled far before clattering against a metal statue. The metallic ping attracted the Red Blood's attention long enough for Ulmus to approach. Ulmus lowered the guard down to the floor and return to the others.

"One more around the next corner, the one patrolling and I think another at the steps to the Imperator's Quarters," Ulmus reported.

"Impossible to take all three at once. We will have to split them up," Iuniperorum declared. "Acernis, draw the one nearest around the corner and deal with him. I will go and deal with the patrolling Red Blood. Ulmus, the other is yours."

Acernis and Ulmus nodded and the three men continued on. Acernis was nervous. He'd only ever taken control of White Bloods as well as the Red Blood he accidentally bumped into. The results were mixed and the Red Blood quickly recovered as soon as the bond was broken. Ulmus, sensing Acernis's concern, drew nearer and placed his hand on his shoulder.

"You can do this," he said reassuringly.

Acernis took a deep breath and crept closer to the corner. He turned to Iuniperorum and signalled he was ready. Iuniperorum and Ulmus retreated to the shadows and dropped one of the Red Blood's gladius swords to the floor.

Just as they had planned, the next Red Blood, alerted by the noise, turned the corner to investigate. Acernis waited for him to pass before rising to his feet. He reached out and placed his hand over the Red Blood's eyes. Anger, resentment and fury permeated into Acernis's own mind. He closed his eyes. He heard every breath of the Red Blood. His heart rate, almost deafening Acernis, began to slow. His mind became calm and his body relaxed. Acernis guided the Red Blood down to the ground and awoke. He maintained his grip on the Red Blood as Ulmus and Iuniperorum raced by.

Iuniperorum darted across the grounds of the palace, heading for the patrolling Red Blood. Ulmus crept quietly towards the large ferns near the steps to the Imperator's quarters.

"Hello," Iuniperorum sneered as the Red Blood turned to face him. Iuniperorum guided him down quietly.

Ulmus gestured for Acernis to join him, but Acernis was afraid that if he let go, the Red Blood would wake. Iuniperorum joined Ulmus behind the ferns and also gestured for Acernis to join them. Reluctantly Acernis let go. He watched the Red Blood intently for any sign of stirring. The Red Blood remained rigid. Acernis gingerly stepped away, glanced back towards the Red Blood, then ran to join the others.

"Is that one of the ones you saw by the tree?" Iuniperorum asked.

"No, none of these men are," Acernis replied, disappointed.

"Perhaps we are too late?" Ulmus suggested.

"Only one way to find out," Iuniperorum jested.

"How will you reach him without alerting him?" Acernis asked.

Ulmus smiled, "Watch."

Iuniperorum guided Acernis back a few paces as Ulmus knelt down. Ulmus placed the palms of his hands against the marble floor and closed his eyes. His breathing slowed, his head dropped. Within a few moments a green aura began to permeate into the stone, originating from Ulmus's hands. The aura began to sprout like the roots of a tree, rippling through the marble. Like a bolt of lightning, the aura then quickly struck out along the floor, to the feet of the Red Blood. He glanced down at the strangely glowing

408

green floor, before clattering to a heap. The three men waited for the cacophony of metal on stone to fall silent before approaching the final steps.

Slowly the three men made their way into the Blue Blood's quarters as the Imperators slept. Treading lightly, they worked towards Tita. The large wine flask on the table and the cup on the floor suggested Tita may be hard to wake. The Green Bloods approached. Her clothes were free of blood, there didn't appear to be any sign of an attempt on her life. Either the Red Bloods had changed their minds, been stopped or more likely, were on their way, the men figured.

"We can probably save her," Ulmus whispered to Acernis. "Are you sure you want to do this?"

Acernis nodded.

"Very well," Ulmus responded softly.

Ulmus placed his hand over Tita's eyes. Acernis was right, she was terrified. The guilt, the blame, the responsibility; it had all taken its toll on Tita's mind. Ulmus decided that he would leave Tita's judgement to the gods and instead, concentrated on preserving her mortality. He slowed her breathing, deepened her dream and brought her heart rate down as far as he dared. Footsteps approached. Ulmus awoke. The three Green Bloods stepped into the shadows and disappeared.

The three Red Bloods entered Tita's room, with Acacia brandishing the Sword of Ravenstone. One picked up the cup from the floor and scoffed with contempt.

"No wonder the guards are dazed," he remarked.

The second removed the bed clothes as Acacia lifted the sword into the air above Tita. The anger inside the Red Blood forced the sword through Tita's chest, pinning her to the bed. She exhaled. Satisfied, the three Red Bloods left.

Iuniperorum Stepped from the shadows and without hesitation grasped the sword. It was heavy and deeply embedded into the bed as well as Tita. Acernis helped him to lift the sword clear and placed it down on the floor behind them. Ulmus placed his hand on her head and began searching for her soul. Iuniperorum placed his hand over the wound. He closed his eyes. A warm green aura filled the room, concentrated and welling in Tita's chest. Acernis watched on as the two senior Magpies began to heal Tita.

Iuniperorum sealed the wound while Ulmus began bringing Tita around from her deep slumber. Her heart was stubborn. It refused to be commanded. Sensing his frustration, Acernis joined his mentor's side. He placed his hand on Tita. He could see not just her soul but that of his mentor's. It was weaker than before, Ulmus was sick. Why had he not told anyone? Acernis wondered. Why was he keeping his pain to himself?

Tita gasped for air. The three men stood back. She struggled violently as her body contorted with pain. Her eyes darted wildly about the room. She looked at the blood on her clothes and the blue-bloodied sword on the floor. She glanced up. Acernis met her confused gaze.

"GUARDS!" she screamed.

Book Two

Chapter One

(Extract)

324 days after the eclipse.

"Sound the alarm!" The Legate cried out, "Ship sighted!"

The buccinas resounded throughout the port as the Red Guard took position at the top of the dam.

"Hold your positions," the Legate commanded.

The six large wooden ships bearing the sigil of the Black Crow, turned towards the port.

"Patience, keep steady," the Legate bellowed, his red crest bending in the gale. "Orange Guard," he roared, "take position."

As commanded, a troop of archers ran to their positions behind the waiting Red Guard; with bow in hand and their quivers brimmed with dipped arrows. A team of Tribunes walked down the lines lighting the braziers ready for the Orange Guard. The Legate stood fast as the ships drew nearer. His face was wet with rain and his hand raised high. All eyes were on him.

The Legate dropped his hand.

"Raise the chain!" echoed around the port.

The heavy metal chain, suspended between the two towers which stood either side of the port, creaked and groaned as it was torn from its slumber at the bottom of the bay. It broke through the surface of the water at the bow of the foremost ship. The Legate grinned.

The port remained deafly silent as the ships continued unhindered.

"How can this be?" the Legate gasped.

Seaweed that had been caught up in the chain, fluttered peacefully as the ships passed through. Their wooden hulls now enthralled the chain with a thick black smoke, emerging wholly intact.

Fear gripped the Legate. The legends were true.

"The archers?" a Centurion asked.

"Yes, the archers," the Legate muttered. "Orange Guard!" he bellowed. "Take aim!"

The archers collected an arrow, and dipped the tip into the flames. Once ignited they each raised their bows and took aim.

"Fire!"

The once blackened sky was now alight as a swarm of fire ascended into the storm clouds.

"Karsch cha," the Black Blood Captain commanded. As instructed, his crew raised their shields and took cover. The arrows whistled through the air. One by one they passed through the hull of the ships into the murky water below. The laugh of the Black Blood captain resounded off the walls of the dam.

All eyes turned again to the Legate. He froze, speechless.

"What do we do?" The Centurion asked.

"What are your commands?" Another pleaded.

The Legate remained silent as he pondered the situation.

"Tell the guard to prepare to board the ships once they land," he commanded. "They will have to stop at the dam. We will board them and take their ships. We will spare no-one!"

"Yes Dux," they replied respectfully.

"They are not slowing down," a Red Guard nearby cried.

The Legate turned to see the ships bearing down on the dam.

"Brace yourself. They intend to ram us," he commanded.

The Red Guard drew their gladius swords and braced to challenge the Black Bloods, who would be forced to jump from their ships as they splintered against the walls of the dam.

"Prepare to fire," the Legate bellowed.

The Orange Guard drew their bows and took aim for the Black Bloods crouched on the decks of the ships.

"Frucha!" The Captain cried.

The mighty ships groaned loudly as they began to rise in the water. The black smoky sails bellowed like captive hurricanes. The men on board remained crouched while chanting in their native tongue. The bow of the ship broke free of the surface, clipping the wooden jetty of the port as it passed.

The Guards could only watch helplessly, as the ships rose clear of the water. Their sodden wooden hulls complaining loudly as they proceeded to sail over the dam.

The foremost ship suddenly dropped, colliding with the edge of the dam. The wall cracked and crumbled. The Guards gathered on top ran for their lives.

The furious Black Blood Captain scanned the deck of his unavailing ship. He saw before him a young boy cowering, crying, abandoning his duties. The Captain signalled his guard who approached the young boy. The Captain ordered the boy to be thrown overboard to demonstrate to the others that there was no room for cowards. The boy collided head first with the wall of the dam. He fell like a rock into the water below.

A crewman down, the ship plunged into the river on top of the dam, sending a wave crashing over the edge. The remaining ships landed gracefully. The sails subsided and the crew awoke from their trance.

The Red Guard could only look on in horror as the ships sailed towards the bridge back to Eagle Blood Shores.

The foremost ship rammed into the struts, sending a shower of wood and stone hurtling into the water. The bridge collapsed as the third ship toppled the remaining support beam.

"What do we do?" the Centurion pleaded. "There is nothing to stop them now from taking the city."

The Legate stared woefully at the fallen bridge, splintered dam and the chain in the port.

"Pray," he replied sincerely.

To be continued...

Appendix

It is the intention of the author that the stories of the Blood Gens can be read independently of one another. Therefore, if it is desired to read the chapters in the order of the Blood Gen's own storylines, please consider the following order:

Blood Gens	**Chapters**			
Aulus – Red Blood	4	11	16	26
Vesnus – Orange Blood	7	10	21	27
Acernis – Green Blood	6	9	18	28
Quinta - Blue Blood	2	14	20	23
Marcus – Purple Blood	5	12	19	25
Petrina – White Blood	3	13	17	24
Max – Demi Blood	1	8	15	22

Glossary

Glossary of Terms

B

Birrus
Short, hooded woollen cloak, worn by the Orange Bloods.

Blood Gens
Group of people, defined by the colour of their blood.

Buccina
A brass horn, used by the Red Bloods to sound the alarm.

Bulla
Amulet worn by male children of Red, Orange, Green and Blue Bloods.

C

Camp
Stone built forts and out-posts.

Codex Vitae
Literal translation: code of life. Used to refer the process by which all livings things live, reproduce, and die.

Concacavi
A very unpleasant swear/curse word.

Cuirass
Protective body armour, worn to protect the torso.

D

Decem Dies Mille

Literal translation: The Ten Thousand Day. The point at which a pure blood becomes an adult in the eyes of the Law, Rytus and her citizens.

Denarius

A small silver coin, the currency of Rytus.

Doctore

The White Bloods of Eagle Blood Shores who train the young Red Bloods in battle craft and weaponry.

Domina

Female master of the White Bloods.

Dominus

Male master of the White Bloods.

F

Fatuus

Literal translation: A fool, or foolish.

I

Imperator

Male leader of Rytus.

Imperatrix

Female leader of Rytus

Ineptus

Insult, meaning idiot.

Insula

Tall, apartment like homes for the citizens of White City.

L

Lacerna

Cloak, worn by the Red Bloods and fastened over the right shoulder.

Lapsae

The highest rank of the Orange Bloods.

Legate

The highest rank of the Red Bloods, only obtainable by the Blue Bloods.

Lena

The madame, or leader of the lupanarium.

Lupanarium

Home of the prostitutes of White City.

M

Maeniana

Narrow walkways between the different levels of the Blue Palace's foundations.

N

Necropolis

The walled city of the dead, a cemetery and crematorium.

Nothus

Curse word meaning illegitimate son.

Nutrix

Wet nurse.

P

Paenula

Long, hooded woollen cloak.

Palla

Shawl worn by the women of Rytus.

Pica

Magpie, a nickname for the Green Bloods.

Pilum

Spear like weapon.

Praeceptor

Teacher, private tutor to the Blue Bloods.

Q

Quiver

A pouch for carrying arrows, worn across the back.

S

Signifiers

Flag bearers and sigil carriers.

Signum Altercations

The banned art of altering the Codex Vitae.

Stola

Worn by the women of Rytus when they came of age, often made of wool or linen. A long dress worn over the tunic, folded and pleated using a belt.

Strigil

Used for cleaning skin. Oil would be applied and a strigil used to scrape the dirt and oil away.

T

Tunic

A garment worn over the body, usually loose fitting. Worn by both men and women.